T0148355

Also by Judith Henry Wall

My Mother's Daughter
If Love Were All
Mother Love
Blood Sisters

The
Girlfriends
Club

Judith Henry Wall

SIMON & SCHUSTER

NEW YORK   LONDON   TORONTO   SYDNEY   SINGAPORE

SIMON & SCHUSTER
Rockefeller Center
1230 Avenue of the Americas
New York, NY 10020

SIMON & SCHUSTER and colophon are registered trademarks
of Simon & Schuster, Inc.

Designed by Jan Pisciotta

Manufactured in the United States of America

ISBN 978-1-4767-7792-4

Acknowledgments

Special thanks go to my "first wives club" friends who
encouraged me to write this book.

I am indebted to Daranna Bradley, JoAnna Wall, Richard Wall,
and Joan Atterbury for their suggestions and encouragement.

And I am grateful to Chuck Adams, my wise and perceptive
editor, and, as always, to my agent and friends of many years,
Philippa Brophy of Sterling Lord Literistic.

In loving memory of my sister, Peggy

The
Girlfriends
Club

Chapter One

I'll kill him if he doesn't come, Dixie told herself as Mary Sue glanced down at her watch for the umpteenth time in the past thirty minutes. Walter was supposed to join them after dinner for a birthday toast.

Dixie rolled her eyes in Gretchen and Pamela's direction as they helped her clear the table and arrange the birthday gifts in front of Mary Sue.

Pamela and Gretchen felt just as she did about Walter. He was an egotistical, overbearing bore of a man, but his presence in Mary Sue's life had brought her out of a serious case of postdivorce despair, so they tolerated him. Pamela and Gretchen did a better job of tolerating him than Dixie. Dixie resented the way the man had taken over Mary Sue's life. They seldom saw her without Walter.

But Mary Sue had decided birthday dinner would be just for the "Girlfriends." Mary Sue had celebrated earlier with her mother and children. Walter could drop by afterward. Dixie had drawn him a map to the lake house and instructed him not to come until after nine o'clock.

Thus far, the evening had gone well. The expensive Merlot provided by Pamela had evoked gasps of delight. They had managed to drink three bottles while dining on pork roast and rosemary mashed potatoes, which had turned out quite well considering how infrequently Dixie now did any serious cooking. Gretchen had driven over to the French bakery in Overland Park for bread and a calorie-laden chocolate-raspberry torte. The moonlight on the water was breathtaking. On the surface at least, the celebratory dinner on the screened-in porch at the lake house seemed quite normal—not so different from other shared evenings, other celebrations. But the normalcy was forced.

Tomorrow, a surgeon would slice off Mary Sue's right breast.

"I think I'll give Walter a call," Mary Sue said, pushing back her chair, "to make sure he's coming."

"You stay put," Dixie said, stacking the plates. "I'll call him."

Aware of all those glasses of wine she had downed, Dixie had to concentrate on each step as she made her way across the living room. And the champagne was yet to come.

From the kitchen phone she listened while Walter's home number rang and rang. She was about to hang up when she heard a thick-tongued "yeah."

"Walter? It's Dixie. Why in the hell aren't you out here? We're ready for champagne and toasts."

"I left a message for you at the store," he said. "I'm a bit under the weather." Then he offered a forced cough to back up his claim.

He was lying. If Walter had left a message, her assistant, Miss McFadden, would have told him to call out here or relayed the message herself.

"So, you're not coming?" Dixie demanded.

"I'm a bit under the weather," he repeated.

"Mary Sue is expecting you."

"I am not coming, Dixie. Tell Mary Sue I'll be thinking about her tomorrow."

"You're not coming to the hospital either?"

"I've got a full day at the office."

"Walter, I don't care if you are double-booked and/or dying," Dixie said, pacing back and forth. "You need to be here tonight and at the hospital tomorrow. You can't let Mary Sue down like this."

A long pause ensued. Then Walter cleared his throat. "I'm not comfortable with this whole thing."

"What *whole thing?*"

"With her being sick. With this whole cancer business. I'm not very good around sick people. That's why I'm a dentist and not a doctor."

Dixie stopped pacing. "What are you telling me? That you are dumping Mary Sue because she's sick?"

"Not just sick. Mary Sue has *cancer. Breast* cancer. That's a real turnoff for a man, you know."

"No, I don't know. Are you saying that if it was some other kind of cancer, you might be able to deal with it?"

"The other night, she wanted to make love. I couldn't bring myself to touch her, knowing that . . . well, you know. They're going to *cut it off,* for God's sake! And God knows what that reconstruction thing is going to look like. I realized then that I just can't deal with it."

"And just when were you planning to inform Mary Sue?"

"I've hinted at it already. Hey, this isn't easy for me, you know. I'd been thinking about proposing on her birthday. I'd even looked at engagement rings, but now I'm having to rethink the whole thing. What if she doesn't get well? What if I'm no longer attracted to her after the surgery?"

Dixie took a deep breath. "I want you to listen to me very carefully, Walter Lampley. If you aren't out here in the next forty-five minutes, I will have a certain photograph of you blown up and put on a highway billboard."

"What photograph?"

"It was taken during some kind of dental meeting a few years back. You guys sure like to let down your hair when you get out of town, don't you?"

"You're bluffing."

"Am I? It was in a hotel room. You boys were being naughty."

"Hey, I've never been *naughty* in the presence of other men."

"Then try this one on for size. I will tell every damned person I know how you dumped Mary Sue Prescott the night before her mastectomy. I will stand outside of your office and tell your patients what an insensitive, godawful son-of-a-bitch you are."

"You can't blackmail me into staying with her."

"Quite frankly, I'll be delighted to have you out of her life, but you are going to ease out of this relationship gradually. You will show up tonight, and at the hospital tomorrow. Then in a few weeks, you can tell her you're still in love with your ex-wife or that you have developed an incurable case of the clap or whatever, but you will not tell her that you no longer find her desirable. Forty-five minutes, Walter. The clock is ticking."

"Fucking bitch!" he muttered before the phone went dead.

Dixie's hands were shaking as she poured the coffee. *The bastard! The goddamned bastard!*

"Walter had fallen asleep on the sofa," she told Mary Sue as she put the tray on the table. "He said for us to go ahead with dessert, and he'll get here as soon as he can."

Gretchen placed the torte in front of Mary Sue and lit nine candles. "It looks yummy," Mary Sue said. "But how did you decide on *nine* candles?"

"Well, there wasn't room for forty-five, but four plus five is nine," Gretchen explained, and kissed the top of Mary Sue's blond head.

Mary Sue was wearing a halter top that left her smooth tan shoulders bare and revealed the contours of her small, firm breasts. Throughout the evening, Dixie had tried not to think of the mutilation that would take place in the morning. She kept herself busy refilling glasses and serving the meal. Mary Sue herself had assumed responsibility for keeping the conversation going. She told a few jokes, then started reminiscing. *Remember at their senior picnic when Pamela dove into the lake and didn't realize the top to her bathing suit had come off. Remember the candlelit ceremonies they held for each other when they had their first period. Remember what a thrill they got just driving by some boy's house or walking by his locker!*

The four of them had grown up together in Garden Grove, Kansas, a prosperous Kansas City suburb where Gretchen's father and Mary Sue's stepfather had been physicians and Pamela's daddy an attorney. While the mothers of her three best friends sometimes helped out in their husbands' offices, they mostly volunteered time for various civic and charitable projects and played golf, tennis, bridge, and mahjong.

Dixie's family owned a store, and her mother worked alongside her father. In fact, the entire Bloom family had worked at Bloom's Flowers and Gifts, which was established by Dixie's grandfather when he returned from military service in Louisiana with his bride, an Army nurse from Baton Rouge and the person for whom Dixie was named. Dixie's brother had grown up helping with deliveries. Summers and peak times, Dixie helped her father with the arranging. Their mother took orders, looked after customers, and managed the gift-shop portion of the business. The store had flourished over the years as weddings and funerals in the flourishing community became ever more opulent. Dixie's parents were able to join the country club and remodel the family home on Choteau Boulevard. And they had built the house on Murphy Lake, where they lived during the summer months, driving back and forth into town. The four friends spent endless hours at the lake, sometimes not going home for days on end. Her father called them the "Four Musketeers." Sometimes, when Pamela's older brother joined them, they were five. Danny had Down's syndrome and liked nothing better than hanging out with his sister's friends.

When it was time for college, the four friends had a tough time deciding between the University of Kansas in nearby Lawrence or the more distant Kansas State University in Manhattan. In the end, they opted for Lawrence because Mary Sue and Gretchen's high school boyfriends were going there. They took a vow that they would pledge the same sorority or not pledge at all. Pi Beta Phi had been their first choice, but the Pi Phi's weren't interested in Pamela, who had been a mediocre student in high school. Thus the four friends from Garden Grove pledged Chi Omega. Dixie had always thought the Chi Omegas took them to get Mary Sue, who had been Kansas High School Cheerleader of the Year and surely was destined for the KU varsity squad. Mary Sue hadn't disappointed them. She was not only a cheerleader, she was named homecoming queen her junior year.

By graduation day, after on-again, off-again courtships, Mary Sue and Gretchen were both engaged to their high school sweethearts. Gretchen moved back to Garden Grove to plan her wedding and decorate her new home. Mary Sue and her husband moved back to their hometown after he had completed his medical training.

Pamela took a job as a buyer for a department store in Saint Louis, where she lived for five years before marrying a partner in her father's Kansas City law firm. Clay Cartwright was divorced, the father of two daughters, and fourteen years Pamela's senior. He told Pamela about his vasectomy on their first date. He loved his daughters, but he'd already been down that road. If he ever married again, he wanted a regulated, sane life unencumbered by high chairs and diapers.

Dixie had followed her college sweetheart to Chicago and took a job at a public relations firm. When she and Arnie married the following year, her parents filled the Garden Grove Episcopal Church with masses of yellow and white blossoms. Pamela, Gretchen, and Mary Sue were her only attendants. By then, Mary Sue and Gretchen were noticeably pregnant.

When Dixie returned to Garden Grove four years ago, she was a divorced woman with a reluctant thirteen-year-old-son in tow, coming home to care for her dying mother and help her father run the business. Now she was pretty much in charge at the store. Her father came in when she needed him, but mostly he fished and golfed and traveled about with his lady friend. Dixie hadn't planned to stay on in Garden Grove, hadn't planned to make Bloom's Flowers a career, but she had no compelling reason to do otherwise.

The centerpiece Dixie had created for tonight's celebration was an assortment of what she considered sweet flowers—freesia, lavender, and sweetheart roses—because Mary Sue was, above all, a sweet person. Even her prettiness had a sweet quality to it. In the soft glow from the hurricane lamps, she still looked much as she had in college. The rest of them had changed more.

Gretchen, the fitness freak, was sleeker now, with Faye Dunaway cheekbones, well-defined muscles, and her blond hair usually pulled into a smooth French knot. She worked out daily and preached nutrition. Tonight she had eaten only a sliver of the pork roast. Her usual fare was steamed vegetables, fresh fruit, and grilled fish.

Pamela had gotten hooked on style. Even tonight, with just four old friends around a picnic table, she looked smart in an expensive silk pants outfit, worn with good jewelry, of course. Good jewelry was Pamela's trademark. And furs. Pamela was the only woman Dixie knew who had a closet dedicated exclusively to furs.

Dixie herself had changed the most of all. Her hair was now short and sensible and had long ago been allowed to return to its natural brunette. Her despised pug nose had been surgically elongated and her front teeth capped, which gave her the confidence to wear makeup only when she felt like it. She was more interested in comfort than fashion and usually wore athletic shoes and well-washed jeans to the store. Tonight, she was wearing a loose-fitting sundress at least a decade old and a pair of Birkenstocks that were even older.

Usually it was Mary Sue who orchestrated their birthday celebrations, even her own. But Mary Sue had spent the past week being biopsied, undergoing lab tests, getting caught up on housework and errands, and installing her mother in her house to ride herd on her two teenagers while she was in the hospital.

The three of them would take Mary Sue to the hospital at dawn and wait throughout the morning while her breast was removed and a facsimile constructed in its stead, using flesh and muscle from her stomach. Not that Mary Sue had much flesh to spare; she hadn't gained more than five pounds since high school. Later on, after everything had healed, the plastic surgeon would create a new nipple, using scar tissue and tattooing to produce a realistic facsimile. Amazing, they had all agreed, when Mary Sue explained the procedure. Absolutely amazing. But inwardly Dixie had shuddered and resisted the urge to touch her own hopefully still healthy breasts.

When Dixie asked Mary Sue if she'd rather postpone the birthday party until after the surgery, she had shaken her head and offered one of her little lopsided grins. "Nope. Let's eat decadent food and drink too much—an evening of excess before chemo."

Spending the night at the cabin had been Mary Sue's idea, even though she knew Pamela's husband would whine. Only Pamela was still married. Dixie had divorced first. Gretchen's marriage ended three years ago when her husband left her for his twenty-five-year-old secretary. Two years ago, after a succession of affairs, Mary Sue's husband had left her for the trophy wife to end all trophy wives.

After a year of near hysteria, Mary Sue began dating Walter, whom she had met through an expensive dating service. Walter, who lived and practiced dentistry in nearby Shawnee, had met his second wife through the same service, but that marriage had lasted only six months.

Gretchen had been too preoccupied with taking her husband to court to spend much time looking for a replacement. She and Paul had made their lawyers rich, arguing over every stick of furniture, every pot and pan. They had even argued over the landscaping, eventually dividing up the shrubbery and trees, with Paul having his half dug up and hauled away. When he wouldn't come by to clean out the dog run, she gave away his bird dogs. Two days later Elvira, her seventeen-year-old cat, was no place to be found. Paul sued Gretchen for giving away the things he had left stored in the attic. She took him back to court, asking for increased child support. When she won, he refused to buy their daughters the car he had promised them. In retaliation, she notified the KU alumni association that Paul had died, and his name appeared under "deaths" in the next issue of the alumni quarterly. He was constantly running into fraternity brothers who were shocked to see him among the living. Even now, whenever mail came for Paul at the house, Gretchen would write "deceased" across the envelope and return it to the sender.

Gretchen and Paul Bonner's much-gossiped-about divorce only served to reinforce Clay Cartwright's low opinion of his wife's lifelong friends. On principle alone, Clay didn't want his wife hanging out with divorced women, even though he had been divorced himself. Usually Pamela saw them only at lunch, unless Clay was out of town, when she was willing to go out to dinner but wanted to be home by ten in case he called. Clay was not out of town this evening. When Pamela tried to beg out of staying the night, Mary Sue dug in. Clay could damned well tuck himself in for just this one night. She wanted an old-fashioned slumber party at the lake house, just like in the old days, and her friends had to oblige her because she had breast cancer.

Of course, it wouldn't be "just like in the old days." They would not be bedding down in sleeping bags on the living room floor with Dixie's parents periodically leaning over the upstairs banister, begging them to please settle down and get some sleep. And the cabin had gotten shabby over the years. Her father still liked to fish out here, but he seldom slept over. Sometimes Dixie's son, Kirk, came with his grandfather, but not as often as before.

Dixie's mother had loved it out here. She read books on the screened porch and decreed that cooking at the lake house be nothing more complicated than hot dogs and egg salad sandwiches. Every summer morning, she would swim across the lake and back—until she got sick.

Her mother's cancer had been in her bones. Much worse than breast cancer, Dixie had assured Mary Sue. And her mother had waited too long to go to the doctor, even though she knew something was wrong. Mary Sue's cancer had been found while it was still small and, they hoped, curable.

Of course, there were no guarantees, Mary Sue had reminded Dixie, not about cancer or anything else. You don't know when you wake up in the morning that a truck won't run over you that day or if terrorists had poisoned the water supply. You don't know if your kids are on drugs or if the husband you loved and trusted is off screwing his brains out with some other woman. They must learn to live each day as though it was their last, Mary Sue had said philosophically. But how did one do that? Dixie wondered. What was life except putting the past behind you and moving forward?

This was the year they all turned forty-five, but more than age, more than divorces and children graduating from high school, more than the death of Dixie's mother, Mary Sue's cancer signified the cresting of a hill. They were now descending. Like their parents before them, they would grow old. And someday, perhaps sooner than they thought and most likely before they were ready, they would get sick and die. Dixie had always known that. With Mary Sue's illness, she *felt* it. She woke in the night feeling it. She felt it now, as Mary Sue blew out nine candles, as she silently wished for the chemotherapy to work and for their beloved friend to get well. Dixie felt it while she watched Mary Sue pull the wrapping paper from her gifts, thinking how many times they had performed this same ritual and wondering how many more times they would gather like this.

She wished now that she hadn't insisted Walter drive out here. He didn't belong, and they didn't need him. Tonight was for four friends facing the future together.

Chapter Two

The air was perfectly still, and the surface of the lake was like a black mirror reflecting the silvery moonlight. They kicked off their shoes and sat on the edge of the pier, dangling their toes in the lake.

Pamela struggled to remove the cork from the champagne bottle.

"Cork removal is a man's job," Pamela said. "Shouldn't Walter be here by now?"

"Maybe he's not coming," Dixie said. "He did have a cough."

"I'm not surprised that he didn't come," Mary Sue admitted. "He's having a hard time dealing with my diagnosis. He admitted that it was a real turnoff."

"He actually said that to you?" Dixie demanded.

"Yeah, he did," Mary Sue said. "He said he's a breast man and wasn't sure how well he was going to deal with a woman who had an artificial boob."

Dixie felt a wave of anger at a man who would say such a thing, who would *feel* such a thing. Mary Sue would have stood by Walter if he'd grown a second head or gotten his dick caught in a meat grinder. But *he wasn't sure he could deal with a woman who had an artificial boob* when the only reason women got any sort of artificial anything was to please a man. She hated Walter and all men like him. She glanced in Gretchen's direction. Gretchen lifted her chin and gave a tiny nod of agreement. Yes, Walter was despicable.

Dixie put a comforting arm around Mary Sue's slim shoulders.

"I never liked the man," Gretchen said, taking the bottle from Pamela and wrestling out the cork with a major "pop" that echoed across the water like a cannon shot. But no lights flickered on in the five other weekend homes that rimmed the small, private lake. On this balmy September night, they had it all to themselves.

"No, I never liked him at all," Gretchen repeated and began filling their cups. She looked like a Norse goddess in the moonlight, her blond hair gleaming silver, her tan shoulders broad and proud.

"I don't like him either," Pamela said, watching Gretchen fill her paper cup. "Now I'd like to kill him."

"What a marvelous idea," Gretchen said.

"The man does not understand the distinction between off-color and crude," Pamela added. "He is not in your league, Mary Sue. Not in your league at all."

Dixie nodded her agreement as she watched Gretchen fill her cup. Then she lifted the cup and said, "Happy birthday and good luck to Mary Sue, the sweetest of us all."

"We'll be with you tomorrow and all the days to come," Pamela said. "You can count on us."

"Your breast cancer is our breast cancer," Gretchen added. "We'll get through this thing together."

Solemnly, they lifted their cups to that thought. To getting through it. To themselves and their friendship of almost forty years.

"And now I'd like to make a toast to Barry," Mary Sue said.

Barry? Dixie was stunned. Why would she want to do that? Mary Sue's ex-husband was getting married the day after tomorrow to a sexy widow who had recently won the state amateur tennis championship and, as it turned out, he had been boinking for years—even before her sixty-three-year-old architect husband conveniently drove his Lincoln Continental into the rear of an eighteen-wheeler.

"Here's to Barry," Mary Sue said, lifting her cup. "I hope that Trish takes a lesbian lover, and the two of them hold him captive. That they make him cook and clean for them and bear their children and change ninety-nine percent of the poopie diapers. And remember to get their cars serviced on schedule. And keep clean underwear in their dresser drawers at all times. And never, ever overdraw his bank account on threat of death."

"Hear, hear," Gretchen said. "How about if they make him wear a ball and chain? And cut off his balls while they're at it?"

Mary Sue held out her cup for a refill. "Does anyone know what time it is? I'm not supposed to have anything by mouth after midnight."

Gretchen held the face of her watch up to the moonlight. "It's eleven forty-five."

"Good. I want one more for the road. In the morning, I'll move on to anesthesia. I hope it purges all memory of Barry. And Walter." Then she paused, but they all kept listening, realizing that more words were coming.

"I dreamed about Barry last night," Mary Sue said, staring out at the lake. "Such an outrageous dream. I dreamed that the three of you—all dressed up in filmy vestal virgin gowns that you could see right through—present him with my breast at his wedding feast. You carry it in on a silver tray covered with a lace doily. Barry is sitting on a throne, with his tennis goddess at his side. When he pulls back the doily, there it is, surrounded by sugared violets with a dollop of whipped cream and a maraschino cherry on the nipple."

Dixie exchanged glances with Pamela and Gretchen.

Pamela offered a nervous giggle. "Does he recognize it?"

"Oh, yes. It brings a tear to his eye. He's left-handed, you know. The right one was always his favorite."

"How would he know it's the right one?" Pamela wanted to know.

"Are you kidding? He runs radiology at the hospital. I'm sure he saw the mammogram. He probably made the official diagnosis—it's breast cancer for Mary Sue."

"He hasn't called?" Gretchen asked.

Mary Sue shook her head, then buried her face in her hands. "I hate him," she sobbed. "Oh, God, how I hate him. I wish he would die so I could stop thinking about him. But I'm the one who has cancer. I'm the one who will probably die."

Dixie and Pamela both moved to embrace her. Gretchen came to kneel behind her and stroked her hair. "Don't say that," Pamela sobbed. "You're not going to die."

Mary Sue was so small, Dixie thought. How could she possibly have the strength in that slim little body to fight off the demon that had possessed her? She seemed to have lost substance since Barry left her. Mary Sue had worked so hard at being the perfect wife, worked so hard at loving her husband and making him proud, only to have him dump her like a used car.

Gretchen broke out of the group hug first, gasping and pointing toward the sky. "A shooting star," she said. "It's an omen. A *good* omen. We'll get through this, Mary Sue, honey. You'll see."

"I love you guys," Mary Sue said. "I really do love you. And we're never going to get a divorce. *Never.*" Then she stood and began to strip.

Wordlessly, the others joined her. And followed her into the silvery water. Mary Sue started across the lake first, the rest followed. They swam as though their lives depended on it, touching the boulder on the opposite shore that they had always called Plymouth Rock, and making the return trip more slowly. Even Gretchen slowed down, making sure she didn't need to help out one of her less-fit friends. They crawled up onto the boat dock, breathless and laughing.

"Best friends forever," Mary Sue gasped.

"Best friends forever," they echoed.

Dixie wasn't sure she believed in omens. Life, to her, seemed pretty random. There was no way to receive glimpses into the future because no plan book existed of what the future was supposed to be. Except maybe that day seven years ago, when she realized the inside of the one-carat diamond that had resided on her left hand for almost seventeen years had shattered—she supposed that she had been seeing an omen of sorts.

At first, she'd thought the diamond was simply coated with hand lotion or some other substance that gave it a milky look. After all, diamonds were forever. Forever was assured in all those DeBeers ads featuring beautiful people celebrating timeless love with diamond jewelry. But no amount of washing or soaking in ammonia or vigorous buffing could restore her engagement diamond to its original high-grade, clear-white radiance.

As realization dawned, Dixie sat at the table of her big homey kitchen, a pot of homemade vegetable soup simmering on the stove, and stared down at the diamond that had once drawn such "oohs" and "aahs" from her sorority sisters, the diamond that had made her mother weep with joy and made Dixie herself walk with her head a bit higher and a heart filled with pride and joy that she would soon become the wife of Arnold Woodward.

The insurance company paid to have the diamond recut, salvaging slightly less than one-half carat and paying the tiny difference between the recut stone's current appraised value and the amount for which the original diamond had been insured.

When she showed her husband the ring with its newly configured stone, he said it looked nice. She had thought Arnie would offer to buy her a new diamond or at least tell her that she should apply the value of the recut stone toward a larger one. Whoever heard of a woman ending up with a smaller diamond after more than a decade and a half of marriage?

Dixie put the ring in her jewelry box and never wore it again. Arnie never noticed. Or maybe he noticed but by then no longer cared.

The shattered diamond came at a time when Dixie was beginning to acknowledge that the magic had gone out of her marriage. And there had been magic, once upon a time. Along with shared goals. Getting Arnie through graduate school. Starting a family. Building their dream home. Taking significant vacations. Getting involved in the arts and in causes. Dixie freelanced an occasional magazine piece on parenthood or the arts, mostly so she wouldn't have to identify herself totally as a wife and mother. She grieved when she realized she would not bear another child. There were advantages to having one child, however. Theirs was a tight little family. They had a good life.

Dixie had always felt fortunate that her marriage was better than most. Certainly it was better than Pamela's with her overbearing husband. And better than Gretchen's with her indifferent one. That was back when they still thought Mary Sue had a great husband and a great marriage, back when Barry still bought her flowers and planned romantic holidays with just the two of them.

Barry had written a poem to Mary Sue that he read at their rehearsal dinner. Every eye teared as they listened to Barry profess his undying love for their Mary Sue. Every head nodded with immense satisfaction. The marriage of Mary Sue Gregory and Barry Prescott was a good thing, a marriage that was meant to be. Dixie had never once thought she and Arnie had a better marriage than Mary Sue and Barry.

Arnie wasn't overbearing, indifferent, or flower-bearing. Arnie was negative.

If Dixie said it was a pretty day, Arnie said it was humid. If she said it had been a good movie, he said it was mediocre. He was negative with her, negative with their son, negative about life. But during her visits back home in Garden Grove, Dixie always made him sound better than he was. She had learned to accept diminished expectations. When she filled out those little tests in magazines that rate such things as marriage and happiness, she never got a ten, but seven or eight was fine. No one could score a ten. Or even a nine. Not if they were honest with themselves. Marriage was more about stability and security than dancing in the dark and consistently achieving mutual orgasms. If anyone had asked what she thought her chances were for 'til death do us part, she would have said 100 percent. Absolutely. Neither she nor Arnie was going anywhere. If anyone had asked her what the chances were for one of the four friends since childhood to be facing a battle with cancer in her mid-forties, Dixie would not have said zero. She was too realistic for that. But she would have said not very likely. Maybe when they were in their fifties or their sixties, one of them might have to face a serious health problem, but forty-five was too damned young. They weren't even postmenopausal. They hadn't figured out happiness yet. Or contentment. Whatever. They were still works in progress.

When divorce came into her life, Dixie had not been devastated like Mary Sue, not hell-bent on revenge like Gretchen. She was just undone by the messiness of it all and profoundly sad at the breakup of their little family. Sad for her son most of all.

But as the divorce cloud gradually lifted, she began to feel other emotions. Relief, for one. Even excitement. She could start anew. And eventually could even wish her husband well in his new life.

The night air suddenly didn't seem so balmy as Dixie grabbed her sundress and pulled it over her wet body. Mary Sue crumpled onto the dock and curled into a fetal position. "I think I'm passing out," she said.

Gretchen draped her shirt around Mary Sue's shoulder, and they half-dragged, half-carried her up the steep hill to the house and up the stairs to Dixie's old bedroom. With only the light from the hall, they struggled to get her into a nightshirt. In the half-light, her lean little body looked pubescent. It always had. Even though she had been the unofficial mother superior of their tight little pack, her body had resisted womanhood the longest. She had been the last to grow breasts, the last to start her period. They had always assumed she would be the last to grow old.

"She's going to be so hung over," Gretchen said, pulling the blanket under Mary Sue's chin.

"Aren't we all," Pamela said. "In fact, I am already starting to feel less than good."

Dixie bent to kiss Mary Sue's smooth forehead, concentrating to control a wave of dizziness that the movement brought. Yes, they were all going to be hung over. No question about that. Her equilibrium regained, she knelt by the bed and kissed Mary Sue's lips. She took one of her limp hands and kissed it. Then the other. "I love you, sweetie," she told the inert form. And shivered when she thought of what would happen to her tomorrow.

Gretchen and Dixie told Pamela to shower first, while they cleared the table and tidied up.

As they started down the stairs, the glare of headlights danced across the room.

"Oh, my gosh!" Dixie said. "He came after all. You get started in the kitchen. I'll get rid of Walter."

By the time she reached the front porch, the headlights had vanished. Maybe it wasn't him after all. Maybe it was just kids necking in the woods.

She heard him before she saw him, cursing as he made his way down the hill. His low-slung car probably didn't take too well to the deep ruts in the unkempt lane that wound its way down to the lake house.

As Walter approached, she could see that he was wearing shorts with no shirt. And was barefoot, for God's sake, carefully picking his way, putting his arms out like a tightrope walker for balance. Not a fine figure of a man.

She realized Gretchen was watching from the screen door. "I told him he had to come," Dixie confessed. "But then I hoped he wouldn't."

The screen door squeaked as Gretchen stepped out with her. "Go home, Walter," she called. "Mary Sue's asleep. The party's over."

"And a good evening to you, too," he said, then stumbled and fell, letting forth a string of fucks and shits and why didn't they have a sidewalk. He had something in his hand. A book, maybe.

"He's drunk," Dixie whispered.

"So are we," Gretchen whispered back.

Yes, they were drunk, Dixie acknowledged, and she needed to proceed with great care. She took a deep breath.

"I want you to go home, Walter," Dixie said. "I'm really sorry I called you. It was a bad idea for you to come out here."

"What do you mean 'go home'?" he slurred. "I am not going home without seeing our little cheerleader. I even brought her a present," he said, waving what Dixie realized was a videotape over his head. "I've turned Mary Sue into a porn queen, and she doesn't even know it. She doesn't look half-bad for an over-the-hill broad with undersized tits. It will be a little souvenir for her of what she looked like before she went under the knife."

When he started up the steps, Gretchen stepped forward. "Give it here, Walter."

"No way. It's my birthday present for Mary Sue."

"I'll see that she gets it. Give it to me, Walter," Gretchen said, holding out her hand.

Walter took the last step and joined them on the stoop. Gretchen drew herself up to her full height and reached for the video.

"No, no, no," he said, taunting, holding the video behind his back and almost losing his balance. "Just cause you're bigger than me doesn't mean you can have my video."

"Just give it to me, Walter, and go home," Gretchen said with forced calmness.

"No way. Madam Tough Lady there told me to get my butt out here, and here it is," he said, turning to offer his rear and patting it with the video.

"Just give me the goddamned video," Gretchen said through clenched teeth.

"Just try and get it," he said, holding it over his head.

Gretchen grabbed at it, but he sidestepped.

She grabbed his fleshy upper arm instead and dug her fingernails hard into his flesh. "Give me the goddamned video, or I'll claw your eyes out."

"Hey, cut that out, you fucking bitch," Walter yelled, swatting at Gretchen with the video.

Gretchen grabbed his left arm and tucked it behind his back while Dixie bit his right hand. *Really* bit his hand. She could feel his flesh open under her teeth, taste his blood. This was an incredible thing to be happening, she thought. She didn't *bite* people.

But this man had done a despicable thing to Mary Sue.

Walter screamed in pain, but she kept biting until he dropped the video.

Then she let go of his hand and scooped up the prize. But Walter twisted away from Gretchen and jerked the video away from Dixie with such force that he stumbled backward, losing his footing.

Arms flailing as he tried to regain his balance, he fell against the wooden railing, which made a cracking sound as it gave under his weight.

Dixie grabbed his arm, but it was wrenched from her grasp as he fell. There was a thud.

Then silence.

Both women raced down the steps.

Walter was on his back, his head leaning at an unnatural angle against a large rock. When Gretchen pressed her fingertips against the side of his neck in search of a pulse, his head rolled away from the rock. Gretchen let out a scream.

Dixie put her hands over her mouth to hold back her own scream. She had never seen a body with a broken neck before, but she knew that was what she was now looking at.

Gretchen pinched his nose and began CPR, and Dixie tried desperately to find a pulse in his wrist. But she knew it was useless. Walter Lampley's life had been snuffed out in an instant.

In *half* an instant.

After several minutes, Gretchen sat back on her haunches and took several deep breaths. "He's dead," she announced, but went back to her task anyway.

"Should I call nine-one-one?" Dixie asked.

On the next inhalation, Gretchen shook her head. "Wait," she said.

After a few more tries, she stopped. "This is futile."

"Are you sure?"

"Well, he's not alive, so he must be dead. And even if he were revivable, he wouldn't be by the time an ambulance arrived."

"I guess I should call the police then."

"I can't think," Gretchen said, rubbing her forehead. "*Police.* God, they'd be all over the place. They'd want to wake Mary Sue."

"We have to do *something*," Dixie insisted. Then she crawled away from Walter's body to vomit in the weeds. She felt as though a cloud were settling over her brain. She needed to close her eyes. Needed to stop moving her head.

The rock that killed Walter was one of a collection. Her mother's idea. Souvenirs from trips to the Ozarks in Arkansas, Red Rock Canyon in Oklahoma, wherever. They used to rest among a growth of sturdy monkey grass, but the monkey grass had died and even sturdier weeds had taken its place.

"You okay?" Gretchen asked.

Dixie managed a grunt in the affirmative, which was a lie.

"The jerk is dead," Gretchen said matter-of-factly. "Which is no great tragedy. Now, where's that damned video?"

They crawled around in the flowerbed feeling for it. Dixie finally found it under the porch.

"I need to take some aspirin," Gretchen said, rising to her feet.

"But we can't just leave him out here," Dixie insisted.

"He's not going anyplace. And maybe we don't know he's here. We didn't hear him drive up."

Dixie could see the logic in that. Just move the timetable back a bit. He's out here dead, and they don't know it. "We probably won't find him until tomorrow after the surgery," Dixie fabricated, but wondered if all that wine was interfering with her logic. "If we come out the kitchen door in the morning, we won't be able to see him."

They were both silent for a moment, staring down at the dead man. "It feels like we should pray or cry or something," Dixie said. "A man just died."

Gretchen nodded. "Yeah, a man who will never screw up another woman's life. What are you going to do with the video?"

"Throw it in the lake, I guess. But for now, I'll stash it someplace."

With Gretchen watching, Dixie put the video behind some cans in the kitchen cupboard. "If we hadn't drunk all that wine, would we be calling the police right now?" Dixie pondered.

"We'll never know," Gretchen answered.

They could hear the bathroom door opening upstairs. Pamela was finished with her shower. Dixie glanced at her watch and realized only ten or so minutes had transpired since they put Mary Sue to bed.

Wordlessly, they went to the living room. Gretchen sat on the sofa. Dixie collapsed into the rocking chair. They watched while Pamela came down the stairs in matching silk pajamas and robe. "I don't know about you guys," she said, "but I had too much to drink."

Dixie and Gretchen looked at each other. "You tell her," Dixie said.

Chapter Three

"Dead! What do you mean, he's dead?" Pamela shrieked.

"Hush! You're going to wake Mary Sue." Gretchen said, pulling Pamela down on the couch beside her.

Dixie glanced upward, half-expecting Mary Sue's head to appear over the railing.

Pamela was sputtering, trying to form her next words. "Take a deep breath," Gretchen instructed.

Pamela did as she was told, then demanded, "Okay, why is Walter dead out by the front porch?"

"I didn't know that he had already told Mary Sue he was planning to dump her," Dixie explained, "and I sort of blackmailed him into coming out here."

"He showed up drunk, mean, and half-naked," Gretchen said. "We kind of scuffled out on the porch. He fell over the railing and hit his head on a rock."

"You were fighting with him?" Pamela's voice was rising again.

"Shhh," Dixie cautioned.

"You mean while I was upstairs taking a shower, Walter Lampley died out there?" she demanded, pointing toward the front door.

Dixie and Gretchen both nodded.

"And he's really dead?" Pamela asked.

Again they nodded. Dixie felt tears rising in her eyes, not so much for Walter himself but for the finality of it all. His deadness made her afraid.

Wordlessly, Pamela rose and headed for the front door. Gretchen and Dixie followed. Dixie switched on the light, and they watched from the porch as Pamela knelt beside the body and poked at his bare chest with her forefinger, tentatively at first, then more stridently. Then she sat back on her haunches and stared down at the still form. Dixie could almost see Pamela's mind shifting gears—away from hysteria and into assessment.

Walter looked smaller than before, as though the removal of his life's force had caused his body to deflate and become even softer than it had been.

"Where are his clothes?" Pamela asked.

"He came like that—to show disrespect, I assume," Dixie said.

"With a body like that, you'd think he'd want to keep himself clothed," Pamela observed.

Yes, Pamela's hysteria definitely was gone, Dixie thought. She joined Gretchen in nodding agreement. Yes, Walter should have kept himself clothed.

"It's hard to imagine him making love to Mary Sue, isn't it?" Pamela said, staring gown at Walter's fleshy gut.

Again they nodded.

"And you haven't called anyone?"

This time Dixie and Gretchen shook their heads.

"Did he tell anyone he was coming?"

"I don't know," Dixie said. "He was at home when I talked to him. He sounded drunk. And he was weaving pretty badly, but the gravel was probably hurting his feet."

"He was stinking drunk," Gretchen said, her voice flat.

"His neck is broken," Pamela said, stating the obvious.

"We thought we'd wait until tomorrow to call the police," Gretchen explained, "until after Mary Sue's surgery. We'd tell them that we had just noticed him—lying there in the weeds."

"What are these marks on his arm?" Pamela asked.

"I guess those are from my fingernails," Gretchen said. "His eyes would have been next." She looked down at her right hand. "It looks like I lost one of my fake nails in the process." She held out her hand under the porch light for Dixie to see.

"There are teeth marks on his right hand," Dixie admitted with a sigh. "Those would be mine."

Pamela rose and sat on the top step of the wooden porch. Dixie and Gretchen sat on either side of her. The wood was spongy with age. No wonder the railing broke. Surely the police would take that into consideration, she thought.

"I don't think we should wait to call the police," Dixie said.

When neither Pamela nor Gretchen responded to her statement, she rephrased it. "I'm going to call the police now." She made a small movement with her body, gathering herself to rise.

Pamela held up both her hands and shook her head, indicating she wanted Dixie to wait. Dixie waited. Pamela was, after all, an attorney's wife and in the past had demonstrated more than a passing sense of the law.

Pamela was still for what seemed like a very long time. Dixie became aware of the insect chorus all around them, and her awareness elevated it to deafening proportions, making the pressure inside her head increase. And through the throbbing pain and unrelenting sound, Dixie was very aware of Walter's silent dead body just feet away from her.

Finally, Pamela offered her assessment. "If we call the police, in twenty minutes, there'll be policemen and police cars all over the place and red lights flashing and yellow tape cordoning off the area. There will be detectives asking questions, trying to decide if Walter's death was an accident or foul play. They will want to know about the scratches on his arm. And the teeth marks on his hand. They will insist on talking to Mary Sue. What if they make us go to the police station for questioning? They do that, you know. They would put each of us in separate rooms to see if our stories match. What if we can't get Mary Sue to the hospital on time? Her surgery would have to be rescheduled. Which would mean more waiting and more apprehension for her, more time for the cancer to spread. But we can't just pretend this never happened and leave him here for someone else to find."

"We can take Mary Sue out the kitchen door in the morning," Gretchen said. "She'll never see him. We can figure out what to do about Walter after her surgery."

"But his car is up there," Dixie said, waving toward the top of the hill. "A bright yellow Porsche is hard to miss, even in the dark."

"Look, Mary Sue's in even worse shape than we are," Gretchen said. "She's not going to be checking the scenery out the car window."

"Yeah, but what about someone driving down the highway?" Pamela asked.

"With all those trees, depending where he left the car, I doubt if it would be visible from the road," Dixie said. "But someone who owns one of the other lake houses might come out here for the weekend and spot it. And when the police do come to investigate, they'll wonder why we didn't see it."

"Imagine how this would look in the newspapers," Pamela interjected. "It will sound sordid—a practically naked man found with a broken neck and unmistakable indications of a struggle. The police will want to know what he was doing out here without his clothes and why he's been clawed and bitten. There will be an investigation. A hearing. We will all be questioned. We will all have to testify. How can we prove this wasn't a murder?"

"A *murder?* Why would we murder him?" Dixie asked, closing her eyes against the blinding flash of pain that shot through her brain.

"Why *wouldn't* we?" Gretchen interjected. "He dumped our friend because she had breast cancer. And he probably bragged to his poker buddies that he was taping him and Mary Sue while they had sex."

"He was *what?*" Pamela demanded.

"He was waving a video around, claiming he'd made Mary Sue into a porn star," Gretchen said. "He probably has a video camera hidden in his bedroom."

"God, what a piece of lowlife scum!" Pamela said. "How could Mary Sue have gotten involved with someone like that?"

"Oh, I suspect we've all had encounters with pieces of lowlife scum," Gretchen said.

"But we wouldn't murder a man for making a video or for dumping our friend," Dixie insisted. "We might turn rats loose in his house or put sugar in the gas tank of his Porsche, but we wouldn't *murder* him."

"Yeah, *we* wouldn't, but they might think Mary Sue did, especially if they found out about the videos," Pamela said.

"But she didn't know about the taping. Walter said it was a surprise for her."

"There's no way to prove she didn't know about it, though," Gretchen said. "Before we even think about calling the police or not calling the police, we need to get inside his house and make sure there aren't any more videos lying around. They could be used as evidence. And think how embarrassing they would be for Mary Sue."

They were silent for a few seconds. Thinking. Dixie shuddered at the thought of strangers—of policemen and prosecutors—watching videotaped encounters of Walter Lampley humping away on Mary Sue. Or worse.

"Well then," Pamela said, slapping her knees, "if we're going to do that, we need to do it tonight, before someone realizes he's missing and the police go to his house looking for him."

"So, what are you thinking?" Dixie asked Pamela.

"One of us should stay here in case Mary Sue wakes up, and the other two should check his house for videos."

"Gretchen and I will go," Dixie heard herself volunteer. "We're the ones most involved."

"Yeah," Gretchen agreed. "I don't suppose you have any gloves out here, do you?"

"Gloves?" Dixie asked. "What for?"

"So we don't leave fingerprints. I haven't read all those hundreds of mysteries for nothing."

Dixie found a pair of rubber gloves under the sink and some brown cotton gardening gloves in the laundry room. Gretchen found two baseball caps in the bin by the back door. "Put your hair up in this," she instructed, handing Dixie one of them. "If someone sees us, maybe they'll think we're guys. You need to take off that dress and change into jeans and a T-shirt. I'll go smear some dirt on my license plate."

"I need something for my headache before I go anyplace or do anything," Dixie said. Pamela had some Tylenol in her purse. The three of them stood at the kitchen sink, downing the tablets with tap water. The water made Dixie's stomach threaten to rebel. Pamela also had Maalox.

Gretchen drove to where Walter's car was parked just over the crest of the hill. He'd left the door open and the dome light was on. Wearing gloves, Gretchen unclipped the garage door opener from the sun visor and closed the door.

On the drive to Shawnee, Dixie had to fight to stay awake. A man had just died, but she was having a hard time thinking about anything except her throbbing head, edgy stomach, and desperate need for sleep. What they were doing seemed disrespectful. But then she hadn't respected Walter when he was alive.

"Are you okay?" Gretchen asked.

"No, are you?"

They had been to Walter's house once before, for a Super Bowl party. He'd told Mary Sue he'd been able to hang on to it through two divorces because it had belonged to his parents. In any other community, the house would have been a showplace, but by Shawnee standards, it was run-of-the-mill.

His garage opened on an alley. Gretchen pulled her Blazer into the garage beside Walter's red pickup and immediately lowered the door behind them.

"Gloves," she reminded Dixie.

With hands properly sheathed, the two women entered the back door of Walter's silent house. Dixie's heart drummed furiously in her chest. She marveled at Gretchen's seeming aplomb in the face of breaking and entering or whatever name was assigned to what they were doing.

The kitchen had dirty dishes and empty beer and liquor bottles scattered about and smelled of sour milk. The den was littered with newspapers, magazines, clothing, and more beer bottles. The living and dining rooms looked unused. They climbed the stairs to the second floor. Of the six doors that lined the hallway, only one was open. The light from a television screen flickered into the unlit hallway. But there was no sound.

Dixie peeked into the room. The bed was unmade. On the television screen, a young Jimmy Stewart in cowboy attire was silently conversing with a bartender. Clothes were piled on a chair and scattered about the room.

She took a step into the room, with Gretchen following so closely Dixie could feel her breath. They stood there for a time, surveying the room. Where would he have hidden a video camera?

A fake fern in a brass planter sat on the top of the television armoire. *There,* Dixie thought, and pulled on Gretchen's sleeve. At that exact instant, the bathroom door flew open, revealing a naked woman, the light from the bathroom backlighting her shapely body.

An instant of stunning silence transpired before the naked woman began to scream.

In their haste to get out of the room, Dixie and Gretchen slammed into one another, and Dixie fell hard against the doorjamb. Gretchen grabbed her arm, and they went racing out the door.

The sound of screaming followed them down the stairs. It followed them as they raced through the house to the back door.

In the Blazer, the garage door noisily rolling upward, Dixie held her breath while Gretchen muttered expletives as she frantically searched her pockets for the keys.

They were on the dash.

"Drive like we belong in the neighborhood," Dixie cautioned. She realized that primal fear had momentarily cured her headache, but the throbbing was coming back. And now her hip hurt where she had fallen against the doorframe.

"The bastard," Gretchen said as she backed out of the garage. "The fucking bastard. He couldn't even wait until Mary Sue had the operation before he started screwing someone else."

Gretchen sped down the dark alley.

"Slow down," Dixie cautioned. "We don't want to get picked up."

The alley was deserted. As was the street.

"You need to turn on your lights now," Dixie said.

"Who was she?" Gretchen demanded.

"I don't know. I couldn't see her face, just her curves. She has good curves."

"Yeah, and red hair. Lots of red hair."

"She's probably already called the police."

"I don't hear a siren," Gretchen said.

"There hasn't been time."

"I'm going to pull in at the convenience store for a few minutes."

"Why?" Dixie demanded, anxious to get the hell out of Shawnee.

"I want to see if she called the police," Gretchen explained, as she drove to the far end of the parking lot and turned off the motor. They sat in silence, listening. Still no sirens.

Gretchen drove back toward Walter's house. From a vantage point three houses down, they watched as the shapely woman with red hair hurried out the front door and crossed the street to a dark-colored BMW.

"She's married," Dixie said matter-of-factly, shifting her weight and gingerly rubbing her right hip.

"Yeah," Gretchen agreed. "If she were a single lady, she would have called the police. Her hubby must be out of town."

With headlights off, Gretchen drove back down the alley. "Jesus!" she whispered when she realized they had left the garage door open.

It took all Dixie's courage to go back inside Walter's house. But it was now or never. By tomorrow, the police might be searching it.

The camera was indeed hidden in the plastic fern. On the shelves below it were at least thirty videos. Most were movies starring Bruce Willis, John Wayne, and Clint Eastwood, plus a few porn titles: *Big Breasted Nurses; Daddy, Daddy, I've Been Bad;* and *The Attack of the Cheerleaders.* Four had no labels. They took the four—and the camera.

On the way through the kitchen, Gretchen stopped at the phone. "What are you doing?" Dixie demanded.

"Eventually, someone is going to look at his phone records. I don't want your call from the lake house to be the last time he ever used the phone."

"But who in the hell are you calling?"

"Time and Temperature," Gretchen said as she awkwardly punched the numbers with her gloved fingertip. She listened for a minute. "Two forty-seven A.M. Seventy-five degrees," she reported.

Then she instructed Dixie to wait by the phone. "To muddy the waters," she said. "It will only take a minute. There's a pay phone just two blocks down the street by that Texaco station."

"But someone might see you."

"The station's closed."

Gretchen wrapped paper towels around an empty gin bottle, careful not to touch its surface, and carried it with her as she headed for the door.

Dixie listened while the garage door rolled up and then down. *Damnation! What in the hell was she doing alone in a dead man's house waiting for the phone to ring!* She desperately wished she could turn the clock back and never have made that call to Walter. That's what she got for interfering in other people's lives. She hated Walter. What the hell had she been thinking—ordering him to drive out there to tell Mary Sue happy birthday? When what she really had wanted was for him to vanish from Mary Sue's life altogether.

Beware of what you wish for, she thought ruefully.

She jumped when the phone rang.

Ever so carefully, Dixie picked it up and held it to her ear. "It's me," Gretchen's voice said. "Go out the front door, turn right, and walk toward the corner. I'll pick you up there. Don't bother to lock the door."

"Why?"

"To make it look like Walter left in a hurry—like maybe someone was after him. Leave the phone off the hook. And the refrigerator door open."

On the way out of town, Gretchen stopped in front of an ice-vending machine and bought a bag. Dixie didn't bother to ask why.

Chapter Four

The yellow Porsche was still parked just over the crest of the hill.

Walter's pale, fleshy body was still in the flowerbed.

Damn him anyway, Dixie thought. If he was going to die, why hadn't he just driven his car into a brick wall?

The front door opened, and Pamela came out on the porch.

"I was right," Gretchen said, holding up the bag with the videotapes and camera. "The bastard had a camera hidden in his bedroom."

"I haven't heard a peep out of Mary Sue," Pamela said.

They went into the house and sat at the kitchen table. "It's time to decide," Dixie said. "I still think we should call the police. In fact, we really *must* call the police." She thought about getting up from the table, walking to the phone, and doing just that. Then would it be her fault if they were arrested? What if they were accused of a crime? And what about Mary Sue's operation?

"Maybe we should put him in his car and drive him away from here," Pamela said. "Far away. And leave him at the end of a country road."

"Then it will look like a murder for sure," Gretchen said. "He wouldn't have a broken neck from sitting in his car."

"Maybe his car ran into a tree," Pamela countered.

"So, we're going to drive his car into a tree for him?" Gretchen asked. "I don't think so. We're talking dangerous here, and besides, his blood has already pooled in the lower reaches of his body. On autopsy, they will be able to tell the position he was in when he died."

"How do you know that?" Dixie demanded.

"Anyone who reads mysteries knows that," Gretchen said.

"We have to do *something*," Pamela insisted. "I can't have my name in the newspaper. Clay would absolutely freak. *The wife of a senior partner in Kansas City's most prestigious law firm involved in mysterious death of Shawnee dentist.* No thank you. Clay is under consideration for a very prestigious judgeship. A scandal like that would ruin his chances. I want that disgusting man's body away from here and out of our lives."

"How about if we bury him and leave the car where it will be stolen?" Gretchen suggested. "Maybe the police will think he was murdered by car jackers."

"Do you have any shovels?" Pamela asked Dixie, her voice full of hope.

"There might be one in the shed," Dixie admitted, "but even if there was, it hasn't rained in weeks. The ground is probably hard as cement. At least, if he's found out there in the flowerbed, it's obvious he hit his head on that rock. We'll just have to explain how it happened, leaving out the video, of course. We'll just say he was drunk and behaving abominably. When we wouldn't let him in the house, he went berserk and fell off the porch in the process."

"Then why didn't we call the police at the time?" Gretchen demanded.

"We could tell the truth," Dixie said. "We could say that we were hysterical and didn't want all that horror to come down on Mary Sue just hours before her mastectomy. Or I suppose we could say that we wanted to get her surgery over with before we called the police—so it wouldn't be delayed."

"Not reporting a death in a timely fashion is probably against the law," Gretchen pointed out. "And no matter what we give as an excuse, it does create an aura of suspicion. What if they ask us to take lie detector tests?"

Pamela held up her hands. "I simply can't be involved in something like this. Clay has a good chance for that appointment and would never forgive me if I screwed it up." The hysteria was creeping back into her voice.

"I cannot be involved," she said. "I need to go home. You two do whatever you want, but leave me out of it."

"We only have one car," Gretchen pointed out. "And everyone knows that you're out here with us anyway."

"Who is *everyone?*"

"Mary Sue, for one, and our kids," Dixie said. "And Mary Sue's mom. My dad. Miss McFadden down at the store. And Clay knows. We all came together in Gretchen's car. You would have driven your own car if you were planning to go home early."

"Well, there's only one solution," Gretchen said, slapping her knees and rising. "Walter and his car are going for a last ride—into the lake."

Dixie opened her mouth to put forward an argument. *Of course, they weren't going to drive a car with a dead body into the lake.* A dead body should be taken care of properly, with reverence. Even Walter Lampley deserved that. Besides, it was the lake her mother had loved and swum across for so many years. It was the lake that had been such a part of her friendship with these two women. And with Mary Sue. They couldn't defile it like that.

"We have to call the police," she said doggedly, rubbing her bruised hip.

Pamela began shaking her head back and forth, tears streaming down her cheeks. "Please no. Not the police."

"Too much time has gone by," Gretchen said, "and when Walter comes up missing, that woman at his house might go to the police. Of course, if he's reported dead, she also might go to the police and tell them about the two people who were roaming around his house."

"What woman?" Pamela demanded.

"There was a naked woman in his bedroom. We made a hasty exit but hung around long enough to see her sneak off into the night. We figure she must have been screwing around on her husband, or she would have called the police from Walter's house to report two intruders."

"Oh, God," Pamela groaned. "Did she get a good look at you?"

"I don't think so," Gretchen said. "Or maybe she did. She was scared shitless though and screaming like a banshee."

"Walter might have told her where he was going," Dixie speculated.

Gretchen shook her head. "But if she goes to the police, her husband will know about her little assignation with Walter."

They argued on. Dixie wanted to call the police. Pamela wanted to take Walter's body someplace else. Gretchen wanted to put him in the car and roll him into the lake.

Pamela and Gretchen finally convinced Dixie that even if the police thought Walter's death was an accident, they would still be obligated to investigate it as a possible homicide. And since there had been a scuffle that left wounds on his body—coupled with the fact that they waited so long to report his death—there was going to be a thorough investigation into how Walter became dead.

Dixie and Gretchen convinced Pamela that taking Walter's body and the car someplace else was a plan fraught with danger. The police would know the body had been moved. And they would check his phone records. They would know that someone at this phone number had called him.

"But a phone call isn't ominous unless they know he died out here," Gretchen insisted.

They argued on about what the police would and would not think, about the logistics of disposing of a body.

At one point Gretchen put on her rubber gloves and went up the hill to get the owner's manual out of the Porsche.

Finally, at a quarter of four, with Pamela using a pair of socks for gloves, they rolled Walter's still limp body onto a blanket and dragged it up the hill to his car, which Gretchen had repositioned at the top of the long incline that led down to the lake. It was an older model, she explained. No air bags. Turbocharged with the motor in the back. Really powerful. A deathtrap for sure.

Gretchen ran back down the hill and returned with a log from the woodpile. She slid behind the steering wheel, and after several attempts at ramming the end of the log against the windshield, managed to crack it.

"Perfect," she said, admiring her handiwork. "If Walter's body is ever found, it will look like he broke his neck when the car hit the water."

It took all three of them to get Walter's body with its wobbly head into the driver's seat. His flesh was rubbery and cool. Dixie kept tasting the contents of her stomach, kept wishing she would wake up from this nightmare.

With Pamela holding the flashlight, Gretchen used the sturdy jack from her Blazer to jack up the back end of the Porsche. "My daddy would be proud of me," she said. "He insisted that my mother and I both had to know how to change a flat tire."

She went loping once again down the hill to her vehicle. When she returned she was carrying the bag of ice, which by now had melted considerably and fused into a solid lump, and the empty gin bottle she brought from Walter's house. She put the bottle on the passenger seat and removed the ice from the bag, handing the empty bag to Dixie.

Dixie watched in amazement as Gretchen got into the passenger seat, started the engine with her gloved hand, turned on the headlights, put the car in gear, and wedged the chunk of ice against the accelerator. The car roared to life, and the back wheels began to spin. Faster and faster, with the roar of the motor growing louder and louder. It roared like a plane speeding down the runway, picking up intensity before the moment of takeoff. The entire car shook precariously, trying to escape. The ground vibrated under her feet and the air around her.

Dixie half-expected the car to take off with Gretchen inside, but the jack held. With great care, Gretchen got out of the shaking car and closed the door. As the three of them lined up behind the jacked-up car with its spinning wheels and roaring motor, Dixie's heart was pounding so hard, she wondered if she was having a heart attack.

Dixie could feel the power of the motor all around her before she placed her gloved hands on the bumper. The car trembled with greater and greater intensity as the motor revved ever higher. It was going to explode. They were all going to be killed.

Dixie couldn't hear Gretchen calling out instructions, so she followed her lead, hunching forward when Gretchen did, pushing when she pushed. With all her might, she pushed.

Dixie couldn't hear her own scream as the roaring car leaped off the jack and took off down the hill. Crashing through underbrush. Picking up speed.

Gretchen took off after it, with Pamela running behind her and Dixie bringing up the rear. Dixie stumbled and fell hands first to the ground.

When she looked up, the Porsche was hitting the water with an enormous spray of water, its headlights creating a swath of illumination across the surface of the lake. The car's forward momentum propelled it away from the shore, the motor still roaring.

Dixie joined Gretchen and Pamela at the water's edge, watching as the car slowly began to sink about thirty feet from the shore. And finally there was silence, which seemed just as deafening. The headlights glowed from the depths. They waited in silence until the lights were extinguished.

"Oh, my God!" Gretchen said. "Incredible. Absolutely incredible."

"The ice was brilliant," Pamela said.

"I read it in a mystery years ago," Gretchen said. "The evidence just melts."

Dixie stumbled over to a clump of cattails and threw up.

She was grateful when Gretchen gave her permission to go take a shower while she and Pamela tried to minimize the damage caused by the car's plunge down the hillside. "Pray for rain," Gretchen said as she and Pamela started back up the hill.

It took all Dixie's remaining energy to climb the stairs and step out of her clothes. Her hip was sore, her head throbbing, her stomach queasy. Even so, a feeling of numbness enveloped her. *Just let this night end. Please let it end.* Gratefully she stepped under the stream of hot water. She would like to stand there endlessly but knew she mustn't use up all the hot water. Gretchen hadn't showered yet. And Pamela might want to shower again— to scrub away the feel and smell of Walter's rubbery dead body. Dixie wished she could take off the top of her head and wash away the images of this night that resided there.

But there was no way to make this night vanish from memory. She and

Pamela and Gretchen would carry it with them always. Would it bind them together or tear them apart?

She stretched out on the bed where her parents once had slept. But as weary as she was she didn't even try to sleep. There was too little time, and she would feel the worse for it. Tonight, she promised herself, she would take a double dose of over-the-counter sleep medication and go to bed at sundown.

Dressed and ready and walking with a decided limp, Dixie joined Pamela and Gretchen in the kitchen for coffee and aspirin. Other than "pass the milk," there was no conversation. Just numbed silence. The dirty dishes were still piled on the counter. The food left out. Gretchen carried her cup to the sink and began rinsing off the dishes. Dixie told her never mind. She'd come back out tomorrow and see to it. Gretchen didn't protest.

Finally, Pamela said, "It's time."

Together, they climbed the stairs, tapped on the bedroom door, and tip-toed to Mary Sue's bedside. "You awake, honey?" Pamela whispered. "It's time to head for the hospital."

"I'm awake," Mary Sue said, opening her eyes. She groaned as she rose to one elbow, then carefully put her head back on the pillow. "Just shoot me," she moaned.

They helped her dress. Pamela knelt to slip on her sandals. Gretchen handed her a wet washcloth for her face. Dixie ran a comb through her hair. "I love you guys," Mary Sue mumbled, which made tears come to Dixie's eyes. "We love you, too," she said and kissed the top of her head.

It was a quiet bunch that headed into town before dawn. Mary Sue held her head and let out a soft moan from time to time. "I'll never drink cham-pagne again—not ever," she swore. "The last thing I remember is climbing back up the hill to the house."

Mary Sue's mother and children were waiting at the hospital when they arrived. Mary Sue asked the admitting nurse how long it would be until anesthesia, and then she hugged them all goodbye. "I'll be fine," she said reassuringly. "See you after a while."

Michelle had a tiny gold angel for her mother to pin to her hospital gown.

Once Mary Sue was out of sight, Gretchen, Dixie, and Pamela made their way to the coffee shop. Gretchen insisted they had to eat toast with their coffee before they took more aspirin. Dixie could manage neither the coffee nor the toast. Each time she thought about Walter on the bottom of the lake, her stomach would begin to roll.

Time in the waiting room crawled by. Pamela took out her needlepoint and occasionally made a stitch or two. When Gretchen's headache eased, she paced about the waiting area, then excused herself for a jog around the parking lot. Dixie holed up in the ladies' room for a time, throwing up for what she hoped was the last time and holding wet paper towels to her forehead. Gretchen brought her a 7-Up and a cup of ice.

As the morning wore on, Dixie began to feel better and even found herself smiling as Pamela slipped into the role of hostess, chit-chatting with Michelle and Michael about school, activities, and friends, and with Mary Sue's mom about how she was doing since the death of her second husband, how she liked living in Florida. Periodically, though, they all went silent and stared blankly at walls or out the window into the small courtyard where smokers stood or walked in circles. Dixie kept shifting her weight, trying to find a position of comfort for her bruised hip, and every few minutes would glance at the clock on the wall and wonder how far along the surgeons were, imagining Mary Sue's small, still form on an operating table.

How would Walter's disappearance affect her? Dixie wondered. Surely she hadn't kidded herself into thinking she loved the man. Surely she wouldn't waste too much time grieving for him, at least not at any deep level. She needed to concentrate on getting well. Her children needed her. Dixie needed her.

In the first grade Mary Sue had slipped her hand into Dixie's and asked if she would join her club. Dixie wore glasses with one frosted lens to correct a lazy eye. She also wore brown lace-up orthopedic oxfords to correct a pigeon-toed gait, and her mother insisted on braiding her hair into dumb old pigtails when other girls got to have permanents and curls. She realized even then that Mary Sue felt sorry for her and had decided to rescue her. And because Mary Sue—with her fluffy blond hair, blue eyes, rosy cheeks, and dimpled smile—was acknowledged to be the prettiest and sweetest girl in the first grade, she had the power to bring poor little Dixie Bloom, the girl with the funny name, strange glasses, ugly shoes, and dumb hair, into the realm of the accepted. The other members of the club were Pamela and Gretchen. Dixie had always theorized that Pamela had been chosen because she had a retarded older brother and Gretchen because—as the tallest student in their grade—the boys had dubbed her "The Monster."

And it was indeed Mary Sue's club. She named it the Girlfriends Club and decided when they should meet and where. She called the meetings to order and decided if the time would be spent coloring or singing or jumping rope. She decided what the password would be and when it should be changed. She decided when it was all right for Pamela's brother Danny to join them for refreshments. No one ever questioned her authority. They might hurt Mary Sue's feelings if they did. And they knew that her every decision was based on what would be best for the club, best for them.

The Girlfriends Club lasted for several years, until they no longer needed the structure of a club, having become all but inseparable. By then, satisfied they were permanently bonded to one another, Mary Sue had relinquished her absolute rule and generally went along with whatever the rest of them wanted. Of course, they continued to want whatever would please her. Mary Sue was the reason they were friends. And in spite of the power of her prettiness, there was a delicacy about Mary Sue that went beyond her small size. Dixie had always secretly worried that something bad was going to happen to her. Mary Sue was like the character you loved so much from the very beginning of the story that you feared he or she was going to be sacrificed to the plot. She was *too* pretty, *too* good. She was Beth in *Little Women,* Alice in *The Last of the Mohicans,* Roberta in *Beaches.* And now Mary Sue had breast cancer. Dixie almost felt as though she had caused Mary Sue's illness by having such thoughts. She almost wished she herself were the one with cancer. *Almost,* but not quite. A part of her was immensely grateful that she was not the one who had been stricken.

When Dixie told her father about Mary Sue's cancer, he had said that at least the cancer was someplace they could cut off. Which was true. So why was it women—herself included—feared breast cancer so intensely? No one wanted the mutilation, of course. It did bring up body issues, tampering with one's image of femininity. But the fear went beyond the mutilation, beyond the loss of a breast. *Every* woman, it seemed, had friends, relatives, acquaintances who had had breast cancer, and some of them had died—not always older women either, but women like Mary Sue with children to finish raising and life issues yet to resolve, with what they hoped were the best years yet to live.

The night after Mary Sue's diagnosis, Dixie had rummaged around in the drawers of her dresser until she found the plastic card she was supposed to have hung in the shower and used to guide her through a monthly self-examination of her breasts. Of course, she didn't quite understand the value of such examinations, when mammograms were supposed to find tumors before they became a threat to one's life. By the time a woman could actually feel a tumor with her fingertips, wouldn't it be too large to cure? But then if that were true, surely the medical profession wouldn't be putting the burden of finding their own tumors on women.

Mary Sue had performed breast self-examination. Her calendar had the appropriate day circled in red. Mary Sue had given Dixie the shower card.

Numerous people had asked Dixie in hushed tones if Mary Sue had done monthly self-examinations and had annual mammograms, as if her not doing these things would somehow have caused her predicament. Dixie remembered when her chain-smoking uncle had died of lung cancer, and everyone had acted so surprised because he had, after all, had annual chest x-rays, as though annual chest x-rays were a talisman that kept the lung-cancer demon at bay.

Dixie was sure that Mary Sue had never once put off her annual mammogram or her annual anything else. She was easily the most conscientious of all of them. Even health-conscious Gretchen, by her own admission, stuck those reminder postcards from doctors and dentists on the refrigerator and put off making appointments for months at a time. She put her faith in prevention, as she was fond of saying.

Ironically, it was Mary Sue's internist who found the lump when she had gone in for her annual physical only two months after her last mammogram, which had been one year almost to the day since her previous one. The friend who had been the most responsible and dutiful had been the one who was stricken.

Dixie carried the instruction card into the bathroom. Following its directions, she first stood bare-chested in front of a mirror, pressing her hands together and flexing the muscles in her arms to observe the contours of her breasts and look for changes. Then she stepped into the shower, soaped herself, and began systematically touching and probing, unsure exactly what she was looking for but hoping she would know *it* if indeed *it* were there. Such a weird thing to be doing. The whole procedure had such a negative feel about it. *Let's see if we have breast cancer today. And if we don't do this every single month, we are naughty little girls.*

There was no male equivalent to this mandated behavior, was there? Was there ever an ominous overtone when men fondled their scrotums? Or were they allowed to do it simply because it felt good? Usually, the only time she touched her breasts with any great intent was when she wanted to arouse herself. She had always wanted Arnie to pay more attention to her breasts during lovemaking, but he seemed to think a few squeezes and a few sucks on one side or the other was all that was required. If he were really into it, he would spend a little time on both breasts but never long enough. Just when she was beginning to feel aroused, he would be crawling on top of her.

Sometimes Dixie wondered if she could have an orgasm just from breast fondling alone. She couldn't quite give herself one, but could some skillful man achieve that for her? Eventually, she discovered the answer to that question, but it wasn't Arnie who provided it.

After the shower, she dried off and, as the card instructed, stretched out on her bed to examine her breasts while she was flat on her back. At the conclusion of the process, she supposed she was okay and reached for her bra and T-shirt, grateful the ordeal was over and she could once again cover herself.

Then she sat on the side of the bed and cried, unsure exactly why. Was it because Mary Sue had cancer or because she herself was, therefore, somehow morally obligated to go through this ritual every damned month for the rest of her life?

And she would do that. Because of Mary Sue, she really would. A sacrament. *Do this in remembrance of me.* Except such a thought made it seem as though she expected Mary Sue to die. She amended the entreaty—*Do this because of me.* Dixie had already circled the days on her calendar. And she would never be late for her mammogram or her yearly gynecological exam again. She would start having annual physicals. She would get her teeth cleaned and her eyes checked on schedule. She would be responsible—the thought of which made her cry all the harder. She rolled back onto the bed and wept into her pillow. She felt as though most of whatever was carefree about her life had just gone flying out the window. Most, but not all.

Gradually, she had gotten the sobbing under control and had calmed herself with lovely thoughts. *She was sitting on a terrace in the mountaintop town of Cornice, a tiny little place that didn't even merit a dot on the map, and lifting a glass of hearty homemade wine to her lips. She felt the golden warmth of the Tuscan sun on her face, a gentle breeze lifting her hair. She could see across the achingly beautiful landscape of vineyards and orchards filled with twisted olive trees that climbed their way up even the steepest hillsides, and of timeless villages, each with the bell tower of an ancient church ruling over a jumble of terracotta rooftops— all the way to the blue, blue ocean twenty kilometers distant. And with just a slight shift of her body, she could feel the solid reality of the man sitting beside her.*

Dixie closed her eyes, shutting out the hospital waiting room and seeing that special place once again. Someday she would like to take Mary Sue there. And the others. But probably she never would.

Pamela had been working on the same needlepoint project for almost two years—not that she wasn't diligent about picking it up whenever she had a chance. The project was an ambitious one, however, a replica of a medieval tapestry featuring a castle in the background and a lady on a unicorn in the foreground. The project required every possible type of needlepoint stitch and dozens of different shades of yarn. When she finished it, Pamela planned to have it framed and hung over the fireplace in the master bedroom. Or maybe she would give it to Mary Sue.

Usually, needlepointing calmed her. She had a hard time sitting still for very long unless she had her current project in her lap. But today, in the hospital waiting room, she had to force herself to sit still while an inner turmoil possessed her. The hideous events of the night before took on a surreal quality when filtered through the light of day.

They actually had put that horrible man's dead body in his car and let it roll into the lake.

Since marrying Clay, Pamela had led a careful, circumspect life, ever aware of the responsibility that came from being married to a prominent, politically connected attorney on his way to an important judgeship. If it ever became known that she had broken the law, that she had helped dispose of the body of a man who had died under suspicious circumstances, she stood to lose everything. *Everything.*

Then she reminded herself that Walter's death and the subsequent disposal of his body were less important than what was now happening to Mary Sue.

When Mary Sue first told her about the cancer, Pamela had been horrified. Women *died* of breast cancer. Good and worthy women still in their prime died of breast cancer. *Mary Sue* could die. Mary Sue, who had been such a constant in her life.

Mary Sue had never once questioned Pamela's decision not to have children, never once said that she was missing the best part of life. Mary Sue was the only person whose number she could dial without planning the conversation in advance. Mary Sue also was the only person who knew that, while Pamela loved the life her husband had provided for her and was incredibly grateful to him for that life, while she did love and care about Clay very much, she was not now and had never been *in love* with him.

Clay was not a lovable man. At some level, Pamela had realized that from the very first. He was impressive, though. A highly regarded partner in her father's firm, Clay Cartwright had an aristocratic look and air about him. One wasn't surprised to learn that his grandfather had been governor of Missouri. That his uncle was a bishop in the Episcopal Church. That he had graduated from Harvard *summa cum laude* and been a Rhodes Scholar at Oxford. That he had been president of the state bar association.

Clay also had two children by his first marriage and was adamant about never having more.

He had met his first wife during his Oxford years. She had taken their daughters back to England at marriage's end, but they had spent summers and Christmases with their father until they turned eighteen.

Clay had told Pamela from the very beginning that he had had a vasectomy. He loved his daughters but was always relieved when they went home, and he could return to his orderly existence. He saw in Pamela an orderly woman who would complement his life. He admired her greatly, he told her when he proposed. She was lovely and had a natural elegance about her that pleased him. He liked the idea of an elegant, decorous wife who would create an elegant, decorous world for him.

Pamela felt honored that such a man wanted to marry her. She never considered saying no to his proposal. And after five years of sharing a shabby apartment with a succession of roommates who never became close friends, after struggling to make ends meet and become self-sufficient but repeatedly having to ask her parents to bail her out, after never being able to afford the fabulous clothes and accessories she helped select for the department store's designer collection, she longed to live well. Longed with a yearning that went all the way to bedrock. And marrying Clay meant she would not have to decide about children. She would never have to risk motherhood.

Her only sibling had been sent to live in a group home when Pamela was twelve. Danny had been seventeen.

Her parents had introduced Danny gradually to the home. The whole Gilbert family went there several times for meals. Then Danny would stay for just the day, with his mother at his side. He was like a parrot, reciting all the reasons why he needed to live in the home, where he would have friends just like himself and have a real job and make money and learn to be a grown-up man.

But the real reason Danny had to go live in the group home was that he wanted to have sex with his sister.

The first decade of Danny's life had been plagued with health problems. He had open-heart surgery to correct a leaking valve and was hospitalized frequently with respiratory illness. Danny's needs always came first. The family seldom went on vacation, fearful of getting Danny too far away from his physician and competent medical care, uncomfortable about the inevitable stares that would come their way.

Their mother, Jessica, spent diligent hours with Danny, maximizing his limited ability. He struggled with *The Cat in the Hat* but eventually was able to do simple computations. Danny earned pats and praise when he knew that twenty take away five was fifteen. Meanwhile, Pamela was chastised if she earned less than straight A's. In the fifth grade, she decided that she would never again be a straight-A student.

Jessica Gilbert's friends, who petted and greatly indulged Danny, considered Jessica saintly. Proceeds from Junior League events were donated to agencies that worked with the mentally retarded. The Gilberts were named Garden Grove's Family of the Year by the local newspaper. But Pamela knew her mother was not happy. She sighed a lot and spent a great deal of time staring out the window. She once told Pamela that sainthood was a trap—once you were elevated to such lofty heights, no one would like you if you climbed down. Pamela knew that when Danny was four her parents had already arranged to adopt a healthy child when Jessica realized she was pregnant once again. They didn't tell anyone about the pregnancy until after she had undergone amniocentesis and the doctor was able to promise them that they absolutely would not have another Down's syndrome child. Pamela had asthma, though. There were frequent late-night visits to the emergency room for breathing treatments.

Her asthma got better after Danny went to live in the home.

Her parents had realized there was a problem when Pamela asked if she could have a lock on her door to keep Danny from getting in bed with her at night. When quizzed, she admitted that he tried to pull up her nightgown and sometimes took his penis out of his pajama bottoms.

Jessica slept with her daughter until they got Danny situated in the group home. And she would return to Pamela's bed when Danny came for overnight visits. Pamela always felt as if it were somehow her fault that her brother had to live in that other house, which wasn't nearly so nice as their family home, but she couldn't help feeling glad that he was gone.

When she became the only child in the house, she thought her mother would have time for her the way she had always had time for Danny. But with Danny gone, Jessica was like a bird let out of a cage. She took up golf after an almost two-decade hiatus. She took tennis lessons and enrolled in watercolor classes. She was elected president of the Friends of the Library and the League of Women Voters. She lightened her hair and lost ten pounds.

At times Jessica went to Danny's room and cried, but mostly she walked with a lighter step and laughed when she talked to her friends on the phone. Pamela's parents started taking vacations, mostly with each other, to Hawaii, Europe, New York. They looked and acted younger with Danny out of the house. They even kissed in front of Pamela, and she could hear her mother giggling in the night. The final part of their metamorphosis came the year after Pamela's marriage to Clay when they sold their home, retired to south Texas's balmy shores and golf courses, and left Pamela in charge of Danny.

Motherhood changed women—of that, Pamela was sure. Even women who had perfectly normal, charming children had to be selfless and saintly. Marrying Clay let her off the hook. And she would never have to disappoint a child, just in case she didn't have it in her to be selfless and saintly. She would never have to undergo amniocentesis and face the monstrous decision of whether to abort a defective child.

Not that she was without regret. She wasn't sure whether it was children that she missed or just love. Of course, she did have children in her life. She doted on her friends' kids and continued to have a reasonably satisfying relationship with her stepdaughters, even though they were now grown up and no longer bothered with trips to Kansas. And there was Danny—he was like her child. She called him almost daily and took him shopping and to the movies. When her parents died, she would become his legal guardian. If she outlived Clay, which was likely since she was fourteen years his junior, she would take Danny on trips and let him stay over on weekends, always with her bedroom door firmly locked, of course.

In many ways, she was the person she was because of her brother. She both wished he had never been born and loved him more than anyone. Danny and Mary Sue were the best and dearest people in her life.

Yes, she would definitely give the lady on her unicorn to Mary Sue, Pamela decided, smoothing the canvas and assessing her work. Each stitch would take on more meaning that way. She was doing something tangible for Mary Sue.

Chapter Five

At eight-thirty, the surgeon came out to say that her part of the procedure went well and Mary Sue was doing fine. Dixie gave Michelle a hug. "It will all be over soon," she promised. "A year from now this will all be an unpleasant memory."

It was close to eleven when the plastic surgeon came out to say the reconstruction was completed, and Mary Sue was in recovery.

It was an hour more before they were allowed to see Mary Sue in the recovery room. Dixie was shocked at how ghastly she looked—so pale, her features distorted under the plastic of the oxygen mask, tubes and wires everywhere. Michelle burst into tears and buried her face against her grandmother's shoulder. Gretchen took Mary Sue's hand and told her it was all over, and her doctors said she had come through with flying colors. Mary Sue mumbled under the mask but didn't open her eyes. They took turns kissing her forehead and squeezing her hand before the nurse shooed them away, assuring them that by evening Mary Sue would be sitting up and smiling.

They all went for lunch at a nearby restaurant, the conversation revolving around what lay ahead for Mary Sue—how long she would have to stay in the hospital, whether she would have radiation or chemotherapy, whether she would lose her hair. Periodically, Dixie's gaze would meet

Gretchen's or Pamela's. *Such a secret they shared.* Forever, Dixie hoped. It must remain theirs alone. Could she pray about that? she wondered. Could she pray that a man's body would rot in the bottom of a lake, rot away until it disappeared?

Over coffee, Gretchen asked Michelle and Michael where their father and Trish were going on their honeymoon.

The teenagers glanced at one another. Michael answered. "To some tennis resort in Bermuda." Oddly, the attempted bravado of his peroxided stand of spiked hair, pierced ear, and baggy clothing only served to make him look younger, like a small child playing dress-up.

"I don't want to be in my father's wedding," Michelle announced, tears filling her eyes. Vividly blue eyes, like her mother's. Michelle was a carbon copy of Mary Sue. And her grandmother. Connie still kept her hair blond, still had a trim figure.

And like her mother and grandmother before her, Michelle was a cheerleader at Garden Grove High School. On Connie's sixty-fifth birthday, the three of them—Michelle, Mary Sue, and Connie—had worked up a routine complete with cartwheels and high kicks. They were so good they had been invited to perform at the homecoming pep rally. Their performance had made the evening news on a local television station, and their picture had been in the *Kansas City Star.*

Michael was dark like his father but had Mary Sue's small stature. He was a handsome boy, or would be when he stopped peroxiding his hair.

"Michael doesn't want to be in the wedding either," Michelle added. Dixie knew that Michelle had been assigned the role of candle lighter, and Michael was to be his father's best man. Trish's sister was coming from Dallas to be maid of honor.

"Are you guys invited?" Michelle asked her mother's friends.

A snorting laugh erupted from Gretchen. "Are you kidding? If I were your father, I'd hire guards to keep us away."

"Dad says that sometimes marriages just wear out and people are better off going their separate ways," Michael put forward in his father's behalf.

"Yes, that's true," Dixie said, putting a hand on the boy's arm. "It isn't that we don't wish your father well, Michael, we're just very sorry that your mother got hurt."

"So, you think he should have hung around and been unhappy for the rest of his life?" Michael challenged.

"What do you think, Michael?" Connie asked her grandson.

He shrugged. "That I'm never going to get married, I guess. I don't want to be unhappy, and I don't want to make anyone else unhappy."

"Trish is making me wear a really dumb dress with *ruffles,*" Michelle said as she toyed with the straw in her empty glass. "It looks like something a six-year-old flower girl would wear."

"I'm sure you will wear it with great dignity," Pamela said. "I think you should have your nails polished blood red, let me put your hair up in a French twist, and carry yourself like a queen. No one will notice the ruffles."

Michelle looked thoughtful, then sat up a little straighter and folded her hands in her lap.

"Besides, you have to be our spy," Connie said. "We want to know who's there so we can mark them off our list of friends. And we need to know about the food and if a windstorm blows away the tent. Or if the maid of honor picks her nose."

Michelle smiled and shook her finger at her grandmother. "You're naughty."

"Yes, and aren't you glad?" Connie said with a grin.

When they got back to the hospital, Mary Sue had been moved to a room but was still too sleepy to say much. Connie sent them all home for a nap. She would stay with her daughter throughout the afternoon.

"I feel like I've missed a year of sleep," Gretchen said as they trudged wearily across the parking lot.

"Now we are joined together as never before," Pamela said.

Dixie kept dozing off on the way back to the lake, her head jerking when she snapped back to consciousness. Gretchen rowed them out to the middle, where one by one, they tossed the videotapes and camera into the lake, along with the blanket they had used to drag Walter up the hill. It was finally supposed to rain tonight, Gretchen observed, looking up at gathering clouds. That should take care of any tracks made by the Porsche.

When Dixie finally got home, there was only time for a short nap before returning to the hospital. She plugged in a heating pad for her sore hip and stretched out on the bed.

She awoke too soon to the sound of her son's voice. He was shaking her shoulder, telling her that she had a phone call, that Dr. Prescott was on the line. He wanted to know how Mary Sue was.

When she arrived at the hospital, Gretchen and Pamela were already there. Mary Sue was sitting up, wearing makeup, looking like her pretty self. "I feel a little dopey, but not too bad," she said.

After Connie had taken her grandchildren to dinner, Mary Sue gingerly touched the right side of her chest. "I'm glad there's *something* there," she said. "The official name for it is 'flap'—at least that's what the nurses call it—but I think of it as my new breast. Anyway, it would have been rough to wake up and have nothing there."

"Have you seen it?" Pamela asked.

"Not yet, but I can *feel* it. That's the important thing."

"Barry called," Dixie said. "He wanted to know how you were getting along. He's sending flowers."

Mary Sue shrugged. "I don't want his flowers."

"We'll give them away," Dixie assured her. "Michelle doesn't want to be in his wedding."

Gretchen nodded. "She told us at lunch. Pamela told her to carry herself like a queen. She'll be fine."

"He's getting away with it, isn't he?" Mary Sue said, carefully easing herself back onto the pillows. "He gets a rich new wife and a mansion. His kids are obligated to forgive him for leaving their mother. I heard Michelle ask her father if she could invite her friends to swim in Trish's pool, which apparently has an island in the center and is big enough to float a battleship. Barry has promised them European vacations, and I have to learn to live more frugally. I'm the only loser."

"You're not a loser," Dixie said. "Now that you know his true colors, you'll come to realize you're better off without him."

"No, I'm not. If I had to choose between divorce and breast cancer, I'd take breast cancer. Now, I've got them both."

Pamela didn't stay long. She needed to get home and see about Clay's dinner, she explained to Mary Sue. "I'll see you in the morning," she said, but lingered a minute longer to hold Mary Sue's hand and smooth her hair.

They watched Pamela leave, then Gretchen said, "I guess there's some unwritten rule about the Lord of the Manor not having to fend for himself two nights in a row."

Dixie and Gretchen stayed until Mary Sue began to doze off, then went to their favorite hole-in-the-wall restaurant. "This morning, I swore I'd never drink again, but I need at least a beer," Gretchen said. "Only one, though. I plan to get a good night's sleep and go to six A.M. aerobics." Then she shrugged. "Life does go on," she said apologetically. "We can't let this . . . this *thing* that happened change who we are, can we?"

"I suppose," Dixie said. "After Mother died, I felt guilty if I caught myself laughing at a joke or enjoying her favorite dessert. I guess the horror of last night will wear off eventually, but the three of us will never be the same."

Gretchen took the first sip of her beer, followed by a deep breath, and said, "It's hard to be sorry when he was such a jerk—a first-class, genuine pain-in-the-ass jerk. And Clay Cartwright is just about as bad. He just hides his jerkiness with eight-hundred-dollar suits and a fake semi-British accent. When I look at Pamela, I wonder if I shouldn't be glad that I'm divorced. But I'm not glad, even though I hate men—really *hate* them. God, they're all such jerks."

"Not all," Dixie said.

"How come you're not bitter, like Mary Sue and me?" Gretchen demanded. "How come you don't hate your ex? How come you're not frantic? Mary Sue and I talk about that all the time. We don't get it. How come you aren't out there looking? How come you haven't joined the dating service?"

"Ah, yes, the same dating service that produced you-know-who for Mary Sue," Dixie reminded Gretchen.

Gretchen nodded. "Yeah. Can you believe I was actually jealous of her because she had a man in her life—even a man who drove a *yellow* Porsche? Do you suppose they really come in that color, or did he have to have it painted? God, what a total ass he turned out to be. But on the other hand, if he *had* stood by Mary Sue in her time of need, we would have fawned over him for being *noble*. We expect so little out of men. If Walter hadn't met his unfortunate demise, the man would have moved on to another cute little ex-cheerleader who would have cooked and fluttered for him. And I will keep looking for a man—*desperately* looking for a man—because I am lonely and scared to death that I will never again feel a man's arms around me, because I don't know who I am anymore without a man in my life. I hate having this last name that no longer has anything to do with who I now am. At least you have a son to justify your last name. My girls will get married and change theirs. My only identity will be as the *first* Mrs. Bonner."

"And if you marry again, you will be the second or third Mrs. Something Else. Change your name to something that has nothing to do with a man, if that's an issue for you. Take back your maiden name or change your name to Gretchen Jones or Gretchen Goodperson and keep it for the rest of your life, marriage or not. You are who you are regardless of whoever it is you are living with or screwing. You are a good friend and a good mother and a fitness freak and mystery buff. If you need something else in your life, get a job. Don't base your future happiness on whether or not you have a man in your life and in your bed."

Gretchen narrowed her eyes. "That's a bunch of bullshit, and you know it!"

She was a bit of a fraud, Dixie admitted to herself as she headed for her car. She paused under a streetlight to look at her watch. It was probably too late to make a transatlantic phone call. But she just might anyway.

With Walter's death, she now had two major secrets in her life—one ghastly and the other so pleasurable she sometimes felt as though she was floating.

Chapter Six

With Dixie living in Illinois, her three girlhood friends had not been witnesses to the demise of her marriage. She insisted to them that her and Arnie's divorce had been mutual. They had grown apart and simply agreed to go their separate ways. That was also what she told her parents and wrote to her brother Joey, who was a regular Army officer stationed in Germany. She was too humiliated to tell them that Arnie had left her for another woman—for Cindy, the Sharon Stone lookalike who painted huge canvases of dark sinister images and didn't own a pot or pan.

Her brother hadn't bought her explanation. He called to ask if he should fly home and beat the shit out of the no-good son-of-a-bitch. To calm him, Dixie insisted that neither one of them had been particularly happy. It was probably for the best.

After hanging up, she had sat there staring at the phone for a long time, wondering if she had spoken the truth. Maybe so. Maybe it really was for the best. But Arnie had ended things so abruptly. He alone made the decision to end their marriage with no negotiation, no talking things over, no second chance, no consideration of what was best for their son.

Her friends also doubted her explanation. In their opinion, no woman ever willingly enters into a divorce—unless, of course, she already has another man in her life.

"Come on, Dixie, you can tell us," Pamela insisted during Dixie's first trip back to Garden Grove after finally owning up to her impending divorce. "Who is he? When will we meet him?"

"Are you waiting until he gets a divorce before you go public with him?" Gretchen speculated.

When Arnie remarried the month after the divorce was final, Dixie's friends backed off. No matter what she claimed, Dixie was living their own worst nightmare. She had been replaced.

Within three years, the same thing had happened to Mary Sue, and then to Gretchen. Dixie wasn't the only one whose husband had been unfaithful. Not the only one whose husband had left her for another woman. Not the only one who had failed at marriage. And Dixie was able to drop her façade and join her friends in their puzzlement and anger. Except that by then, she was down the road and able to look back, to assess. Divorce no longer seemed like the end of the world.

She hadn't really planned to move back to Garden Grove. That came when it became apparent that her mother was dying. And then she thought it would just be temporary. Kirk stayed with his father and Cindy in their smart, newly restored loft apartment with a view of the lake, while he finished out the school year, using car service to transport him back and forth to his school in suburban Sauganash. The arrangement made Dixie nervous. What if Kirk liked Cindy more than he liked her? What if he wanted to live with them always? Losing her husband was one thing, but she'd rather die than lose her son.

Poor Kirk. He didn't know what he wanted. When she told him she planned to move to Garden Grove, he cried.

"Grandpa needs us, and you can have a dog," Dixie said, playing her trump cards up front.

"Dad needs me, too," Kirk countered.

"I don't have enough money for us to stay in our house," she admitted. "I'm going to have to sell it. If we stay in Sauganash, we'll have to move into an apartment or buy a house in a cheaper neighborhood. In either case, you won't be able to go to the same school. In Garden Grove, we can live with Grandpa, and I can make enough money for us to take trips and not have to watch every penny. It's only an hour flight to Chicago. You can see your father almost as often as before."

In the end, Kirk relented. Cindy was almost too nice, he admitted. Sometimes he wondered if she was just putting on an act.

Of course, Dixie had mixed feelings about moving back and living with her father. It seemed as though she were going backward. But what she had told Kirk about her financial situation was true. What she had thought was a fair divorce settlement turned out to be inadequate. The house needed a new roof, and every month, it seemed there was a new budget buster. New tires. A dead refrigerator. Squirrels in the attic. A broken garage door. Frozen pipes. Five hundred dollars to have a dead tree removed. And no matter how hard she worked, her income from freelancing wasn't enough to make up the difference between her settlement and reality. Her Ford station wagon was six years old, and her husband's second wife was driving a new Mercedes. When Kirk told her that Arnie and Cindy had bought a cabin cruiser, Dixie came unglued and went on a rampage, breaking china and screaming like a crazy woman, with Kirk begging her to stop.

But through the fear and rage, other feelings would surface.

She would experience moments of sheer giddiness that she didn't have to negotiate what television program to watch, what time she went to bed, what constituted an evening meal. She didn't have to listen to Arnie carping at her when she forgot to close the garage door or pick up his dry cleaning or buy his favorite cereal. She no longer had to put up with his rebuttals and put-downs.

But there also were those times when she woke in the night feeling unbearably sad that Arnie wasn't there beside her, when she thought of something she wanted to tell him and realized they would never again just converse, never again laugh together or tease each other. It seemed such a short time ago that she had assumed they would be together forever.

Dismantling their home had been devastating. Dixie was left with the task of deciding what to do with every item. Each room, each closet, each drawer contained memories. It was hard to decide what to keep and what to throw away. She would discard something only to go dig it out of the trash and find a place for it in one of the boxes. When the van arrived in Garden Grove, she didn't have the heart to change her mother's house, and most of her possessions ended up in either the basement or the attic.

Her dad stayed on in the first-floor bedroom. She and Kirk had the second floor to themselves. They and Betty the beagle puppy were just beginning to settle into new routines when her father started keeping company with a widow down the block. Dixie was shocked. Her mother had been dead less than six months. Myrtle Simpson's husband hadn't been dead much longer. It was unseemly and disrespectful.

George Bloom ignored his daughter's objections and within the month had moved in with Myrtle. But they wouldn't be getting married, he told his daughter. Marriage would screw up their Social Security.

Dixie hadn't seen her father this happy in years, and it made her seethe. Perhaps she should be glad for him, but her pain over losing her mother was too raw. How could he just toss grief aside? Her parents had been married for almost fifty years, for God's sake! They had been good friends with the Simpsons for most of those years. The four of them always went together to the home football games in Lawrence and played in the same bridge clubs. And now, her father was *living* with Myrtle. Dixie wondered if he was getting senile. Surely he and Myrtle didn't have sex.

Gradually, though, she became accustomed to the arrangement and had to admit that his relationship with Myrtle had given her father a new lease on life. He and Myrtle took up ballroom dancing, enrolled in watercolor classes, went on cruises, gambled in riverboat casinos.

But why hadn't he done those things with her mother? The last trip of any consequence Dixie remembered her parents taking together was almost ten years ago when they went to Colorado. Her mother had taken along a stack of books to read while her father fished. She had brought back a rock to add to her collection at the lake house. And now her widowed husband was dancing the tango with Myrtle Simpson on cruise ships.

Always before, Dixie had assumed her parents had the perfect marriage. Now, she wasn't so sure. She couldn't remember her father ever looking at her mother with the adoring eyes with which he now gazed at Myrtle Simpson. He and Myrtle held hands. And hugged. Even kissed. Right there in front of her! She had to look away.

She wished she had asked her mother how she felt about marriage. Had she been happy? Did she have any regrets? What did she wish for her daughter?

In those last weeks, Millie kept forgetting that Dixie was now a divorced woman and would fret about how long she was staying in Garden Grove. She really should be getting on home to her husband and son.

When Dixie's brother arrived, it took Millie the longest time to realize who he was. "But you grew up," she had said. Then she wouldn't turn loose his hand.

They waited together with their father for their mother's last breath. When it came, it seemed anticlimactic. Dixie was shocked that she didn't cry uncontrollably but mostly felt exhausted and relieved that it was over. The uncontrollable tears came at the funeral. Mary Sue, Pamela, and Gretchen sat with the family. After all, Millie Bloom had been like their second mother.

When her father insisted she and Kirk should eat Thanksgiving dinner at Myrtle's house, Dixie finally had her say. He was helping her rake leaves in the backyard, with Betty the beagle making a game of it. Kirk would be with his father, George pointed out. Dixie shouldn't be alone on a holiday. "Myrtle is a great cook," he added.

The words stung. No one ever would have called Millie Bloom a great cook. Dixie's mom avoided real cooking like the plague. She was a devotee of Hamburger Helper and recipes that called for canned cream of mushroom soup and no more than four other ingredients. She was on a first-name basis with three generations of the family who owned the Greek deli. When Dixie and her brother were growing up, they always ate holiday dinners at their grandparents'. Her grandma Dixie was a fabulous cook, who deep-fat-fried turkeys Cajun style in the backyard and made pecan pies that tasted of bourbon. Dixie could never recall her mother cooking a turkey or making a pie.

Dixie kept raking, Betty doing her best to undo the effort. "I'd rather not," she told her dad, her voice cool.

"Look, honey," he said, kneeling to pet the dog. "I know you're not crazy about me and Myrtle getting together so soon after your mother's death, but Myrtle is the best thing that could have happened to me at this stage of my life."

"I suppose," Dixie said, not looking at him. "But it's hard for me to see you so happy, like Mother doesn't matter anymore."

"My being with Myrtle doesn't mean I didn't love your mother. I loved her since grade school. I grew up knowing I would marry her. She was a wonderful woman, and I wish like everything that she were still here with us now. But she's not. Does that mean I have to stop living, too?"

Dixie stopped raking and leaned on her rake. Betty sat at her feet, waiting. "You could have waited a year or two. It seemed like you hardly spent any time grieving for her or missing her."

"Honey, I'm seventy-two years old. I want to enjoy what time I have left."

"Do you love Myrtle?"

"Yes, I love her. She's funny and kind and takes damned good care of me. A man likes a woman to fuss over him. Your mother wasn't much of a fusser. She preferred reading to cooking. But don't you go asking me if I love Myrtle more than I loved your mother. It's not the same. Your mother and I had all those years. We shared our youth and grew old together. What Myrtle and I share is a reprieve, which is a wonderful gift when you think about it."

"Don't you miss Mother at all?" Dixie asked.

"When I think about her, I miss her so much it hurts. That's why I don't go down to the store anymore. It seems like she should be there with me. But mostly my mind is filled with what is happening right now. I'm living in the present, honey."

"And what about that grave marker for two out in the cemetery?"

"That's where I belong when the time comes, just like Myrtle will be buried next to her Ralph. But in the meantime, we both have life and each other. Now, will you have Thanksgiving dinner with us? Her son and his family are coming."

"No, I really can't, Daddy. Maybe next year."

Mary Sue had invited her to have Thanksgiving dinner with her, Barry, and the children. Pamela said she was sure Clay wouldn't mind if Dixie came to the catered dinner they were having for assorted friends and relatives. Gretchen, Paul, and their kids were heading for Springfield to have turkey with his brother's family—but Dixie was welcome to come along.

Dixie appreciated their offers but decided to stay home and paint the pantry. When she took everything off the shelves, she counted eight cans of Campbell's cream of mushroom soup and numerous boxes of Hamburger Helper. She opened a can of the soup for her Thanksgiving dinner. And ate a whole bag of Hershey's kisses. No, her mother hadn't been much of a fusser, she acknowledged as she gathered up the foil wrappings from the candy and threw them in the trash. Her mother bought pies at the bakery and expected her husband and children to carry their own dinner plates to the kitchen and participate in the tidying up. Dixie had tried to be a different sort of wife. She wasn't any good at pies, but except for her writing, she played the role of the traditional wife. Maybe she should have been more like her mother. At least she would be a well-read divorcée.

Midafternoon, her father brought her a plate of turkey and dressing and the remainder of a bottle of wine. She thanked him and, as soon as he left, gave Betty a slice of turkey and put the rest down the disposal. She drank the wine, however, and it made her maudlin. "I love you, Mother," she said, projecting her voice throughout the lonely old house. "I'll never be unfaithful to you. No one else could ever take your place. You're the best mother a girl could ever have. The very best. The very, very, very best."

✳   ✳   ✳

With Dixie's status changed from a temporary to a permanent resident of Garden Grove, she realized that her friends were having a hard time fitting her into their very established lives. She was, after all, a *divorcée*. Had she not already been a fixture in their lives, they probably would have kept their distance. As it was, they weren't sure just how to structure this new phase of their friendship. No divorced woman belonged to the Garden Grove Junior League. The only unmarried women who were members of the country club were widows. Mary Sue, Gretchen, and Pamela's social lives were couples-oriented. Nevertheless, the three of them began to invite her to dinner parties, casting far and wide for a suitable single man to pair her with—until Dixie asked them to stop. She had dated before moving back home. She'd had enough of dating for now. Her announcement to that effect occurred after Pamela had talked her into going to the law firm Christmas party. She wanted Dixie to meet a recently widowed senior partner. "He has a real interest in flowers and is on the board of the botanical gardens," Pamela explained. "He would really like to meet you."

The morning after the party, Dixie was still in bed when Pamela called. "Why did you leave—without even telling us? And don't give me that headache stuff."

"You should have told me he was old," Dixie said, rolling to a sitting position, staring at the clock.

"Foster is not *that* old," Pamela insisted. "And even if he was, it was unbelievably rude for you to leave like that. Before dinner even. Clay is furious. He says I'm never to arrange an escort for you again."

"The man must be at least *seventy*," Dixie retorted, carrying the phone to the window and opening the blinds. It had snowed. Her backyard was a pristine snowscape. She wondered what Betty would think of the snow. "That pitiful strand of hair he combs across the top of his bald head must be ten inches long. And his false teeth *click* when he talks. You'd think a man as well off as he is could at least get himself a set of decent teeth."

"He can't help it that his teeth fell out. Foster is a lovely man. He's old Kansas City. Old money."

"Pamela, he is old *everything*. I'm curious. What did you have in mind when you insisted that I had to meet him? Did you think I would have an affair with him? Or marry him? Could you really imagine me kissing this man? Or in bed with him?"

"My God, Dixie. All I did was arrange for the two of you to be dinner partners at a Christmas party."

"Well, you forgot to tell him that," she said, slipping on her bathrobe and sitting on the side of the bed. "As soon as you and Clay drifted away, Foster said he hoped my nipples were as big as silver dollars and asked if I liked 'to perform fellatio.' He didn't whisper either. I heard the woman standing behind me gasp."

"You're making that up."

"No, I am not. Now you know why I insisted on driving myself into the city—so I'd have a means of escape. Blind dates are almost always a disaster. There's usually a good reason why a heterosexual man is single, and I refuse to be desperate, Pamela."

"Well, I hadn't realized you have such a low opinion of men," Pamela said, her voice huffy.

"Not *all* men. Just most of them. I'm trying to raise Kirk to be a decent man. I think my brother is decent, but I haven't been around him enough in recent years to know for sure. Maybe he's been screwing around on his wife for years. Mr. Graham was a good guy. And maybe there's a few more, but I can't think of them."

"*Mr. Graham?* Who's he?"

"Our high school chemistry teacher."

Pamela was silent for a long minute. "I guess my Clay wouldn't make your short list of nice men," she said.

"I'm sure Clay has some redeeming qualities; I just haven't figured out what they are."

"Don't you get afraid?" Pamela asked.

"Of what?"

"Living the rest of your life without a husband."

"At first, I did. Now, it doesn't sound so bad."

"You don't mean that, Dixie Bloom Woodward. Every woman wants a man in her life."

"A man in my life is one thing. A husband is quite another."

"But you never go out. I thought you'd be thrilled to dress up and go to a big party like that. Mary Sue and Gretchen did, too. We worry about you."

"I used to get thrilled. Now, I don't expect much. But thanks for thinking of me. Have you seen the snow? I wonder if Kirk is too old to go sledding with his mom."

By the following Christmas, Mary Sue and Gretchen were both living alone and embroiled in their respective divorces. Only Pamela was still married.

Chapter Seven

*A*s *Gretchen drove home*, she tried to remember the last time she had been this exhausted, the last time she had missed an entire night of sleep. She had napped some this afternoon but had been too agitated to sleep soundly.

She didn't even bother with a shower. After washing her face and brushing her teeth, she crawled into bed, every muscle in her body crying out for sleep.

But when she closed her eyes, an avalanche of images tumbled past her mind's eye, the unpleasant and pleasant following one another in no discernible order. Images of Mary Sue in the recovery room. Of herself taking a victory lap after winning state in the fifteen hundred meter her sophomore year in high school. Walter Lampley dead among the weeds and rocks. Her beloved grandpa dead in a casket, with his hair parted on the wrong side. Skiing down an Aspen slope with Paul on a glorious sunny day. Paul smashing their wedding portrait on the banister. Lighting birthday candles on Robin's first birthday. Walter's obnoxious yellow car sinking into the lake.

Would what had happened to Walter be considered homicide or manslaughter? For sure they were guilty of illegally disposing of a body. Of concealing a crime. Could she and Dixie stand trial? And Pamela? Could they go to jail?

But no matter how many times she replayed the scene on the front porch, a different ending depended on giving in to Walter and allowing him to see Mary Sue, allowing him to get away with making that video. Dead or alive, he was disgusting and she hated him. She found it difficult not to think less of Mary Sue for becoming involved with such a man, yet—in spite of Walter's shortness, beer belly, and arrogance—she probably would have been willing to date him herself if she had met him first. Walter, she was beginning to realize, was a member of a rare species—an unmarried man willing to go out with a woman over forty.

Finally, Gretchen gave up on sleep, pulled on a pair of sweats, and jogged over to the high school track. The moon peeked in and out of clouds. Unlike last night, there was a cool breeze that suggested summer was slipping away. Fallen leaves were even scooting across the sidewalk.

Every crack in the sidewalk was familiar to her, every tree and house that lined it. Except for the years she had been away at college she had lived her entire life in this town, in this neighborhood.

She circled the high school, then climbed over the fence into the track and field complex. Kneeling at an imaginary starting block, she waited for an imaginary shot from the starter's pistol. As her body tensed in expectation, she could feel the adrenaline flowing, exhaustion being overridden. She was Gretchen the Runner. Gretchen the Strong.

When the shot came, she took off full throttle but after a hundred yards began pacing herself. She needed to run a long time. An hour. All night. Forever.

The chilled air and solitude were intoxicating. Around and around she ran, not bothering to count. Lap after lap. Her wind was good, her legs strong.

Maybe she should train for distances. The ten kilometer. Even the marathon. She could join a running club. Learn the newest training theories. Meet a nice lean male runner who would help her move on from divorce and victimhood.

Her father had been the first to realize she ran faster than other kids. He bought a stopwatch and starting timing her. She loved running, loved making her father proud.

She'd run track in junior high and high school but dropped out before her senior year. Running made her different. Boys didn't like girls who were jocks. Paul had actually told her that after she'd gotten up her courage and asked him to a Pep Club dance. He told her that even though he was backup center on the basketball team and a jock himself.

She and Paul sat next to each other in world history. The teacher always started class with questions about the day's assigned reading. When no one raised a hand, the teacher usually called on Paul, who always knew the answer, always knew more than what had been assigned. He knew that Alexander the Great was a pupil of Aristotle and that Peter the Hermit led the First Crusade. Gretchen became quite diligent about studying her assignment, fearful of being called on, fearful of making a fool of herself in front of Paul, who was smart, handsome, and taller than she was.

She didn't quit track just because of Paul. His remark simply reinforced what she already knew. It was a surefire path to popularity to be a cheerleader, pompom girl, or majorette, but at Garden Grove High School in the 1970s, popular girls did not participate in sports. Of course, tall girls could never be cheerleaders, pompom girls, or majorettes. Tall girls were supposed to take modeling classes and cozy up to tall boys, except tall boys always seemed to end up with girls who came to their armpit. Boys liked a girl to be short enough for them to drape their arm possessively around her shoulders as they strolled along.

Tall girls mostly were out of luck. Like overweight girls, their best bet was to be good friends with popular girls and hope some of their aura rubbed off. In that regard, Gretchen was lucky. Her best friends were all popular. Mary Sue was head cheerleader, and she, Dixie, and Pamela were chosen to be class favorites their senior year—Pamela was named "Best Dressed," Dixie was "Most Friendly," and Mary Sue "Most Popular." They were never without a boyfriend, not from grade school on, while Gretchen had never had a real boyfriend, not one who hung out at her house and called her all the time.

She fully realized that, if she was to have a chance with a boy, she must act a certain way. Mary Sue, Dixie, and Pamela changed when they were around boys, their voices and expressions becoming coquettish as they looked up at some guy. Dixie now denied ever having acted that way, but Gretchen remembered it well. She remembered being painfully jealous of her three best friends because they actually could look up at boys. If there were a way to shorten her long legs, she would have jumped at it, even if it hurt like hell. She understood why the Little Mermaid in the fairy tale was willing to have her tail split into legs and suffer unending pain so she would be acceptable to the handsome prince.

In junior high, Gretchen had towered over all but a few boys. In high school, boys seldom admitted to being less than five-ten. Those who were five-ten claimed to be six feet. But at just under six feet, Gretchen was taller than most boys and all the girls. It felt as if the whole world was short. Mary Sue was a perfect five-foot-five. When she got married, her husband would be able to carry her over the threshold.

Gretchen never wore high heels and had poor posture—except when she was running. Her parents insisted that tall was beautiful. They would rattle off the names of tall women—Jane Russell, Sophia Loren, Eleanor Roosevelt, Esther Williams, Ingrid Bergman, Babe Didrikson Zaharias. Her coach told her she should get down on her knees and thank God every night for her wonderfully long legs. Mary Sue said she looked like a goddess—like Athena, who was wise and strong and beautiful. But nothing anyone said could ever convince Gretchen that being tall was anything but a curse.

But maybe, just maybe, if she gave up her jock status, a tall boy or two might look at her differently. She did have nice hair and skin. And thanks to orthodontia, her teeth were perfect.

Not that she didn't go out at all. She did have dates—usually double dates arranged by her friends. But the boys seldom asked her out again. And when they did, Gretchen wondered why. Did they think she would be easy?

She wouldn't be. Or at least she didn't think she would be. She had never had a chance to put her principles to the test.

She knew that, on dates, she was supposed to get boys talking about themselves and ask their opinion about all manner of things—and if at all possible, agree with whatever they said. She wasn't very good at it, though. She, too, had opinions about hot pants and Twiggy, about busing and the draft. And if a boy said that Dallas was the capital of Texas or didn't know the difference between the Revolutionary War and the Civil War, she was damned sure going to correct him. Mark Garrison had insisted that men had one less rib than women and had gotten mad when she demanded he show her where in the encyclopedia it said such a thing. Jimmy Cochran called her a know-it-all when she told him Mozart was a composer, not a painter.

She had never gone out with any boy more than twice.

When she told her coach she was quitting the track team, he begged her to reconsider. She had a good shot at a college scholarship. If she worked hard next year, she could be a star.

A star to whom? she wondered. When she won state, they hadn't even put her picture in the newspaper—not the school newspaper or the *Garden Grove Gazette.* She hadn't tried as hard her junior year, hadn't qualified for state. If she had had a boyfriend cheering for her in the stands, it might have been different. Not even her parents and friends came all the time, especially to the out-of-town meets. She didn't blame them, she supposed. The meets were long and boring.

She developed a way of standing around boys—with her pelvis thrust forward and her weight more on one foot than the other so she would seem less tall, so she wouldn't tower over whatever boy she was standing next to. It was quite tiring to stand that way for very long, and she had to keep shifting her weight from one foot to the other, but what choice did she have?

Before their senior year began, she asked her friends to help her with a makeover. She couldn't change her height, but maybe she could change her look. On the first day of school, she was ten pounds lighter, had flowing, blow-dried hair, and was wearing eyeliner and mascara. Mary Sue hung a mirror in Gretchen's locker so she could check her mascara between classes. Pamela told her that she was *never* to go without earrings. When Gretchen insisted that earrings pinched her ears, Pamela took her to get them pierced. Dixie told her to make eye contact with boys in the halls between classes. "You don't even have to smile or say a word. Just look 'em in the eye to let 'em know you're interested."

This time, when she asked Paul to go the Pep Club dance, he accepted. With Mary Sue's help, Gretchen made a mental list of questions to keep the conversation going. Did he like Stevie Wonder? Where was he going to college? Had he seen *Dirty Harry?* She was not to bring up Gloria Steinem or the war in Vietnam.

By the end of the first semester, she and Paul were going steady, necking endlessly, and talking about everything under the sun. He believed in equal rights for women but didn't want his wife to be a feminist. He supported the war in Vietnam and was thankful for college deferments. If he said something she didn't quite agree with, she kept her mouth shut.

All Gretchen wanted out of life was to marry Paul Bonner and have his babies. She was supremely happy, the happiest she had ever been in her life. She didn't miss running at all. She worked on standing up straight. She wore shoes with modest little French heels to the prom.

She wanted to die when Paul broke up with her during their freshman year at KU. He didn't want to hurt her, he explained, and still wanted to see her some, but he needed to date around. They were too young for commitment. Gretchen came perilously close to dropping out of school. If it weren't for Mary Sue, she would have. Or worse. It was a terrible time. A dark time.

Mary Sue was her roommate. The four of them had drawn straws to determine who would room with whom, but really what they had been doing was see who got the privilege of rooming with Mary Sue. "Wait a month and see how you feel," Mary Sue told her.

"Are all boys jerks?" Gretchen wanted to know.

"Most are, but even jerks have their moments."

Paul still called her off and on even though he was indeed "dating around." Gretchen still went out with him, still necked until her lips were bruised and swollen, her nipples raw, and her clothes a mass of wrinkles. She was too weak not to. He told her that other girls let him go all the way. She told him she would never go all the way with him or any boy until she had a ring on her finger. But even as she said it, she wondered if she really believed her own words. If Paul told her he loved her, and if she really believed him, she might. She'd rather be Paul's steady girlfriend than a virgin.

One Saturday night, she saw him with a really pretty girl at a campus hangout—a really pretty *short* girl, with masses of auburn hair and a great body. Paul had his arm draped possessively around the girl's shoulders, his fingertips brushing the top of her right breast. She slapped his hand but looked up at him with flirtatious eyes.

Gretchen allowed a football player who looked like a Neanderthal to buy her a beer. She pretended that she recognized his name. Joe something from St. Louis. He was a second-string linebacker who claimed he was a sure bet to be first team next year and was planning on a sensational pro career. His tone told her she was supposed to feel damned privileged that he was sitting with her and buying her beer.

They both drank a lot. Gretchen lost count of how many beers she downed as her tongue became thicker and thicker. When she went to the rest room, she had a difficult time navigating the narrow hallway and getting herself into the even narrower stall. She missed the toilet and peed all over the floor. When she walked back down the hall, her shoes squished.

She remembered the wet shoes and remembered bumping into tables and people as she made her way across the crowded room. She did not remember arriving back at the bar. Didn't remember leaving the bar. The next thing she knew they were in Joe's car driving someplace. She put her head against his beefy arm and dozed.

And then he was pulling into a seedy motel. "There's a party in one of the rooms," he explained, leaving her in the car while he went in the office to find out the room number. But there were no lights on in the room he parked in front of. There were no other cars.

Technically, Gretchen supposed what happened was a rape. But she had known he wanted sex while she downed all that beer. She was constantly pushing his hand away and turning her head when he tried to put his tongue in her ear, but she did so with a giggle. And she didn't get up and leave.

And she hadn't screamed when he pulled her out of the car and carried her into the dark room. He yelled at her, though, when she threw up all over him and wiped off the vomit with the bedspread. When he began pulling up her skirt, she begged him not to and tried to push him away, desperately tried, feeling as though she were going to choke to death on the fear that welled inside her chest and head and heart. But her arms were made of Jell-O. All she could do was cry. And say the word "no" over and over again.

When he was finished, Joe asked if she wanted him to take her someplace. She said no. "The room's paid for," he told her and left her ten dollars for cab fare. After he left, she called Mary Sue. She had to put down the phone and go outside to find out the name of the motel and the room number.

When she arrived, Mary Sue asked if she should call the police. Gretchen was adamant. *No police.* Then everyone would know. And she felt responsible. He should not have done that to her, but she had been an idiot to let herself get in such a predicament.

Mary Sue went to an all-night drugstore and returned with a douche bag. Gretchen stood in the shower, while Mary Sue filled and refilled the bag over and over again. Gretchen wasn't sure if she was cleaning herself or trying to prevent pregnancy. Maybe both. She simply did as Mary Sue said.

From that day to this, they had never spoken of that night. Gretchen knew absolutely that Mary Sue had not mentioned it to anyone else and never would. She wondered how much the experience had altered her. Would she hate all men and be frigid for the rest of her life? She couldn't allow herself so much as a flicker of a sexual thought without reliving the ugly scene in the motel room. She hated herself. And men. Mostly she hated Paul. She hated him more than she hated the football player. She knew his name now. Joe Markowski, who did indeed make the first team the following year and had gone on to a credible professional career. In the years that followed, Gretchen would hear his name over and over. Paul would sing his praises while he watched *Monday Night Football*. A former Kansas Jayhawk. One of their own.

Toward the end of that semester, Paul had called. She told him she didn't want to talk to him and hung up. The next day, a dozen roses arrived for her at the sorority house. The next time he called, he said they needed to talk. Again she said no.

Over Christmas break, he came over and sat with her in the living room. Her father and brother were watching a football game in the family room. Her mother brought a tray with glasses of milk and generous slices of chocolate cake.

He wanted an agreement. She was the girl he wanted to marry. Those other girls were just for dating. Just for screwing around. But Gretchen was a woman for the rest of his life—an intelligent woman who would wear well over the years, who would be a good mother, whose love would be abiding and deep. He knew that now. He just didn't want to give her his frat pin until their junior year. If he could sow his wild oats now, he would be a better husband for her later on.

Gretchen put down her glass of milk and went upstairs without even saying goodbye. She listened at the top of the stairs until she heard him tell her parents good night, heard the door open and close. *Damn him to hell.* She wished she were Catholic so she could go live in a convent.

But she couldn't stop thinking about Paul, even though thinking about him made her chest hurt. Her thoughts weren't all damning, though, weren't all of him screwing a succession of girls while she was lonely as hell. She also thought of the good times. Of endless kisses. Of meaty discussions during which they had challenged each other. Of silliness and laughter. When it came right down to it, she missed him so dreadfully it felt like a disease.

Why did she love him so much when he wasn't worthy? Mary Sue wanted to know. "Are you sure it's not a case of wanting what you can't have?" she asked.

Gretchen had no answer.

The summer before their junior year at KU, Paul dropped by her house.

They sat on lawn chairs under the walnut tree, and he said he was ready to settle down. He'd like for her to have his pin. Theirs could be the first pinning serenade in the fall.

A pinning serenade. Such a sweet ritual. She closed her eyes and imagined the men of his fraternity coming en masse at midnight to the Chi Omega house. The housemother would unlock the door and let Gretchen go outside to stand with Paul, with all her sorority sisters crowded around the upstairs windows, while Paul's fraternity brothers reverently sang songs in praise of their brotherhood and of true love. The serenade would end with the song that made their fraternity famous. *The girl of my dreams is the sweetest girl of all the girls I know.*

She listened while Paul mapped out their lives. An engagement ring the following summer, a wedding the summer after that. They would live back east while he earned his MBA. He wanted to work for a Kansas City brokerage firm, but they could live in Garden Grove. Family was important for both of them. It would be good to live away for a while, but they needed to come back home so their children could grow up with their grandparents close by.

In the end, he had gotten just what he wanted. He'd had his two years of dating, of screwing every coed who would let him in her panties. Then he took up with Gretchen just where they left off. She even got a prescription for birth control pills.

The first time was not going to be in the backseat of his car, she told him. And not in a roadside motel. They checked into a small hotel in the nearby town of Leavenworth. He'd brought a bottle of wine.

"Are you a virgin?" he asked when the lights were out.

"No."

"Would you like to tell me about it?"

"You've got your nerve," she said rolling away from him.

"I don't mean names and dates. I just want to know how experienced you are. If there's anything you like or don't like."

Gretchen felt panic rise in her throat. She could not do this. Not tonight. Not ever. She would always remember that other time with that huge grunting animal pushing himself into her. A part of her would always associate sex with fear and loathing. But it was Paul here with her tonight. God, she had invested so much emotion in him, had given him such power over her. What happened here tonight would set the tone for the rest of their life or end their relationship altogether.

She turned back to face him. "I had sex just once, and it was horrible. I need for you to hold me for a long, long time and kiss me like we used to do back in high school when kissing was all there was, when I believed the first time for both of us would be the night we got married."

He kissed her face. Kissed her tears. "I'm sorry," he said.

"Me, too." She didn't say that her horrible first experience would not have happened if he hadn't broken up with her. But she was thinking it.

She had not been responsive. She wanted to be but just couldn't make herself. The next time was better, even though it was in the backseat of his car. It actually seemed more natural there.

It was not until New Year's Eve that she experienced her first orgasm. He made her come with his hand. "Oh, my God," she kept saying over and over. "I had no idea." Suddenly, she realized that sex could be good for her, too. For that she would always be grateful to Paul. She loved him and needed desperately to be his wife, needed for him to love her, but she was never able to expunge completely an impervious seed of hatred for him that she kept buried deep in her heart. She was never able to forgive him for those two years they were apart. Her hate became ever more retroactive as she learned that he had never been faithful to her. *Never.* Now that her marriage had ended, people kept dropping little tidbits here and there for her to piece together. Even when she wore his frat pin and then an engagement ring, the whole world had known he was screwing other girls behind her back. All up and down Greek Row. Later, it was women from the tennis club. Women at his office. Women in their neighborhood. Wives of his partners. And all that time she had felt proud to be his wife and felt appreciative of how hard he worked for her and the kids. She thought of all those phone calls about staying late at the office, all those times she had waited up for him to serve him a snack and rub his neck. Now she'd like to wring his neck. Or cut his throat. Take every cent of his money. Forbid their daughters to see him. Teach them to hate him.

All she could do, though, was take him to court again and again for every damned reason she could think of. Her goal was somehow to ruin his life as he had ruined hers. She had invested her life in their marriage, in being a good wife and mother. She had given up any plans of a career. She had an accounting degree that she'd never used. She had never tried to become a world-class track star because of him. And he dumped her for a young secretary with big tits. The secretary was short. Paul had been a lie from start to finish.

She thought of all this as she circled the same high school track she had circled as a high school student. She should have listened to Coach Harvey and kept on running.

Gretchen hadn't taken up running again until after Robin was born, and she couldn't stand her overweight, flabby body. She bought seventy-five-dollar running shoes and a three-hundred-dollar baby stroller with bicycle tires and headed for the jogging path around a nearby park. The first time, she had to walk most of the way—and could barely do that. But she got better. That was a good feeling—getting better. She timed herself and set goals. She grew lean and tan. Since then, running had been a part of more days than not. When she was pregnant with Debbie, she ran into her seventh month, when the doctor insisted she settle for brisk walks. Her labor had been less than two hours.

Running became an important part of who she was. She was proud to be a runner, to be strong and healthy. She loved the feel of her own lean body. Paul did, too. He said she was a knockout. He said he loved walking into a restaurant with her on his arm.

They were in a restaurant when he told her he wanted a divorce. She hadn't had a clue. Everyone else had, apparently. Even their children.

The day that Paul packed up and left her, she had put on her running shoes and run until she literally dropped. She crawled under a bush and wept until she was empty and exhausted. Then she crawled out of the hiding place and ran some more. That had been the week after her forty-second birthday. Now she was almost forty-five, no longer young, not yet old, poised in the middle of life on what she hoped was a vast long plain and not a peak she would have to descend too quickly. She no longer timed herself. She simply ran two miles three or four times a week and went to aerobics the days she didn't run. She needed to stay strong so she could do a better job of hating Paul.

Dixie said she had to let go of the hate. No man was going fall in love with her if her heart was black with hate. Her daughters, each in her own way, told her the same thing. Intellectually, she supposed they were right, but in her heart and mind and gut, she needed to hate Paul.

But she was so lonely—very, very lonely in a way that friends and family could not fill. And sometimes, she worried that her friends and children would grow weary of her venom and simply give up on her. She knew she should get on with her life. If that took forgiving Paul, however, she never would. He had hurt her so deeply that she could never be the person she was before. The hurt became an integral part of who she was.

The day Mary Sue got her diagnosis she had called Gretchen. In response to Mary Sue's polite, "How's it going?" Gretchen launched a tirade about the latest correspondence from Paul's lawyer, requesting she return his grandmother's emerald dinner ring. "His grandmother gave me that ring after Debbie was born," Gretchen ranted. "I'd throw it in the river before I'd give it back so he can give it to that witch. That ring will go to Debbie."

It took Gretchen a while to realize that Mary Sue wasn't saying much. "Are you okay?" she asked.

"Not exactly," Mary Sue said in a small voice. "May I come over?"

Gretchen fixed coffee. They sat at the kitchen table like always. Gretchen waited.

"I have breast cancer," Mary Sue said.

Gretchen had been stunned. And had a hard time keeping her composure. She knew that breast cancer was rampant. Her mother's oldest sister had eventually died of the disease, but Aunt Olga had been almost eighty. Not still young and vibrant like Mary Sue, someone Gretchen counted on always to be a part of her life.

She wanted to blame the cancer on Mary Sue's divorce. On Barry. If that son-of-a-bitch hadn't put her through all that pain and embarrassment and stress, this probably wouldn't have happened.

Mary Sue shook her head. "I'm not going down that road. I'm not going to blame Barry or God or bad genes. I loved my life up until the day Barry stopped loving me. Maybe the pendulum will swing back again. Maybe not. But I don't want to spend whatever is left of my life mired in blame and bitterness. I want to handle this thing with dignity. It happened. It happens to lots of women—to saints and sinners. A random thing."

Gretchen knelt beside Mary Sue's chair and wrapped her arms around her friend's slight body and wept. Gretchen had always known she loved Mary Sue the best. They had all had their fallings out from time to time. Dixie had become remote for a time, living too far away for daily phone calls and weekly lunches; now Gretchen sometimes wondered if Dixie, as a working woman with a business to run, didn't feel a bit superior to the rest of them. And Gretchen sometimes became irritated with Pamela's obsession with social status and her constant quest for impeccability. Her car, house, yard, and person were always perfect. Dixie accused Pamela of having a car wash in her garage and a manicurist chained in her attic.

But the only thing for which Gretchen could fault Mary Sue was her niceness. It was unnatural for anyone to be so damned nice. She was nice to telemarketers and rude salespeople. She managed to discipline her children without raising her voice. And now, goddamn it, she was being nice about breast cancer when any normal woman would be frustrated or angry or looking for someone or something to blame. A normal woman would be wondering, "Why me?" But Mary Sue wasn't normal. Mary Sue was Mary Sue, and Gretchen loved her like the sister she had never had. As did Dixie and Pamela. The four of them had no sisters of their own so Mary Sue had created their sisterhood.

Mary Sue had cancer. Walter was at the bottom of Dixie's lake. Three of the four of them were divorced, and Pamela was married to a turd. As Gretchen let herself into her quiet, lonely house, she wondered what lay ahead for their friendship. For her life. She had been so sure that putting Walter in the lake was what needed to be done. Like disposing of a dead mouse. Now she no longer felt sure.

What she felt was fear.

Chapter Eight

Dixie scanned Friday evening's *Garden Grove Gazette,* but there wasn't a word about a missing Shawnee dentist. She turned back to the first page and looked more carefully. Not a word.

Kirk, with Betty at his heels, came wandering into the kitchen to grab a bottle of juice and ask what was for dinner. In the doorway he paused. "You okay?" he asked.

Dixie pulled her gaze from the newspaper, and her heart did a flip-flop at the sight of her son standing there, concern on his still boyish face. Kirk was wearing cut-off jeans and a well-washed navy T-shirt, with his dark hair tousled, his feet bare. She supposed the correct way to describe her son would be "good-looking" or "handsome," but to her he was beautiful. At seventeen, he was a younger, taller version of Arnie. Everyone said so. He had his father's dark curly hair, dark eyes, square jaw, long legs. He even had the same cleft in his chin. But when she looked at her son, she saw his uniqueness. His grin, his laugh, his frown were his own. And his sincerity. His openness.

Oddly enough, divorce ultimately had brought her and her son closer together. Maybe it was because Kirk was her only child and because the two of them had had to either grow closer or drift apart with Arnie gone from their daily lives and the status quo no longer an option. At first Dixie continually had to fight the urge to back away from confrontation and not

87

tell Kirk when he was out of line, fearful he might resent her and pull away. Which he did. Frequently. After a rocky year or so they had arrived at a comfortable place where he usually accepted that she was both parent and friend. Dixie considered him to be the nicest male person she had ever known. And when he wasn't nice, when he slipped into disrespect or surliness, she told him so, even though it still made her stomach knot with apprehension. What if he stopped loving her? Who would she be if her son stopped loving her? She needed his love, needed him to be the most important part of her life. She dreaded the day he would go off to college and become a visitor in her home and life.

Dixie longed to tell Kirk that yes, she was worried, that the man Mary Sue had been going with was at the bottom of Murphy Lake and she and Gretchen and Pamela had put him there. She and Kirk had shared secrets before. He'd told her that he'd gotten a girl pregnant and used the money he had saved toward a car to pay for an abortion. He'd told her that his father was fooling around on Cindy. And he knew where she went when she told everyone else she was going to a convention or on a buying trip for the store. He knew she was going to see Johnny. Sometimes, he went with her.

But Dixie would not burden him with this new secret. More out of concern for him than for her own future, she hoped that he would never have to know what his mother and two of her best friends had done. They had not been thinking of their children when they rolled Walter and his car into the lake.

Dixie shuddered to think of what it would do to their children's lives if their mothers were arrested for illegally disposing of a body. Maybe even for murder. She still felt as though she should call the police and take her chances. It wasn't just a matter of *her* chances, though.

Yes, she was worried. Worried sick. But she could not tell her son the reason why.

"I'm worried about Mary Sue," she said, which was the truth, just not all of it.

"But she'll be okay, won't she?" he asked.

"I hope so. I guess that only time will tell."

Kirk put down the can of juice and knelt beside his mother's chair. "I'm sorry," he said, and put his arms around her for a minute of comforting closeness. "Mary Sue is lucky to have friends who really care about her."

After dinner, Dixie drove to a nearby convenience store and bought the *Johnson County Evening Courier.* She sat in a parking lot and scanned its pages, but there was nothing about Walter.

The same was true of Saturday and Sunday's newspapers.

But Monday evening, there was a story on page two of the *Courier.* Walter's office manager had reported him missing. He had not come to work on Friday, but it wasn't the first time he had taken the day off without alerting his office staff, who assumed he had taken a long weekend.

When he didn't come in on Monday, however, his office manager had called the Shawnee police, who had checked his home and were making inquiries.

With a pounding heart, Dixie looked up the phone number of the Shawnee Police Department.

The next morning she took the newspaper with her to the hospital and told Mary Sue that Walter had been missing since Friday. Then she handed her the newspaper and stood looking out the window while Mary Sue read it.

"I'd been wondering if he would call," Mary Sue admitted. Her hair was freshly washed, her makeup on. Her robe was pink and soft. She looked lovely. The lull before the storm. Before chemotherapy robbed her of hair and vitality. "I wonder where he is," she said pensively.

"He was home when I called him from the lake house," Dixie said. "He sounded kind of drunk."

"You probably need to tell the police that you talked to him."

"I called the Shawnee police as soon as I saw the story. They are checking the road between there and the lake and looking in all the ditches and gullies. The detective I spoke with already knew that you and Walter had been dating. I imagine they will want to talk to you at some point."

Mary Sue leaned against propped-up pillows. "I feel so strange. He might be hurt or sick or dead." Then she paused. "Or he might be off with another woman."

"Walter was not a worthy man," Dixie said.

"No, I suppose not." Mary Sue stared at the ceiling for a time, tears welling in her eyes. She reached for Dixie's hand. "I hope he's okay, though. I wouldn't want anything bad to happen to him."

"I know," Dixie said, squeezing Mary Sue's hand. She hated to see Mary Sue sad. Hated what had happened to Walter, and the mess they had made of things, and the anxiety that grabbed at her throat and infiltrated her brain.

Tuesday morning, when Mary Sue was released from the hospital, Dixie helped her mother pack up Mary Sue's things and get her home. Pamela brought lunch. Gretchen dropped by. They looked uncomfortable when Mary Sue kept bringing the conversation back to Walter. Dixie found herself avoiding eye contact with Pamela and Gretchen. She was relieved when Connie announced that her daughter needed to rest and shooed them away.

Walter's disappearance was covered in the Wednesday morning edition of the *Kansas City Star*, which reported there was no sign of foul play at Lampley's Shawnee home. His pickup truck was parked in the garage, but his Porsche was missing. Neighbors had not noticed any disturbances at the house. Lampley's office staff said that he frequently patronized the local casino and also made frequent visits to Las Vegas. According to an unnamed source, Lampley was known to bet large sums of money. His office manager was quoted as saying that the dentist often carried a "roll of bills." The article went on to say that Lampley drove a yellow 1989 model 911 Porsche, and both his ex-wives—Darlene Lampley of St. Louis and Joyce Lampley, a resident of North Kansas City—had not heard from him in some time. Darlene, who had two children with Lampley, indicated the Shawnee dentist was in arrears with his child-support payments and had not seen his children in several months.

✲   ✲   ✲

It was Gretchen who showed Mary Sue the *Star* article. Mary Sue sighed and acknowledged that Walter had avoided talking about his children. And he considered himself a high roller. He liked to brag about how much he had won. And lost.

"I know you're wondering what I saw in him," she said.

"Oh, not really," Gretchen said. "He was a man—marginally acceptable, but a man nonetheless. And having a man in your life made you feel less rejected and lonely. I just wish there were a pill to cure the feeling so we could just bypass all that crap."

Mary Sue knew that the police eventually would seek her out. Still, it was a shock when an attractive young woman from the Shawnee Police Department came to the front door, flashed a badge, and introduced herself as Detective Mosley.

Connie poured two cups of coffee and disappeared up the stairs.

Yes, she had been a friend of Walter Lampley's, Mary Sue told the detective. They had been dating for about six months.

She admitted that she had sometimes feared that Walter would come to a bad end. He carried a lot of cash and liked to flaunt it. He usually paid tabs with hundred-dollar bills. On two occasions, he had even paid with a five-hundred-dollar bill and on one of those occasions made a bit of a scene when the restaurant couldn't make change.

And yes, Mary Sue was aware that he liked to gamble. Since she had known him, he had gone to Las Vegas on three different occasions and apparently reveled in the VIP treatment he received at the casinos. Once he had wanted her to go with him on a gambling trip to Bossier City in Louisiana, but she needed to help her daughter get ready for the prom.

Mary Sue knew little of his friends—mostly he had entered her world rather than pulling her into his. She had visited his home in Shawnee but never his dental office, never met his children or any member of his family.

When asked about his ex-wives and children, Mary Sue hedged a bit, saying that Walter didn't seem to have a particularly amicable relationship with either one of his ex-wives and did not spend a great deal of time with his children. The unvarnished truth was that he spouted venom about his former wives and, to her knowledge, he hadn't seen his children in the months that she had known him.

"Do you have any leads?" Mary Sue asked as the woman began making motions to leave. "I don't see how someone can just drop off the face of the earth."

Detective Mosley hesitated, then asked, "Is that your natural hair color?"

Puzzled, Mary Sue touched her thinning hair and nodded.

"Was he seeing another woman?"

"Not that I know of. Why do you ask?" Mary Sue wanted to know.

"We found some long red hairs in his bathroom. Do you know who they might belong to?"

Mary Sue shook her head.

The detective gave her a card and asked that she call if she thought of anything that might be helpful. Anything at all.

Mary Sue showed the woman to the door, then went back to the kitchen table for a second cup of coffee. "Where in the hell are you, Walter?" she said. Then she digested the knowledge that Walter had already been screwing another woman. Maybe he had been all along.

At first Mary Sue had convinced herself that Walter was away on a gambling binge. Then she speculated that some Mafia type was after him, and he had gone into hiding. But as the days and weeks went by, she began to wonder if there was a more ominous reason for his disappearance. Gretchen, Pamela, and Dixie were reluctant to theorize with her but admitted they thought Mary Sue was better off with him gone.

She had realized her friends didn't like Walter and could even understand why. Walter was a bombastic know-it-all. He had other attributes, of course, a few of them good. He could be generous, fun-loving, and even thoughtful on occasion. But for Mary Sue, his chief virtue was that he had come along at a time when she was desperately needy and in a state of continuous grief and pain over Barry's departure from her life.

Walter had saved her. It had been nothing short of amazing. In a dizzying short period of time, she had gone from knowing that, if it weren't for her children, she might have sunk to the deepest depths of depression and despair, to worrying about what to wear and what to cook and whether she should have her eyebrows arched. She was ashamed that she hadn't had the strength of character to heal herself. After all, she had two beautiful children and wonderful friends. She had always prided herself on being calm and stable, as being the sort of person who—short of something happening to her children—should have been able to count her blessings and get on with her life.

Sometimes she was sorry that she couldn't be angry like Gretchen. Anger gave Gretchen strength.

Barry had left her because he didn't love her anymore, because he had found a more beautiful and exciting woman. She should have paid more attention to her appearance, should have been more alluring and seductive. Sometimes while she chattered away at the dinner table, telling him about her day, asking about his, getting Michelle and Michael to tell him what they did that day at school, she could feel his boredom radiating across the table. Which made her chatter all the more. Made her see herself through his eyes. Her husband found her ordinary. Foolish even. When once he had looked at her with love. When once he had adored her.

She could feel his restlessness as he bought and traded vehicles—sports cars, pickups, SUVs. As he went from sport to sport—golf, tennis, skiing, handball—attacking each one with such passion, as though mastering it would bring him peace or satisfaction or whatever. And then, although she didn't know it at the time, he went from woman to woman. Always searching for whatever it was that was missing in his life, whatever it was that she could not supply.

But who could compete against the likes of Trish Cabbiness? Trish Prescott now. Her children referred to her as their stepmother. She was rich and gorgeous and had won the state amateur tennis tournament year before last.

Instead of feeling angry Mary Sue had felt deeply and incapacitatingly inadequate and sad. When she looked in the mirror, she saw a woman who was no longer pretty, no longer worthy of her husband's love. She listened patiently while her friends heaped blame on Barry, and perhaps justifiably so. But the bottom line was he was gone, and there was nothing she could do about it.

So she dated Walter, slept with Walter, and convinced herself that she cared for Walter. All those mythical men that various friends said they would fix her up with—all those brothers and brothers-in-law, all those cousins, uncles, neighbors, friends, colleagues—never materialized, so she had set out with great determination to find a man on her own. Her very survival seemed to depend on finding a man. She visited chat rooms, read singles ads, and joined an upscale singles club that held monthly social events. She met Walter at the first event she attended—an old-fashioned Sunday afternoon tea dance held in the ballroom of a Kansas City hotel. Each attendee was given a dance card with dance partners selected by computer.

The conversation with her various dance partners was carefully neutral. She lived in Garden Grove, had a teenage son and daughter, was a good cook and a terrible tennis player. Her partners talked about what they did for a living and their hobbies, dogs, favorite team. She got a bit uneasy when a portly insurance salesman from Independence asked if she had accepted Christ as her savior.

Walter Lampley was the sixth name on her program. When he came to her assigned table to fetch her, he said she was the prettiest woman in the room and how about ditching the rest of the party and heading for the bar.

They had cocktails in the hotel bar and dinner at a nearby restaurant. It had been easy. All she had to do was listen to Walter drone on about Porsche rallies, his golf game, and his rotten luck with women. His first wife had been a fat bore. His second wife played around on him. He was looking for a sweet little stay-at-home wife who put him first and didn't carp when he played cards all night with his friends.

Very quickly, before she even had time to think about it, Walter became a fixture in her life. At the urging of her attorney, Mary Sue had insisted that Barry pay for a separate country club membership for her and the children. Since her divorce, however, she and the children had used the club only for swimming and tennis. Now she had an escort for the social events. She could hold her head up. She had a man at her side for all the world and her ex-husband to see. Walter also took her to nightclubs, which she didn't enjoy, and to lovely restaurants that she enjoyed very much. She even enjoyed the weekends when he camped out in front of the television in her family room, watching one sporting event after another, while she kept him supplied with snacks and beer. With a man in the house, she felt whole.

If he had asked her to marry him, she would have said yes, even though her children would be displeased. And her friends.

If Walter had come home from wherever he had disappeared to and said he was sorry that he hadn't handled her illness better, that of course he wanted to be with her always, she would have welcomed him. Even now, after all these weeks, she imagined him calling her from someplace, telling her he was coming back to her. When he arrived, he would pull a ring from his pocket and tell her that he loved her. She didn't care about the ring, but she did want to be loved, even if she didn't exactly love him in return. She did appreciate him, and she didn't expect for true love ever again to come in her lifetime and was willing to settle for less. For a great deal less, actually. It was safer that way. It was too painful when what one had trusted to be the real thing turned out to be false.

The chemo room at the Cancer Center was a depressing place, with ashen people installed in recliners, chemicals dripping into their veins, their thin bodies covered with old-fashioned crocheted afghans, their hairless heads covered with bandanas or baseball caps. Like Mary Sue, the patients were usually accompanied by a family member or friend who hovered about, bringing them glasses of juice, helping them make their way to the bathroom with IV stands in tow, making sure the nurse was administering the correct chemical.

Mary Sue, who often was the youngest and seemingly most fit patient in the room, still had enough of her hair that she got by with cutting it quite short and wearing it pixie-style. On her chemo days, however, she wore a baseball cap anyway to fit in, not wanting to flaunt her good fortune in the face of all that baldness.

Other than nurses asking questions and explaining things in their soft, neutral voices, background noise was provided by a big-screen television featuring a game show or soap opera. Many patients would doze in their recliners with mouths hanging open, looking even older and sicker than they did when they were awake.

Because Mary Sue could not abide a social vacuum, she would try to visit with any nondozers at her end of the room. Some—after they got over their surprise that she was breaking the code of silence—would share the entire history of their illness and its impact on their lives. And Mary Sue would respond in kind, bringing her mother or whichever friend was accompanying her that day into the conversation, explaining how her mother's uncle had lived with leukemia for more than twenty years. Or how Dixie's mom had been doing so well in her fight against bone cancer until she developed pneumonia.

Mary Sue was surprised how frankly some people discussed their disease. One man explained that he knew he was dying but hoped to hang on until the book on genealogy he had written was published. A woman named Daisy hoped to live until her first great-grandchild was born. Most, though, like Mary Sue, were hoping for a cure.

Whatever their situation, she and her fellow patients all had a fascination with their own disease. They could recite the ups and downs of their white blood cell count and the ups and downs of the all-important cancer markers. They discussed which foods they best tolerated and whether Fibercon worked better than Metamucil. They discussed the pros and cons of various antinausea and blood-pressure drugs and what a pity it was they couldn't take steroids continuously. They knew the exact day of which chemo cycle their hair started falling out. They knew the day and hour after a chemo treatment that they would begin sinking into the inevitable valley of total malaise and the day and hour they could expect to start the climb out again.

The chemo would hit Mary Sue the second morning after the treatment, when she would wake up nauseated and too weak to do more than go to the bathroom and either go back to bed or curl up on the sofa under a quilt. Food tasted strange and she mostly lived on canned chicken noodle soup and Sprite. By the seventh evening of her twenty-one-day cycle, however, she was feeling a bit better. The second week her energy and appetite gradually improved. The third week she was able to take short walks and add sips of tomato juice and a bit of rice to her diet. The following Monday, the cycle began anew.

When she tried to help with the housework, her mother insisted that she rest. Most of the time, Mary Sue obliged and found it satisfying simply to be in her mother's presence, watching Connie clean, fold laundry, cook, boss the kids. Her mother overstepped, of course, rearranging furniture, throwing out centerpieces and houseplants she considered past their prime, but Mary Sue didn't protest. She just hoped that someday when her own children needed her to help them through the rough spots, she would be there for them. Always before that had seemed a given.

Her mother was actually quite amazing—never running out of energy or conversation. She gossiped, reminisced, and offered unsolicited advice as she bustled about. Mary Sue hadn't spent this much time with her mother since she came to help out after each of the children was born. This time was different, though. Not joyous. Not full of promise. Connie would stop in the middle of whatever she was doing and say that she just couldn't understand why this was happening to Mary Sue. "I should be the one with cancer, not you," she would say, grabbing a tissue to blow her nose and wipe her eyes.

Filtered through the new reality of Mary Sue's life, the reminiscing became especially poignant. Her memories of her father, who had been killed in a hunting accident when she was three, had been mostly manufactured from photographs. She needed to hear her mother retell the Daddy stories she had so loved during her childhood. She needed to hear that her father called her "princess," played hide-and-seek with her, took her sledding, and amazed her by finding coins in her ear.

And Mary Sue needed to talk about Dwight, her physician stepfather, who had died only last year. Almost twenty years older than Connie, Dwight had been a quiet, somber man who read a great deal and pretty much left Mary Sue to her mother's care. "I felt bad that I didn't grieve for him more," Mary Sue confessed.

"I know, honey. Dwight was a good man, but he never knew what to say to you. I don't know what would have happened to us if he hadn't come along, though. Your father was the love of my life, but he never took care of things. He never bought life insurance, and he was always looking for ways to get rich without having to work. When he died, we were months in arrears on the rent, and the tires on the car were bald. Dwight had been a friend of my older brother. He came calling a month to the day after your daddy's funeral. I got down on my knees after he left and prayed to God that he would marry me."

Mary Sue took the pillow Connie had propped behind her head and cradled it carefully against her tender torso, which was a study in raw, red scars—around the implanted flap and across her abdomen where the plastic surgeon had harvested the skin and tissue to create it. The skin on her abdomen was now stretched so tightly that Mary Sue found it impossible to stand up straight and had to walk hunched over like an old woman.

"But you loved Dwight, didn't you?" Mary Sue asked her mother, shifting her weight in search of comfort.

"Not like I loved your father," Connie said as she folded towels and placed them neatly in a stack. "I don't think Dwight expected that of me. He said he wanted to live in a house with the sound of voices and the aroma of food cooking when he came in the door at night. His first wife had been pretty worthless, apparently. She ran off with a rodeo cowboy— you didn't know that, did you? She'd been gone for ten years when Dwight and I met. He had to hire a private detective to track her down and paid her to sign the divorce papers. Dwight needed a home, and I needed someone to support me and my daughter. Without him, I probably would have become a weary old saleslady with varicose veins and a dour outlook and you would have been a latchkey kid. As it was, we lived in a big handsome house in a fine neighborhood and belonged to the country club. Instead of being a charity case myself, I got to be the grand lady who volunteered at the hospital and helped put on benefit galas for the less fortunate. I thanked God for Dwight every day of my life. Before he died, I told him that I loved him more than I ever loved your daddy, and I don't think God is going to send me straight to hell for saying that."

"Do you miss him?" Mary Sue wanted to know.

"Oh, yes. I miss him and the life I used to have. After Dwight died, everything changed. I had been living in a couples' world, and suddenly I didn't have a husband. It was as though I didn't exist anymore. That's why I so wanted you to work things out with Barry. A woman needs to be married. Even a not-very-good marriage is better than no marriage at all. I thought Barry was such a good husband, and then he takes up with that Trish person. I've seen her type before. She'll spend all his money and have affairs behind his back."

"Mother, Trish has more money than Barry. Lots more. And given Barry's track record, he'll probably be the one fooling around on her."

"Then he should be giving you more money. It breaks my heart to have you alone and sick like this and worrying about money. I'd like to see that Barry and give him a piece of my mind. You don't know how many times I thought about calling him and telling him just what I think of a man who leaves a wife after she's given him the best years of her life. I was hoping that dentist would turn out to be a good man like Dwight, but I don't think a middle-aged man who drives a yellow sports car can be trusted."

Connie carried a stack of dishtowels to the kitchen. "Yes, I do miss Dwight, and I miss being married," she said as she returned. "It's not as bad now that I'm down in Florida with your aunt Nelda in the retirement community. I get tired of being with older people all day long, but we do keep busy. There's an activity every evening and an excursion every week-end. Dwight is still taking care of me, you know. Because of him I have enough money to live in Florida and to fly back and forth whenever I need to be here."

During her mother's stay, Mary Sue not only learned that Dwight's first wife ran off with a rodeo cowboy, she found out that her cousin Rachel had been born only five months after Aunt Nelda married Uncle Bob. She found out that her grandfather had gotten an Army nurse pregnant during the Korean War and that her aunt Daphne had once been arrested for shoplifting. She wasn't sure just why her illness made it now okay for her mother to tell her family secrets, but it was oddly satisfying and certainly entertaining.

Mostly, though, she liked hearing about her father—how he sang like an angel and could identify a bird by its song and mimic it perfectly. How he wept with happiness the night she was born. How it was his idea that she be named Mary Susan for her grandmothers. How everyone smiled when he walked into a room.

How strange life is, Mary Sue thought. Because of cancer, she had some of the best times she'd ever spent with her mother. She felt emotionally and physically closer as they hugged and kissed for no particular reason, as they linked arms when they strolled about the yard. In the evening when they watched television, Connie had Mary Sue sit on the footstool in front of her so she could rub her back.

After two months, however, it was time to send Connie on her way and once again become the lady of her own house. At the airport, Connie broke down. "It should be me," she kept saying. "It should be me." They clung and cried, with people going around them to get on the plane. "I love you so much," Connie said. "I never said that enough, never hugged you enough. I was always too busy with all my clubs and projects. I'm sorry about that now. I wish I'd been more like Dixie's mom, with all the time in the world for you kids."

"That was because she was always at the store," Mary Sue said, "and we could run in for Band-Aids or to borrow a dollar or get snacks from the refrigerator in the back room. But you were the car-pooling queen. Nobody drove us more miles than you did."

Connie smiled through her tears. "That was fun, wasn't it, with you girls always singing. I still remember the words to all those songs. It makes me feel young to sing along with the radio."

In the car, Mary Sue had to cry a bit more, already missing her mother. Finally, though, she wiped her eyes and started the motor. Before backing out of the parking place, however, she tuned in to the seventies station on the radio. As she drove home, she sang along with the dated songs of her youth that still made her mother feel young. "Bad, Bad Leroy Brown." "Delta Dawn." "Rocky Mountain High."

Chapter Nine

"*This is morbid*," Pamela insisted.

"I know," Gretchen admitted. "But I need to see how deep the water is out here."

"So what are you going to do if the car is just below the surface?" Pamela demanded. She was sitting in the front of the boat, watching Gretchen row. "We have no way to move it."

"I just want to know how much I need to worry," Gretchen said, looking back at the shore to judge the distance. "About here, don't you think?" she called to Dixie, who was watching them from the dock, her hand shading her eyes against the sun's glare.

"Maybe a few feet farther out," Dixie called back.

Pamela lifted a fishing pole and dangled a line in the water, just so some unknown person watching from the shore would not wonder why two women were in a rowboat in the middle of November. Of course, it was a warm, bright day, the first time they had been to the lake since they had returned to throw Walter's sex videos in it and clean up after Mary Sue's birthday party, and the last, as far as Pamela was concerned. Which was a shame. It was a lovely place. An oasis that had been such an important part of their growing-up years.

Dixie's father wanted to sell the lake house, but she kept talking him out of it, fearful that new owners might discover a submerged car just thirty yards or so from their boat dock. It had been Gretchen's idea to come check on the car's location. And she had volunteered to do the diving. Pamela herself never wanted to put so much as a toe in the lake again. Nor did Dixie.

Gretchen stripped down to her bra and panties and rolled out of the boat. Pamela watched anxiously as she dove and surfaced half a dozen times before announcing that she had found it. "It's about ten or twelve feet to the roof of the car," she said as she crawled back into the boat. Pamela handed her a beach towel to wrap around her shivering body.

"Did you look inside?"

"Hell no! I'm not that morbid. Anyway, it's hard to see down there. The water is murkier than you realize. And there're a lot of plants—waving around in the current. It's pretty creepy."

"Do you think the plants will eventually cover the car?" Pamela asked hopefully.

"Maybe. But I keep remembering that year the lake was so low that the dock was stranded on dry land. That's bound to happen again someday."

"Maybe not for years and years," Pamela said hopefully.

"Maybe. Remember in *Fried Green Tomatoes* when they found the car in the river years later? At least Walter's been down there long enough that the scratches from my fingernails and Dixie's teeth marks are gone."

Pamela shivered at the image of Walter's body decaying in his car. "It's sad that no one really gives a damn about the man, isn't it? Except maybe Mary Sue."

"I suppose. When you're dead, you can't change. Maybe if he'd lived he would have turned into a nice guy, but I don't think so."

With her teeth chattering, Gretchen peeled out of her wet underwear and pulled on her sweatshirt and jeans. "Someday, sooner or later, Walter and his car will be found. I think we can bank on that. Hopefully it will seem like he broke his neck when the car hit the lake. Otherwise, we may still have some tall explaining to do, but the more time that goes by, the less likely that is."

❋   ❋   ❋

With her mother gone, Mary Sue and her children began to forge new routines. Michelle and Michael took up tormenting one another once again. Mary Sue made it clear that they had to help her more around the house, and they agreed. They knew she needed help. Michael would vacuum and Michelle would dust. They took turns with kitchen duty. But they never did their chores without being reminded at least once. Often more than once. Mary Sue would have to seek out Michael in his basement music room and Michelle in her bedroom.

Always before, when Barry wasn't home, it was an excuse for them to order pizza or eat out. After he moved out, the dining room became a room for special occasions only, with the kitchen table seeming more appropriate for their newly configured family. But Mary Sue insisted the table be set, that the three of them sit down together, no matter how simple the meal.

The nights and weekends the children were with their father, Dixie or Gretchen would stop by in the evening with carry-out. Pamela came during the day. Always, their first words were, "How are you feeling?" She wondered if the four of them would ever get back to being lighthearted. She could use some of that in her life.

As it was, she would complete her chemotherapy, then wait to see if it had worked. If it hadn't, she would be treated with more chemo, but it would be only a matter of time—months or years—until the cancer killed her. She internalized this knowledge and made it part of who she was.

It surprised her that, except for the moments of unbearable sadness when she thought of leaving her children, she could live fairly normally with the prospect of death hanging over her head. Maybe she was in denial. But whatever the reason, she felt almost calm—certainly more so than her mother and friends. It was like flying on an airplane. She was always nervous before a trip, but when the plane took off, she didn't think about a plummeting plane carrying her to her death. There was no point in worrying about stalled motors or terrorist bombs. What would be would be. That's how she felt now. She would live each day, continue to put one foot in front of another, but other than by taking a hormone that was thought to keep stray breast cancer cells from forming new tumors, there was no way to change whatever lay ahead. She would either be cured or not. If she wasn't cured, she would live on as best she could.

She prayed some—for strength and acceptance. But she could not bring herself to pray that a God who had become vague to her in recent years single her out for a cure when he let others die. If he had the power to cure her, then obviously he had the power to prevent her from being stricken in the first place. She figured that he either didn't care one way or the other who got cancer and who was cured, or he had a policy of just sitting back and letting things randomly take their course. Mary Sue would smile and nod when people told her to put her life in the hands of God or Jesus, just as she would smile and thank people when they told her they had added her name to the prayer circle at their respective church or when they recommended meditation, visualization, acupuncture, herbal remedies, cancer diets, yoga, therapeutic massage, rolfing, or green tea. People would call to tell her about a certain physician or cancer clinic they'd just heard about on television or to report on some marvelous cure they had just read about—injections of scorpion venom, drinking a gallon of distilled water every day to flush out the cancer cells, putting magnets under one's mattress, electrodes on one's head. Gretchen wanted her to take walks every day when she was able and eat steamed vegetables on the days she wasn't too nauseated.

Pamela wanted her to go to the Mayo Clinic and undergo a bone-marrow transplant and downloaded all the information on the procedure from the Internet, which Mary Sue promised to read, but it seemed to her that experimental protocols were something you did if standard, less drastic treatments failed. Or maybe she just didn't have the energy to do battle with an insurance company and didn't want her friends to hold fund-raisers on her behalf.

Dixie wanted her to play beautiful music whenever she wasn't watching television, but beautiful music—whether Beethoven or Simon and Garfunkel—made Mary Sue melancholy. After a time, she would have to turn off the stereo and get back to CNN—but never to silence. Silence was too cavernous, too ominous. She used a sound machine to help her through the night; her favorite sound was ocean waves, which seemed a bit odd for someone raised in Kansas. The sound of Kansas was the wind and chirping crickets.

Busyness was her favorite therapy. On her good days, she cooked, mended, knitted. She cleaned out closets, bookcases, her desk, and her recipe box. And then there were the photo albums and drawers and boxes of photographs. What should she do about all those mounted and waiting-to-be-mounted photographs that portrayed what no longer existed? Had all those pictures of their handsome, smiling family of four been a lie? Should she sort them into two separate categories of before and after—when Barry still loved her and after he stopped loving her? Or had the lie always been there, waiting to surface?

She couldn't bring herself to throw away her wedding photographs—or the pictures of their family at christenings, birthdays, family vacations. There was no way to eliminate all the pictures that had Barry in them.

In the end, she left the completed albums intact and carefully selected photos for a new album that covered the last years of their marriage—photographs that showed Barry only on the fringe. The ones with just Barry and the children she put in a box for him—not that she had any illusions about him putting them in albums or selecting ones to put in frames. The box would be put in the top of a closet, but maybe someday he would take them down and remember what good kids Michelle and Michael were and experience regret that he had distanced himself from them by divorcing their mother. She wanted that—wanted for him to feel regret.

She had only a few photos of Walter Lampley. She selected the best of them and tucked them away in a drawer, just in case he was still alive and one day came back to her.

Then she bought a new album with blank pages to chronicle the post-divorce years, an album in which there would be no pictures of Barry. If the children wanted current photos of their father, they would have to take them. Or would Trish take care of that? And what would happen to this collection of albums anyway? Would Michael and Michelle even want them? And their children?

As Mary Sue went about her busyness, she wondered if she was tidying up her life before she died or making a fresh start on the rest of her life. Whichever, it felt like the correct thing to do.

The first of December, Detective Mosley returned, wanting to know if she had recalled any additional information about Walter—perhaps the names of friends and associates he might have mentioned.

Mary Sue wasn't very helpful. Walter knew several maître d's by their first names, and he spoke about the people in his office some. He had mentioned a half-brother, but she had no idea where he lived. Mostly she had introduced him to her friends, not the other way around.

The detective admitted that Walter seemed to have disappeared without a trace. And no, they still did not know the identity of the redheaded woman who had been in his house. "It must have been difficult for you to find out he had been seeing someone else," she said.

Mary Sue wasn't sure if the woman was being sympathetic or discreetly probing. "At first it was, but I'm kind of accustomed to the idea now," Mary Sue admitted. "I realize I was wearing a pair of blinders when it came to Walter. But I do hope he's all right, even if he's living with the redheaded mystery woman on some tropical island."

When Mary Sue came to the end of her chemotherapy and the final touches had been made on her reconstructed breast with what almost could pass for a nipple tattooed at its crest, she called her three best friends together for a commemorative event and holiday get-together. There would be no holiday decorations, she warned them. With the children spending most of their school break with their dad, she hadn't bothered to drag all those boxes down from the attic and instead made do with a table-top tree.

At the end of a really fine meal that she'd taken two days to prepare, she announced she was ready to get on with her life. She wanted to find both a job and a man—and would appreciate their advice on how she might go about accomplishing those goals.

They talked about getting a job first.

"I'm going to have to either get a job or sell the house," Mary Sue admitted. "Eventually, I'll have to sell it anyway, but I'd like to hang on to it until Michelle and Michael are on their own."

She looked around the family room with its hardwood floors, stone fireplace, and floor-to-ceiling bookcases. It was a handsome room in a handsome house. Once she would have said that she loved her house. She had certainly lavished a great deal of loving care on it. But a wonderful house didn't make a marriage work and didn't make a husband stay. If it weren't for her children, she would prefer to move. The house seemed like a monument to failure.

"The house aside, though," she continued, "I really *want* to get a paying job if anyone will hire me. I have a degree in sociology, but I pretty much majored in cheerleading and sorority. The only money I've ever made in my life was when the park department paid me for running the Little League program. I was absolutely thrilled to think that someone thought my services had value. The following spring when Barry filled out our tax forms, he claimed the money I made was just enough to put us into the next tax bracket. He said it cost us more in taxes than I made. The next year I ran the program for free. It wasn't the same, though. I was just a mother helping out and not a valued employee."

They talked for a time about possibilities and strategies. Mary Sue took notes. She needed to read want ads and go online. She should let all her friends know that she was looking. She needed to develop a résumé that emphasized her organizational skills and experience working with groups. For references, she could offer the head of the park department and the high school principal.

At nine-thirty, Pamela said goodnight and hurried home to her husband because she lived by her husband's rules—just as Mary Sue herself once had done, perhaps to a lesser degree. Just as Dixie and Gretchen had done during the years they were married. It was nice not to have to do that anymore, Mary Sue realized. It made her feel like a fully franchised adult for the first time in her life. She brewed the coffee the way she liked it and put bell peppers in almost everything she cooked, when before she had seldom bought bell peppers because Barry hated them. But without the structure of a husband, without her life being wrapped around his comings and goings, his needs and dislikes, she was left rudderless—a ship wandering aimlessly with no regularly scheduled stops as it sailed about.

With Pamela gone, Mary Sue opened another bottle of wine. "Now, we can talk about men," she said. "I don't know if there's a good man out there willing to take a chance on a woman who's had breast cancer and has a reconstructed breast. He would be shallow if he minded the reconstruction, and I don't want another shallow man in my life, but I certainly would understand a man's reservation about getting involved with a woman who has an uncertain future. *But* if there are any such brave souls out there, I would like to find one who is close to my age and passionate about life. So, tell me, how do women our age find nice men?" she asked.

"Yeah, how is that done?" Gretchen chimed in.

Then both Mary Sue and Gretchen turned to Dixie for an answer. Dixie had been divorced for almost six years. She wasn't dating anyone now, but she had before she moved back to Garden Grove.

Dixie looked at Mary Sue and Gretchen's expectant faces. And cringed. They actually thought she might be able to tell them how a woman facing middle age finds an acceptable man.

Dixie knew that both Mary Sue and Gretchen would claim they had no great expectations, that a kindly man who wasn't old enough to be their father would do just fine. This man would have to get along with their kids, and he shouldn't be obese or have any disgusting habits. He needed to be reasonably successful and not be a freeloader. Each wanted a man who would fit into her existing life, not someone who would uproot her or expect her to change her religion or politics, not someone who would expect her to take up sky diving or frequent nudist colonies.

And Dixie knew that, deep in their wounded hearts, Mary Sue, Gretchen, and even Pamela, whether they realized it or not, didn't really want a generic nice man who was not yet elderly. No matter that they told themselves any respectful man without a beer belly would do. Each was hoping for an exceptional man who would lift her heart. They had all sighed as young girls when Cinderella sang that someday her prince would come. In her heart of hearts, each was still hoping that someday a princely man would show up at her door.

Like Dixie herself, they all thought at one time that they had found him, but either they had been kidding themselves or even princely guys can turn into jerks. Not that Dixie ever would have ended her marriage. She would have stayed with Arnie no matter how distant and contrary he became. Just as Mary Sue and Gretchen would each have stayed married no matter what. Just as Pamela continued to stay married to a man who kept her on a short leash and often was barely civil to her. If not a someday prince, they had, at least, all been waiting for a change—for a time of renewal in their marriage. Maybe after the children grew up or their husband had reached a point in his career when they could spend summers in the south of France, provided, of course, there were golf courses and ESPN, and they would find greater fulfillment in life and marriage.

But Dixie doubted if there was a woman out there—married or otherwise—who had not dreamed about a princely person riding into her life. He would fall madly in love with her and be willing to give up his throne if only she would let him spend the rest of his days loving her.

Even if she decided—for the sake of family and marriage and being a good woman—to stay in her marriage, she at least would have a wonderful memory to pull out when she was feeling unloved. Probably even a nun in a convent wanted a princely man to fall in love with her so she could make the ultimate sacrifice by sending him away. Then every night for the rest of her life, after she finished her prayers, she would take out the memory of the man who had loved her more than anything and hold it close to her heart while she fell asleep on her chaste little cot. Unrequited love was the most romantic kind. It stayed frozen in time with nary a moment of disillusionment. That nun was lucky because she would never have to compete with the television remote control. She would never find her beloved's toe-nail clippings on the bedside table, never become the laundress of his smelly socks and soiled briefs, never wonder who he was thinking about when they had sex, never reach the point where she herself was thinking about some real or imagined lover.

Chapter Ten

Dixie *hated the cynic* she had become. She desperately wanted to believe in the package deal of love and marriage, more now for her son than for herself. She wanted Kirk to find the right young woman and live with her happily ever after. She wanted her grandchildren to grow up in a home where their parents loved and respected each other. Surely such marriages were out there. *Surely* they were. At one time Dixie would have said she wanted Kirk to have a marriage like her own parents had. But her father seemed happier now with Myrtle than he ever had been with her mother, a situation that made Dixie wonder if all along she had been looking at her parents' marriage through rose-colored glasses.

She was the wrong person to tell Mary Sue, Gretchen, or anyone else how to proceed with their lives. She herself had decided against proceeding, decided against finding a man to marry, settling instead for an occasional escape from reality. Not that she wasn't apprehensive. Escapes from reality generally were not long-term propositions. Someday, she would be old and lonely, with nothing on her horizon, with nothing to which she could escape.

But wasn't that what happened to most women? The great majority of them outlived whatever happiness or unhappiness marriage had brought to their lives. Her mother was an exception. Most women were widows when they died.

Fragile Mary Sue, with her scarred body and uncertain future, and seething Gretchen, who hated her ex more than she had ever loved him—these women who were like sisters to her believed that the key to their future was held by some man. And they felt a desperate need to get out there and find him. *Soon.* While they were still young enough to compete.

Sitting on a stool in Mary Sue's kitchen, Dixie looked into the family room. The Prescott family portrait over the mantel had been replaced with a mirror. Barry's recliner had disappeared for a time but reappeared when Walter came onto the scene. Now, it had vanished a second time, with the furniture moved about to compensate for its dismissal. Mary Sue's collection of ceramic owls was gone. In fact, the bookcases were devoid of bric-a-brac altogether and held only books and a scattering of photographs. The abundance of throw pillows had been reduced to the few that might accidentally serve a purpose. The arrangement of dried flowers had disappeared from the coffee table, which now was adorned with only a stack of magazines and a bowl of nuts. The room had a sleeker, more pared-down look about it.

The same could be said for Mary Sue herself. She was thinner and had decided to keep her hair, still drab and lank from chemotherapy, closely cropped for now. Without her fluff of shining blond hair and with her newly acquired penchant for faded jeans and turtleneck sweaters, with the caution that now came with her dimpled smile, she no longer looked like the cheerleader they all remembered. For so long now, they had counted on Mary Sue to make them look on the bright side, to count their blessings, to inspire them to be thoughtful and kind. For four decades, she had been the glue that bound them together. She still was, but with a difference. She was subdued—no longer Wendy Darling clapping her hands to save Tinker Bell and saying, "I believe."

Dixie watched while Mary Sue refilled her wineglass—with jug red wine, when once they all had been wine snobs. Now only Pamela could afford the good stuff. Dixie took a couple of sips and nibbled on a piece of ordinary cheddar cheese. Both tasted pretty damned good.

How did women their age find a nice man? They were still waiting for her answer.

"What about that running club you joined?" she asked Gretchen.

Gretchen shrugged. "Mostly, the men are married and/or small. And believe it or not, a lot of them are old. One man in the club holds the state record for the mile run by men over seventy."

"I thought you said there was a great-looking tall guy who said he was divorcing," Mary Sue chimed in.

Gretchen allowed herself two peanuts from the open can on the bar before answering. "Yeah. Tall, dark, and handsome and not a day over fifty. But he came just that once. Every time the phone rang, I actually said a prayer, but beautiful Yves never called. Apparently the business opportunity he was looking at didn't pan out, and he went back to St. Louis and probably to his wife."

"Finding a good man who's close to one's own age can be a problem," Dixie admitted. "Just look at the men we ourselves married. Pamela is the second wife of a man a decade and a half older than she is. Barry, Arnie, and Paul—who, as it turned out, weren't such good men after all—but that aside, they, like Clay Cartwright, are typical in that they all found someone younger to make them feel younger."

She paused and waited for a comment.

When none came, she went on, with no idea where she was going with all this. "Once I went out with a man who was my exact age. When I happened to mention the year I graduated from high school, he was horrified. 'But I thought you were much younger,' he protested and grabbed his coat. He actually slunk out of the bar like a thief in the night, petrified that— horror of horrors!—someone might see him out with a woman his own age. Believe me, there are damned few, if any, heterosexual unmarried men who aren't sexually dysfunctional or just plain weird willing to date someone their own age. Except for the widowers, these men left their wives for someone younger. Of course, the younger wife or girlfriend soon discovers that her new man isn't such a prize after all, no matter how deep his pockets. Some of these second-wife types make up their minds that a man belching in front of the television is better than no man at all and settle in for the long haul. But some of them can't take it and jump ship. First wives seldom leave their husbands, but second wives do. The men left by second wives are usually the ones floating around singles bars. They are the ones putting singles ads in the newspaper, prowling around in chat rooms on the Internet asking women what size bra they wear and if they sleep naked. They're the ones showing up at singles Sunday School classes and Parents Without Partners meetings. Maybe this time around they are willing to settle for a woman just five or so years younger than they are, but unless the woman happens to be an old flame from their younger days, they won't even consider women their own age."

"You mean in the years since your divorce, you have not come across even one man you'd like to hook up with?" Mary Sue asked.

"Not one I would marry," Dixie hedged. "But then, I'm not sure I ever want to get married again."

"I refuse to believe that there aren't single men out there who are sweet and sensitive and caring—and don't have one foot in the grave," Mary Sue said, with a defiant tilt to her chin.

"Of course there are," Dixie allowed, "but most of them have boyfriends."

Mary Sue groaned. Gretchen rolled her eyes.

"For the most part, the dating scene is pretty scary," Dixie continued, "like the time Pamela insisted I meet that man at the law firm Christmas party. I knew better, but every so often, I guess I need to be reminded. Before that, a sales rep from my floral distributor talked me into going out with her brother-in-law. I met him in the city at some trendy bar on the Plaza. We chitchatted a while, and he seemed nice enough until he started telling really disgusting jokes. I got a sudden headache and left. One time back in Sauganash, I was so desperate to dump a blind date, I crawled out the window in the restaurant bathroom."

"How many men have you gone out with anyway?" Gretchen demanded. "We need some details here. Did you sleep around? Is that why you won't talk about it? Are you embarrassed?"

"I don't talk about it because I am too cynical. No woman wants to hear that, for every good guy floating around out there, there are hundreds of Walters. I really have only one piece of advice. Whether you find men through a dating service, singles Sunday School class, singles bar, or online chat room—the first time you go out with him, meet him for lunch. That way you won't ruin an entire evening if he turns out to be boring or boorish. If he insists that you meet him at a bar after work, make it clear you have plans later on in the evening and make your exit, even if he seems nice enough, even if he seems like the greatest thing since Kris Kristofferson in *The Sailor Who Fell from Grace with the Sea*. Then if he never calls back, at least you haven't gotten drunk and gone to bed with him. Even the dysfunctional guys are after sex. They think that finding the right woman will cure them."

Dixie drove home wishing she had kept her mouth shut. She wasn't an expert on anything, much less midlife dating. It would be just fine with her if she never went on another date as long as she lived. What she had with Johnny wasn't dating. It was a relationship.

Johnny was at least part of the reason why she wasn't out there looking for a man—for *any* presentable man who would make her get over rejection and humiliation and diminish the fact that her husband had left her for someone younger and firmer.

Even though she had used every delaying tactic she could think of just in case Arnie changed his mind, Dixie had known all along that she was kicking a dead horse. She could either turn into a pathetic victim or get on with her life. Not that she hadn't had moments of agonizing pain, but it came more from being rejected than from the prospect of facing life as an unmarried woman.

Of course, Dixie's own husband had left her more discreetly than Mary Sue's and Gretchen's had left them. Arnie and Cindy had kept their affair secret. They were both divorced before they went public. Close friends knew better, of course, but went along with the charade. Close friends, for the most part, abandoned Dixie in favor of the second Mrs. Woodward. As it turned out, they hadn't really been *her* friends at all. When it came right down to it, her only true friends had been Mary Sue, Gretchen, and Pamela—the ones who knew her before she became Mrs. Arnold Woodward.

Like other women who had been left for a younger woman, Dixie lost too much weight and bought clothing that was borderline sex-kitten. Not for long, though. Her son saw to that. Kirk told her she was too skinny and showed her a picture he had taken with his Polaroid to prove it. The woman in the picture looked like a forty-year-old anorexic. And one evening, before they left for his school carnival, Kirk asked her if she would please wear a longer skirt and a sweater that wasn't so tight.

Her first date as a divorced woman was with a man she met at that very carnival. Ivan Fisk was his name. His daughter was in Kirk's homeroom. Ivan called the morning after the carnival to ask her out to dinner. She got all giddy and spent hours fixing her hair and deciding what to wear.

Ivan, the rare man whose first wife had left him, was a civil engineer and talked at great length about structural steel. On and on, Ivan talked about structural steel, while Dixie studied the other diners, toyed with her drink, played with her salad.

When the entrées were served, he abruptly switched gears. "I suppose you want to know about my divorce," he said.

"Not really," Dixie said, but he told her anyway. What it boiled down to was that his wife had left him for his best friend. But he had a lengthy presentation that Dixie suspected he had delivered before. While his food grew cold and she discreetly nibbled at hers, he told her in excruciating detail about every missed clue, about all the trips he and his wife had taken with his best friend and his wife, how Jinny and Phil were always running to the liquor store together or heading for the greenhouse to buy bedding plants or fertilizer. Ivan and Phil's poor wife never had a clue.

"God," Ivan said, with a slap to his forehead that made the diners at the next table turn and stare. "God," he said again, "how trusting we both were!"

Dixie declined coffee, saying she had to get home because her son wasn't feeling well, when actually Kirk was spending the night with Arnie and Cindy.

When Ivan pulled into the circle drive in front of her house, Dixie already had her hand on the door handle and was ready to make her exit the minute the car rolled to a stop.

But he put a hand on her arm. "I had a good time," he said. "I'll call you," he added. And he leaned forward with his lips pursed.

"I enjoyed meeting you," Dixie had said, averting her face, fumbling with the door handle, "but I'm not ready for dating yet."

She really got her hopes up when she received a call from a man she had known back in high school who was now living in Chicago. She had dated Robert Olson before his family moved to California. They had even talked about forever and ever.

Robert was heavier but not fat, his hair startlingly white. They shook hands. He told her he would have recognized her anywhere.

Almost the moment they were seated in the restaurant, he began his tale. His first wife never understood him, but his second marriage had been absolutely perfect until his wife got a job and had an affair with her panties on.

Dixie asked him to repeat that last part, which he did but without explanation.

"Are you saying there was absolutely nothing wrong with your second marriage until the morning your wife went to work and had an affair with her panties on?" she asked, genuinely curious.

"That's right. We'd never had a single argument. We lived in a great house. She got along with my kids and was a great cook. And we had wonderful sex almost every night."

"Come on, Robert, every marriage has problems."

"We didn't. It was the best five years of my life."

"Well, if everything was so great, why did she have an affair? And why did you get a divorce?"

"Well, I wasn't going to stay married to her," he said indignantly, "not after she did a thing like that."

"If you had had such a great marriage, maybe you should have tried to save it. Or maybe you thought it was great, and she didn't. It couldn't have been all that perfect or she wouldn't have succumbed."

"*Succumbed?* That's a fancy word for adultery."

"With her panties on," Dixie reminded him. "Tell me about your kids."

"They live with their mother."

"Has their mother remarried?"

Robert nodded.

"What about wife number two?"

"She's remarried, too."

"To the guy she had the affair with?"

Again, he nodded. "Did you forgive your husband?" he asked.

"For what?"

"For succumbing. He did, didn't he?"

"So it seems. I didn't exactly forgive him, but I was willing to give him another chance. He wasn't interested, though. But enough of adultery and divorce. Tell me what you do for a living."

Robert spent the rest of the lunch talking about his construction company.

Dixie ate her sandwich and half-listened. He never stopped talking, never asked a single question about her life, never reminisced about their high school years, never said he missed her when he moved to California. When the check came, she insisted on paying for her own lunch.

She was surprised two days later when he called, inviting her out for dinner and a movie. "I enjoyed seeing you again," she told him, "but I'm not ready for dating."

"What do you do for sex?" he asked.

"Goodbye, Robert."

Eventually, she did have sex. With another man named Robert—J. Robert Foreman, an English professor on the Northwestern University Evanston campus. Dixie met him at her branch library when she attended his lecture on Jane Austen. Professor Foreman felt Austen had wasted her talent writing about ineffectual people but admired how skillfully she portrayed those people.

He gave a short reading from *Pride and Prejudice* that included the quotation: "A lady's imagination is very rapid; it jumps from admiration to love, from love to matrimony in a moment." Apparently he was quite taken with the quotation, because he repeated it at the end of the reading.

After the event, Dixie strolled over to the fiction section and sought out the shelf with Austen's books, most of which she had read and loved as a young woman. As an older person, would she share Professor Foreman's disdain for her characters?

"You win the prize," a male voice behind her said.

She turned and there was the professor himself.

"For what?" she asked.

"For being inspired to revisit Miss Austen."

Dixie smiled. "Yes, I thought I might. I loved her books in high school. But now that I think about it, what I really loved were the courtships. I wonder why I wanted to read about courtship when most of the marriages she portrayed were rather grim."

They walked across the street to a coffee shop and chatted for a time—about books and movies. Before they parted, he asked if she would accompany him to a Little Theater production of *Laura* the following week.

Dixie enjoyed the play and thought it quite polished for an amateur production. They went to a bar afterward and discussed the play over a glass of wine. Or mostly Robert discussed the play. The role of the detective had been miscast. The sets were amateurish.

She had thought he might ask her out again but was surprised when the invitation was for dinner at his home. When she hesitated, he said, "Please, I get tired of spending my evenings here alone."

She expected pizza or some other carry-out meal. But when she arrived, the table was covered with a fresh white linen tablecloth. The silverware was polished and correctly placed. Candles were lit in their holders. And the meal itself was nice—grilled chicken breasts, wild rice, baked squash, tossed salad, hot rolls—all served with good Chablis in crystal wineglasses. She remembered how Arnie would open a can of soup for her if she was sick in bed. The entire time they were married, he had never once cooked an entire meal for her.

Robert wouldn't even let her carry her plate into the kitchen. He served her coffee and cookies in the living room. She found it all quite touching. He had gone to all this trouble just for her.

Robert's wife, Elsie, had been a pillar-of-the-community sort of woman, he explained. She had founded both the local Little Theater group and library support group. She had volunteered for years with Meals on Wheels and Habitat for Humanity. A real saint. At her funeral, the sanctuary had been full to overflowing.

Over brandy, he told Dixie about Elsie's sudden death. In great detail, he told her. Elsie had cooked a hearty beef stew for dinner—she always used marinated sirloin for her stew. A wonderful cook. After dinner, they had watched a PBS documentary on apes, sitting side by side on the sofa, holding hands like always. When Elsie complained of a headache, he had rubbed her shoulders and neck. Then she had taken two aspirin and gone to bed before the news. An hour later, he went upstairs, put on his pajamas, brushed his teeth, crawled into bed—and realized she was dead. Just like that, he said with a snap of his fingers, his lovely wife of twenty-seven years was gone—the finest woman he had ever known.

Dixie thought of Ivan-the-engineer. Like Ivan, Professor J. Robert Foreman's every expression, his every gesture seemed rehearsed. She had the uncomfortable feeling that he had told other women his sad story in this very living room, after cooking the exact same meal.

He finished his presentation by saying how much he missed his wife and how difficult it was for a man who had loved and respected his wife so very much and had so enjoyed being married to carry on. Then he paused, bit his lip, and looked away.

His performance was a real turnoff, but Dixie was still feeling a glow from the meal and the wine. And over dinner Robert had asked if she had children. He even asked what year Kirk was in school and what his interests were. That earned the man points. And she had thought that tonight would be The Night. She had spent sixty dollars at the beauty shop on a pedicure and leg waxing and was wearing good lingerie. When Robert solemnly took her hand and led her up the stairs, she didn't resist. She wasn't attracted to him, but he wasn't unattractive, and maybe the first postdivorce coupling was just something to get over with.

After he assured her that this was not *the* room, not *the* bed, in which Elsie had died, Dixie timidly took off her clothes and crawled under the covers. J. Robert undressed quite openly. Dixie assumed that she was supposed to be thrilled by his body, which was rather nice. But she didn't like the way he strutted naked around the room, pausing in the shaft of light from the hall so Dixie would get the full effect and see that his penis was already at half-mast.

In bed, he touched her a bit but mostly wanted her to touch him. His penis stayed pretty much as it had during the prebedding viewing, but suddenly he was stuffing it inside her. The act itself ended very quickly, but apparently J. Robert was quite pleased with his performance, for to Dixie's astonishment, he scrambled onto his knees and began beating on his bare chest, letting forth a Tarzan yell that echoed throughout the quiet house.

Dixie didn't know if she was supposed to laugh or join in. One thing she did know, however, was that J. Robert was *weird*. And he had never once touched her silky smooth legs.

She couldn't get dressed fast enough, grabbing a corner of the sheet to wipe his semen from the inside of her thighs while firmly declining his offer of a nightcap. She thanked him for a lovely dinner and left him in the bed. "I'll let myself out," she called from the top of the stairs.

When he called to invite himself over to dinner—apparently it was her turn to cook for him—Dixie explained that she realized that she wasn't ready for an affair.

Number four was a banker—Thad Bartholomew, whom she also met at the library. Thad was nice looking and took her dancing. He was the kind of dancer who made a woman feel like Ginger Rogers. Dixie relaxed and let the music take her. And allowed herself a lovely fantasy of her and Thad dancing their way into the future. On cruise ships. In ballrooms. After intimate dinners at her house when Kirk was spending the night at his father's.

In the wake of the J. Robert experience, however, she didn't consent to sex until she and Thad had been dating for a couple of months. When he took off his clothes, he didn't strut. He kissed her for a long time, but it wasn't inspired kissing. In fact, it was rather dull kissing. Then he took a break and explained that his analyst had given him a ten-step program to follow to achieve complete arousal.

He turned the clock face where he could see it, then proceeded to time himself as he went through the ten steps, which involved a certain number of minutes of deep kissing, then caressing each breast, and so forth. Nothing was required of her. If fact, it was best if she remain totally passive.

When Thad was finished with the big number ten, he excused himself and took a shower. The last sound Dixie heard as she hurried toward the front door buttoning her blouse was that of Thad gargling.

That was it, she decided. *No more sex.* At least not until she got to know a guy and find out if his analyst had him on a ten-step program.

Then she and Kirk took their big trip, and she met Johnny, who didn't have an analyst and had never heard of performance anxiety. Odd that her son was the only one who knew about him.

While she was trying to decide where Johnny fit into her life, there had been other men, other dates. She was never even tempted to go out with any of them more than once or twice, never tempted to go to bed with them.

By the time she moved back to Garden Grove, she realized she might very well live the rest of her life as a single woman. The prospect did not frighten her, but maybe that was because of Johnny. She'd never told her friends about him. One reason was that he wouldn't be a secret anymore if she did, and she was wise enough to realize that secrecy was part of his allure. If the pros and cons of Johnny were being discussed by her friends, he might not seem nearly so romantic. But mostly she didn't tell them because Johnny was married.

But having Johnny in her life protected her from desperation, protected her from making foolish mistakes with flawed men. Mary Sue and Gretchen would have to make their own mistakes. That was part of the process.

Of course, there was the possibility that Johnny himself was a mistake and that she would someday regret him. But for now, if she had romantic thoughts, they featured him in the starring role.

Chapter Eleven

As $Pamela$ $drove$ $away$ from Mary Sue's house, she couldn't decide if she was irritated or relieved. Her friends had waited for her to leave before addressing the topic of men.

So often now, Pamela felt like the odd person out when she was with them. It reminded her of the years after the three of them were married, and she was single and living in St. Louis. They thought she was living such a glamorous life as a single career girl; in fact, she had been underpaid, overworked, and homesick and was starting to realize that she had a finite number of years before she became one of those career women who never married. She saw them all around her. The successful ones wore Armani suits and three-hundred-dollar shoes and became tyrant bosses who expected their underlings to put in the same impossibly long hours they did and then take work home with them. The others became drab and bitter. Pamela had found herself greatly regretting the men she hadn't married when she had the chance.

Yes, she had lots of practice being the odd person out, first as the only one of her friends who hadn't married, and then as the only one who didn't have children. Pamela couldn't contribute to discussions of stretch marks and teething.

Since marriage, she had been an attentive stepmother to Paul's two daughters, but that wasn't even close to the real thing, especially after their mother took the girls to live in England. As a result, she grew to care deeply about her friends' children, lavishing gifts on them at every opportunity and taking them to magic shows, circuses, and plays. Michelle especially had become her pal. Michelle would ask Pamela if she looked better in pink or red lipstick, if it was okay to mix gold and silver jewelry. Pamela took her to style shows and theatrical productions. Mary Sue's illness had given Pamela the chance to do even more for Michelle. She helped her practice her lines for the senior play and went shopping with her. But of course it still wasn't the same as having a daughter of her own. Her childlessness set her apart from the other three. It always had. Probably it always would.

Pamela still sometimes found herself dreaming about a baby, about Clay having his vasectomy reversed or them rescuing one of those Eastern European babies from its crib prison.

Clay would be sixty next summer, and while he was still youthfully handsome, he didn't like noise and disruptions. And of course, she hoped she would never be single again—at least not until she was too old to care.

Dating for women her age seemed undignified—having to turn on one's rusty radar and go on the prowl. The thought of flirting gave Pamela the creeps. She had seen middle-aged women doing that—trying to look perky and cute and available. She found it cheap and degrading. Apparently Dixie thought so, too—by her own admission, she had pretty much bowed out of the dating game. But now, Mary Sue and Gretchen wanted to give it a try. The second time around for Mary Sue. You'd think after Walter Lampley, she would feel burned.

Walter. Wouldn't it be ironic if Mary Sue were the only one to get over him? The other three all would have memories of the disgusting dentist from Shawnee hanging over their heads forever.

He had been "missing" almost four months now. One of the local television stations recently had run a series on the evening news about the area's more notorious missing-person cases. The series had ended with a segment on Walter. The reporter, standing in front of Walter's house, said that the Shawnee dentist had a reputation as a big spender and compulsive gambler. Pamela had wanted to switch the channel, but Clay insisted on watching. "Mary Sue is better off without the likes of him," he decreed. Pamela had quietly agreed with him.

At least Mary Sue was no longer brooding about Walter, Pamela thought as she turned onto County Line Road. Mary Sue was ready to find someone else. Both she and Gretchen could not imagine living the rest of their lives without a man, which was something Pamela understood completely. She supposed if she were in their shoes, she also would be launching a campaign.

When she tried to think of men Mary Sue and Gretchen might date, Pamela could not think of a single eligible man who wasn't elderly or an avowed philanderer—or both. Pamela did want Gretchen and Mary Sue to find someone, though. Dixie, too. Pamela would like for all of them to be married again, preferably to men that Clay approved of and would enjoy being with. She missed the couples' activities they once had shared—the backyard barbecues, football treks to Lawrence or Manhattan, dinner dances at the country club.

She and Clay had lots of other friends. They had a busy social schedule and sent out hundreds of Christmas cards. But she had never managed to achieve the same level of emotional closeness with other women that she enjoyed with Dixie, Mary Sue, and Gretchen. She was stiff with other people—too proper, she supposed. Overdressed. Never informal. She wasn't comfortable in jeans and sneakers. She never walked out her front door without full makeup and appropriate accessories. She turned to Dixie, Mary Sue, and Gretchen for sympathy, validation, and encouragement. She needed them, she suspected, more than they needed her. Which was odd. She was the one with her social status intact. She had the prerequisite husband and bank account to maintain her position in the community. Her husband was now a justice on the state court of criminal appeals, while her three best friends had been all but dropped from the town's unwritten social register.

Dixie had overseen Pamela's holiday decorations and created a spectacular centerpiece for the annual holiday reception she and Clay hosted, but Dixie had declined to attend the event itself. The house had never looked more beautiful. Even Clay had been impressed.

Mary Sue and Gretchen were both talking about selling their houses and moving someplace more affordable. Pamela couldn't imagine doing such a thing. Part of her identity came from being the lady of her fine vintage Tudor on the spacious wooded lot. She cherished her house. She had taken such pleasure in restoring it, caring for it, and continually finding ways to make it even more handsome.

Pamela felt a rush of pride now, as she turned down her street. Every single house on the block was decorated for the holidays—not with just a few strands of light in the bushes and around the door, but professionally done, with the steeply pitched roofs and front walks of every house outlined in red lights, with white icicle lights dripping from the eaves, and the trees and shrubs laden with thousands of twinkling lights. A veritable fairyland of lights, it was truly beautiful.

And her house was the most beautiful of all.

The outside of poor Mary Sue's house had not been decorated at all, the only house on her street without so much as a string of lights around the front door. Surely Michael and Michelle could have helped her put something up so the house wouldn't look so dark and gloomy.

Mary Sue had come to the reception, but she seemed a bit forlorn and hadn't stayed long. Pamela had wanted to invite her over for Christmas dinner, but Clay insisted that Christmas dinner this year be just the two of them. Last year, her parents and Danny had joined them. But this year her parents had decided not to make the trek back from south Texas for the holidays.

Two days before Christmas, Pamela put her excited brother on a plane to Harlingen after going over his instructions a dozen times. *Don't leave your backpack on the plane. Don't get off the plane in Dallas when everyone else does. Wait for a flight attendant to take you to the plane for Harlingen. Mother and Daddy will be waiting for you when you walk off the plane.*

She put cards with her name, address, and home and cellular phone numbers and those of their parents in both his backpack and shirt pocket.

Pamela had tears in her eyes as she watched him walk down the boarding ramp. A fifty-year-old child. His first solo flight.

Christmas morning, she and Clay called his daughters, who were spending Christmas with their mother and stepfather at their country home in West Sussex. Pamela had enjoyed her stepdaughters when they were children, but now she felt intimidated by them. Janet was married to a viscount. Prissy was a successful journalist. Their accents had gotten more precise with each passing year, whereas once they had acted and sounded like American girls. Their summer visits had always been something to look forward to and plan for, but they hadn't come for a visit in more than five years. The last time she and Clay had seen the girls was when they went over for Janet's wedding, which had been an impressive affair attended by several second-tier royals.

Pamela had ordered the roast duck but prepared the rest of Christmas dinner herself—even the steamed pudding and brandy sauce using her grandmother's recipe. Clay had selected a superb wine and made a lovely toast about them sharing yet another gracious and fulfilling holiday season together.

They exchanged gifts in the living room with the tree lit, carols playing on the stereo, and a fire in the fireplace. Clay gave her a Rolex—her third, but this one had sapphires instead of diamonds. She had knitted him a ski sweater and presented him with a first-edition copy of John Hersey's *Hiroshima*. Then they bundled up and walked over to the annual neighborhood gathering on the greenbelt, where there was a bonfire, wassail, and caroling—an idea that Pamela herself had conceived and launched ten years ago.

All in all, it had been a good Christmas, Pamela decided as she pulled her Mercedes into the garage next to Clay's Jaguar. Next year, she wanted lights strung in the greenbelt trees and a harpist to accompany the singing. And she planned to talk her parents into coming home for the holidays so she wouldn't have to send Danny away. He would have loved the fire and the singing.

After hanging up her coat, she headed for the study. Clay was in his robe and pajamas, a brandy at his elbow, a fire in the fireplace. Pamela leaned over the back of the chair and kissed him on the top of his head. His hair was still damp from the shower. He smelled clean and manly.

"How was your evening?" he asked.

"Fine. Mary Sue must have cooked for days. Her children are skiing with Barry, so she fussed over us. She's ready to get on with her life and wants to find a job. I think it would be good for her."

Clay had no comment. Already, his gaze was back on his book.

"Did you warm up the food I left for you?"

He nodded.

"Can I get you anything?"

He shook his head.

Pamela poured herself a finger of brandy. She didn't really care for brandy, but it was Clay's nightcap of choice, so she pretended that she liked it. It seemed more companionable for them to have the same thing.

She kicked off her shoes and curled up in a corner of the sofa. After several minutes of gazing hypnotically at the fire, she abruptly asked, "Do you love me?" She hadn't planned to say the words. They were out of her mouth before she knew they were coming.

Clay looked up. "Pardon?"

She started to say "never mind." But it wasn't necessary. He had already refocused his attention on the pages of his book.

Pamela cleared her throat. "I asked if you love me," she said.

He stared at her over the top of his reading glasses. "Now what kind of a question is that? You are my wife. Of course, I love you."

She wanted to tell him it was a perfectly valid question. After all, he had stopped loving his first wife. Being a man's wife did not ensure his continued love. But she didn't have the courage to say such things.

Instead she said, "I tell you that I love you all the time, but you hardly ever say it back. It is nice to hear the actual words once in a while."

Clay sighed and, holding his place in the book with his forefinger, asked, "So, were you complaining to your divorced friends that your husband never says he loves you?"

"Of course not. But when I'm around them, I feel afraid. They are lovely women, but their husbands divorced them. Maybe I need reassurance."

"Maybe they weren't such 'lovely women' as you think, at least not to their husbands. Maybe that's why they are now divorced."

"Oh, come on, Clay. We're talking about Dixie, Mary Sue, and Gretchen. They loved their husbands and were good and faithful wives. It's not fair what happened to them."

"And you're afraid the same might happen to you?" he asked, not unkindly. He actually closed his book and put it on the table next to his glass.

"Sometimes," Pamela said, making herself look at him and not at her hands. "It would be nice if you reassured me once in a while."

Clay opened and closed his mouth, apparently thinking twice about the next words that should come out of his mouth. "You are a fine wife, Pamela. You've always seen to it that I have the orderly home life that I need. Of course, I do get out of sorts when you aren't here with me in the evening. No man likes to come home to an empty house and have to warm his own food. I don't understand why you can't see your friends during the day. I don't like you being away from home on *my* time."

"Dixie works during the day, and Mary Sue wanted all of us there to celebrate the end of her chemotherapy. It's the first time I've gone out on my own in the evening for months," she reminded him. She started to add, *since the night before Mary Sue's mastectomy.* But she didn't. She did not want to speak about *that* night. If Clay ever found out . . .

She took another sip of her brandy to distract herself from such thoughts.

"What about that photography class?" Clay demanded. "It was at night."

"That was last year and only for three nights. And I wanted you to take it with me. I thought we might enjoy having a shared hobby. It's nice when a husband and wife do things together."

Clay was looking at her oddly, and Pamela realized there were tears rolling down her cheeks. Hastily, she wiped them away.

Clay put down his book and opened his arms.

It took her several heartbeats to realize what he wanted. Then she flew onto his lap, curled up in his arms, and began to cry. "I get scared sometimes," she sobbed.

"Don't," he said, kissing her forehead. "I'm not like those other men."

But he had been, Pamela thought. He had left Jane and married her.

"You are everything I want in a wife," Clay said, "and I would never leave you. Now you go upstairs and get ready for bed. I'll bring your brandy upstairs."

She soaked in the tub a long time. If Clay had taken a Viagra, she wanted it to have time to work.

He didn't know that she knew about the Viagra, but how could she not? Suddenly one night his erection was firmer than it had been in years. Pamela had wanted to thank him, to tell him that she admired his courage in trying something new, in actually going to his physician and admitting he had a problem, in actually asking for help. She realized how hard that was for a man, especially a proud man, like Clay.

But if he had wanted her to know, he would have told her, so she said nothing. And marveled. His erections had never been this nice before. She had been faking orgasms for years. An orgasm had become something she gave herself on the nights Clay was away on a business trip. She would take a leisurely bath, oil her body, drink some wine, and think of the one man from her past she had never been able to forget.

Martin Leonard was the first boy with whom she'd ever made love.

She'd dated him on and off in high school and had sex with him the summer after their freshman year in college. Martin didn't want to become a doctor like his father. He wanted to be a writer. Pamela did, too. Martin was the only one she ever let see her pages. Poetry mostly. And she read his chapters. She said they were good, but they really weren't. He rambled too much, and she could never find the story. And she didn't trust him when he said her poetry was good. He was probably lying, just as she was. But they dreamed together. That summer, Pamela got a prescription for birth control pills, and they screwed themselves raw. She never told her friends. She wondered if they had gone all the way with their boyfriends and if they were wondering the same thing about her.

Sometimes she and Martin talked about marriage, but he was Jewish, and their parents didn't like them seeing each other, especially once they were in college. The sneaking around made their encounters all the more exciting. She wondered if Jewish weddings were like Gentile ones. Did the bride get to wear a wedding dress with a train and a veil? She went to the library and read about Judaism, about converting.

In the fall, Martin went back to Harvard, and she returned to KU. They wrote letters that didn't say much of anything. He didn't come home for the holidays that year. When his father died, she spent hours writing a letter that was so awful she tore it up and sent a sympathy card instead, with a note on the bottom saying how much she missed him. She never heard back from him. She didn't see him again until their twenty-fifth high school reunion. But she had never stopped thinking about him.

She hadn't realized he would be at the reunion. Her heart almost stopped beating at the sight of him. He was gorgeous. So was his wife. They had five kids and seemed to be crazy about each other.

When the band began playing "Best of My Love," Martin asked her to dance.

"You remember?" she asked.

"Of course, I remember. That was our song. That was our time."

Pamela realized twenty-five years too late that she should have followed him back east. Except her grades were terrible and no out-of-state college would have accepted her.

A life with Martin Leonard obviously had not been in the cards for her, but seeing him once again threw her into a funk that she had a long and difficult time crawling out of. She finally accomplished it when Mary Sue's breast cancer was diagnosed, and she realized she needed to count her blessings and not lament a lost love. Clay was a man for always. Martin had been about lust, not enduring love. His wife supported him and the kids while he wrote novels that never got published. They didn't wear good shoes. His wife wore department-store jewelry.

After the reunion, Pamela had written a poem—the first one she had written in years. She had thrown away her early writings years ago, after she had married Clay and she decided it was time to put adolescent daydreams aside.

She tucked the reunion poem away in a high school yearbook, safe from Clay's eyes. Her husband was allowed to have a past—two engagements and an ex-wife—but she was not. But then, she had pretended that she was a virgin when she married him at age twenty-seven.

The poem had helped put her encounter with Martin in perspective. She still reread it from time to time. It had been cathartic, but she had not written another:

In middle life, she saw him once again—
her first love.
So long it had been.
He was heavier, his hair gray.

But when she looked twice,
she could see him still—
the adorable boy who had loved her
on a blanket under the stars.

They talked. The remember whens.

To dance with him,
to hear his voice,
to touch his face—
such unexpected joy.

Why had she not married him back then?
She could not recall.

If she had,
would the sight of him this day have
filled her with such aching?

If she had,
could there have been the moment,
the oh-so-perfect moment
of seeing once again?

Clay came to bed with an erection. "See what holding you on my lap did to me," he said, his voice husky. "Don't ever doubt that I love you, Pamela. You are the most important person in my life."

Pamela wondered briefly if it was her husband or the Viagra talking, but quickly got beyond such doubts. Her heart soared, and her body responded. And she told him that she loved him over and over again. Their life together was perfect.

She promised herself before sleep that she would never again have sexual thoughts about Martin Leonard. She would stop imagining scenes with her running into him on a plane or in a restaurant, stop imagining what she would be wearing if that should ever happen, stop playacting little conversations with him, stop thinking about him when she wanted to be aroused. She loved her husband. And Martin's eyes had danced when he looked at his wife, which made Pamela admire him all the more.

Chapter Twelve

*Y*ou want a glass of wine?" Gretchen asked, as they settled themselves at a tiny table in the bar to wait for seating in the dining room.

Dixie shook her head. "No, it would slow me down, and I have a busy afternoon. We're working on a wedding and two funerals for tomorrow."

"I guess I should abstain, too," Gretchen said. She paused before adding, "I've got an appointment with my lawyer. I haven't gotten any child support from Paul in the last two months."

"You're not going to court again, are you?"

"He doesn't answer my phone calls or letters. I'm going to have two daughters in college this fall. It was a struggle with just Debbie. I need to spend as much outfitting Robin for rush week as I did for Debbie. Paul needs to buy them a car. Debbie's had to bum rides everywhere she went. She'll be the poorest girl in the Chi Omega house next fall."

"None of us had a car at college," Dixie reminded her.

"Yeah, but that was back then. Times have changed. And it's not just the clothes and car. Robin's obsessed with her nose. We'd always promised her she could have the bump smoothed out when she graduated from high school, but I certainly can't afford to pay for it. All I do is worry about money. I'd like to hang on to the house at least until the girls are out of college. Paul and that woman live like royalty, and I have to use coupons from the newspaper to lower my grocery bill. It's just so damned unfair."

In a diversionary effort, Dixie began looking around at the paneled walls and brass chandeliers. "I haven't been to Lemuel's since they remodeled the place," she said. "Mr. Lemuel used to keep his bowling trophies on a shelf behind the bar, and there was a juke box in the corner."

Gretchen froze for a minute, her shoulders tense. "I guess you get tired of hearing about it, don't you?" she asked. "But doesn't it stick in your craw that Arnie and his wife are living better than you are?"

"Of course it does. But I'm not going to let it ruin my life. Remember how we'd sit in here listening to John Denver and Diana Ross by the hour."

"Yeah," she offered, "*Ain't no mountain high enough to keep me from you.* I hear those songs on the radio and can't decide if it was a hundred years ago or yesterday. I can't decide if I'm wiser or stupider. I wish Mary Sue didn't have cancer. I wish Paul hadn't turned out to be a disgusting, evil human being." She paused, glancing over at the next table where a group of businessmen were talking shop, leaned toward Dixie, and lowered her voice. "And I wish Walter Lampley had never come out to the damned lake house."

Dixie felt an all-too-familiar stab of guilt. "He wouldn't have come if I hadn't forced his hand," she said softly. The men at the next table were discussing the IQ of their new boss, who was apparently making unwarranted changes that had a negative effect on their work lives. No company cars. Shared secretaries. One of the men used the word "bitch."

"I wish I didn't have to think about that despicable man ever again," Gretchen said.

Dixie signed. "Me, too. The irony of it is that a man I loathed will be forever in my thoughts."

"I hope we don't have a dry summer. I have nightmares about that car suddenly becoming visible."

"I drove out there the other day to look at the dam and make sure it was solid," Dixie admitted.

After a server took their order for iced tea and left two menus, Dixie changed the subject once again. "So, how'd your date go Saturday night?"

Gretchen shrugged. "He lied on the dating service questionnaire."

"How do you know?"

"I was expecting a fifty-year-old, five-foot-ten optometrist who works out three times a week. When I walked in the bar, I looked right past him, thinking that he couldn't possibly be the guy I was supposed to hook up with. He had to be at least fifty-five, probably older, and is inches short of five-ten, and there may have been a week in his dim, dark past that he worked out three times, but not recently. His upper body is just short of pitiful. I couldn't tell about his legs. Actually, though, he was reasonably nice, and he didn't have a pot belly. I hated his mustache, though. It was big and bushy and made him look like a clown. He reminded me of that man on the *Today* show who does the movie reviews."

"Gene Shalit."

"Yeah, I wonder if Gene's wife minds his mustache. This guy had a cold. Every time he blew his nose, I thought how unsanitary the thing was. I don't think I could ever kiss him without thinking about the snot and food that must be trapped there."

"If you started going out with him, you could ask him to shave it off," Dixie suggested.

"I suppose," Gretchen said with a shrug.

Gretchen was wearing a white sweater set with pale blue slacks. She was tan, fit, and beautiful—easily the most beautiful woman in the room. Dixie wondered if she didn't intimidate men with her cool good looks and athletic body. She wondered if Paul had ever truly appreciated what a magnificent woman he was married to.

They watched as the server put the glasses of iced tea on the table, and both took a sip. "What was you date's name?" Dixie asked.

"Gus."

"Are you going out with him again?"

"I gave him my phone number, but now I wish I hadn't. And it's not just his fudging on the questionnaire—I lied a little, too, just not as much as he did. It's just that there's no point in going out with someone I'm not attracted to. In addition to the mustache, his shirt was open one button too many—to show off his gold chain and chest hair, I suppose. It turned me off. And you're talking to a woman who hasn't had sex in over two years. My standards aren't what they once were. In bed last night, I even tried to have a fantasy about old Gus, but it didn't happen. I had to cast about for someone else."

"I'm sorry," Dixie said sincerely and thought of how easy it was for her to conjure up a fantasy. Johnny seemed to float into and out of her mind at will. "Care to tell me who got the part?" she asked.

Gretchen grinned. "Someone safe. I watch this soap opera sometimes over lunch. There's this really sweet, sensitive man with a great body whose nutcase wife is cheating on him."

"Does *he* work out regularly?" Dixie asked.

"Yeah. Sometimes they give the viewers a treat and show him without his shirt. Of course, in real life, he's probably a self-centered, egotistical son-of-a-bitch. On the soap, though, he gets tears in his eyes sometimes because he still loves his wife, which makes me think he may be sweet and sensitive in real life and gives me faith that such guys really exist. Paul Bonner was never sweet and sensitive. He was always self-centered and egotistical. I keep trying to decide if I really loved him back then or just thought I really loved him."

"I think they amount to the same thing," Dixie said. "Have you talked to Mary Sue? How did her date go?"

Gretchen made a face at her for changing the subject again.

"I'm going to limit you to two mentions of Paul an hour," Dixie explained. "What about Mary Sue's date?"

"She said he was a little older than she expected but quite distin-guished-looking. He wants to take her dancing. Apparently he and his late wife were really into ballroom dancing."

"That would be fun for Mary Sue."

"Yeah. I thought so, too. But she said he never shut up about his wife. She thought it was sweet to be with a man who'd been deeply in love with his wife, but he kept having to wipe the tears from his eyes. It was a little much."

"How long has she been dead?" Dixie asked.

"Seven years. He wants to take Mary Sue to see her grave. His wife's favorite color was pink. The tombstone is of pink granite that he had imported from Egypt."

"You're kidding. She's not going, is she?"

"No, she told him she heads a statewide organization that advocates cremation and the abolishment of cemeteries."

"Our little Mary Sue said that? *Mary Sue,* who doesn't have a devious bone in her body?"

"It's in keeping with her pathological need to be nice to everyone," Gretchen said. "She didn't want to tell him he was weird, so she made herself unacceptable to him."

Dixie had to smile. Dear Mary Sue, who was above all nice. "I'm famished," she said, opening the menu.

She was trying to decide between pasta and a veggie burger when she heard Gretchen's sharp intake of breath and hurried whisper, "Don't look up!"

"Why? What's going on?" Dixie asked, keeping her gaze carefully focused on the menu.

"It's *her!*" Gretchen whispered.

"*Her* who?"

"Shhh! The naked redhead."

"The woman in Walter's bedroom?" she whispered back, darting her eyes left and right without moving her head. "Where?"

"Sitting at the bar."

Dixie stole a look. A statuesque redhead in a form-fitting green dress was sitting on a barstool, talking to a man in a business suit. "How can you tell?" she asked. "We only caught a glimpse of her that night."

"I parked next to a BMW in the parking lot."

"God, Gretchen. There are thousands of BMWs around here. Garden Grove is a BMW kind of town."

"The one parked out front is a late-model, dark-blue, four-door sedan. Ever since *that* night I've become very aware of late-model, dark-colored, four-door BMW sedans."

"Seems to me most BMWs are dark and have four doors," Dixie argued.

"The one out in the parking lot has one of those professional medallions attached to the license plate—you know, like that snake thing on physicians' cars. Only this one says American Dental Association."

"You don't know it's the redhead's car," Dixie protested. "And even if it is, it doesn't prove she's the same redhead."

"That woman is *her*," Gretchen insisted. "I can *feel* it."

Dixie stole another look at the couple at the bar, trying to decide if either the man or the woman looked like a dentist. The woman had a great figure and at first glance appeared to be younger than she probably was, thanks to artful makeup and four-inch heels that definitely weren't dentist shoes. Her companion was older, balding, and wearing an expensive blue suit, expensive shoes, expensive tie. Dixie decided he looked more like a banker than a dentist.

They both watched over the top of their menus while a waitress led the couple toward the dining room. Dixie wondered if she really was the woman from Walter's bedroom. "What now?" she asked Gretchen.

"We pay our tab and go stake out the BMW."

"And why will we do that?"

"So we can follow her," Gretchen insisted. "We need to figure out where she lives and find out what her name is."

"To what end? Even if she is that woman, she apparently has decided to keep her mouth shut."

"We need to know why."

"We figured that out when she didn't call the police and went creeping off into the night," Dixie said, not trying to keep the irritation out of her voice. "She was having an affair with Walter and didn't want her husband to find out."

"But what if she decides to get a divorce? What if her husband dies?"

"Come on, Gretchen. It's been—" She paused to calculate. "It's been almost *eight* months since . . . since Mary Sue's birthday."

"This may be our only chance to find out who she is," Gretchen said.

"Can't we at least order a sandwich? I'm hungry."

"I don't want to be waiting for a server to bring our check while they walk out of the restaurant and drive away."

Gretchen left money on the table for the drinks. She stood and watched impatiently while Dixie took several sips of tea, ate the orange slice garnish, and gathered up her purse and jacket. Gretchen led the way toward the front of the restaurant.

As they passed by the short corridor to the rest rooms, the door to the ladies' room opened and out came the redhead. She looked right at Gretchen. *Really* looked at her, and glanced in Dixie's direction before heading back toward the dining room.

Dixie felt her empty stomach take a lurch.

But even if she was the woman from Walter's bedroom, she couldn't possibly recognize them, Dixie told herself. The bedroom had been dark.

But light had streamed out the bathroom door.

The woman was naked, though, and in the presence of intruders. She would not have been in an observational mode. Probably all she had noticed was two people in baseball caps. And she would have noticed that one of the intruders was taller than the other.

Dixie pulled herself to her full height and directed her attention to her purse, pretending she was digging around for keys or whatever as she followed Gretchen out the door.

"Christ," Gretchen said. "She looked right at us."

Dixie took a deep breath. "No, she looked right at *you*. One attractive woman appraising another. She was taking in your hair, your makeup. She was deciding if you lightened your hair and if you shopped at Neiman's or Penney's."

Gretchen moved her Blazer to the far side of the parking lot, where they could observe at a discreet distance. Dixie walked across the street to a Burger King and bought two hamburgers and two bottles of water.

Gretchen, with her gaze glued to the front of the restaurant, barely touched her food.

It was almost an hour before the redhead and her companion exited from the restaurant. They walked toward the BMW.

The woman drove. Gretchen followed.

When the car stopped in front of a multistoried office building, Gretchen also pulled over, keeping a discreet distance. She and Dixie watched while the man got out of the car and entered the building. The BMW drove on a few more blocks and pulled into the parking lot of a new, one-story professional building. The sign in front announced "Dental Clinic." Four names were on the sign—three male names and "Grace B. Corona, DDS." When the redhead got out of the car, she was wearing shoes with more modest heels.

They watched her unlock a private side door and go inside.

"She and Walter probably met at a professional meeting," Gretchen speculated.

"I wish she didn't practice in Garden Grove," Dixie said.

When Gretchen pulled up in front of Bloom Flowers, Dixie offered a sarcastic, "We'll have to do this again real soon."

"Are you upset?" Gretchen asked.

"Yeah."

"Me, too. It bothers me that she's a dentist."

"Why is that?" Dixie asked.

"She has an income—a good income most likely."

"So?"

"Women with good incomes aren't so desperate to stay married no matter what. If our redheaded dentist gets fed up with her husband, she might be tempted to divorce him and tell the police that she was at Walter's house the night he disappeared. And while she was there, one tall woman and one not-so-tall woman broke in and may know something about what happened to him."

"I don't think we should mention our little excursion to Pamela," Dixie said as she opened the vehicle door.

"Agreed," Gretchen said. "She's been a basket case lately and will either say we shouldn't have followed the woman or be upset because we don't have her under twenty-four-hour surveillance."

Dixie stood in front of the store and watched Gretchen drive away.

Walter Lampley was going to haunt them forever, she feared. Pamela kept track almost to the day of how long it had been since *Mary Sue's birthday*, a term that had become euphemistic for the night Walter died. Pamela tried to find comfort in passing time, reasoning that the more of it that went by, the less likely that anyone would ever learn about their role in the dentist's disappearance.

Dixie had thought that Pamela would relax a bit when Clay got his appointment to the state court, but she was more on edge than ever. Clay's reputation must be protected at all costs. He might climb higher still in judiciary circles. He could even sit on the state supreme court someday. Or the U.S. Supreme Court. Walter Lampley had become an obsession with her.

And with Mary Sue, too. She continually pondered Walter's fate. "But what do you guys think might have happened to him?" she would ask.

Such situations were beyond uncomfortable. They made Dixie's skin crawl. But the three of them had been Mary Sue's best friends since first grade and would protect and love her until their last breath. Even though they had rolled Walter's dead body into the lake and knew full well that it was rotting away inside a rusting yellow sports car, they had to sit there making up plausible reasons why the man had vanished without a trace:

Perhaps mounting gambling debts forced him to change his identity and leave the country.

He could be wandering around aimlessly, suffering from amnesia.

Car thieves murdered him and buried his body in the Flint Hills. Or dumped it in the river.

He had a wreck on his way to Vegas in which he, the car, and all his identification burned, and he was lying unidentified and comatose in a hospital between here and there.

Once when Gretchen suggested flippantly that aliens had beamed him up, Mary Sue chastised her. "I know you never liked Walter," Mary Sue said, "but I don't think you should make light of his disappearance."

Gretchen had apologized.

Damn you, Walter Lampley, Dixie thought. Why couldn't the man have had a heart attack or been struck by lightning?

Dixie shook away thoughts of Walter and picked up a crumpled cigarette package from the sidewalk. Then she regarded the freshly painted exterior of her store. Her father had a fit when she painted the ancient bricks, citing some unwritten law against putting paint on masonry. But the cream color looked great.

Dixie's grandfather had bought the building back in the late 1940s, and over the years, the Blooms had restored the building to its turn-of-the-century look, which started a trend. Façades came down up and down Main Street. With the restored buildings, the stately trees, the handsome Presbyterian church with its soaring steeple, City Hall with its quaint cupola, and the old-fashioned bandstand in the park, the hilly downtown had the look of New England about it.

The rest of the town had spread like oil on water, with housing additions covering the landscape all the way to Shawnee on one side and the river on the other, and the main thoroughfares were lined with discount stores, shopping centers, and fast food establishments. But downtown still felt the same. Dixie wondered how many thousands of times she and her three best friends had ridden bicycles or roller-skated up and down the street.

And now they were at midlife. No longer girls or even young women. Dixie tried to decide what she, as a young woman, had thought this stage in her life would hold. Certainly she hadn't expected to be divorced. Or to be running Bloom's Flowers. But oddly enough she was, for the most part, at peace with both turnings. At times she still thought about a journalistic career, and sometimes a sweet memory from the years that she and Arnie enjoyed being a family with their son would fill her with sorrow that it was no more. But she would be quite contented with what life had brought her were it not for two things—Mary Sue's cancer and Walter Lampley's death.

The bell jingled merrily as she opened the door. "I'm back," she called.

"We don't have enough yellow roses for Mr. Jamison's coffin piece," Miss McFadden responded.

They would have to fill in with white, Dixie decided as she hung up her jacket and pushed up the sleeves of her sweater.

Chapter Thirteen

When Dixie walked in the back door with her stack of Styrofoam containers, Betty greeted her with a thumping tail. Kirk was sitting at the kitchen table, schoolwork spread out around him. "Johnny called," he said.

Dixie put the containers on the counter and tossed her jacket and purse on a chair. "When?" she asked. Because of the seven-hour time difference, Johnny usually called in the morning before she went to work or on weekends.

"Right after I got home from school."

"But he knew I wouldn't be here."

"He wanted to talk to *me*," Kirk said with a teasing grin. "He wants me to spend the summer with him, doing slave labor and learning about the grapes—and working on my Italian. He said he'd pay for my plane ticket and see that I was well fed."

Dixie poured a glass of wine and leaned against the counter. "What about the job in Chicago at your dad's office? What about the car you were planning to buy?"

"Granddad said he might give me Grandma's old Buick. He says that between Myrtle's car and his truck, they really don't need it."

"I seem to recall that when I suggested you ask him about Grandma's car, you indicated that you wouldn't be caught dead driving around in a ten-year-old Buick sedan."

"Yeah, it would be humiliating all right, but I'd rather spend the summer doing physical labor in an Italian vineyard than being an overpaid gofer in a Chicago accounting firm."

"What would you tell your father?"

"That I'm going to spend the summer with your Latin lover."

"Don't be fresh. What would you tell your father?"

"Why don't you want anyone to know about Johnny?"

"You know why, Kirk. So, you really want to go?"

"Yeah, I really want to go. Johnny said I wouldn't even be allowed to curse in English. It will be total immersion on the language front, which would be a great start on becoming bilingual. But mostly, I'd like to live there for an entire summer—working with my hands, spending evenings in the square, bicycling to places that tourists never go."

"So, what would you really tell your father?" she asked again.

"That I'm going to study Italian in Italy."

"I doubt if he'd see the value of that. He wants to show you off, son. He wants you to meet people and learn about his world, meet people who might give you a job someday."

"I know. Maybe I'll do that next summer. But I want one last summer with my shirt off."

Dixie put down her wineglass and leaned over the back of Kirk's chair to embrace him. He smelled of youth and soap. God, how she loved him! How empty her life was going to be when he was no longer living under her roof. How lucky she was to have raised such a good kid.

"Please be fully clothed when you are around the village *signorine,* who are all going to fall madly in love with you as it is," she said, returning to her wine. "Just remember that every one of them has male relatives willing to kill to keep her virginal, and, if that fails, willing to kill to make sure she marries the guy who deflowered her. A wife in Italy would put an end to your college plans."

"Then it's okay if I go?"

"Haven't you already told Johnny yes?"

Kirk grinned. "I told him I could talk you into it. Johnny said that while I'm talking you into things, I'm supposed to get you to promise that you'll come for the entire month of August. He and I will do the cooking. All you have to do is drink wine and soak up the sun. And he promised to take us to more of those places that the guidebooks never heard of. You can get Granddad to take over down at the store. August is always slow. No holidays. No weddings. Just an occasional funeral."

A month in Italy with Johnny and her son. Dixie felt weak at the thought.

His name was actually *Gianni*.

Dixie hadn't realized that at first, although she probably should have. She had taken two semesters of Italian at KU to fulfill the language requirement of the general education curriculum. But she had long since forgotten that there was no J, H, or Y in the Italian alphabet. The soft "j" sound in Italian was made with the letters "gi."

She had enrolled in Italian with the intention of studying abroad her senior year either in Florence or Rome, but when her senior year rolled around, she was madly in love with Arnie and couldn't imagine being away from him for even a few days, much less an entire semester. The notion of studying abroad had fallen by the wayside, along with her dream of working for a major metropolitan newspaper and maybe becoming a foreign correspondent someday and traveling the world in search of stories.

When her divorce became official, Dixie had felt an incredible need to do something wonderful with her son—to show him that life went on for the children and wives of divorce. He already knew that husbands got on with things. He had known about his father's infidelity before Dixie did. By the time Dixie found out, Cindy was already a fixture in Arnie's life.

Dixie had gone to the travel agency with Italy in mind. Surely there were some lingering Italian words and phrases buried in her head waiting to surface with the right stimulus.

The travel agent told her about the tour she had put together for the Northwestern University art museum—"Italian Art and Culture." It hit all the high spots—Rome, Florence, Venice—but the brochure also promised "enchantingly beautiful out-of-the-way places untarnished by tourism that will fill your senses and heart."

Dixie called the art history professor who was in charge of the tour. The professor assured her that several other youngsters were taking the trip, including his own son and daughter, and there would be fifteen college students, several faculty members, and their spouses. He was filling up the remaining spaces with area residents. The guide would be an Italian art historian from Florence, who had been a visiting professor at Northwestern several years back. This was the third trip on which the two of them had collaborated. Participants would stay in cheap-but-clean hotels. Dixie shouldn't expect bathtubs or even a private bathroom in some locales. One suitcase per person. Comfortable shoes were a must.

Dixie ordered a set of Italian language tapes and promised herself that she would master the eight hours of language instruction they offered before the departure date. She never found the time, but she did locate her old Italian textbook and brushed up on a few verb conjugations and some basic vocabulary. At least she would be able to ask where the bathroom was and how much something cost, although she wasn't sure she would understand the answers.

Benita Fabrizi, their Italian guide, met the plane in Rome. A woman well into her sixties, Benita was robust and handsome. She had been born the day that Benito Mussolini declared victory over Albania and was named for him, she explained. "Of course, I'm not even sure that Albania had an army," she said with a laugh, "but at the time my parents and grandparents worshiped the man. He made them proud to be Italian, and apparently he really did make the trains run on time."

Benita now lived in Florence but had been raised in the tiny mountaintop town of Santo Stefano, which was one of the untarnished places they had been promised in the brochure. But first, they made what she called the "tourist triad"—Rome, Venice, and Florence, or more correctly, *Roma*, *Venezia*, and *Firenze*.

The days in Rome with its ancient ruins and the Vatican with its endless jumble of art were almost too concentrated to be digested. A person should spend weeks there, not just two frantic days.

Enchanting Venice was like going through a time warp. Benita insisted they rise before dawn to hear their footsteps echo in the empty vastness of San Marco Square and to experience the sunrise over the San Giorgio Maggiore.

The high point of their visit to Florence was a magical hour they spent watching the sun go down over the city from the tiny hilltop village of Fiesole. The terra-cotta rooftops of Florence seemed to glow in the golden light. The light truly was different there. Not scientifically but magically so. One could understand why the likes of Leonardo da Vinci, Giotto, Fra Angelico, and Michelangelo came there for inspiration.

But looking back on the trip, what Dixie remembered most fondly was their visit to Santo Stefano. If *Gianni*/Johnny hadn't been a resident of Santo Stefano, she still would have felt that way.

After homage had been paid to the antiquities and masterpieces of Rome, Venice, and Florence, they left the *autostrada* to wind their way into the mountains of Tuscany. Every curve in the road revealed another photo op, but Dixie finally stopped taking pictures and sat with the camera in her lap, then put it in its bag. She wanted nothing between her and the beauty that surrounded and absorbed her.

As they drove along, she saw several mountaintop towns in the distance, most with a castle, all with a church spire. "I want to come back here," she told Kirk. "I want to go to every one of those hilltop towns."

"Yeah," he agreed. "It would be cool to go through those castles."

Finally they came around a curve, and there it was: Santo Stefano. A scene from another time. An imposing castle ruled over a tiny walled city that had been perched on its mountaintop for more than a thousand years. Surrounding the town were vineyards—miles and miles of vineyards. It was Chianti country, Benita told them. Red grapes like the mountain air.

"Tonight, we drink t.   wine and eat the food that I was raised on. And yes, I grew up drinking wine. Tonight, your children will drink the wine.

Tonight, you will think that you never want to go home. But remember, before you begin making plans to sell your fine homes and come live on an Italian mountaintop, you need to know that a person can't sneeze in a town like this without everyone knowing about it. If a woman misses one week scrubbing the family graves and putting flowers on them, she loses respect. And day in and day out, week in and week out, life has a sameness here that breeds restlessness in the young. There is no life of the mind here. Just *la tradizione*. And tradition can be stifling. Those of us who grew up in places like this have to go away before we gain an appreciation of the beauty and the thousand years of footsteps that wore the paving stones smooth. Then we come back for pilgrimages, and when we die, we want to be buried here. Now, I want you to put away your cameras and enjoy your visit here. Make memories, not photographs. Tomorrow, I will allow you to take pictures, but not tonight."

The tiny hotel just inside the city walls didn't have room for them all. Seven of the students were sent to stay in private homes. Dixie and Kirk rode a minuscule elevator to the second floor, which was really the third floor, but in Italy the ground floor doesn't get a number. The room was so small that Dixie had to walk sideways to make her way around the beds to the armoire. The bathroom was the size of a closet. The showerhead jutted from the wall across from the toilet and its companion bidet. Kirk joked that it would be possible to use the toilet and take a shower at the same time.

Once they had stashed their bags and freshened up, Benita marched her charges to the *piazza*.

Against the medieval backdrop of castle walls, the piazza was decorated for a *festa*. Italian flags had joined the masses of vining geraniums on the balconies that graced most of the buildings. Plank tables had been set up in the square. Each was covered with a white tablecloth; each had a vase of flowers. Dozens of people—mostly women in aprons—were scurrying to and from two *trattorias* that faced the square, putting the finishing touches on the table settings, placing baskets of bread and bowls of fruit.

The evening was magical. They ate and drank the bounty of the land. The local band, in green uniforms resplendent with gold braid and brass buttons, serenaded them throughout the evening. After dinner, they learned to dance the *tarantella*. Around and around the square they danced. Young and old. Kirk hung around with two other teenage boys from the tour, but as the evening wore on, the boys timidly made friends with boys from the village and even danced with a couple of the braver village girls. Almost without exception, the Italian youngsters were beautiful—the girls especially. She couldn't help but stare at those young girls, who were as ripe and perfect as the pear she had eaten earlier.

The American college students mingled even more, trying out their classroom Italian, learning to dance to the polkalike music. Soon, the young had separated themselves from the rest, talking, flirting, dancing—all under the watchful eyes of a squad of old women in shapeless black dresses. The less arthritic of the chaperons would occasionally pair up with each other— or sometimes with a child—and dance with surprising sprightliness. But some of their number always kept watch over their ripe young charges.

From out of the recesses of Dixie's mind the word *vedova* came perking to the surface. Widow. These watchful ladies were the village *vedove*.

Several of the village men asked her to dance. That was how she met Johnny. Earlier she had noticed him noticing her. He was one of a contingent of men helping the women serve the food. And keeping the wineglasses full, replacing the bottles of water. He was like a character in a Fellini movie—a man of the earth, with powerful arms and hands, weathered skin. His wavy hair was damp with all the rushing around, and it clung to his broad forehead. The muscles in his forearms tensed as he lifted kettles and carried trays of food. He was always talking to someone, always joking and laughing. His dark eyes danced as he bantered with the matronly and not-so-matronly women in their aprons.

She found herself wishing he would come fill her glass. Several times, he caught her looking at him. At first she was embarrassed. Then, it became a game, as she would watch him then look away the instant he glanced in her direction. The others at her table noticed. She felt the disapproval of two of the women—faculty wives who sat with their purses clutched to their chests and did not take part in the dancing even though their professorial husbands were out with the others, learning the steps, laughing, having a good time. The husbands would pay for their fun, Dixie thought, and felt a moment of profound sadness for the husbands and their inhibited wives. She had been like that at times—not capable of enjoying a situation and resentful because Arnie was more adaptable. She remembered a Christmas spent at his parents' home, with his entire family playing poker far into the night. It was the first Christmas she had ever spent away from her own family, and she was hell bent on being miserable. She refused to join in, refused even to kiss Arnie goodnight when he finally came to bed in his old bedroom, elated with the evening, not yet aware he had an out-of-sorts wife. He had tried to court her, wanting her to make love in the bed where he had first experienced erotic thoughts, but she would have none of it.

"How do you say 'hunk' in Italian?" she asked Benita.

"You are saying it with your eyes," Benita said with a smile.

"Who is he?"

"We will visit him tomorrow. Your 'hunk' runs one of the vineyards. He grew up in Santo Stefano but for many years lived away from here."

"Does he have a family?"

"Which means, 'Is the man married?' if I am not mistaken."

Dixie felt herself blush.

"All Italian men are married," Benita explained with a laugh. "Most of them marry quite young, about seven or so months before they become fathers. Strange how most first babies in Italy are said to be 'premature' no matter how robust they happen to be."

Benita paused, taking a sip of wine, before continuing. "The 'hunk' over there was one of those horny young men whom I suspect became an unwitting bridegroom and father. The bride lived two villages away. He would have met her when he was bicycling through, or making a delivery, doing farm work, whatever. He moved there when they married, and they lived with her widowed mother for a time. But then he grew restless and left to see the world."

"Did she live here when he came home to Santo Stefano?"

"Not to my knowledge. I don't think she's ever set foot in Santo Stefano. Apparently she prefers to stay in the house where she has spent her entire life."

"So why didn't they just get a divorce?" Dixie asked.

"Ah, that is not so simple here," Benita said. "She would never sign the paper. He loves his daughter and would not want her to live with the stigma of having divorced parents. And if he and his wife did divorce, she would get half his pension, which would leave him without enough money for his old age."

"So he has affairs?"

Benita laughed. "Supposedly most Italian men have affairs, but I do not believe there are sufficient numbers of Italian women who are willing or daring enough to have an affair to account for all the men who want their cohorts to believe they have a woman or two on the side. But if your *Signor* Bernardi over there does have affairs, I imagine he takes care not to repeat the stupidity of his youth." Benita paused and looked in *Signor* Bernardi's direction. "He is appealing, isn't he?"

"Yes, you could say that."

Dixie tried to remember the last time she had been this attracted to a man. Not since college, she decided, when Arnie entered her life, when she had experienced such a need to be where he was, to hear his voice, to feel his touch.

Now once again, years past young love, she found herself floating on a sexual high because a man was as aware of her as she was of him. Not a man who would fit into her life. Not a man with whom she could build a future. But a man who was making her skin tingle.

When he was finally finished with his chores, she watched him amble toward her table, just as she knew he would. He stopped along the way to talk to people, to draw out the anticipation. When finally he arrived, he asked, "Please, we dance." His voice was deep, gravelly, sexy.

"Yes, we dance," she said and gave him her hand.

The dance steps were complicated and took heavy concentration. But her partner was accomplished, and he guided her skillfully around the area cordoned off for dancing. It was energetic dancing. Exhilarating dancing. Soon their clothes and hair were soaked with perspiration. And still they danced on.

I am having such fun, she thought. *Such incredible fun!*

At one point, she realized Kirk was watching her. He waved and gave her a thumbs-up.

The evening ended with the town residents standing in front of the bandstand and lifting their voices in a patriotic-sounding song. She recognized the word for fatherland. At the end of the song, the band members packed up their instruments. The silence that fell over the *piazza* was startling.

"I am Johnny," he said.

"My name is Dixie."

"Dik-zee," he said carefully. "A pleasure."

He pointed in Kirk's direction. "Your son?"

Dixie nodded and waved for Kirk to come over. "We walk now," Johnny announced.

As the three of them wandered up and down the narrow streets of the now quiet town, their footsteps echoed from the stone walls of houses built along streets so narrow a car would not be able to pass. Clotheslines were strung overhead. Dixie could hear an occasional toilet flush and televisions playing, as they walked by open windows. At one point, she recognized the theme music for *Bonanza*.

"Not much privacy, is there?" she whispered.

When he didn't understand, she pointed at the houses, then indicated with her hands the narrowness of the street and said, "No secrets."

He chuckled. "No secrets."

"Did you study English in school?" she whispered as they walked along.

"No. I learn little here, little there. I drive ten years for American people in *Napoli* and *Roma*."

When they reached the city wall, Kirk scrambled up the ancient stone steps ahead of them and went scurrying over to the nearest tower. From the top of the wall, the moonlit panorama took her breath away. "Your country is very beautiful," she said.

"*You* are very beautiful," he responded, and softly rubbed a fingertip down her cheek. "And you like to be happy."

She wanted to touch him back. God, how she wanted to touch him back, but she didn't dare. "Everyone likes to be happy," she said.

"No, not everyone."

Kirk came racing back. "Can we go inside?" he asked.

"The castle is always locked," Johnny said.

"Always?" Kirk asked, disappointment in his voice.

"Always," Johnny said, "but I have the key. Tomorrow you go inside."

Johnny took her arm, and they picked their way back down the uneven steps. At the door of the hotel, he said, *"A domani."*

"Yes, *a domani.*"

By this time, Kirk had convinced Johnny to show him some of the castle tonight. She watched the two of them head down the dark, narrow street, Kirk all but dancing with excitement. *A castle at midnight.*

Johnny Bernardi was both sexy and nice, she decided.

She took the stairs to her room and for a long time stood on the tiny balcony and stared out at the astounding moonlit countryside. Beauty was like a drug, she realized. It filled you up and played with your mind. She took a deep breath and inhaled all that wonderfully intoxicating beauty.

Finally, she tore herself away from the night and went to stand under the spitting water of the rusty showerhead. She stood there for a long time, between the toilet and the bidet, taking enormous pleasure in the feel of the tepid water on her body. She felt happy and alive because a man had been nice to her and her son, because he had touched her cheek and called her beautiful.

Then, as she stood there, a memory came unbidden of another shower in another hotel bathroom. A luxurious bathroom in a five-star hotel. She and Arnie had driven down to Indianapolis for a two-day business conference. It would be her first time away from Kirk since his birth six weeks before. Her mother had flown up from Garden Grove to look after him.

She remembered standing in that shower, crying. Milk was oozing out of her breasts, even though she had just pumped them. Her chest hurt with missing her baby. And then there was the other hurt. The more ominous one.

She had been preparing for this trip for days—getting the house ready for her mother's visit, laying in groceries, pumping herself repeatedly to bank enough breast milk for Kirk to have in her absence, writing out instructions and phone numbers, and searching through her closet for clothes that would fit her postpartum body. The day before, she'd had her six-week checkup from her obstetrician and gotten the okay for sex.

Arnie had been anxious to be on the road. He wanted to be out of town before the rush hour traffic. There was a baseball game he wanted to listen to on the way.

He kept telling her what time it was and insisted on closing the suitcases and putting them in the car, even though she wasn't sure she had finished packing.

He came back in and followed her around while she put missed odds and ends in a plastic bag. Then he said, "Let's go," and walked out the door.

Dixie kept remembering things to tell her mother. About Kirk's bowel movements. About his bath. His diaper rash. Where the extra pacifiers were. It had been years since her mother had looked after a baby. What if she forgot to burp him? What if she didn't wake up in the night when he cried?

"Motherhood is like riding a bicycle," her mother finally declared. "It comes back to you. Kirk and I will be fine."

Then both women tensed at the sound of a car horn from the driveway. *Arnie was honking the horn.*

Her mother looked away, embarrassed for her daughter.

"I'm not going," Dixie said.

"Yes, you are," her mother said and hurried her out the door.

On the drive she had been spared talking by the baseball game.

When they arrived, Arnie wanted to go straight to bed.

They hadn't made love for months. She still felt raw and swollen from the delivery. She needed romancing. A glass of wine. A nice dinner. Words of love. She felt as if a hole in the mattress would have served him just as well.

Afterward, he asked, "What's wrong?"

"For starters, you honked the horn."

"Geez, is that why you're acting like an iceberg? Because I honked the fucking horn? When you knew how horny I've been for you? I managed to take care of a stack of paperwork, make a dozen phone calls, and still get myself home by noon. I couldn't believe you weren't ready. My God, Dixie, you've had nothing to do for days but get ready."

She went into the bathroom to cry. And stood under the shower, trying to calm herself, knowing that she had to suck it up. She also knew that he wouldn't dare knock on the door and tell her to hurry up, so she stood there endlessly, even allowing the water to ruin the hairdo she had struggled to achieve. Eventually she would have to get dressed for the banquet in the ballroom even though she didn't want to go, and no matter how hard she tried, she would be the frumpiest woman there. She would have to be pleasant at dinner. And after dinner, when they came back to the room, she would have to have sex again. She would have to pretend she wasn't still angry, pretend that she wanted him, pretend that she had an orgasm. She would have to because, since it would be impossible to make him understand how she felt, there was no point in trying.

My God, Dixie, you've had nothing to do for days but get ready. She shuddered, remembering his words. She had stood under the shower for a very long time, trying to decide if she hated her husband or if it was just a postpartum thing, like her lumpy body and her lank hair. Perhaps it was inevitable in every marriage that a woman simply backed away from expectations and settled for what was attainable.

And now, with Kirk a rambunctious twelve-year-old, Dixie found herself wondering about an Italian man's wife two villages away. Was that how it was for her—settling for the attainable? Was she lonely, or was she grateful that her husband came home only once a week?

One thing Dixie knew for sure was that Johnny's wife was not a happy woman.

When Dixie learned that Arnie was leaving her for another woman, she had made a vow that she would never get involved with a married man, *so help her God.* She would never do to another woman what Cindy and Arnie had done to her.

She wondered if Johnny and his wife made love on Sunday.

Kirk was stretched out on his bed when she came out of the bathroom. He wanted to talk. On and on, he talked. The castle was incredible. It still had beds and tables in it. Johnny had a lantern and took him down into the dungeon where they used to torture people. And there was this big hall where they ate and some duke was stabbed to death. It was cool. *Really* cool. Johnny was nice. He wanted them to stay in Santo Stefano for the rest of their trip. He would stay with his cousin in the village and let them have his house. He would show them other castles. There were castles all over the place.

"He likes us, Mom. He says you're a happy lady and I'm a happy kid."

"He's married, Kirk."

"Can't he still be our friend? We'll never get another chance like this again."

Chapter Fourteen

*G*retchen *tried to put the encounter* with the woman from Walter's bedroom out of her mind as she headed down First Street to her lawyer's office. She needed to get her thoughts organized for her appointment.

Sometimes she wondered if she needed to find a new lawyer. Too often Joe Rollater seemed uninterested—even irritated. "You know, Gretchen, divorces aren't supposed to go on forever," he had told her at the end of her last appointment.

Joe had played golf with her father every Wednesday afternoon since before Gretchen could remember. Joe had been with her father when he died in the men's locker room after one of his best rounds in years. That had been almost twenty years ago. Joe took care of things then—and later when her mother died. She had always felt that he would be on her side, no matter what.

Joe kept her waiting longer than usual. She wondered if it was intentional.

She looked through the stack of magazines on the end table, but they all had guns, fish, or golf courses on the cover.

Joe collected antique clocks, and since his wife wouldn't let him keep them at home, they filled his waiting room and office. He kept all of them operating, but apparently synchronization was impossible. As a result, the coo-cooing and chiming had nothing to do with the actual time. Gretchen had never paid much attention to the clocks in the past, but today she found them annoying. As was the waiting.

She got up and paced.

Finally she was allowed into Joe's cluttered office, in which the clocks' ticking seemed even louder.

"Did you talk to Paul?" she asked as she seated herself.

"No, but I looked over the divorce decree again and talked to his lawyer. You can't make him pay child support after the girls are eighteen, Gretchen. The law says that offspring stop being children on their eighteenth birthday, whether they are in college or not."

"But Debbie's almost twenty, and he kept sending the checks until two months ago."

"Yes, but apparently he's decided now that both girls are over eighteen, he's not going to pay anymore. Like I explained to you on the phone, he doesn't owe you a dime in child support. Your divorce decree stipulates that he pay their tuition for four years at either Kansas State or KU or the equivalent amount would be applied toward tuition at an out-of-state or private college. That is all he has to pay, Gretchen, and there's not a thing you can do about it. If the girls don't finish their degree in four years, or if they decide to go to graduate school, they are on their own."

"What am I supposed to tell them?" Gretchen demanded. "We were counting on that money." She wanted to scream and rage. About Paul. About men in general. Joe seemed so smug sitting there behind his huge desk, his wispy hair giving him a mad-scientist look, the damned clocks ticking away, with their wooden birds and milkmaids with pails and boys with fishing poles popping in and out. It reminded her of a scene out of some horror movie.

"I suggest you tell your daughters their father's only financial obligation to them is their college tuition," Joe said, his voice irritatingly reasonable.

"What about his pension plan?" Gretchen demanded.

"You waived any claim to that when he agreed to give you his half of the house."

"Yes, but as *I* explained to *you* on the phone, that house was more mine than his. I applied most of the money I inherited from my parents toward building that house."

"But you have no proof that's what you did with your inheritance. You should have kept those funds separate from the marital estate and kept records to show that's what you used it for. For all the court knows, you used it to buy stock or put it in a Swiss bank account."

"But how was I supposed to know that I should keep my inheritance separate from 'the marital estate'? You never told me to, and I never planned to be divorced. Besides, I don't see what difference it makes what the specific money was used for. I put it all into a shared pile the year that we bought the lot and started the house. My inheritance didn't pay for the entire house, but we certainly wouldn't have been able to afford a home like that for years on what Paul was making at the time. It stands to reason that some of the money we used was *my* money."

"Then does that make the money that Paul was earning *his* money?"

"No, he was the wage earner for the family."

Joe sighed. "I guess we can try. Bring in all the financial records you can find for that time period and jot down all your recollections about how your inheritance was used, and I'll take a look at them. And I'll have a look at your folks' wills. Just be aware, Gretchen, that the court probably isn't going to make Paul pay your legal bills on this one. And I'm not going to do it for free."

"You don't have to be so crotchety," Gretchen said, standing.

"It makes me crotchety when I see someone I care about ruining her life. You seem hell bent to be miserable so you can prove what a goddamned son-of-a-bitch Paul is. And he very well may be a son-of-a-bitch, but in my book, what you are doing is called 'cutting off your nose to spite your face.' And you have a damned nice nose, Gretchen. You're a damned fine-looking woman. And a smart one, too, with two wonderful daughters. Go find yourself another man. Join the Army. Go back to college. Whatever. Just do *something* beside spitting venom all the time.

Now, go search for those records, and I'll help you if there's a prayer of getting any more money out of Paul, but it's the last hurrah. The *very last* hurrah. Your daddy was one of the very best friends I ever had, but I'm not doing his daughter any damned good by helping her stew in her own juices."

A ballerina popped out of the clock behind Joe's desk and made three jerking pirouettes in cadence to three tinny-sounding bongs. "You finished?" Gretchen asked.

"I'm finished," Joe said, slumping in his chair and brushing his hair back with his hands in a gesture of exasperation.

Gretchen marched to the door. "You need to get some different magazines in your waiting room," she said over her shoulder.

From Joe's office, she drove back down First Street and turned onto Highway 19. The BMW was still parked by Grace Corona's private door. Gretchen had planned to run before dinner but parked in the shadows of a large elm instead. While she waited for the woman to appear, she pulled a crumpled envelope out of her purse and on the back of it began to create a log of how the money she had inherited from her parents was used.

Such a difficult time that had been. Her grief over losing her father had been profound, and her mother suddenly became inept and pitiful. But Gretchen had two little girls who filled her heart. And Paul's. They shared their love for their daughters.

Paul had been very kind to her mother. He had been better with her than Gretchen, cajoling her into playing golf again, into living again. He wouldn't take no for an answer when she insisted she didn't feel like going out for a pizza or to the park for a picnic with her granddaughters.

Sitting there in her vehicle, stalking a woman who could make serious trouble for her and her friends, Gretchen was irritated to find herself thinking kindly thoughts about Paul. But he had kept the deathwatch with her at her mother's bedside. And he had cried with her when she died. Really cried.

❖   ❖   ❖

Gretchen had waited until Debbie was home for the weekend to tell the girls their father was no longer going to send a monthly check to help support them. And explain about her new plan to make him live up to his responsibilities.

They ate dinner in the breakfast room off the kitchen where they had always eaten evening meals when their father wasn't home. It was a wonderful room with a bay window overlooking the terrace and pool. The room had been Gretchen's idea, as had most of the house's other really interesting touches. It was a wonderful house, a good house for raising children and entertaining friends.

Now her children were all but grown, and without a husband she had a vastly diminished social life. But she hated to give up the house. It was so much a part of her. She had worked with the architect for months getting the house plan just as she wanted it. She had landscaped the yard herself, planted every shrub, every tree.

For dinner Gretchen roasted a chicken and made a squash and eggplant casserole and homemade rolls. For dessert, she served raspberries with a low-fat custard sauce. Actually most of the fat grams for the meal came from the olive oil and feta cheese in the casserole. But she didn't mention fat grams. The girls thought she was a bit obsessive about that.

Debbie had been a bit pudgy during her early teen years, but both girls were now tall and lean—not as tall as Gretchen, but almost. But they didn't seem to mind their height. The acceptance and even pride with which her daughters viewed their height and bodies still amazed Gretchen, who still felt more feminine if she was standing next to a very tall man and still preferred to wear low-heeled shoes.

Debbie had brown hair and eyes like Paul, whereas Robin had Gretchen's blond coloring. Yet they looked alike. They both had their mother's cheekbones and jaw, their father's brow line and full mouth.

They had hated each other growing up, but when their parents' marriage began to dissolve, they had started operating as a team, sharing friends and activities.

Gretchen had wanted them to kick and scream about having to spend a weekend a month and every other Wednesday evening with their father, but they hadn't. And when they returned home from a visit, they refused to be drawn into a conversation about how their father and Mona were living and how much money they were spending.

Debbie drank coffee now. Robin said she'd have a cup, too, with lots of milk. They sat with their coffee cups like three adult women, a scene that filled Gretchen with its poignancy. She was deeply proud of them and loved them very much. And she would be unbelievably sad next fall with both of them gone. For many years, she had focused her life on her children, husband, and home. She no longer had a husband. Robin would join Debbie at college next fall, and her house, even if she got to keep it, would become an empty shell.

That was when she would start serious athletic training, she reminded herself. Her goal was to run in a marathon before she turned fifty.

And get a job. She was definitely going to have to do that. With both daughters in college, it was time to get her life in order.

They would still be the most important part of her existence, of course. She would travel to campus for athletic events and sorority functions. Debbie had pledged Chi Omega, and Gretchen had had the supreme pleasure last spring of attending the initiation and pinning her own sorority pin over her daughter's heart. She looked forward to performing the same ritual for Robin.

Now that Debbie was a full-fledged member, she would be moving into the sorority house in the fall. She had been voted assistant rush chairwoman and would be hovering when her sister went through rush, making sure Robin got every consideration, seeing to it that she was extended a bid. Being in a sorority cost money. Having nice clothes cost money. Debbie had a steady boyfriend and had needed formal dresses last year for the Chi Omega Christmas party and his fraternity's spring dance.

"I need to talk to you before you head out with your friends," she told them as she refilled their cups. "Since you both are now over eighteen, your father has decided not to pay any more child support. He will pay your tuition and that's it—which precipitates a major financial crisis for us. I talked to Joe Rollater on Monday. Most of the money I inherited from my parents was used when we built this house, and there's a possibility we can force your father to reimburse me at least part of that money. I've spent the last four days going through old financial records and trying to construct a paper trail on how the money was used. Getting the reimbursement might mean another court battle, but it would be worth it if I can send you girls off to college in style."

Robin and Debbie exchanged glances. Robin nodded at her sister, and Debbie took a deep breath. "Daddy said that he thought you would try to get more money out of him."

"He *told* you that he wasn't paying any more child support?"

"Yeah. Mona found out that he wasn't legally obligated anymore. And she's pregnant."

"With twins," Robin added. "She wants him to start trust funds for their kids."

Paul was going to have twins. Gretchen closed her eyes to ward off a wave of lightheadedness. It didn't help.

"Mother, are you all right?" Debbie asked, jumping out of her chair.

Robin rushed to the kitchen for a glass of water.

Gretchen took sips of the water and took several deep breaths as they instructed. "I'm fine," she said. Which wasn't true. She wasn't fine at all. She was approaching menopause, and that son-of-a-bitch was getting to start all over again. He got a second chance at happiness. It was as if he was erasing her and their daughters. As if they never happened. As if they had no meaning.

She'd read about how men were much better fathers with their second families. This time around, Paul would probably even change diapers and take night feedings. His second set of children would have trust funds. *They* would have plenty of money for college.

Gretchen's hate for Paul had never been more intense. She wished he were here so she could kill him. She wouldn't even care if she went to prison. Even if she were put to death, it would be worth it.

Why couldn't it be Paul's body on the bottom of Dixie's lake? She had thought of that while they were chasing that car down the hill and watching it sink. *If only it were Paul.* If he were dead, she would still hate him, but she wouldn't have to think about him all the time.

"Over my dead body will your father use money that should go to you girls to start a trust fund for *that* woman's children," she told her daughters through clenched teeth.

"We want you to stop the war," Debbie said, her voice soft, loving even, but firm.

Robin nodded her agreement, tears filling her eyes.

"But I have to fight him," Gretchen said, her voice trembling. "I *have* to. You girls need money for clothes and your house bills. You need a car. Robin wants the bump taken off her nose."

Her daughters were both shaking their heads at her. Which made her angry with them, too. They were willing to just roll over and allow Paul to have his way. Willing to let pint-sized Mona with the big boobs have her way.

"I have to fight him," Gretchen said again. "I'll take ads out in the newspaper if I have to, telling the world what a son-of-a-bitch Paul Bonner is. I'll send letters to everyone in his firm. He can't get away with this. He has a responsibility to you girls."

Debbie held up a hand. "No more attorneys, Mother. No more going to court. It has to end. Robin and I have discussed this—a lot. We want it to end. We want you to stop being angry all the time and learn to be happy again."

"All any of the fighting has accomplished is to make you crazy and us embarrassed," Robin said, taking her mother's hand. "We can manage without Daddy's money."

"No we can't," Gretchen wailed.

"Robin and I will get jobs and apply for financial aid. Lots of kids do that."

"But what about living in the sorority house? What about having nice clothes to wear and a car to get back and forth?"

"We will manage, Mother," Robin said. "And you don't have to wait for us to finish college to sell the house. You need to do that now and invest the money so you'll have an income. Debbie and I will get jobs and rent a little apartment."

"I already put down a deposit," Debbie said. "We both plan to go to summer school."

"But I'd looked forward to having you both home for the summer," Gretchen protested. "And what about the Chi Omega house."

"Not being in a sorority won't be the end of the world," Robin said.

"It's not fair," Gretchen sobbed. "Damn him to hell, it's not fair!"

Debbie took her mother in her arms. "This financial crisis can either tear us apart, Mother, or make us strong. Robin and I want the three of us to be strong together."

"Tell me that you hate him," Gretchen begged. "Please tell me that you hate him."

Robin stroked her mother's hair. "No, we don't hate him. He's our father. We need to love him."

"And Mona's babies? What about them?"

Robin shrugged. "They're his babies, too. How can we hate babies?"

"It wasn't all bad, was it?" Debbie asked, her voice quivering. "We were a good family for a long time. We want to remember the good times."

They offered to stay home with her for the evening, to rent a movie and pop some corn. But Gretchen shooed them on their way.

Then she went to the telephone answering machine and listened again to the message that had been waiting for her when she got home from the grocery.

"Hello, Gretchen. This is Gus from last Saturday night. I was wondering if you were doing anything tomorrow evening. I thought we could have dinner and go to a movie. Give me a call."

Gretchen had written down the phone number he had recited. She picked up the scrap of paper and stared at the number.

She had to do something, she decided. She was desperate to do something. She could either jump off the roof or call this man.

But she hated men. Perhaps not all men—but most of them. She hated men because they could shed wives like automobiles and get away with it. Maybe, though, she should at least find out what sort of person Gus was before she judged him. They hadn't talked about their divorces. Maybe his wife had dumped him. Maybe he was wounded, too.

She knew she would never fall in love with him. Never have soul-searing sex with him. She had that sort of man once, and he had dumped her. Maybe the Guses of the world were safer.

So what would she say to him? *Hello, Gus. This is Gretchen. I'll be glad to go out with you if you shave off your mustache and button your shirt and have an acceptable explanation for why you are a divorced person.*

She didn't say those things, of course. She was disgusted by the syrupy sweet voice that came out of her mouth as she suggested they meet tomorrow evening for a drink at the same bar.

Then she marched upstairs to look through her closet and decide what to wear. She spent the next two hours trying things on, trying looks that ranged from daring to sophisticated. Most of the clothing she tried on, she put into boxes for Goodwill—clothing that was contaminated with memories.

Finally, she made her choice. She would wear Robin's white sundress. Her only decent sandals made her at least an inch and a half taller, but if Gus wanted a short woman, he wouldn't have called her back.

Then, because she had to tell someone that she had a date, she called Mary Sue. "Are you excited?" Mary Sue asked.

"Yeah, I am. He is not Mr. Right, but I need something right now, and he's available."

"You want to get laid, don't you?"

"I don't know. Maybe I do."

"Me, too. I find myself wishing Walter would come back, even though he wasn't a good lover. He would come too soon and assume I thought it was wonderful. I had learned to beat him to the punch, but even so, I sometimes wondered if a vibrator wouldn't be more fulfilling. But there's just no substitute for a man in your arms."

"That's the first time I ever heard you speak ill of old Walter."

"Sometimes distance makes things clearer. He was a jerk, and I was pitiful. I got myself tested for AIDS."

"You did?"

"He wouldn't wear a condom and wouldn't have an AIDS test. I got away with being stupid this time. Have a condom in your purse, just in case. And if he refuses to put it on, don't do it."

Chapter Fifteen

On the plane coming home from that first trip to Italy, Dixie tried to deal with her confusion. She was smitten with a man who lived half a world away. Any sort of lasting relationship with Johnny was out of the question. She had to finish raising her son and get him through college.

Johnny didn't have a college education. She wasn't even sure if he had finished the Italian equivalent of high school. He drove an old car and had a terrible barber. Of course, he loved opera and seemed to be quite knowledgeable about grapes, wine, and European politics, but in reality he was a peasant. A simple man. Not a man over whom to disrupt one's life.

So why did her heart feel so tender? Why had it been so hard to say goodbye to him?

She had been quiet on the early morning drive to Milan, with horrendous traffic through one ugly industrial zone after the other, not the Italy with which she had fallen in love. Kirk and Johnny exchanged sports information, trying to make each other understand their respective country's passions. For Johnny, the only sport that mattered was soccer—or *calcio*. Kirk couldn't believe that Johnny had never heard of Barry Sanders and Troy Aikman. At one point, Johnny pointed out the turnoff to Le Roncole, the birthplace of Verdi, and seemed stunned that Kirk had never heard of the composer. Or any of Verdi's operas. Not even *La Traviata*.

Johnny explained that the opera was *una tragedia*. Even though Alfredo loves Violetta more than life itself, Violetta cannot decide if she wants to be in love with him.

"I didn't think people *decided* about love," Kirk said. "I thought it just happened to them."

"Sometimes people do not listen to their hearts," Johnny said. Then he sang *"Addio del passato"* in a rather fine baritone and explained that in the song Violetta says goodbye to happiness.

"You have been happy in *Italia,* no?" Johnny asked.

"Yeah," Kirk said with genuine enthusiasm. "It's been cool."

Oh, yes, Dixie thought. She had liked it. Too much. Four days with her son and a man with whom she would be having an affair were it not for her son's presence. For four days, she and Kirk had worked with Johnny in the vineyard, picked the food from his garden and gathered eggs for their meals. The pears from his trees were so luscious their juice dripped down their chins. For four days, her son managed to survive without soda pop, hamburgers, and MTV and never once complained.

Each afternoon they went on an excursion to a hamlet even more remote than Santo Stefano, each with a charming *piazza,* a small castle to be explored, and a church that seemed far too grand for such a tiny, isolated place. Johnny knew people everywhere they went—the bartender, the mayor, the priest, the person who had the key to the castle or the ancient hilltop church.

But as enchanted as she was by the country, it was Johnny who captivated her, who made her wish she could stay. Her fingertips tingled with the need to touch him. She was in a continuous state of arousal, yet she also felt supremely content, as though she could just float here with this man indefinitely, taking immense pleasure in watching Johnny be Johnny, enjoying the sound of his voice and laughter.

Kirk was only twelve, but she could see in his eyes that he was aware of her attraction for Johnny. And she could see his acceptance. Johnny made them both happy.

At the airport, Johnny walked with them to security and embraced Kirk first, telling him that he was a fine boy and his father was fortunate to have such a son, and he extracted a promise that Kirk would return and bring his mother. Then he wrapped his arms around Dixie and she melted into the solid strength of him and kissed his cheek. "Thank you. It may have been the best four days of my life."

"Please, I very much want you to return. You and your son."

On the other side of security, she began to cry. "I'm sorry," she told Kirk.

"It's okay," he said. "He's a really nice guy."

Arnie came for Kirk the first Friday after they returned home. Dixie called up the stairs, telling Kirk his father was here. Arnie stepped inside the door but didn't want to sit down. Cindy was waiting in the car. They were going to Grass Lake for the weekend.

"Kirk says you had a great time in Italy," Arnie offered, staring up the stairs.

"Yes. I actually remembered some of my college Italian."

"That's nice," he said, shifting from one foot to the other, obviously not caring to hear anything more about her trip. He yelled up the stairs, "How you comin' up there, pal?"

Dixie felt a familiar wave of discomfort at his dismissal. So often in the past he had done that to her—arriving home in the evening, opening a beer, turning on the news, and picking up the newspaper while she prattled away, all but begging him to talk to her, to tell her about his day, to listen while she told him what the pediatrician had said about Kirk's cough or the mechanic had said about the ping under the hood. His only comments would be "Fine," or "That's nice," which he uttered without looking up at her. Without really listening.

Suddenly, she was glad that she had lusted after a man in Italy.

On Tuesday, she received a postcard bearing a picture of the Santo Stefano castle. On it was written *"Ti penso sempre."* And was signed "Gianni." That was the first time she realized his name had an Italian spelling.

Ti penso sempre. I think of you always.

She sat on the hall bench and clutched the card to her chest. Johnny thought of her always. Which was how often she thought of him.

Driving home from work, she had talked herself out of going to aerobics. But suddenly she was full of energy and raced up the stairs to change.

She practically floated through the class. With every move and every kick, Johnny's words danced through her head. He thought of her always. He thought of her always.

The next day she called Benita Fabrizi in Florence.

"So how was your extended stay in Santo Stefano?" Benita asked in her almost accentless English.

"Confusing. Tell me about Johnny's wife. Was what you told me in the square his actual story or just hypothetical?"

"A little of both. I have known Gianni all my life. In fact, we are even distantly related. I do not know his wife, but I know of women like her. Twenty or thirty years ago and even still today, many women who grow up in small villages quite literally never go anyplace. Gianni had traveled about and worked for the American military in *Napoli.* But he came back home to settle down. Or maybe he settled down after he got her pregnant. I am sure she was lovely and shy, and he fancied himself to be deeply and spiritually in love with her, but it was a tragedy for them to marry. So tell me, Dixie, why do you ask about her?"

"I want to see him again, but I don't want to do to some other woman what was done to me. I don't want to ruin another woman's marriage."

"Ah, I see. Well, I am sure that if you asked *Signora* Bernardi if it is all right for you to sleep with her husband, she would say no, even if she has not slept with him in years. The story, as I recall, was that she almost died when their daughter was born and she was told not to have any more children. And for a devout woman who follows the papal dictates on birth control, the best way to prevent another child is to close the bedroom door. Gianni's job in Santo Stefano gives them a way to live apart."

"He *never* spends the night with her, *never* has sex with her?" Dixie asked.

"I do not know this, Dixie. Maybe they have sex on Sunday afternoon and practice withdrawal. Maybe he stays overnight sometimes. Maybe she has finished with menopause, and they have begun anew. The only way you know what goes on between a man and a woman is to hide in their bedroom, and I have not done that. But I do know one thing for certain. You should not expect Gianni Bernardi to move to America. Even if he thinks he wants to, you must not let him. I have seen what happens to men like him. In Santo Stefano, Gianni has stature. He is liked and respected there. He probably will be the mayor someday. In America, an uneducated Italian man becomes a caricature. He would become a cook or a gardener. He would have to bow and scrape to get by. He would not have respect, not even from you. So tell me, have you heard from him?"

"He sent a postcard," Dixie said, picking it up from her bedside table and staring at its three lovely words.

"Did he ask you to return?"

"He did that before we left."

"And you would like to do so without guilt?"

"Something like that," Dixie admitted, turning the postcard over and looking at the castle. It was a bad picture—not quite in focus, the colors too bright.

"But you know it could not last," Benita said. "A relationship cannot be sustained with just an occasional visit."

"You're probably right. Right now, however, I'm not looking into the future. I'd just like to get on a plane tomorrow and see him again. But I keep thinking about his wife. Do you know her name?"

"No. I've never met her. So what will you do?"

"I'm not sure," she said, then corrected herself. "No, that's not so. I probably will go back at least once."

Johnny called the following Sunday. *"Ciao, Dick-zee."* His voice was soft, yet he sounded as though he was standing beside her.

"Johnny?" she said just as softly. And put her hand to her chest to still her pounding heart. "Is it really you?"

"*Si.* You are well? And your beautiful son?"

"Yes, we are well. And you?"

"*Bene. Molto bene.* When do you come again in *Italia?*"

"I just got back from *Italia,*" she said breathlessly.

"But you come again?"

"Yes."

"Soon?"

"In a couple of months maybe."

"*Couple?* I do not understand *couple.*"

"A few. *Qualche.* Actually, more than a few. Next spring probably. *Nella primavera probabilmente.*"

She didn't tell Kirk what she planned. She would find some excuse to explain her absence.

Johnny was a married man. She could not come to terms with that, could not tell her son that she was going back to Italy, when he would realize full well what that meant. Which made her very uncomfortable. Having an affair with a married man made her no better than Cindy. She found herself wondering if Arnie had wanted Cindy as much as she now wanted Johnny.

But as time passed, the wanting would come and go. For days, she would be able to rein herself in and allow reason to take charge. *Of course, she would not go back to Italy.*

Then Johnny would call again, and each time the sound of his voice melted her resolve.

Sometimes Kirk was the one to pick up the phone. She could always tell by his grin that he was talking to Johnny. The look on his face when it was his father calling was less open. More careful.

Finally, she told Johnny it made her very uncomfortable to "visit" a married man.

"I cannot change who I am," he said.

"I understand that."

"Do you want to be my wife?"

His question startled her. "No. We have separate lives."

"Yes. But we can have the visits. Beautiful visits. When we are old, we can remember the visits and smile."

It was almost a year before she returned, after her mother died, and she and Kirk had moved to Garden Grove.

Chapter Sixteen

$\mathcal{T}$*he gynecologist introduced herself* as Sally Gibson and addressed Pamela as "Mrs. Cartwright," which seemed odd to Pamela since the convention seemed to be just the reverse. Patients were expected to address their physician as "Doctor," and physicians generally called patients by their first names. Or at least that had been Pamela's experience. Maybe it was just female patients who were marginalized in this way.

Dr. Sally Gibson was attractive and young. She had taken over the practice of old Dr. Fremont when he finally retired. Dr. Fremont had been perfunctory with his examination, dismissive of questions, and referred to Pamela's genitalia as her "little thing." Even so, Pamela had actually wondered if she wanted a female physician, especially one so young and therefore inexperienced. At the conclusion of her first visit, she was embarrassed to have had such thoughts.

Dr. Gibson was respectful, thorough, used a speculum that had been warmed, and asked numerous questions as she gently prodded Pamela's pelvis and breasts. Were her periods regular? Did she have any breakthrough bleeding? Had she ever experienced night sweats or hot flashes? Did she ever experience pain during sex? Were her breasts always this tender? With the end of her reproductive years approaching, did she think about having a child?

To the last question, Pamela had responded, "My husband had a vasectomy before we married."

177

"Is that the only reason why you have not had a child?" Dr. Gibson asked as she helped Pamela to a sitting position and to cover herself—not with the customary paper sheet but with a cloth one that draped about her body and allowed her a bit more dignity.

"There seemed to be no point in even thinking about it," Pamela responded with a shrug. "Clay already had children when we married and was quite up front about not wanting a second family. And my brother has Down's syndrome. I would hate to ever face the decision about whether to have an abortion."

Dr. Gibson nodded. "Those are understandable reasons," she said. "And it's well documented that the instance of Down's syndrome rises with the age of the mother."

"Do you have children?" Pamela asked.

Dr. Gibson smiled. A lovely smile. "Four. I'm still breast feeding my last one. My husband brings her down to the office twice during the day. He stays home with the kids—and designs Web sites when he finds the time."

"That's very modern," Pamela said. "I'm sure my husband never changed a diaper."

"My father, too. He can't believe that Carl is a stay-at-home dad and keeps asking when that husband of mine is going to get a job."

Dr. Gibson told Pamela the nurse would call with the report on the Pap smear and was preparing to make her exit when Pamela asked, "Could I still have a child at my age?" Then she hastened to add, "Not that I even want to."

She felt herself blush. What had possessed her to ask such a thing? She wasn't about to have a baby. She didn't even *want* to have a baby. Not any-more. "I'm just curious," she explained.

Dr. Gibson took her hand from the doorknob and leaned against the instrument cabinet. "Perhaps," she acknowledged. "You are healthy, have a youthful body, and still have a few years before you enter menopause. It's not too uncommon for a woman to conceive into her late forties, some-times with the help of a few extra hormones. The issue is, I suppose, would you want to do that, especially considering your husband's age?"

"And his vasectomy," Pamela reminded her.

The doctor suggested that Pamela might want to do some soul search-ing over the next months. And her husband might ask his urologist about the possibility of having his vasectomy reversed.

Clay would never do that, Pamela thought as she dressed. She was cer-tain of that. Just as she was certain that Clay would never allow her to be artificially inseminated. And he would divorce her if she did it on her own. And being divorced was far more disturbing a specter than going childless.

The next day, however, when Pamela turned on her computer to pay some bills, she went first to the Internet and searched for information about sperm banks. Not that she would ever have need of one. She just wondered if there were any in the Kansas City metro.

There were two.

How strange it would be to have a child with a mystery father, she thought, staring out the window at her backyard. Donors filled out ques-tionnaires about their family and medical history. Supposedly, they would say if there were a history of genetic disorders, such as Down's syndrome. Still, that would be no guarantee. Neither of her parents had known of a Down's syndrome child in their families. Her mother had been in her twenties when Danny was conceived.

She realized that the thought of an abortion didn't concern her as it once had. At her age, there would be no question. She would not take on the raising of a Down's syndrome child, especially one who would not have a sibling to serve as the child's legal guardian after her death.

In years past, Down's syndrome children died in early adulthood and did not live on into their fifties as Danny had done. He'd had a heart valve repaired as an infant, but a murmur had continued into adulthood. And now, he was taking medication for congestive heart failure. But other than tiring more easily than he used to, Danny seemed fine. He still rode his bicycle five days a week to the same neighborhood grocery where he had bagged groceries and mopped floors for almost thirty years and would have gone seven days a week if they had let him.

She'd never told Clay about Danny's heart problem. She feared he would say something callous—like questioning the wisdom of keeping people alive when they contributed nothing to society—that she would have to hate him for.

Maybe her concern over Danny's health had precipitated these sudden thoughts of having a child after all. If anything ever happened to Danny, she would have no one to mother.

She wished that Dr. Gibson had never brought up the topic of childlessness. It was none of her business. At least Dr. Fremont had minded his own business.

Then, with a firm click of the mouse, she closed out the sperm-bank site and moved on to her bank's home page. Back to reality. She wasn't sure what she would do with a child if she had one. Her life was set. If it hadn't been before, it certainly was now that Clay was a high-ranking judge. Being the wife of such a man came with a clear set of responsibilities.

And she had never been one to rock the boat. Courageous people rocked boats. She was not courageous.

For more than a month, she gave little thought to her conversation with Dr. Gibson. Then, on a Thursday afternoon, Clay startled her by coming home early, a wide grin on his face and a bottle of Dom Pérignon under his arm. He put the champagne on ice and refused to tell her what his good news was until it was chilled and the glasses were poured.

She imagined all sorts of things. He was to receive some high award. Or had been selected to give the commencement address at the KU law school. They finally were going to take that trip to Australia that he'd been talking about for years.

But when he lifted his glass, it was to announce that he was going to be a grandfather. Janet was pregnant.

Pamela had never seen her husband so animated. Clay admitted to being surprised himself at his elation over Janet's news. At first it hadn't sunk in. The court was halfway through the afternoon docket before it hit him. At the first opportunity, he called Janet back and sobbed like a baby. A *grandchild*. She had made him so very happy.

"Maybe we should look at property in London, as a second home now and for retirement later," he told Pamela. "I want to be part of this child's life. I am going to be a better grandfather than I was a father."

Pamela emptied her glass and downed another, while Clay jabbered on about going over for the child's birth, about establishing an endowment for its college education, imagining the joy he would feel holding a grandchild in his arms. He planned to find out the name of Janet's obstetrician and check his credentials.

"Or *her* credentials," Pamela corrected, sipping the champagne.

Clay paused, obviously not comprehending her comment, and continued his monologue. He speculated about possible names; maybe they'd name the baby for him if it were a boy. He'd like a house by a park. Or maybe in an area where they could keep a pony. He'd had a pony when he was a boy.

"You're getting a little carried away," Pamela finally said. "You can visit the child all you want, but I am not moving to London. My friends and Danny are here."

Clay looked surprised. "Isn't that a bit selfish of you?" he asked. "I realize that since you've never had a child, it's hard for you to understand what this means to me. But this is a monumental event for me, Pamela. There is something quite wonderful in the idea of progeny and knowing that something of me will live on. I want you to help me pick out a special piece of jewelry for Janet, then let's have a celebratory dinner at the Country Club."

"I've already started dinner," she said.

"Then I'll change into something comfortable and help you finish up. We can go shopping tomorrow."

A few minutes later, dressed in khakis and golf shirt, Clay reappeared and began bustling about, uncharacteristically helpful, getting in her way as he put ice in the glasses, sliced the bread, stirred things that didn't need stirring. Pamela didn't trust herself to speak more than a word or two at a time lest some of her internal seething erupt. Of course she didn't know what it was like to be a parent. Not having children had been a prerequisite for their marriage. And it made her angry as hell for the man who kept her

from having children now to talk to her about progeny, about how important it was to be a parent and a grandparent. How *monumental* it was.

By the time they sat down at the table, however, she had calmed herself. She would be hurt if he *didn't* want to share his happiness with her.
Of course, she would help him celebrate. Tomorrow she would guide him
in selecting some appropriate piece of jewelry for Janet. She was happy
for Janet and her husband. Happy that Clay was happy. A baby would be
wonderful.

Asking him if he had ever regretted his vasectomy had been the farthest
thing from her mind. The words came unbidden. And hung there in the air
between them. In the silence that filled the room.

"Not really," Clay said finally, irritation creeping into his voice. "Why do
you ask?"

"I was just wondering if it ever bothered you that I never had a choice
about whether or not to have children?"

"Yes, you did, Pamela. You decided not to have them when you
accepted my proposal of marriage."

She said nothing as she gathered up the dishes to take to the kitchen.
Clay was right, of course. If she had insisted on having children, he never
would have married her.

And what would she be today if she had never married Clay? Probably a
bitter old spinster who terrorized underlings. If there were underlings. She
might still be a lowly assistant buyer. She certainly wouldn't have a grand
house or a closet full of furs, a safe filled with fine jewelry, a new Mercedes
every fourth year, a painting by Winslow Homer over her fireplace.

"And now do you regret that decision?" he asked.

She hesitated. *Did she?* "I have thought about it some over the years,"
she admitted. "Whenever my friends had a baby, I thought about it. And
sometimes when I see a mother looking at her child's face with such ado-
ration, I wondered if I was missing the most important part of being a
woman. And a part of me would wish that you'd change your mind and
decide we should have a child or two of our own. I even checked into the
possibilities of having a vasectomy reversed. But that was years ago. The

longer we were married, the more I realized that you didn't like being around children—or childlike adults—and that children would never work for us. I guess I'm a little stunned by your excitement over the prospect of a grandchild. More than a little stunned. And jealous, I guess."

While Pamela cleared the table, Clay remained in his seat, stoically sipping his wine, no longer the helpful husband.

She turned on the coffeepot, put the dishes in the dishwasher, and removed a carton of sherbet from the freezer, the ice cream scoop from the drawer. Then she stopped to stare at her reflection in the window over the sink. She had really made a mess of things. She supposed she should feel worried or afraid. But she was pretty devoid of feelings right now.

She was still staring at the window when she heard Clay push open the door, heard his footsteps crossing the kitchen, saw his reflection appear behind hers.

"Are you sorry you married me?" he asked, his tone a careful neutral. Not challenging. Just inquiring.

"Of course not," she said, turning to face him. "It's just that I've reached that now-or-never stage when it comes to childbearing. I know it is never, but the finality of it does give me pause."

"Aren't you excited at all about Janet's baby?"

"Yes, of course, I am. A baby will be lovely."

He watched while she dished up the sherbet, then he poured the coffee and carried the dishes on the tray to the study, where he turned on the financial news to fill the silence. When they had finished their coffee, he poured two brandies.

When he handed a glass to Pamela, she shook her head. "I would prefer a finger of Crown Royal, if you don't mind."

"But we always have brandy."

"I know. I never really liked it, though."

"You have been drinking brandy with me for almost nineteen years, and now you tell me you never really liked it?"

"I know," she said, reaching for a magazine. "I should have told you years ago."

"What else have you not liked that you never told me about?" he asked, still holding the unwanted brandy. "Do you not like the way I drive? What about my kisses? And the way I make love?"

She suppressed a sigh. She should have just taken the damned brandy like always. Now she would have to do damage control.

She stood, took the glass from his hand and put it on the table, and slipped her arms around his neck. "Please, don't get upset over a little brandy," she said.

She pressed her body against his. At first his body stiffened, but he soon relaxed and began automatically running his hands up and down her back, accepting her demonstration of contrition.

His hands strayed down to her fanny. And Pamela could feel the beginnings of an erection. But without Viagra, it would fade. He would take a pill while she was bathing, then take his time showering and shaving, giving it plenty of time to work.

"I'm sorry if I seemed insensitive, Pamela," he whispered into her hair.

"You are?" she asked.

"Of course I am," he said. She could hear his anger. She had ruined his celebration; now she doubted his sincerity.

But when he stepped back from their embrace, it wasn't so much anger she saw as puzzlement.

"What's gotten into you, Pamela?" he asked. "Are you mad because my daughter is pregnant, and you will never have a child? I wanted this evening to be such a celebration. I wanted you to share my joy."

Pamela knew she was supposed to crumble. Supposed to apologize for ruining his evening. Promise to make it up to him. He was waiting for her to do that.

But the words would not come. Instead, a thunderous silence filled the room and sucked away the air.

She took a step backward, thinking she would open the French doors. Maybe she could breathe on the terrace.

Clay reached for her hand. "Why don't you let me pour you that finger of Crown Royal?"

Pamela shook her head. "I am sorry to ruin your celebration," she said. "Let's try again tomorrow night. I'll meet you in the city. We can go to the jeweler's and eat at that new French place on the Plaza. But right now, I'm going over to Mary Sue's."

"Now?" he asked. "You are going over there *now?*" She could see the indecision in his face. He wanted to challenge her. She could do whatever she wanted during the day, but in the evenings, he expected her to be at home with him.

He was going to tell her not to go. *Forbid her to go.* She waited for his words.

But he didn't say them. She kissed his cheek and left him there.

When Mary Sue opened the door, Pamela said, "I need a friend."

"And here I am," Mary Sue said. "Michelle has play practice, and Michael is having a jam session, or whatever it's called nowadays, over at a friend's house. I was just thinking about a glass of wine. Care to join me?"

"Do you have any bourbon?" Pamela asked, following Mary Sue into the kitchen.

"Clay out of town?" Mary Sue asked, pouring a finger of Jack Daniels for Pamela and a glass of red wine for herself.

"No. He's at home," Pamela said, accepting the glass, taking a sip.

"Oh?" Mary Sue inquired with a lifted eyebrow. "Trouble in paradise?"

"Not really. I just needed a little space." Pamela lifted her glass. "Here's to space."

She downed her glass and helped herself to a refill. "I love my husband," she said.

"I know you do, honey."

"But sometimes I hate him."

Mary Sue put down her glass and opened her arms. Pamela buried her face against Mary Sue's shoulder and wept. She wasn't sure exactly why she was crying. Was it because she would never bear a child? Or because she could no longer pretend that her life was fulfilling and that if she had it all to do over again she might not have gone down the same road?

Eventually, after a third shot of bourbon, she told Mary Sue her disjointed tale of the new gynecologist and Janet's pregnancy and Clay wanting to buy her jewelry and move to England. Mary Sue reassured her that she was entitled to feel the way she did, which was confused and sad and a little bit afraid.

"More than a little bit," Pamela admitted.

"Do you want to have a child yourself?" Mary Sue asked.

"At this point in my life, probably not. But it bothers me for Clay to suddenly decide that his grandchild is the most important thing that ever happened to him. I want to be happy for him, but there's this little voice that says I'll never have those kinds of feelings for myself."

"And you have about fifteen minutes on your biological clock to decide if you are going to back up and try a different direction?"

"Yeah, something like that."

"Well, I need to tell you something that isn't going to help things one bit."

"What's that?"

"Martin Leonard is back in town. He called me today. The people who bought his folks' house defaulted on the loan, and he got it back. He said that he and his wife have separated, and he's living there alone. And he asked that I pass this information along to you. I told him I'd think about it, but of course I have to tell you before someone else broadsides you with the news or you see him walking down Main Street."

Pamela closed her eyes. Her head was already spinning from the liquor. Now the room was spinning, too.

Dear God. Beautiful Martin, with whom she had the best sex of her lifetime. He was here in Garden Grove. *Alone* in Garden Grove. *And he wanted her to know.*

Chapter Seventeen

Mary Sue followed Pamela out the front door. "You're not going over there, are you?" she asked.

"Probably not," Pamela said. She hugged Mary Sue and headed down the walk toward her car.

"I don't think you should be driving," Mary Sue called, trailing after her.

"Don't worry," Pamela said over her shoulder. "I'm not drunk. In fact, I am stone cold sober. I have never been more sober."

"If you're going over there, I think I should go with you," Mary Sue insisted.

With her hand on the door handle of her car, Pamela paused as though considering the offer—a companion to make sure her visit with the man she had once loved, and maybe still loved, was just a friendly one, and would not turn into something that might alter her life.

"It would be best if I went along," Mary Sue said, putting a restraining hand on Pamela's arm.

Pamela shook her head and pulled her arm away.

Mary Sue watched Pamela's immaculate silver Mercedes back out of the drive and take off like a sleek, shiny bullet. Maybe a policeman would stop her for driving too fast. Maybe he would test her breath for alcohol and arrest her. Then she would have time to come to her senses.

Of course, all hell would break loose on the home front when Judge Clay Cartwright had to bail his wife out of jail. But he'd get over it. Mary Sue doubted, however, that he'd get over his wife having an affair.

An affair was all it could be. Pamela was not going to marry Martin and live happily ever after. Martin would either go back to his wife or disappoint Pamela when she realized the man she thought he was had never existed at all. She would end up more unhappy than before or be left only with herself. Of course, being left only with herself was what eventually happened to most women. Maybe it was better for a woman to find herself alone while she still had time to figure out who she really was and how to live the rest of her life based on her own sensibilities. She no longer had to pretend she was voting for the same candidates as her husband or spend evenings with people she did not like. But what women who were alone really did was forage around until they found a Walter.

With a sigh, Mary Sue started back up the walk toward her house—her *empty* house. A portent of her life to come. Her fear of being alone was why she had taken up with Walter in the first place, why any single woman of a certain age takes up with a man. She was looking for a hedge against loneliness after a lifetime of living for others.

At least Pamela had a husband in her house.

Mary Sue remembered how relieved she had felt when Walter started hanging out at her house. It calmed her to have a man in the family room or underfoot in the kitchen. It gave her a reason other than guilt to clean and cook. She went over to his house only when they were going to have sex.

Entering the house, she thought again of how empty it felt. Maybe she should get a cat. Or adopt a greyhound from the rescue place in Wichita.

She left the porch light on for Michael and Michelle and turned on the television to keep her company while she tidied up. She wiped the counters, started the dishwasher, and put away the almost empty bottle of bourbon.

Pamela really had had too much to drink. She shouldn't be driving a car, much less making a decision that could affect the rest of her life.

Mary Sue dialed Pamela's cellular phone, but it was turned off. She couldn't remember Pamela ever turning off her cell phone, but tonight she had cut the tether.

Mary Sue jumped when her own phone rang. The caller ID screen showed Pamela's home number. That would be Clay checking on his wife's whereabouts. Mary Sue let it ring. Clay Cartwright was the last person in the world she wanted to talk to.

When the ringing stopped, she picked up the phone and, on a whim, dialed Walter's number, taking pleasure in selecting the familiar numbers. She hung up as soon as she dialed the last number; his phone had been disconnected months ago. She stood there with her hand on the receiver remembering how nice it had been to pick up the phone and have a man to call. They saw each other or called almost every day. Even when he was off gambling, he would give her a call to brag or lament. She wondered if his possessions were still in the house. And if they weren't, where were they? She would have liked to have his blue terrycloth bathrobe that she wore after sex.

She still imagined hearing from Walter. Imagined him calling to say he was sorry he had been such a butt about her cancer and would she please come live with him on some little Caribbean island, where he was safe from mobsters and ex-wives. She wouldn't live with him, but she might go for visits. Or maybe not. Maybe all she wanted was a more palatable ending to their relationship.

She didn't love Walter. At times, she didn't even like him. But she had felt incomplete without a man in her life. Her circle of friends had shrunk to those few who predated her marriage and a few loyal neighbors, plus some folks at church. Most of the couples with whom she and Barry socialized had embraced the second Mrs. Prescott. Trish now belonged to the doctors' wives' club, when only three years ago Mary Sue had served as club president and considered launching a climb toward the state presidency. She even thought she might like to be national president someday, when her children were grown and she had the time to travel.

And there were other organizations that once had filled her calendar. But since she could no longer count herself among the community's society matrons—among the women who had the money, time, and inclination to do good works and plan benefits—she had let memberships lapse. Or maybe she'd let them lapse because it was hard to see people from before. She was a victim of both divorce and cancer, and that made people smile too broadly and lie about how good she looked and ask if there was anything they could do, when what they really wanted was to get the encounter over with as quickly as possible. She had become their worst nightmare.

But for those six months before her cancer had been diagnosed, she had felt almost normal with Walter at her side. They attended parties at the country club and had gone to a benefit auction for the women's shelter and the city's annual jazz festival. Having him beside her at Michael's baseball games made it easier when Barry showed up. Sometimes Barry brought Trish, who even in faded jeans and sneakers always managed to look as if she belonged on the cover of a fashion magazine. Mary Sue hated it when Trish cheered and jumped up and down as if she were a real mother. She desperately hoped that Barry was just as annoyed when Walter cheered for Michael. She cringed, though, when Walter yelled, "Kill the bastards," or demanded the umpire get his head out of his ass. Mary Sue understood well those pitiful divorced women who concluded that any semiacceptable man was better than no man at all—even an ill-mannered man with a penchant for vulgarity. She had become one of them.

She had sex with Walter because it was expected of her. Mostly she faked orgasms with accompanying moans and trembling. But sometimes, if she had drunk enough to lessen her inhibitions, but not so much that she had become anesthetized, she could steer her body into familiar waters and paddle her way to climax.

Now Walter had dropped off the face of the planet. She probably would continue to meet men when the dating service called, but her expectations diminished with each "date." The men were either pitiful or annoying. Or both.

She took a last look around the downstairs, then turned off the television and headed up the stairs. Where was Pamela now? she wondered. Was she at home, apologizing to Clay for being late and seducing him into forgiveness? Or was she lying naked in Martin Leonard's arms?

Pamela and Martin had been lovers that summer after their freshman year in college. Mary Sue had been certain of that. Gretchen and Dixie thought so, too. One minute Pamela would be flitting around like a hummingbird on diet pills, then abruptly get a dreamy look on her face and sit there motionless for minutes on end, her mind definitely elsewhere. That was before the football player had raped Gretchen and she had started sleeping with Paul. It was before Dixie and Arnie had started living together in Chicago. Pamela had been the first of their little foursome to have sex. And Mary Sue had been the last. She was the only one who walked down the aisle a virgin. She'd thought virginity would give her a leg up on happily every after.

When she, Gretchen, and Dixie concluded that Pamela had indeed fallen off the wagon and was screwing Martin almost daily, they worried themselves into a tizzy about birth control. What if she got pregnant? Did she have enough sense to insist Martin wear a condom? What was their responsibility? Should they say something to her? Gang up on her and insist she go to a doctor for pills or a diaphragm?

They were relieved when Dixie found birth control pills stuffed under the lining of Pamela's purse. At least pregnancy was being avoided without any intervention on their part. In the end, they said nothing and pretended they didn't know.

But they did have endless discussions about whether or not they would ever screw a boy they weren't going to marry. Or had Pamela and Martin decided to go against their parents' wishes and get married after all? Or maybe they just wanted the memory of a beautiful summer affair to carry with them always.

Pamela had scarcely mentioned Martin in the years since. While she was working in St. Louis, she would sometimes mention men she was dating— a fourth-year surgery resident at George Washington University Hospital, a stockbroker, even a fireman. As time went by, however, they heard less and less about her social life. If asked, she would say there was no one special.

She had gotten thinner, more stylish, more brittle, while the other three girlfriends gave themselves over to the all-consuming state of motherhood. Then suddenly, Pamela showed up at a Fourth of July gathering at the lake house with an engagement ring.

She seemed genuinely pleased over their squeals and hugs and kisses. But she hadn't seemed thrilled. Dixie asked her about that. "I'm more relieved than thrilled," Pamela admitted. "Clay is a fine man, and it's time for me to get married. And I get to move back home without my tail between my legs."

They met Clay at an engagement party hosted by Pamela's parents. Dixie had made a return trip from Chicago for the event. Gretchen and Mary Sue were there with their husbands. All three were pregnant, Gretchen for the second time. Clay did not beam when congratulated. He did not cast adoring looks in Pamela's direction. Afterward, Gretchen and Mary Sue sent their husbands home and headed with Dixie to a nearby bar. That was in the years before anyone had heard of fetal alcohol syndrome, and they enjoyed their beer guilt-free.

Mary Sue defended Pamela's choice. She had given up on finding Mr. Right. She was afraid of never finding anyone at all. Clay represented security and position in the community. "And she can have a baby or two," Mary Sue pointed out. It was more than a year before Pamela told them about Clay's vasectomy, about agreeing to a childless marriage.

Clay insisted on a simple wedding in the small side chapel at the Presbyterian church. The senior partner at his firm would be his best man. One attendant each was sufficient.

Pamela came to Mary Sue's house to lament. How could she get married without her three best friends at her side? Pamela had wailed. "We'll all be there," Mary Sue assured her. "We'll draw straws to see which of us will represent the Girlfriends."

Pamela didn't know the drawing had been rigged. Gretchen and Dixie insisted that Mary Sue must be their representative at the altar. She would become appropriately dewy-eyed during the ceremony. Gretchen and Dixie weren't sure they could pull that off. "And in her heart of hearts, you're who Pamela wants," Dixie had pointed out. "If Gretchen and I could have had only one attendant, we would have wanted it to be you. You're the one who made us friends and kept us that way."

As Clay had wanted, the wedding was small, but Pamela's parents invited everyone they knew to the reception at the country club. Mary Sue knew that Pamela had planned for Danny to stand in the receiving line alongside Clay's daughters, but Danny was nowhere to be seen at the wedding or the reception. Pamela got tears in her eyes when Mary Sue asked where her brother was.

"Danny's not feeling well today," Pamela's mother hastily explained.

"Oh, dear, are you thinking what I'm thinking?" Mary Sue had whispered to Dixie and Gretchen.

"I will never forgive the man for this," Dixie declared.

Gretchen was more to the point. "I hate his guts," she said. "I hope Clay Cartwright chokes on his silver spoon."

After they had dutifully thrown rice and seen the newlyweds off on their honeymoon, Mary Sue, Dixie, and Gretchen drove out to the lake house and took their pregnant bodies skinny dipping just to prove to themselves that they still had control over their own lives, that their marriages were not and would never be like the one Pamela had just entered into.

Which was only partly true, Mary Sue now had to acknowledge. There was no such thing as a fifty-fifty marriage. One partner always worked harder at pleasing than the other. And that partner was usually the wife. Was it something they had been born with—a gene that predestined them to be accommodating at all costs? Or had they learned it at their mother's knee?

Mary Sue never used to think such cynical thoughts. It was out of character for her.

She had changed, though. Her friends still wanted to think of her as sweet little Mary Sue, but that person no longer existed. She didn't want to have a low opinion of men. She was, after all, the mother of a son. As was Dixie. They had tried to raise Kirk and Michael to be sweet, sensitive men. Except that Michael had gotten surly and disrespectful of late. When she tried to discipline him, he would threaten to go live with his father and Trish. On several occasions, she had come within an inch of telling him to go.

If she hadn't gotten breast cancer, she probably would have married Walter. Or some other man she didn't love. But cancer, chemo, and the passing years had put an end to the fresh-faced prettiness she had enjoyed all her life. Being pretty had been an elemental part of who she was. All things had sprung from the prettiness well.

Not that she was now ugly. She just wasn't pretty anymore, and all the makeup in the world wasn't going to change that. Men didn't look at her the same way. Often all she got was a glance. Some even looked right through her as though she wasn't there. If she ever married again, it would not be because of her looks. Which might be a good thing.

If she ever got married again. She was less frantic about that now. Sometimes the thought of sharing her life and space with a man—any man— seemed oppressive.

But that night at the lake after Pamela's wedding, the old Mary Sue had made excuses for Clay. That was her role. She was Mary Sue the Good. She was Tinker Bell, sprinkling her magic fairy dust, and Pollyanna, always looking on the bright side. And, of course, she was the cheerleader. Always the cheerleader. They counted on her to encourage them and keep them from straying too far from the beaten path. And to mend them when they had a falling out. That night she was right in character as she pointed out that Clay Cartwright had a failed first marriage under his belt and only God knew what wounds he was concealing. Maybe he had to learn to trust again. Maybe that was why God had brought him and Pamela together. Clay needed a caring woman at his side to heal him. A year from now, he would be a different man. When they had a party to celebrate Pamela and Clay's first anniversary, Mary Sue was sure that Danny would be there.

She had been wrong about Clay, Mary Sue acknowledged. He had, if anything, become more overbearing over the years, holding Pamela on an ever-shortening leash. She couldn't even begin to imagine how Clay would react if Pamela were unfaithful to him.

Mary Sue tried Pamela's cellular phone once again to no avail.

"Don't do it, honey," she whispered into the silent phone. "Not yet. You need to think about it first and consider the consequences."

But if Pamela was with Martin, they probably were already making love, already trying to recapture that long-ago summer.

In the middle of her dark bedroom, with only the light of the moon illuminating the pale walls, lying in the bed she had once shared with her husband, Mary Sue wrapped her arms around her body and remembered young love, remembered wanting love so much she thought she would die if she didn't get it.

She wasn't sure she would ever get married again, but she didn't want to go the rest of her life without the incredible feeling of becoming one with a man she wanted very, very much.

She didn't like self-gratification. She avoided even thinking the word "masturbation," which was what adolescent boys did while looking at girly magazines. And what husbands did in the shower while thinking about women other than their wives. That last year she and Barry were together, he took very long showers. And he had taken to waking her in the night for wordless sex—until she could stand it no more.

But this was one of those late-night moments when she desperately needed something to fill the emptiness.

Walter never once had been her phantom lover. She still had to push away thoughts of Barry and remind herself that the man she had been married to for twenty-two years and had planned to love forever didn't want her anymore. She would have to remind herself that he was with Trish and erase him from her mind, conjuring instead the body of a faceless generic man who would pound his flesh against hers and make her feel.

Then an unbearably heavy blanket of suffocating sadness would envelop her, and she would curl her body tightly around a pillow to weep and vow never to do that to herself again.

She swung her feet to the floor. No, she wasn't going to resort to that, she decided. and marched into the bathroom. In the cruel hundred-watt light, she removed her clothes and examined her altered body. She hoped to make love again at some point in her life, but she doubted if she would ever want to show herself to a man again.

The most noticeable thing was the hipbone-to-hipbone scar across her belly, where the plastic surgeon had harvested the tissue for the reconstruction. She hadn't really had the tissue to spare, and the remaining flesh had been pulled so tightly over her abdomen, she hadn't been able to stand up straight for months. Even now, her tummy was hard as a rock and almost concave. If she threw back her shoulders and tucked under her hips, to carry herself the way she had been taught in all those ballet classes and cheerleader clinics, she still felt an uncomfortable pulling sensation. As a result, her once-perfect posture was no more. Her daughter nagged her about it. And during her mother's last visit, Connie had suggested she walk around with books on her head. Mary Sue ignored them both. She accepted the fact that no one was ever again going to tell her that she carried herself like a dancer.

Maybe because of all that pulling, the incision across her abdomen had not scarred well. It was jagged and red and interspersed with ugly keloids. The plastic surgeon had revised it once and wanted to work on it again.

The scar that completely circled her reconstructed breast was keloid-free but still quite red. In spite of the final-touch liposuctioning that was supposed to make it match its mate, the reconstruction was a bit saggier and a bit smaller than her real breast. But Mary Sue figured the left side was going to shrink and sag with age. Maybe eventually they would match.

A facsimile nipple had been made by tattooing color onto tissue that had been deliberately roughed up into a puckering scar. The result was certainly better than the blank Barbie-doll look, but it never quite matched the ever-changing left nipple with its erectile tissue able to respond to temperature changes and touch. The manufactured nipple stood perpetually at half-mast. If a T-shirt was at all snug, the mismatch was apparent. The tattooing would fade, Mary Sue had been warned, and she might want to have it redone in five or six years.

But she didn't want anything else done. No scar revision or retattooing. She supposed the scars would get less harshly ugly and red as time went by, but that mutilated body in the mirror would be hers for the rest of her life.

Looking at it was still a downer and probably always would be. But at least it was a cure for horniness, which came in handy when a gal lived alone.

If she ever made love again, it would be in the dark.

Chapter Eighteen

P*amela sped away from Mary Sue's house*, momentarily relishing the roar of the engine, the feel of power. But then she took a deep breath and lessened the pressure on the accelerator, turned the corner at a sane speed, and pulled into an unlit parking lot by a neighborhood park.

She put her hands to her face and was startled by how hot her skin felt. So what now? she asked herself.

She took her cellular phone from her purse and called information, but there was no listing for Martin Leonard. Probably he hadn't been in town long enough to establish service.

And even if he had a phone, what would she say to him? That she was thinking of him and her skin was on fire?

She put down the phone, hesitated, then picked it up again to press the off button. The tiny screen went black.

She was unreachable.

Clay would call Mary Sue, though. And Mary Sue would say that she had just left. Which meant she still had time to get herself home, to settle back into the rut that had become her life.

But what if she didn't do that? What then?

She could tell Clay that she had forgotten to recharge the phone. That she was upset and needed time to think. She had gone to a bar or was just driving around. Maybe not going straight home would not be the end of life as she knew it.

Clay didn't know that Martin Leonard was back in town. She wasn't sure Clay even knew who Martin Leonard was. She was fairly certain she had never mentioned his name. She had mentioned Tim Blaine, a tenth-grade boyfriend who now taught English literature at Drake. And Clay had met Greg Reynolds, whom she had gone with briefly her junior year in high school and who was now the Garden Grove city manager. But she hadn't had sex with Tim or Greg. It was safe to talk about them.

Clay had been out of town during her twenty-fifth high school reunion. She had told him about it beforehand, even asked him if he wanted to go with her, but had been relieved when he declined.

She didn't know if Martin would be there, but there was always the possibility. When she saw him, she had to struggle to appear unflustered. His wife had said, "So this is the Gentile girl you were so smitten with back then."

She was an attractive woman with a sincere smile. Clara was her name. And now they were separated. Maybe Clara had gotten tired of supporting a husband who wrote books that never got published. Maybe she told him to get a job and he refused. Maybe they had gotten tired of each other and were just giving things a rest.

Just start the car and go on home, she told herself. Maybe she would have an affair with Martin, and maybe she wouldn't, but she didn't have to decide tonight. If she did have an affair, she needed to plan, needed to be levelheaded about it. It was not something to be done spur of the moment. An affair required preparation. It required secret phone calls and clandestine meeting places. She couldn't just drive over there and park her car in front of his house. Not a late-model silver Mercedes sedan.

She made a U-turn and headed toward home. But when she got there, the light was still on in the study, and she kept driving. She wasn't ready to face her husband. Not after her skin had been hot for Martin Leonard.

She would drive back to Mary Sue's and spend the night there. She would call Clay from there and explain that when she started home, she realized she'd had too much to drink. And no, she didn't want him to come for her. She was already in bed.

He would be pissed. But after this evening, she could handle pissed. She might even tell him to cool it. Or she might apologize.

But she did not drive back to Mary Sue's.

The Heritage Park area used to be silk-stocking, but it had gone downhill after the city let Wal-Mart raze two square blocks to build a superstore nearby. The tree-lined street where Martin's family had lived was now a thoroughfare with traffic lights and turn lanes. The once-gracious old homes were decaying, many divided into rental units.

The tree in front of the house where Martin grew up, where he apparently was living once again, was dying and the shrubs were seriously overgrown.

Pamela slowed the car as she drove by the house, feeling an overwhelming sense of déjà vu. When she was in grade school, she would ride her bicycle down this street just because Martin Leonard lived there. In the seventh grade, Martin had starred in her first carnal imaginings.

In high school, she would drive by. Usually alone. After dark. Her friends realized she and Martin were friends, but she always claimed that their mutual interest in writing was the basis of their friendship. They never officially dated, but they necked some when the opportunity presented itself. Even when she was going with another boy, she would hang out with Martin, neck with Martin. He came to her house sometimes, but she never went to his house. He said his parents wouldn't understand him having a Gentile girl as more than just a school friend.

Martin had given a talk about Judaism during a multicultural assembly program. He'd even worn a yarmulke, which made him seem like someone else. He said his family wasn't Orthodox but they kept a kosher home and explained about the two sets of dishes. It seemed to Pamela that his mother must spend a lot of time in the kitchen.

His Jewishness made him seem more exotic, which made their clandestine necking sessions all the more exciting. During their freshman year in college, with her in Lawrence and him in New Haven, they had intense, late-night telephone conversations that raised their yearning to a feverish pitch.

While she was still in Lawrence, she had gotten a prescription for birth control pills, which hadn't been the horrible ordeal she had thought it would be. The elderly family physician commended her for being responsible. She had the prescription filled and called Martin at Yale. "Guess what I'm holding in my hand?" she said.

Martin had been astounded. And lowered his voice to a whisper. "You did that? You went to a doctor?"

"Isn't that what you wanted me to do?"

"God, yes. But I didn't think you really would. I would have worn a condom."

"I know. But it will be nicer this way."

"It will be perfect. Oh, God, Pamela. I never knew I could love anyone the way I love you."

It was the first time he had ever said he loved her. She melted inside. She would spend the rest of her life with this man and do anything to make him happy.

Finals week, he called to say his mother would be going to Wisconsin to be with her terminally ill father.

Martin's older sister was married and living in New York. His older brother was spending a year in an Israeli kibbutz. During the day, his surgeon father was either at the hospital or on the golf course. They would have privacy and a bed in which to consummate their love. Martin said his bedroom would become a temple. He wanted candles burning and beautiful music. They would promise never to make love to any other human being as long as they lived. They belonged to each other for a lifetime, which she both believed and disbelieved.

Pamela's mother also was gone much of that summer—on a mission trip to Mexico. Pamela dutifully had a meal on the table every evening for her father, then would go hang out with her friends. Weekends, she would visit Danny at the group home, sometimes taking him swimming or to play video games at the mall. Afternoons were spent in Martin's bedroom. When they weren't screwing, he'd read his pages to her. Mostly she praised his writing, but sometimes she offered critiques. He did need to curtail the descriptions; everyone already knew what sunsets looked like. Maybe he should have the story better in mind before he began.

After his grandfather's funeral, Martin's father stayed in Wisconsin to help settle the estate, and they screwed into the night, in every room in the house. When the air-conditioner broke, they took a blanket out in the backyard.

They talked about getting married. Martin said he could live without kosher. Pamela had all but decided to convert, even though she doubted if he would ever be a successful novelist and worried about how he would support them. She was still writing poetry, but at least poets didn't expect to support themselves with their words. All Pamela hoped for was to get something published someday. But Martin actually expected to be rich and famous, with six-figure contracts and a Bentley in his garage. He said that Jewish writers had a leg up because of the love-hate relationship they had with modern American society. And with their parents. With sex. Just look at Saul Bellow and Philip Roth.

Pamela read *Portnoy's Complaint* and found it disgusting. If Martin was determined to be a writer, maybe he could be a Jewish Ross Macdonald.

She thought that Martin would surely give up his dream and go to medical school as his parents expected. Pamela would change her major to elementary education and teach school while he earned a medical degree. She had even called a rabbi to ask how one became Jewish. He wanted to make an appointment for her to come see him. She wasn't ready for that. But Elizabeth Taylor managed it almost overnight when she married Eddie Fisher, so it must not be too hard.

On the day of her deflowering, she had almost changed her mind. Martin led her up the stairs, but in the hallway outside his bedroom, she began to tremble. She asked him to promise that it would be all right if she changed her mind, if she decided she really didn't want to go all the way. They could just take off their clothes and enjoy feeling each other up without the restriction of clothing.

He said yes, of course. Whatever she wanted was what he wanted. Then he drew her into his room and locked the door behind them. The room didn't look like a temple. It looked like Danny's room at the group home—a boy's room with sports posters on the wall and even a model airplane hanging from the ceiling. But the bedspread was pulled back to reveal snowy white sheets. A folded, dark-colored bath towel was waiting on the nightstand, just as he had promised, along with a candle and a book of matches.

They just stood there for the longest time, not looking at each other, not quite believing the much-anticipated moment had actually arrived.

So what now? How did they proceed? "Maybe this isn't such a good idea," she said, wondering if she was going to cry.

Martin turned on the stereo, and suddenly Olivia Newton-John was singing "If You Love Me." His hand shook as he lit the candle. Then he pulled her into his arms and kissed her. A stand-up kiss, which is an entirely different thing from a kiss in the front or backseat of a car. A stand-up kiss was a grown-up kiss, like in the movies. Like Robert and Barbra in *The Way We Were*.

And suddenly, they were tugging at each other's clothing, falling onto the bed. He kept telling her she was beautiful, even more beautiful than he had imagined. Over and over he said it. For years afterward, she would remember Martin saying those most seductive of all words. Never since that summer had anyone said them to her with such conviction. Never since that summer had she felt so uninhibited about showing herself to a man, about making love in every way imaginable. In fact, she had become more and more inhibited over the years. She and Clay made love exactly the same way every time, steering clear of unexplored territory. It was safer that way. When Clay finished, he thanked her and rolled onto his side. She would reach for the hand towel she had placed on the bedside table and wipe away the semen. When he was asleep, she would go wash herself. With Martin, they had gloried in the semen and rubbed it on their bellies and on her breasts.

The sex she had experienced with Martin that summer had become her gold standard; she had never experienced anything quite so remarkable since. She no longer expected to. Only infrequently did the specter of great sex rear its troublesome head and taunt her with memories of what she was missing.

Like now. Here she was again, parked in front of that same house of that long-ago summer. She put her head against the steering wheel and groaned.

He was in that house now. *Waiting for her.* She knew that he was. That was what his phone call to Mary Sue had been about.

She imagined herself walking up the front walk, knocking on the door, walking up that same flight of stairs.

But she didn't want to be unfaithful to her husband. And besides, she was due for a leg waxing and pedicure. Because of the heat, her lingerie was cotton. Not silk. Not what a woman would wear to begin an affair.

And her body wasn't the same as before. She weighed about the same, and her stomach was still flat, but her skin no longer fit as tautly over her frame, and her breasts were lower on her chest. Of course, Martin had been a bit fleshly at their high school reunion. He had changed, too.

Clay was waiting for her at home right now. Her husband would either be livid that she had left abruptly or would assume the role of a tolerant father willing to listen to her apology and her promise never to be a bad girl like that again. Neither possibility was satisfactory. No longer.

She sensed that something monumental had taken place between her and Clay tonight. Or at least something monumental had happened to her. She had told him she didn't like brandy. What a simple thing, but God, how liberating that had been! And she went over to Mary Sue's without first laying the groundwork, without telling him the week before of her plans for the appointed evening and being an especially sweet wife in the interim to soothe his ruffled feathers.

Would he divorce her if she didn't come home tonight? Would she be jeopardizing her future if she went inside the house where Martin was waiting?

Pamela began hitting her head against the steering wheel—hard enough that it made stars shoot across her closed eyelids. If she got out of this obscenely expensive car and started up the walk, she would not find her lost youth or that long-ago passion behind the screen door.

What she did find might be worth risking all. Or it might not. Even so, she was too needy to turn around and go back home. She would steal one hour from her marriage. That didn't seem so awful. Just one hour. Then she would decide if she would ever come back again.

She peeled out of her cotton panties, then unhooked her bra and pulled it out of the armhole of her blouse.

She got out of the car and like magic the front door opened.

As she pulled into the driveway, Pamela saw with a sinking heart that the light was still on in Clay's study. He was waiting up for her. She could only imagine his fury.

She would tell him she hadn't been ready to come home. She needed time to drive around and think. She had driven all the way to Lawrence and back.

She puttered in the kitchen for a time, then squared her shoulders and marched down the hall.

The television was turned to CNN. His easy chair was empty. He wasn't sitting behind the desk.

Then she saw his body sprawled on the floor by the desk.

Chapter Nineteen

G*retchen met* G*us at the same* Prairie Village restaurant where they had met on their first "date." She wasn't ready yet to tell him where she lived—or her last name. And he had not supplied this information about himself.

He was waiting at the bar and stood while she approached. "Nice to see you again," he said formally, extending his hand.

His graying hair was freshly cut, but his mustache was, if anything, bushier than last time. And he still had his shirt unbuttoned to the middle of his chest, exposing a heavy mat of graying chest hair and a heavy gold cross.

After the bartender had taken their orders, Gretchen reached over and buttoned one of the buttons.

With a puzzled frown, Gus asked, "Why did you do that?"

"Because I like it better that way. Humor me."

"Well, if I told you I'd like it better if you wore a miniskirt up to here, would you humor me?" he asked, touching a point on her thigh just below her panties.

"No," she said, pushing his hand away. "But that's not the same."

"Why not?"

"Because I want you to cover up, not expose more of yourself."

Gus became very still, a vein throbbing in his neck. He stared at his folded hands while the bartender placed two foaming glasses of beer in front of them. "What else don't you like?" he challenged. "Would you like me to grow a couple of inches?"

Gretchen picked up her purse and pulled out her wallet, ready to pay for her beer and leave, but Gus put a hand on her arm.

"The last woman I went out with told me she was crazy about hairy chests and thought that men didn't show them off enough."

"Why aren't you still going out with her then?"

"She found someone else she liked better. Which has become a pattern. You're the seventh woman I've met through the dating service and the first one who gave me her phone number. I don't exactly have a way with women."

"What happened to your wife?"

"She ran off with my younger brother."

"You're kidding," Gretchen said.

"I wish," Gus said. "It turns out he was the father of the baby I thought was mine. I lost my kid, my wife, and my brother all in one fell swoop."

"God, I'm sorry," Gretchen said, groping for words. "I know that must have been terrible for you."

"My first wife left, too. She said she still loved me but didn't like being married. But the day after our divorce became final, she married her boss."

"Usually it's men who leave," Gretchen observed, staring at their images in the gold-tinted mirror over the bar. The tint was flattering. If it weren't for the mustache, the mirrored Gus would be nice-looking—maybe even handsome. The white sundress accentuated her tan. She had even used hot curlers and worn her hair down for a change. She looked better than she had in a long time.

"I decided I was too nice," Gus wistfully told their mirrored images.

Gretchen turned to look at the man himself. "Too nice? How can anyone be too nice?" she demanded.

"I've been reading Harold Robbins. Women like men to treat them rough."

"Oh, come on," Gretchen said, ready to reach for her purse again.

"Harold Robbins writes like that because he's a misogynistic son-of-a-bitch."

"Nice guys finish last," Gus stated emphatically, then took a long swig of beer.

"Look, Gus, maybe some women are masochistic, but most of us want to be treated with respect." Her hand closed around her purse. This had been a mistake. And she'd spent more time getting ready for tonight than a sixteen-year-old would getting ready for a prom. "Tell me, have you always worn a mustache?" she asked.

"Yeah. All the men in my family wear mustaches. Don't you like it either?"

"Not really. I think you would be better-looking without it. And I imagine most women prefer to kiss men without all that bristly hair hanging from their upper lip."

Gus drew in his breath and squared his shoulders. "Both my wives said it was sexy."

"But they left."

"Not because of the mustache," he insisted. "If you don't like my mustache and my chest hair, why did you agree to meet me again?"

"I was really down when you called. It helped to have a man want to be with me."

"Even if you weren't particularly attracted to the man?"

She shrugged. "I wanted to see how I felt when I saw you again. The first two men I met through the dating service were pricks. I wasn't attracted to you, but you didn't seem like a prick. I thought maybe I wouldn't mind the mustache so much when I got to know you."

"And the unbuttoned shirt?"

"It wasn't a major problem."

"But the mustache is."

"It wouldn't be if we were just friends. But neither one of us is looking for someone to be just friends with."

"If I shave it off, will you go to bed with me?"

"I might, but I can't make any promises, so I really think it would be a bad idea for you to do that. That should be something you do because you want to."

"I think I'll go on home now," Gus said, throwing money on the counter for their beer.

"I understand. I'm sorry. I didn't mean to be unkind, but I couldn't stand the way my husband didn't pick up after himself. He did that from the very first day we were married. And I never told him. I never said, 'Goddamn it, hang up that wet towel and put your dirty clothes in the hamper!' Then suddenly I realized I'd passed the statute of limitations on speaking up. It would do more harm than good for him to know I'd been seething for ten years and never said a word. It would make him angry and make me seem like a gutless idiot. Well, I'm never going to be a gutless idiot again."

"Yeah, whatever," Gus said, standing. "Happy hunting."

Gretchen watched him leave, then finished her beer. And wondered if she should smile at the man at the end of the bar. He was fiftyish, with a full head of salt-and-pepper hair. No wedding ring. Expensive knit shirt. Nice shoulders. A tennis player maybe. She mentally rehearsed doing that—looking his way and nodding, then offering just a suggestion of a smile. Did she have the courage to do that? She checked her reflection in the mirror. She hated for all the effort she'd put into getting ready to go to waste.

She wished she knew how tall the man was.

Just as she was about to risk a smile, a woman came in the front door and slipped onto the stool beside him. "Sorry I'm late," she said and kissed his cheek. Gretchen watched in the mirror while he nuzzled her neck and whispered something to her, watched the woman laugh and slip her hand to his lap. She was petite and young enough to be his daughter. No dating service necessary for the likes of them. Dating services were for marginal men and women over forty.

Gretchen nodded when the bartender asked if she wanted another beer. Maybe she would just sit here for a while and see if a marginal man came along. Except the one and only time she had hooked up with a stranger in a bar, he forced himself on her. Which she realized would now be called "rape."

But it was hard for her to give it that name. She didn't want to be a woman who had been raped. That was too much baggage to drag around. Guys took advantage of drunken women; that was the way of the world. She had known that then, and she'd certainly made sure that her daughters knew it now.

Joe Markowski was a second-string sportscaster now. She'd be flipping through the channels, and there he would be giving the play-by-play on some regional game. It still had such an effect on her. She would have to go off and be by herself for a while. Calm herself. She hated herself more than she hated him. Sometimes she would call Mary Sue, who would remind her how long ago it had happened, how not one cell of her body had even existed back then. She was a different person now. She had a husband and two daughters. She had a beautiful home. She was strong and proud. Joe Markowski was an obnoxious, fat has-been.

Probably not a day had passed in Gretchen's life without some thought of Markowski and that night. If he thought of that night at all, no doubt it would be a vague memory of one of the many nameless, faceless broads he screwed whether they wanted him to or not. His name was emblazoned in her memory; he didn't know hers.

The beer in its frosted mug was wonderfully cold and elemental. She would enjoy it, perhaps have another. She was not going to let thoughts of an asshole ex–football player run her off. But if some man came to sit beside her, she would leave. She no longer wanted male companionship. She no longer found any satisfaction in her reflected image. Her white sundress was too bare, too come-hither. She would never wear her hair down again.

As she emptied the glass, she realized Gus was standing beside her. "I'm sorry about the crack about your height," he told her. "I think you're stunning. With your hair like that, you look like Ingrid Bergman in *Casablanca*."

"Yeah," she said, spinning the stool around so she could face him, "but Humphrey Bogart had to stand on a box when he kissed her. No one says he was too short. They just talk about how tall she was."

He gave a weary nod. "I was hoping that you'd been wearing shoes with thick soles last time—that you weren't really taller than me. And you were hoping I'd shaved off my mustache."

Gretchen shrugged. "I guess that makes us both shallow."

"Good luck," he said, holding out his hand.

"Same to you," she said.

As soon as he was gone, she paid her tab and left. If she was going to meet Mr. Right, it wasn't going to be in a bar. And she seriously wondered if there was such a thing as an unmarried Mr. Right. Dixie had warned them about that. The nice men are all either married or gay. She still thought about that man she'd met at the running club. *Yves.* He wasn't gay, and he had presented himself as a man about to become unmarried. She had allowed herself to fantasize about him. The first man since her divorce she'd had sexual thoughts about. Yves had touched her arm. Twice. And asked for her phone number. But he never called.

When she arrived home, there was a message from Robin fastened to the refrigerator door with a magnet. "Mary Sue called. Call her on her cellular phone. Clay Cartwright had a heart attack."

"Where are you?" Gretchen asked as soon as Mary Sue answered.

"In the intensive care waiting room at St. John's."

"How bad is it?"

"Clay was unconscious when Pamela found him and had stopped breathing by the time the paramedics arrived."

"How's Pamela?"

"Surprisingly strong."

"I'll change and be right over."

"No, Dixie is here now. We'll stay through the night. Why don't you relieve us in the morning? Someone needs to be here with Pamela. Robin said you had a date and looked really nice. How was it?"

"I met Gus the Mustache Man again. He won't shave it off, and I can't shrink a couple of inches. We are not a match. I thought about picking up someone, but the one time I picked up a man in a bar, it didn't go well. You know, I've only had sex with two men in my life. Joe Markowski forced himself on me, and Paul Bonner walked out on me."

"You need to be courted."

"Courted? God, that sounds so old-fashioned. But wouldn't it be wonderful? I read once that Gloria Steinem said that's the time in a woman's life when she has the most power—during courtship. You know, that's the first time I've said that ghastly man's name out loud in all these years. You're still the only one who knows."

"And I always will be unless you decide to tell someone else."

"I love you, Mary Sue. You're the keeper of all our secrets and the best friend any of us have ever had."

"I love you, too, honey. I don't know what I would do without my friends. Get some sleep. I'll see you in the morning. We'll have breakfast before I go home."

"Is Clay going to live?"

"It's touch and go."

"Why couldn't it have been Paul."

"You don't mean that."

"Yes, I do. I would have waited before dialing nine-one-one."

Pamela couldn't sit still, so Mary Sue and Dixie took turns walking with her up and down the fifth-floor hallways. Mary Sue was with her when she stopped at a pay phone to place a transatlantic call to stepdaughter Prissy, who would have the task of telling her pregnant sister about their father's heart attack. Mary Sue listened while Pamela tried to be hopeful, telling Prissy that her father's underlying health was good and he had the will to live, especially with a grandchild on the way. But this was a major heart attack. "No, don't hop on a plane yet. Let's see how things go tomorrow."

Pamela took a deep breath as she hung up the phone. "She said she was grateful her father had such a loving woman to look after him. I'm not feeling very loving right now, however."

Mary Sue took her arm, and they began walking again.

"I went to Martin's house last night," Pamela confessed.

"I thought you probably did."

"The place is a wreck. Nothing is the same as before."

"It's been a long time."

"We screwed on a mattress, then he propped up the pillows behind his head and said he needed help on the plot for his next book. It was unreal. He's lying there stark naked, telling me that he always got good ideas when he talked writing with me, and the only thing he'd ever sold—a short story to *Esquire*—was one I had doctored for him. It had taken him years to acknowledge I had been right and finally to send the thing off. He said I was always able to point out flaws and call him down when he got too pretentious. I told him to write in his own voice—in the voice of a pork-eating American Jew from Kansas who loved movies, football, and rock-and-roll and was facing lifelong guilt because he was not a good Jew like his brother. Now Martin realizes I was right. He needs me to keep him on track. He wants us to get married and be a team. I would get to be the woman behind the great man and get my name listed in the acknowledgments. Did you know that Martin and I had sex that summer after our freshman year?"

"I thought you might have."

"Did Gretchen and Dixie know?"

"You were pretty distracted, but no one knew for sure."

"Well, we did. All summer long. Monday through Friday while his father was at work. He said his bedroom was a temple for our love. Anyway, I've been remembering the greatest sex of a lifetime and turning to mush every time I hear Olivia Newton-John sing 'If You Love Me,' and he's been longing for all those discussions about writing he had after we screwed. The first time I went over there he had clean sheets and a candle, but the 'temple' got skuzzy after that. He claims that he wanted to propose back then but wasn't strong enough to stand up to his parents and to his brother, Jake the Holy One. Then back at Yale, he got a lot of encouragement from a creative writing professor and decided he didn't need me after all. There was no point in upsetting his family. So he never answered my letters. Never called. His wife's family has old money."

They stopped by a bank of vending machines and dumped coins into the hot beverage machine.

"I don't want my husband to die," Pamela said, punching the hot chocolate button.

"I know you don't."

"Yes, but you don't know the reason why. I want Clay to get well so I can sort out how I feel about him and myself—about being married. *I* want to make the decision about whether or not to stay married. I don't want it made for me."

Mary Sue resumed her seat in the waiting room while Pamela went back to her vigil at her husband's bedside.

Yes, she had been the keeper of the secrets, Mary Sue thought, picking up a magazine to thumb through. And now she had another one. Pamela had stepped out on her husband, on the exalted Judge Clay Cartwright. Who would have ever dreamed such a thing? It was absolutely amazing. She had to suppress a giggle.

Years ago, the secrets had been about small things. Dixie confessing that she had cheated on a spelling test. Gretchen admitting she spied on her parents while they were having sex. Pamela losing one of her mother's pearl earrings down the bathroom drain and allowing poor retarded Danny to take the blame.

Then as they grew older, the burden of their secrets grew heavier. Mary Sue knew why Pamela's brother had been sent to live elsewhere. She had been the one Gretchen called after she was raped. She knew that Dixie had secret trips abroad, which must surely involve a married man—why else would they be a secret? And now, she alone knew that Pamela had been unfaithful to her husband.

But there was one secret they hadn't shared with her. Not one of the three had told her what happened to Walter. Mary Sue knew that they knew; otherwise they would tell her to shut up with all her speculation about what could have happened to him. They would tell her they were tired of listening to it. Tired of talking about it. *Just cool it, all right,* they would say. *The jerk was either dead or hiding out.*

But someday one of them would tell her. They always did. It was a habit of almost forty years' duration.

Did they never wonder about her own secrets? They came to her because they could not bear the burden of their secret alone and knew she would not betray them. Which was true. They thought she was so good, so above reproach. What she was, however, was a fraud. Oh, she kept their secrets all right. But she was their very best friend and the safest of confessors because she needed them to love her best of all and would never do anything to jeopardize that love. Their love defined her. Without it, she wasn't sure who she would be. Her husband had left her. Her children were perched on the brink of adulthood and would soon go their own way. But her friends would be with her always.

Clay regained consciousness about 5:00 A.M. "He opened his eyes and said 'I thought you weren't coming back,'" Pamela told Mary Sue.

"And what did you say?" Mary Sue asked.

"I told him that I had considered it and wanted him to get better so I could see what it felt like to not be afraid of him."

"Incredible," Mary Sue said. "What about Martin? Are you going to see him again?"

"No. For a quarter of a century I'd been dreaming of screwing him again, and when I finally did, it was boring. Which was a liberating revelation. I'm not afraid of Clay, and I've discarded my Martin baggage. It feels quite wonderful. And frightening. I feel like I've just jumped out of an airplane without checking to see if I have a parachute on, but God what a view."

Chapter Twenty

$\mathcal{D}$ixie *spotted her the minute* she entered the hospital waiting room. *Grace Corona.* The redhead from Walter's bedroom.

Dixie put on her reading glasses by way of disguise and walked with her face turned away from Grace's side of the room. She seated herself so that she wouldn't be in the woman's line of vision but could lean forward every so often to steal a glance.

Grace was with two men, one middle-aged, the other younger. Dixie was able to catch snatches of their conversation from across the room. They talked about a patient in intensive care. His name was Andy. Was Andy the man who'd been with Grace in the restaurant? The man who might or might not be her husband?

The wheels in Dixie's mind were turning so fast, it was difficult for her to follow the conversation of Mary Sue and Pamela, both seated next to her. She did notice, of course, how *un*hysterical Pamela was. Her husband was in intensive care, but her hands were not wringing and her eyes were dry.

When Pamela left for Clay's bedside, Dixie asked Mary Sue what was going on. Mary Sue shrugged. Pamela was just being strong. That's what Clay needed right now—a strong wife. And if he died, she needed to be strong for herself.

"Do you know that woman?" Mary Sue asked.

"Who?"

"The glamorous redhead."

"No," Dixie said. "I was just admiring her coloring. She reminds me of that movie star who played in Westerns with John Wayne."

"Maureen O'Hara?"

"Yeah. Or was it Maureen O'Sullivan?"

"She's a dentist," Mary Sue said. "I'm sure she doesn't remember me, but I met her when Walter took me to a county dental society banquet. Her husband is an orthodontist."

As it turned out, Dixie could see that Grace did remember Mary Sue. When Mary Sue headed for the ladies' room, Grace's gaze followed her all the way down the hall. When Mary Sue came back up the hall, she looked away. Fingers of worry picked at Dixie's mind.

At midnight, Mary Sue told Dixie to go home. She had a store to open in the morning and a son to get off to Italy. "I'll call you if there's any change," Mary Sue promised. "Pamela knows you need to get Kirk off. I'll stay until Gretchen comes in the morning. You can take the afternoon shift."

"It isn't so much getting Kirk off as all those floral displays for the Robertson funeral I need to finish up in the morning. Miss McFadden won't work overtime anymore. I'll have to get up at dawn to have them ready, but I'll stay here a little longer. I'd like to know Clay's out of danger."

Dixie headed for the bathroom next. When she was out of Mary Sue's sight, she used her cell phone to call Gretchen. "Sorry to wake you. There's no change with Clay, but I just wanted to give you a heads-up. Dr. Grace Corona is in the intensive care waiting room."

Dixie waited for Gretchen to respond. "Are you still there?"

"Yeah. Did she recognize you?"

"I don't think so. But she stared at Mary Sue. Mary Sue says they met once at some dental thing."

"I'm more noticeable than you are."

"Maybe she'll be gone by the time you get here," Dixie said. "I didn't say anything to Pamela. She's got enough on her mind. I don't suppose in all your sleuthing, you found out Grace's husband's name?"

"Yeah. It's Andrew. He's an orthodontist."

"Oh, dear. Andrew is in intensive care," Dixie said.

"Jesus. I hope he doesn't die. If he dies, she might go to the police and tell them she was in Walter's house the night he disappeared, along with two weird women, one of whom was tall."

Pamela was sitting with Mary Sue when Dixie got back from the restroom. "Clay's sleeping," Pamela reported. "Or drugged. He looks like a gray ghost, but the nurse says he's stable. You go on now. I'll see you tomorrow."

Dixie hugged her. "I'll be thinking about you every minute. And I'll keep my cell phone close."

"Turn the damned thing off and enjoy seeing Kirk off on his wonderful adventure," Pamela said. "Tell that darling boy that adulthood sucks, and he should stay a kid as long as he possibly can."

Dixie arrived at home to find that Kirk had left a note on the kitchen table saying that he was packed and ready but needed to stop at Wal-Mart on the way out of town. He couldn't find his flip-flops or a Frisbee. And he probably should buy some muscle shirts to give the signorinas a thrill. Dixie found the flip-flops and several Frisbees under the back porch. The night air felt so nice she poured a glass of wine and carried it out to the picnic table that resided under the backyard's only landscaping—an oak tree the home's original owners had planted in the 1930s that now canopied over almost the entire backyard. Her mother said she spent her days among flowers and had no desire to plant any at home. The front yard had shrubs that got trimmed in the spring; the backyard with its glorious tree demanded only mowing and raking. The one so-called flowerbed out at the lake house was landscaped with rocks and monkey grass. The monkey grass died. One of the rocks killed Walter.

No thoughts about Walter, Dixie chided herself. *Or the redhead.*

She stared at the moon through the branches, remembering how she and the girlfriends used to spend many a summer day out here—hammering boards onto the tree's lower limbs and draping blankets over others to make a tented tree dwelling of sorts. And they would spend hours digging in the bare dirt under the tree. Dixie's mom was the only one who allowed backyard digging. Sometimes they even flooded the area under the tree and made a mud swamp. One summer they dug an enormous hole in the side yard that became a hideout, cave, or crater on the moon, depending on the game they were playing. Dixie lifted her glass to her easygoing mother. And wondered about the memories her son was going to have of his mother when he was forty-five.

After locking up, she climbed the stairs. Kirk's room was dark, his door open. "I'm awake," he called out by way of invitation.

She sat on the side of his bed and stroked his thick, dark hair. "Just yesterday you were my little boy learning to ride a bike and playing T-ball. Now you are eighteen and going off on your own to a foreign land. How come you grew up so fast?"

"It wasn't fast. I've been working at it my entire life. How's Mr. Cartwright?"

"Alive. In intensive care. I guess the next twenty-four hours will tell the story."

"That must be strange for you."

"How do you mean?"

"Well, you don't want him to die, but you still won't like him very much if he lives."

Dixie kissed his forehead. "You are wise for your tender years, my darling son. I might like Clay more if he weren't married to one of my best friends. Or if Pamela weren't such a wimp and didn't allow him to bully her all the time. I was a bit of a doormat wife myself, but nothing like Pamela. Maybe Clay's brush with death will make him a nicer person."

"I hope so, for Pamela's sake," he said.

"She said for me to tell you to put off adulthood as long as you can."

"Make up your mind. Am I grown up or just a kid?"

"Both. You get to go back and forth as you please until you graduate from college. Then you have to stop wearing baseball caps indoors and become a man."

Kirk touched his mother's cheek. "Hey, you going to miss me?"

"Big time. And you better miss me at least a little. But mostly I want you to have an absolutely glorious time and savor each moment of your beautiful youth."

"It will be fun in August when you come."

"You know, some people might think it pretty weird for you to be vacationing in Italy with your mom and a man who can't make an honest woman of her."

"Yeah, and I think it's weird that some people vacation at manicured golf resorts or made-up places like Disney World."

"You look like your father, but you got all your other genes from me. You know that, don't you?" she demanded, punching his arm. "Tell me that you know that."

"I am my mother's son," he acknowledged. "I think even Dad is beginning to realize that."

"You and Johnny are the two nicest males I know."

"And Grandpa. He's a nice guy, too. It's time for you to forgive him for being happy."

"We'll see."

"Ah, yes. *We'll see.* The great maternal nonanswer."

"What was the paternal nonanswer?"

"Dad didn't have one. He would automatically say 'no,' so I always asked you instead. If I kept after you and offered a bit of clever bargaining such as promising to clean up my room or rake the leaves, you'd eventually give in. And if it required approval from Dad, you could make him think it was his idea in the first place. After I read *Huckleberry Finn*, it took me a day or two to convince you that we should go to Hannibal. Then you got to work on Dad. You guys were getting along okay back then, weren't you?"

She would have liked to gather this boy of hers in her arms and hold him against her breast as she had done when he was small. But the mother of a grown son had to satisfy herself with a pat or a touch here and there. She took his hand and rubbed it against her cheek. "Yes, we were getting along. We all enjoyed that trip. And all the other trips. Trips were good."

"I think married people don't work hard enough at keeping passion alive."

Dixie laughed. "Hey, buddy, you were batting a hundred until you came up with that remark. Passion is something married people sometimes experience on the rare night they are away from their offspring in a hotel room."

"You wouldn't marry Johnny even if he were free, would you?" he asked.

"No, I would not."

"You're afraid it would ruin things, aren't you?"

"There's more to it than that. I'm not going to move to Italy. Johnny would be a fish out of water in Kansas. But that aside, marriage would alter things. That's inevitable, and I like the way Johnny and I are now. As long as I can go there and float above reality for a time in that beautiful land with that beautiful man, I will do so. And when it ends, I will remember that time in my life fondly."

"Sometimes I think Dad is sorry he didn't stay married to you. If he and Cindy ever got a divorce, would you take him back?"

"It's not even worth thinking about. Your father would find someone else to make him feel young. I wouldn't even make his short list of possible partners. Now, you'd better try to get some sleep. You've got a long journey ahead of you."

She leaned over and kissed him lightly on the lips, then put her face against his hair and felt the ache that comes from loving someone absolutely. "You've done a pretty good job raising your mother," she told him, "and she greatly appreciates it."

She walked down the hall to her bedroom, the same spacious corner room where she had slept as a girl. After her father moved to Myrtle's house, Dixie had considered moving downstairs to the large bedroom her parents had once shared. But her mother had died in that room, and she had already redone the upstairs room to suit her, with wooden blinds and built-in bookcases and desk.

She opened the windows and stared out at the oak tree. When she had grandchildren, they could dig in the dirt all they wanted.

"I miss you, Mother," she whispered, "but your grandson tells me it's time for me to make my peace with Myrtle and Daddy. If Daddy would just stop going on about what a good cook she is, it might be easier. But I guess I could tell him that, couldn't I?"

In bed, she replayed her conversation with Kirk. *His father automatically said no.* It was true. They could never approach Arnie directly with a request. She remembered telling Arnie about Kirk being so taken with *Huckleberry Finn* and wanting to visit Mark Twain's birthplace. She explained to Arnie that she told Kirk a trip to Hannibal was out of the question, that they had already taken a trip to Colorado Springs and his father was much too busy for another trip. Arnie had vetoed her decision, just as she knew he would, and they took Kirk on a riverboat cruise to Hannibal.

Dixie let out a deep sigh. And experienced a moment of euphoria that she was no longer a married woman. No, she would never marry Johnny, for she feared she would face that inevitable day when she found herself telling him why they should not do something just so he would overrule her.

At the airport, when Kirk's flight was announced, Dixie had to cling for a moment, finding farewell harder than she'd thought it was going to be. She'd never been away from her son for two whole months. And when he came back from Italy, he'd be off to college. This was the first step in leaving the nest, which made her feel sad. And old. The pages were turning. Too fast, they were turning.

After she and Kirk had returned from their first trip to Italy, Dixie had enrolled in Italian for Travelers, an evening class held at a nearby community college. She was embarrassed to discover that several of her classmates were also women who had met men in Italy. She felt like a cliché. The instructor, *Professore* Rebori, an aristocratic-looking gentleman from Genoa, warned the ladies that there was no such thing as a sincere Italian man. That was why his wife always accompanied him to class, he explained. She kept him from engaging in insincere behavior.

The formidable *Signora* Rebori collected fees from the students and sold them their grammar book the first night of the class. During subsequent class meetings, she sat in the back of the room with her knitting. And at every class meeting the *professore* would warn his female students about insincere Italian men.

One night *Professore* Rebori told them a story about an American lady who was mistakenly sent to hell when she died. In hell, she found that the police were German, the chefs were English, the mechanics were French, the government officials were Italian, and the lovers were Swiss. When it was discovered she had been misdirected, the American lady was whisked up to heaven, where she happily discovered that the government officials were Swiss, the mechanics were German, the police were English, the chefs were French, and, *of course,* the lovers were Italian.

Dixie had laughed and squirmed at the same time. Would she be just a notch on Johnny's belt?

She continued to accept the occasional date that came along, hoping someone would appear on this side of the ocean who would make her forget all about an Italian man who might very well be insincere. Even if Johnny's marriage was a sexless one, as he implied, he was still a married man. And did she really want a serious relationship with a man she would see only occasionally?

All the while, however, postcards from Johnny continued to arrive, with photographs of *bella Italia* on the front and sweet messages in Italian on the back. And Johnny kept calling to say he missed her and greatly anticipated her next visit. He had the most wonderfully sexy voice—deep and gravelly, with a chuckle to match. She would be euphoric for days after those calls.

And she called him—always late at night her time, when it was early morning in Santo Stefano and he had not yet left his little house in the middle of the vineyard. She would have scripted a few Italian sentences to try out on him, to which he always said, *"Brava!"* and insisted that all it would take for her to be fluent was a month in Italy. By then, however, she realized she would never be fluent, that the time in her life for actually mastering a second language had long passed. But she would do the best she could. The last night of the evening class, she told the Reboris that she would be back for the next session.

By the time the next session started, however, she'd been called home to Garden Grove for her mother's final illness. In the months that followed her mother's death, she sold her home in Sauganash and moved back home for good. It was April before she made her return trip to Italy. Her cover story was a florist convention in Toronto.

The day before she left, Dixie gave Mary Sue an international phone number with no explanation other than to call her if there was an emergency. Mary Sue promised that she would check on Kirk and her father periodically to make sure they were getting along okay.

Going back to Italy was the most outrageous thing she had ever done in her life. As the time grew closer, she realized the trip was about more than seeing a nice man once again. It was about finding the courage to live on and not join the ranks of divorced women for whom bitterness becomes their life's blood.

Johnny was waiting when she emerged from customs in the Rome airport. He was all dressed up, and she was in blue jeans. They had a moment of acute shyness until he wrapped his arms around her and told her it was the happiest day of his life. Even so, a little voice in Dixie's head wondered how many other gullible American women he had met at the Rome airport.

The first hour, it took all of Johnny's attention just to navigate his small car through the maze of traffic and reach the *autostrada*. By the time they exited the autostrada and began winding their way into the foothills, it was midafternoon.

They stopped for lunch at a small roadside *trattoria*. At first the elderly *signora* insisted she was not open for *pranzo*. But Johnny went to the corner cabinet and began taking out dishes and silverware. Dixie understood part of what he told the woman—the American lady was hungry and had come a long way just to eat Italian food and drink Italian wine. Soon he had the woman laughing and playfully shaking her finger at him. Johnny took Dixie's hand and they followed the woman into her kitchen, where she put a pot of water on the stove to cook the pasta. Johnny helped her put out the food on the roughhewn kitchen table. The three of them ate and drank together. Johnny and the *signora* compared the dialects of their respective towns, laughing uproariously at some of the words, which Dixie decided must be sexual in nature.

It was early evening when they arrived at the tiny house in the middle of the vineyard. Johnny had painted it inside and out. The wooden floor was scrubbed, the furniture polished, the windows spotless. Containers with fresh flowers were on the table, bookcase, china cabinet, and shelf over the bed. The bed in its alcove had been made with military precision.

Suddenly she was shy again. How did they proceed? Did she even want to?

She could not have sex with him in daylight. Not the first time anyway. She would prefer to wait for darkness.

But again his arms came around her and he whispered, *"Mio tesoro."*

Tesoro. He was calling her his treasure. Which was lovely. Now he was kissing her. Really kissing her. Her mouth, her eyes, her throat. And a sweet, syrupy warmth she had not felt in oh so very long began to seep into her veins and flow through her body.

The solid, earthy reality of him was overwhelming—his muscular body, his warm breath, his male scent, the timbre of his voice, the evidence all around her of just how greatly he had anticipated her arrival. And there was reality in moisture between her legs, the pounding of her heart, the tingling in her skin. She was alive and wanted this man very much. In daylight or darkness.

The armoire by the bed had a mirror on the door. She could both feel and see them making love. Two people in middle life who were fortunate enough to taste genuine passion once again.

Afterward they dozed. And when they awoke, they made love again. Dixie would have been perfectly content to spend the entire evening there, eating whatever food Johnny had on hand. But Johnny had other plans. They were expected in town. She was to wear a pretty dress.

They went to his aunt's house and ate mountains of wonderful, hearty food. The windows of the aunt's apartment overlooked the entire valley. Several friends and cousins were there. "But you are married," Dixie whispered, acutely conscious that her lips were swollen and the skin on her face was burnished from lovemaking. She felt as though she had the word "sex" written across her forehead.

"Yes, but they understand about my life. They know that you have made me happy."

How odd, that she was being made to feel welcome in a country that made divorce next to impossible. Or maybe because it was so difficult, they had learned to look the other way when someone stole a bit of happiness. But welcome or not, she felt uncomfortable and was relieved when they said goodnight.

Dixie had arrived on Friday. On Sunday, when Johnny said he planned to spend the afternoon with his wife and daughter, she almost packed up and left.

Johnny could not understand her fury. Dixie had known his situation. He had never made it a secret. He went to his wife's house once a week to eat a meal and help with the chores and spend time with his daughter.

Dixie watched while he loaded a case of wine and one of the containers of flowers in his car. Dixie wanted to protest that those were *her* flowers. He took a basket and picked salad greens that had already ripened in his garden.

When he tried to kiss her goodbye, she slapped him. "I don't want to be the other woman."

Of course, he didn't understand the term "other woman."

She told him she felt no better than the woman who had stolen away her own husband. She felt like a bad person.

"If I do *not* go to my wife and daughter, you will feel like a good person?" he asked, picking up a bag of laundry from beside the armoire.

"Oh, my God! Does your wife do your laundry?"

"Yes, she wash the laundry. Do wives in America not wash the laundry?"

"What about the sheets?" she shrieked, pointing at the bed. "Did she wash the sheets on the bed? Have we been making love on sheets that your wife washed?"

When he didn't answer, Dixie began ripping the bedding from the bed and throwing it on the floor. She was crying uncontrollably. Johnny left her like that.

She packed her clothes and put the suitcase by the door.

She needed to call the airline and change her return ticket but didn't know how to use the phone. And she didn't know how she was going to get herself from Santo Stefano to Rome.

She carried the remaining flowers outside and threw them onto a compost pile. Then she opened every drawer and cabinet in the house, examining his possessions, looking for some other reason to hate him, for evidence that she was only one of many women he had brought to this house, evidence to reinforce her decision to leave. She found meticulously kept ledgers and crop records. She found no lingerie tucked in the back of drawers, no feminine toilet articles in the bathroom cabinet. His books were mostly about World War II, and there were several titles dealing with agriculture and winemaking. In a drawer, she found an envelope with three photographs. A young, somber-looking Johnny with an even younger, frightened-looking bride in a homemade wedding dress. The second was of an overdressed baby with huge, solemn eyes. Dixie saw those same eyes in the third photograph of a frail-looking girl of about twelve holding hands with Johnny. Dixie wished for a magnifying glass to better examine the pictures, to better understand this pathetic family that gathered every Sunday afternoon two villages away.

She carried the bridal picture to the window and stared at it in the sunlight. "So what did you expect?" she asked the young Johnny. "That you could screw this young thing and never pay the price?"

Was there always a price? Had she come here thinking she might find a lovely relationship with no price to pay other than a plane ticket? Apparently the price for her was self-esteem. And the sickening feeling that she would now have to forgive Arnie and Cindy for what they had done to her.

She unpacked her clothes once again. Then she rinsed out the bed linens as best she could in the shower and hung them sopping wet over bushes to dry. She walked down the lane and found some sprays of green-ery to replace the missing flowers and set out a simple meal.

They barely spoke over dinner. Dixie's stomach was in knots. Afterward, she asked him to tell her about his daughter.

Her name was Teresa. She had a difficult birth and never had been nor-mal. But she could do more if his wife would just let her. His wife still dressed Teresa and combed her hair. She still bathed and fed her like a baby, claiming the girl would make too much of a mess if left to her own devices. For years, he had begged his wife to let Teresa come here to live with him. He would help her plant a little garden of her very own and teach her about insects and birds. She could have the puppy she had always wanted. But when his wife accused him of wanting to have sex with the girl, he never asked again.

Johnny put his hands on his face and cried. Tears poured from his eyes and between his fingers. Dixie had never seen a man shed so many tears.

The sheets were still wet. Dixie left them on the bushes and smoothed a blanket over the bare mattress. When she led Johnny to the bed, he protested that he had hoed his wife's garden and needed to bathe. Dixie sat on the edge of the bed and pulled him down beside her. For the longest time, she held him in her arms and rubbed his tired muscles. He smelled of earth and hard work.

When he entered her, they both wept.

She realized now that Johnny's life was oppressively sad, but he refused to let the sadness rule his life. He looked for and found what joy there was. He loved his job, his village, and its people. And at this point in time, he did sincerely love her.

They would never marry or even make a home together. Their time together would always be limited, and someday she would be too old to make the journey. But whatever time they had together would be sweet.

The next day, she awoke filled with a need to hear her son's voice. Every-thing was fine, he told her when she called. "Where are you?" he asked.

When she hesitated, when she didn't say she was calling from Canada fast enough, Kirk asked if she had gone to see Johnny. Her first instinct was to deny. Instead she said, "This first time I had to come alone to find out if he was as I remembered."

"Is he?"

"Yes. He wants us both to come during your fall break and has offered to help pay for the tickets. He's still married, Kirk."

"I know. He told me that he always will be."

"Johnny has to be our secret, honey. Other people would never understand. How could they when I don't understand myself? And I don't want your father using it against me."

"I know, Mom."

"What did I ever do to get a son like you?"

"Just lucked out, I guess."

Chapter Twenty-one

Gretchen approached the waiting room cautiously, fearful that Grace Corona might still be there. She couldn't make herself shorter, so in hopes of making herself less noticeable, she had tried to look older and plumper. She was wearing a sack of a dress and no makeup and had tied her hair at the nape of her neck with a piece of yarn.

It took her eyes a minute to adjust her vision to the glare of morning sunlight streaming through the windows. The room was almost empty, with only a nun fingering her rosary, an elderly woman staring at nothing, and Mary Sue smiling, rising, crossing the room. She was wearing jeans and a wrinkled white shirt, her purse dangling from her shoulder, dark smudges under her eyes.

"You look beat," Gretchen said with a hug.

"You don't look so good yourself. Do you feel okay?"

"I'm okay," she said. "How's His Highness the Judge?"

"Pamela says he seems to be doing okay," Mary Sue said. "He's awake, and she's with him now. The doctor says that with no setbacks he probably can go home in four or five days. The wife of one of his other patients didn't get such good news. Remember the redheaded dentist? Her husband died early this morning."

"Oh?" Gretchen said. She had to remind her feet to keep walking. The

230

major reason why Grace Corona would never admit that she had been in Walter Lampley's bedroom the night he disappeared was now dead.

"The man's name was Corona. His wife's name is Grace," Mary Sue explained as they rode down to the basement cafeteria. "I didn't think she remembered me and hadn't even bothered to nod in her direction. But during the night, she asked me if the police were any closer to learning what happened to Walter. And she told me how shocked she had been by his disappearance. Mostly, though, I talked to her brother. He and her son by a previous marriage stayed here with her. The doctor had warned them that her husband probably wouldn't make it through the night. Grace's brother—his name is Jared—said that the man had been as healthy as a horse, or so they thought, until he had a heart attack in his office yesterday morning. Scared the kid he was working on half to death. The poor man never regained consciousness."

"What did you tell her about Walter?" Gretchen asked, as the elevator door slid open.

"That I hadn't heard from the police in months. I also told her that Walter dumped me when he found out I had breast cancer, even though I was probably the only woman around willing to put up with him. She agreed that Walter could be a real jerk but said he was fun at a party."

"Would you put up with him now—if he came back?"

"I like to think that I'd send him packing. But having a man want you is the most seductive thing in the world. I guess that would be doubly so for a woman with a scarred body."

"You're still the same Mary Sue," Gretchen said, immediately regretting it. None of them were the same as before.

Mary Sue linked arms with her. "No, I'm not, but it's not just the scars. What really changed me was divorce. Just like it changed you. The big D. It's like a huge tornado sweeping through one's life. Nothing is the same as before. There's nothing but debris scattered across the landscape, and I never even saw it coming. I thought Barry loved me. I thought we were happy."

"Yeah, sometimes I wonder how Dixie managed to adjust," Gretchen said. "How come she isn't among the walking wounded?"

"She is calm for a divorced woman," Mary Sue agreed.

After they had gone through the cafeteria line and seated themselves, Mary Sue continued the story of Grace. "Pamela recognized her brother," she said. "Jared was two years ahead of us at Garden Grove High. I don't remember him, but he remembered all four of us. Pamela said Jared was a beanpole in high school—now he has a nice build. And owns an art gallery in the city. He and his wife are getting a divorce."

"And?" Gretchen asked, pouring skim milk into her coffee.

"The first part of the evening he kept talking on his cell phone to someone named Tiffany, who I'm sure is under thirty and probably has augmented boobs. Having someone to talk to helped pass the night for us all, though. When Pamela wasn't with Clay, she was restless and wanted to pace up and down the halls. I walked with her sometimes, but other times she said she needed to be alone. I think she was composing her speech for Clay. She says his heart attack is a chance to start over. She wants new ground rules for their marriage."

"Such as?" Gretchen asked, emptying a packet of honey into her oatmeal.

"Going out in the evenings with us. Spending more time with Danny. Getting a job. That kind of thing, I guess."

"Did Grace remember us from high school?" Gretchen tried to make her voice sound casual.

"She was two years behind us, but she ran track in junior high and remembers seeing you win state. She was quite impressed and thought you would go to the Olympics someday."

The bite of oatmeal in Gretchen's throat threatened to choke her. *Grace Corona saw her win state.*

Was that why she stared at her in the restaurant? Maybe she realized that the tall athletic girl who won state in the fifteen hundred meters was the tall athletic woman she saw in Walter's bedroom.

❋ ❋ ❋

Josh Kamp, the cardiologist, was an old friend of Clay's dating back to their crew days at Harvard. After his morning rounds, he took Pamela to the lobby snack bar for coffee.

"You have your work cut out for you," he said.

"How do you mean?"

"Well, that husband of yours is a stubborn man. It's going to be up to you to see that he takes his medication on schedule, loses weight, eats right, and exercises every day, and I do mean *every day*—no exceptions. And it's essential that he give up lunchtime martinis and restrict himself to just a little wine in the evening. At least he doesn't smoke—we have that to be thankful for. I want you to get a blood pressure cuff and take his pressure every morning and evening. I'll have my nurse give you information about his diet and include tips for heart-healthy cooking."

"I can't follow Clay around to see that he has grilled fish and iced tea for lunch instead of pork chops and martinis," Pamela protested. "I can't make him go to the health club or swim laps. I'll see that we have 'heart-healthy food' at home, but other than that Clay needs to be responsible for his own health."

"Isn't that a little callous?" Josh asked, his left eyebrow arched in disapproval.

"If it were I who had the heart attack, would you be having this conversation with Clay? Would you be telling him it would be his job to take my blood pressure and see that I take my medicine on time and eat plenty of fruits and vegetables and exercise every day?"

"That's different."

"How?"

"Well," he said, sputtering a bit. "Most wives want to fuss over their husbands."

Pamela shrugged. Maybe so. Or maybe they didn't want to lose their meal ticket. Maybe they just pretended to fuss while they spiked their husband's mashed potatoes with butter and told him the ice cream was no-fat frozen yogurt.

If Clay had had his heart attack one day sooner, Pamela realized that she probably would have been hanging on every word Josh said. She would have made Clay's health her mission. Whether he lived or died would be her responsibility.

But she was tired, Pamela realized. Tired of always being fearful that she would anger him. Tired all the way to bedrock. Probably she should have been the one to have the heart attack. Suddenly all those years of being fearful felt as though they were pushing down on her, grinding her up, taking away her substance and her ability to want things other than not making her husband angry.

With Josh's assurances that Clay was out of danger, Pamela went home to bathe and change from the clothes she had been wearing since having sex with a man who wasn't her husband. She had committed adultery with Martin Leonard, a man she used to consider the great love of her life. But she knew now that she never had a great love. Not really. Never even a mediocre one. Not Martin. Not Clay. Not any of those men who came after Martin and before Clay. But Lord, had she tried to turn every one of them into a great love, when maybe if she could have been more realistic in her expectations, she might have found something genuine.

The crotch of her panties had still been damp from sex as she rode in the ambulance to the hospital with her unconscious husband. Now she needed to wash Martin from her body. She needed to douche and shampoo her hair. And it had nothing to do with feeling guilty. She just wanted to be clean.

She felt surreally serene. If Clay died, he died. If he lived, she would either leave him or change the rules of engagement. She had risked all by fucking Martin. The experience gave her distance.

Walking up the front walk of the former home of the Leonard family, Pamela had been on fire. She had been nineteen years old again, on her way to the first time. Every step, every breath was a sexual act. When Martin opened the door, she had all but swooned into his arms.

He accepted her embrace, returned her kiss. "Would you like to go upstairs?" he asked breathlessly.

She didn't want him to ask. It took her back a notch. Maybe he hadn't wanted to have sex at all.

The house had an empty, echoing feel.

Manuscript pages were scattered over two card tables in the dining room. Along with a bottle of wine. Two glasses. Two folding chairs.

Probably he had planned for them to discuss his latest book. Then go upstairs. She was probably rushing him.

But she had too much forward momentum to stop, too much built-up frustration with the woman she had become. She wanted to be that nine-teen-year-old again, with possibilities awaiting her, not a middle-aged woman locked away in a box of her own making.

So up the stairs they awkwardly climbed, not to the same room as before, but to the room that once had been his parents'. There was no bed, just a mattress on the floor. No candle was waiting to be lit, but the sheets were clean. That reassured her.

She expected immediate passion, but Martin needed to talk first. He talked on and on, about how stunned he was when his wife told him he either had to get a job or leave. She no longer believed in him. He needed a woman who believed in him. He needed Pamela. He had never been more on track than that wonderful summer they spent making love and reading and discussing. Every word he had written had been written to show to her, to have her praise him and help him see how he might make it better. He needed that again. What a fool he had been to let her get away. But he had been young and concerned about his parents, his brother, and his immortal soul.

Finally he was rolling on top of her, entering her. Still he kept talking. How different his life would have been if he had married Pamela. He would be somebody by now.

He kept talking while she went into the bathroom, while she put her clothes back on.

He was still lying on the mattress talking, his arms under his head, when she told him she was leaving. "But I thought we could go downstairs and look at some pages," he said.

"Get a day job, Martin, even if it's driving a taxi. And in the evenings, try writing a book from a female viewpoint. Write a book about a woman married to a man who sat home all day writing books that never sold. Write about her feeling herself getting older and needing something more. How she needed for him to look at her once in a while and really see her, and really listen to her, and try to understand how she felt. How she finally had the courage to kick him out. How that day was the most glorious day in her entire life, because even if she took him back, it would be on *her* terms."

"Will you come back tomorrow?" he asked, sitting up now, pulling the sheet across his middle.

"No."

"You're not coming back at all, are you? After I came back here to be with you?"

"You came back here because you had no place else to go."

On the way down the stairs, she had started laughing. She had come here in search of a life-changing event. And that was what she had found. She just hadn't expected it to be a goddamned farce. But God, it would make a perfect short story. Martin would never write it, though. He wouldn't know a good story if it hit him in the face.

Driving home, she thought of the confrontation with Clay that awaited her. He would demand to know where she had been. She wished she had the courage to tell him she'd been fucking an old boyfriend. Instead, she would tell him how upset she had been by his insensitivity. And somehow try to defuse the situation. As she always did. Probably she would end up apologizing. And hate herself for it. But what was her alternative?

She didn't want to find sustenance in hate, as Gretchen had done. She didn't want to be like Mary Sue and settle for a run-of-the-mill jerk just so she could have a man in her life. And she didn't want to be an ordinary shopkeeper, like Dixie. Years of being Mrs. Clay Cartwright had molded her. Without her marriage, who would she be?

When she found Clay on the floor by his desk, she made the 911 call and sat on the floor beside him holding his unconscious form in her arms, telling him she hoped he would be all right because she wanted them to start over.

That had been only ten hours ago, she thought as she parked her car in the gracious circle drive in front of her gracious house. She went to the study and looked at the place on the floor where Clay had been lying. He had been waiting for her at his desk, apparently. Ready to give her a tongue-lashing from a position of power. And to set limits on her future behavior. Perhaps his anger had triggered the waiting heart attack. Which served him right.

Under a hot, stinging shower, she washed Martin from her body, and then she transferred to the tub for a long soak. She was achingly tired and the hot water felt therapeutic. Erotic even. Better than sex, she thought with a rueful chuckle. Sex was probably the most overrated of all human activities. Eating and drinking were far more dependable. And genuine friendship. That was the best of all.

In spite of the warm weather, she put on a black suit with a choker of pearls at her throat—serious clothing for a serious conversation that could set the tone for the rest of her marriage.

Mary Sue thought Pamela should put off her "conversation" with Clay until he was up and around and she was sure he was thinking clearly. But Pamela had this last-train-out-of-the-station kind of feeling. And she didn't care if Clay was thinking clearly or not. All that mattered was that he listen to her and understand her message. If she was going to change her marriage, it was now or never.

If the sex had been glorious with Martin, she might have decided to end her marriage, but she would have been leaving one self-centered man for another. She thought of a joke that Gretchen had told her: *How many men did it take to change a light bulb? Only one. He just stands there and waits for the world to revolve around him.*

Clay knew all the judges and would outmaneuver her in any divorce court. She would end up in greatly diminished circumstances like her three best friends. And she'd lose her status in the community, which was based 100 percent on being Clay's wife.

She didn't want diminished circumstances. She had too much invested in this marriage to throw it away. And who was Clay going to find to replace her at his age? She had seen a crack in his armor yesterday. He was afraid of losing her. She, too, had power, it seemed.

At the hospital, she squared her shoulders and marched to his bedside. She hadn't planned to bring up Danny. Not yet. She would start with a job. She wanted to work at least a couple of days a week. Maybe at an art museum in the city. Or maybe she would go back to school.

But as soon as she kissed Clay's forehead, she announced, "When you're up and about, I'm going to drive Danny down to Texas to see Mother and Daddy. Daddy's not well, and Danny hasn't been on a motor trip in years. Not since we were kids. And I'm going to fix up Janice's old bedroom for him. I want him to spend every other weekend with us and stay with us during holidays."

Clay was frowning. "Why are you bringing this up now?" he said. "I've just had a heart attack and here you are deliberately trying to upset me."

Pamela hesitated. He did seem weak, as if it was an effort to speak. And his color wasn't good. Maybe she should wait a day or two.

"Well, I'm waiting," he said.

She answered with a question of her own. "Why does Danny upset you? I've never understood that. He's my brother, and you wouldn't even let him come to our wedding. I should have stood up to you then. And last Christmas—just think how Danny would have enjoyed the singing and the bonfire. But you didn't want him. You didn't want him to have Christmas dinner in our home, and I was too gutless to stand up to you."

"Your brother is better off with his own kind," Clay said.

"What if Janet's baby is Down's syndrome? Would you want her to send it to live with its 'own kind'?"

His face registered his horror. "God, Pamela, what a despicably horrible thing for you to say."

"Hey, it happens. It happened to my parents. It could happen to Janet and Phillip. Danny is not a monster, Clay. He's a sweet, lovable man who happens to be mentally challenged. I love my brother, and I plan to include him more in our lives. Or if you prefer, in just my life. But he will come to my home whenever he wants to."

"Goddamn it, woman, it's my home, too. I bought and paid for it."

Pamela glanced at the heart monitor. The lines were busier, spiking more.

He followed her gaze. "Do you want me to die?" he demanded.

"Of course not. I want you to change. I am forty-five years old, and I still have to ask permission to go out at night. No longer, Clay. I will enjoy the time I spend with you a lot more when it isn't mandatory. Wouldn't you rather be with a wife who *wants* to be with you and who isn't there just because she's afraid of making you mad?"

She watched the anger slowly leave his face, leaving it sagging and older. He prided himself on being youthful, but at this moment Clay looked like an old man—a pathetic old man, with tears welling in his eyes. "Have you ever loved me?" he asked.

Pamela remembered asking him the very same question the evening of Mary Sue's surgery. The night after they'd put Walter Lampley's body in the lake. "I certainly loved you for rescuing me from spinsterhood," she offered. "Which you unquestionably did, even though I made it seem I was giving up a busy social life and lots of gentlemen friends. And I *wanted* to love you, even convinced myself that I loved you. I loved having your name and loved our home. But you were my warden, and it's hard to love your warden."

Chapter Twenty-two

$\mathscr{M}$ary Sue had taken a sleeping pill—not the over-the-counter variety but one that had been prescribed after her surgery.

When the ringing began, she had to fight her way back to consciousness.

At first she thought it was the telephone and reached for the receiver, only to hear the dial tone.

She glanced at the clock. It was 2:32 in the morning, and her doorbell was ringing. She bolted upright.

Her children!

Someone had come to tell her something had happened to one of her children.

She grabbed her robe and rushed down the stairs. Michelle was attending cheerleader camp in Lawrence and would be locked away in a dorm. Michael was spending the night at his father's and should be sound asleep.

Maybe one of her friends was having a crisis. Clay had been out of the hospital for two weeks, but maybe he'd had another heart attack. But that would have warranted a phone call, not someone coming to the house.

She turned on the porch light and opened the door a chain's length. She half-expected to see a policeman standing there. But it was Barry and Michael in the pool of white light. Michael's right arm was in a cast.

"Oh, my God," Mary Sue gasped, closing the door to unlatch the chain, then jerking it open again. "What happened?" she demanded, reaching for her son.

Michael winced when she touched him. "I skidded on my motorcycle," he said, putting his left arm awkwardly around his mother, leaning into her embrace.

Mary Sue looked up at Barry. "What motorcycle?"

"I bought two small street bikes for us to ride when Michael is with me. We were riding along the river, and he skidded on some gravel. He has a simple fracture of the radius and a couple of cracked ribs. Some abrasions. When we left the hospital, he asked me to bring him home."

Mary Sue followed as Barry helped Michael up the stairs. She pulled back the covers on Michael's bed while Barry helped him in the bathroom.

"He's had some Demerol," Barry said as Mary Sue took off Michael's shoes and tucked him in. "He shouldn't have any trouble sleeping, but he's going to be pretty sore for several days. I'll leave some pain pills and come by in the morning."

Mary Sue sat on the side of the bed and gently kissed her son's battered face and stroked his stiff, peroxided hair. She couldn't hold back the tears. He could have been killed. The doorbell in the night could have been announcing Michael's death.

Barry cleared his throat. "I'll . . . ah, wait for you downstairs," he said and backed out the door.

"Don't be mad at Dad," Michael said. "I talked him into the motorcycles. I told him you didn't need to know."

She used the tail of her bathrobe to dry her tears. "Which makes me very angry, but we'll discuss that later when you're feeling better. For now, I'm very grateful it wasn't worse. And I'm glad to have you home. I've missed you, son."

"Even though I've been a butthead lately?"

"Well, I must admit I've missed the old Michael more than the new one, but I knew the old one was still in there someplace."

"Is it okay if I stay at home while I'm getting well?"

"Of course, it's okay, but you will have to clear it with your father. You're on his and Trish's time now."

"Trish never knows if I'm there half the time."

She kissed him again, on the mouth this time. "I'll go talk to your dad, then check on you before I go back to bed. Just yell if you need me."

"I will. I love you, Mom."

"I love you, too, Michael. I always have, and I always will. Now I'd like to trust you as well."

Before heading back downstairs to face Barry, Mary Sue went to her bathroom, to splash cold water on her face and run a comb through her hair.

Then she squared her shoulders for battle. With each step on the staircase, she felt the fury building within her. *A motorcycle!* Barry knew how she felt about motorcycles. He'd been at her cousin Jack's funeral.

"You son-of-a-bitch!" she said as she marched into the family room with clenched fists, spitting out her words. "You Goddamned, lying son-of-a-bitch!"

Barry's eyes widened at her venom. "Hey, I'm sorry," he said, holding up his hands as though to ward off blows. "I'm really sorry."

He was standing by the window, apparently uncomfortable in the house where he once lived and unsure if he had the right to sit down. Usually he came no farther than the front door. In bad weather, he stepped inside the entry hall if he needed to wait for one or both of the children.

"You bastard, you could have gotten him killed!" Mary Sue said as loudly as she dared, with their injured child upstairs. She wanted to hit Barry. To pick up something and throw it at him.

"I'll get rid of the motorcycles," he told her. "I just thought they would be something for me to do with Michael. Michelle is easier. She drives back and forth to see her friends and sometimes Trish takes her shopping—and she's a pretty good tennis player. But Michael isn't old enough to drive or interested in tennis or golf, and I can't stand that music he plays at a hundred decibels. The motorcycles were fun for both of us. We camped out at Clinton Lake last weekend. It was the best time we'd had since . . ."

Barry's voice trailed off. Mary Sue finished the sentence for him. "Since you moved in with Trish and divorced his mother."

He did not respond.

"For God's sake, Barry, you knew how I felt about motorcycles. You promised me at Jack's funeral that no child of ours would ever have one. You promised me again when Michael was born. And when Jenny and Bob Bertram's son was killed. Of course, you also promised to cleave only unto me and 'til death do us part, so maybe I shouldn't be so surprised. But I hate you for it. You risked our son's life."

"Isn't that a bit melodramatic? He was wearing a helmet."

"So was Mark Bertram."

He shrugged.

"Sit down," Mary Sue commanded.

"Why?"

"We need to talk—about something else."

"*Now?*"

"Yes, *now.*"

He sat down and waited while she went into the kitchen for a drink of water. She started to ask if he wanted anything but changed her mind.

"You've changed things," he said when she returned. "The room looks kind of bare."

"I like it that way." She sat in the rocker facing him.

"What did you do with the family portrait?" he asked, nodding toward the spot over the mantel where a mirror now hung.

"It's in the attic. I thought one of the kids might want it someday."

"It was a good picture. I always liked it."

"Yes, the all-American family, complete with dog. Did you think I was just going to leave it there?"

"I don't know. It just looks odd with it gone. Shep died not long after it was taken."

Mary Sue took a couple of swallows of water then put down the glass. And began to rock. "I found a lump in my left breast. I thought you should know, since what happens to me affects you and our children."

His eyes widened, and he stiffened for the instant he took to shift into his professional mode.

"When did you find it?" he asked, his voice a careful neutral.

"The day before yesterday."

"Where is it?"

"Right there," she said, lifting her arm and pointing to the outside region of the breast.

"Would you mind if I feel it?"

She started to say no. She didn't want him to touch her. But he was after all a physician. She shrugged.

He asked her to lie on the sofa. Then, without exposing any flesh, he reached inside her gown and prodded. "Have you been to see Jose Gomez yet?"

"I have an appointment tomorrow. But it's just a matter a time, isn't it?"

He helped her to a sitting position and sat beside her. "It's just a matter of time for us all, Mary Sue. This could be a benign cyst."

"But you don't think so?"

"Probably not. You'll have to start all over again with the chemo, probably more aggressive treatment this time."

"Do you really think treatment is worthwhile?"

Barry sucked in his breath and tried to grab her hand, but she pulled away. "God, yes, Mary Sue. You don't just give up."

His voice was trembling. Tears were welling in his eyes.

"Except for the kids, giving up doesn't sound all that bad. But I'd like to see them on their own. I'd like to know my grandchildren."

Mary Sue carried her glass to the kitchen and brought Barry a handful of Kleenex. He thanked her and blew his nose. She sat back down in the rocker, needing to keep her distance.

"I hope you are happy," she said.

He looked puzzled. "Unless you're being sarcastic, that's gracious of you to say."

"Not gracious. It's just that I'd hate to think you put me and the kids through all this anguish for an unsuccessful second marriage."

Barry slumped forward, with elbows on knees and hands clasped between his legs in a gesture that reminded Mary Sue of Michael. "Trish is remarkable," he said. "We have a busy social life. Tennis is very important to both of us. And travel. We like traveling. She wants to go to Hong Kong next."

"Yes, you travel the world, and I struggle to pay for a new roof," she observed. "But you didn't answer my question. Are you happy? Or maybe 'happy' is not the right word. Do you still feel that you made the right decision?"

He stared at the mirror over the mantel. "I wanted an exciting new life with Trish, and we have had some good times together. She gets along well with Michelle—Michael can be a problem, but he is with me, too. But I should have been the one to take care of you during the chemo. I thought about it all the time. Maybe if you'd kicked some sense into me when I started pulling away, it never would have come to divorce. Why didn't you put up a fight?"

Mary Sue was stunned. "So the divorce was my fault?"

"No, mostly it was my doing," Barry admitted. "But you didn't try to stop it. You didn't stand up to me or fight for our marriage."

Mary Sue stopped rocking and reminded herself once again of Michael upstairs. She could not scream at Barry.

"By the time I realized what was going on," she said, "you had already seen a lawyer and sheltered your assets. Now you're saying that if I had been more suspicious, maybe hired a private detective and caught you with your pants down and insisted we get counseling or pray together or whatever, that you wouldn't have left me? But you married me because I believed in happily ever after, for God's sake, because you knew I would be your sweet little unquestioning wife. I realized you were restless, but I thought if I just baked more pies and planted more flowers and did enough sit-ups and had a tuck taken in my eyelids, I could make it all better. When I first realized your mind was elsewhere when we made love, I bought *The Joy of Sex* and tried my damnedest to be kinky. I did every weird thing you asked of me, but if I asked you to talk to me, you got mad, even though at the beginning we used to talk about everything. We used to be soulmates and best friends.

But there at the end, you found me repulsive. You even used that word. *Repulsive.* I don't know any word in the entire language that could have been more hurtful. Now you're telling me I should have put up a fight and tried to keep a man from leaving who found me repulsive? Then, after you left, I find out that everyone knew you were being unfaithful to me. It wasn't just Trish, either. You had been screwing around on me for years while I was baking those fucking pies. And now you're telling me that if I'd just tried harder, you wouldn't have divorced me?"

Looking down at his folded hands, he shook his head. "The others were just a game."

"And Trish?"

"I couldn't get over her."

"Go home, Barry," she said.

He stood. "I'll be by to see Michael in the morning."

She nodded.

"I'm sorry, Mary Sue."

"For what? For divorcing me or for the cancer?"

"Both. I wish I were the one with cancer," he said. "I deserve it and you don't."

"For God's sake, Barry, cancer is a crap shoot. You see that every day reading those X rays and scans. It has nothing to do with deserving or not deserving." She covered her face with one hand and shooed him away with the other. "I need for you to leave. *Now!*"

After the front door closed behind him, she wearily got up and turned the lock, engaged the chain guard. Then she turned out the lights and climbed the stairs. Each step was a chore. Just the thought of more chemo made her feel weary and weak.

Michael was sleeping. She touched his hair, then his cheek and throat, just to feel the living flesh of him—*needing* to feel the living flesh of him. Her anger at Barry came surging back. And her horror at realizing how close she'd come to losing her son. She leaned forward and kissed his forehead. So smooth. So young. Her poor wounded little bird. He had wanted to come home to his mother. Which went a long way toward making up for the disrespect of the last months. Punishing her children had never come easily for her. Michael, especially, had been such a willful child that finally Gretchen told her that if she didn't start making him mind, she was going to end up with a monster for a son. Michael had to be punished for the subterfuge, for enticing his father into breaking his promise to her. No matter how repentant Michael was, he had to be reminded that she was still in charge. And she knew just how to do it. She would make him wait until second semester to take driver's education and get his beginner's permit, even if he told her he hated her and threatened to live with his father.

In her dark bedroom, she curled up on the window seat and stared down at the backyard. The moonlight was kind. It didn't show how overgrown the lawn was, how neglected the flowerbeds were. It camouflaged the rotting boards in the deck and the blighted hedge. Mary Sue still managed to keep up with the front yard, but she couldn't keep up with both. Her children helped only under duress and were seldom at home.

Mary Sue was studying for her real estate license, and the first house she planned to sell when she passed the exam was her own. She had dreaded telling her children, but now she felt more focused. They hadn't done their part in helping her take care of the house, and she had to do something to keep the wolves from the door. That meant moving to a more modest neighborhood, which Michelle and Michael would resent. And that resentment would be directed toward her, not the father who had put them in this position. Michael and Michelle had been perfect children the months after her surgery. Then they started carping because there wasn't a cleaning woman and yardman like before, because they had to change their own sheets or sleep on dirty ones, because they couldn't have every damned thing they wanted.

Except now she would probably be starting chemo again. That would change everything. Stronger chemo than before, when she herself was not as strong as before. Not even close. She still tired so easily. Still had problems with her appetite. She would have to rely on her friends to find her a house, to move her. Which they would, of course. Her children, she had to beg or pay, but her girlfriends would do anything for her. She hadn't told them about the lump yet. She hated to be the bearer of such bad news. But she would. Except for Barry, they would be the first to know, before her mother even, and her children. She would call them after she had talked to the oncologist. Except she'd like for Dixie to go with her. She needed a hand to hold.

She reached under her nightgown to feel the lump that would change everything. Just a small bulge about the size of an olive. Barry had not reassured her when he felt it, had not said that she didn't have anything to worry about.

She had not beaten cancer. Probably the best she could hope for was a postponement. Maybe it was irrational, but she felt that, whether it came sooner or later, she now knew the cause of her own death.

Death was too big and dark for her to comprehend, but she felt its presence all around her, felt its breath on the back of her neck, and its fingers tickled her awake in the night.

When the phone rang, Dixie assumed it was Kirk and Johnny, who sometimes gave her a wake-up call. But it was only five-thirty-seven, she realized when she looked at the clock. They wouldn't be that mean.

She almost asked, "Barry who?"

She pulled on her jeans, brushed her teeth, and ran a brush through her hair, and padded downstairs to put on the coffeepot. *Barry Prescott.* What the hell did he want?

When the doorbell rang, she pulled open the door and announced, "This had better be good."

"I'm sorry," Barry said as he followed her to the kitchen. He was quiet while she poured two cups of coffee.

He took a sip, then put down the cup.

Dixie hadn't seen Mary Sue's ex in three years. Not since that last Christmas he and Mary Sue were together. He looked older. And exhausted. But still a very handsome man. Almost too handsome. The sort of man a woman should admire but never trust.

She remembered Barry sitting at this table many times before. Often they would come here after high school parties to eat popcorn and wind down. Her parents allowed her and her brother to bring friends home no matter what the hour. During the college years, her mother kept cots down in the basement so that anyone who shouldn't be driving could spend the night.

"You look beat," she said.

He told her about Michael's motorcycle accident. And about Mary Sue's anger.

Then he was silent. But Dixie knew he hadn't come here at this early hour to tell her about his son's accident.

"I want to go home," Barry finally said, the words coming out in a gasp. Then he buried his face in his hands and started to sob.

Dixie wondered if he was drunk. She thrust a wad of tissue in his hand. Got him a drink of water. He took a sip and choked. Then drank it down.

Dixie reseated herself and waited.

He put the glass on the table and stared at it. "I want to go home," he repeated.

Dixie felt herself frown. "Is there some reason you can't do that?"

"I want to go back to Mary Sue. Mary Sue is my home."

Then Barry started sobbing again. He looked at her with tears streaming down his face. "She's got cancer in her other breast."

Dixie felt herself go rigid. "But the prognosis was good," she protested. "Only a few lymph nodes were involved. She's been taking tamoxifen. Isn't that supposed to keep it from coming back?"

Barry nodded. "Tamoxifen is a good drug, but it's not a guarantee."

"What's going to happen now?" Dixie asked in a whisper, icy fear infiltrating her heart, her mind screaming a silent protest.

"Aggressive chemotherapy," Barry said. "Maybe there's an experimental protocol that will help. She may have years. Many years. Or she may not. Whatever, I want to be with her. When I saw the mammogram of her first tumor, I wanted to be with her. But I was supposed to get married in two days, and she had that dentist hanging around all the time. I couldn't believe she hooked up with him. It made me sick to my stomach to think of her with him."

"She 'hooked up' with him because she was lonely and desperate," Dixie said, grabbing a tissue for herself. "How did you find out about the cancer coming back?"

"She told me when I took Michael home. No one else knows. Not her mother. Not the kids."

"Has the oncologist seen her yet?"

"No, but she let me feel the lump. I could be wrong, but I don't think so." He leaned across the table and grabbed Dixie's hand. "I want you to talk to her, Dixie. Tell her I want to divorce Trish and come back home to her. She doesn't even have to marry me again if she doesn't want to. I just want to live with her and the kids under any terms she sets. Will you do that for me? I know how Mary Sue values your judgment, your pragmatism. She'll listen to you. I need for you to tell her that nobody can take better care of her than I can. I *need* to be the one taking care of her. Please ask her if I can come home."

"Why can't you just ask her yourself?" Dixie said, pulling her hand away.

"Because she hates the sight of me and will instantly say no and tell me to leave without even thinking what it would mean for me to stay."

"And what would it mean?" Dixie demanded.

"That I know how wrong I was. That I am sorry. That I want to start over. That I know I need her more than she needs me. Life has no meaning without her at its center. She was my life. My comfort. My mirror to make me like myself. I don't like myself anymore. In fact, I can't stand myself. You'll do it, won't you? You'll reason with her and let her know how sincere I am?"

"You think she's going to die, don't you? You want to help her die."

"God no. I want to help her live. And as much as humanly possible, I want to make it up to her for what I did. Believe me, Dixie, trying to get her back is the most selfish thing I've ever done in my life, but I feel like I'm going to suffocate if I don't at least try."

"What does Trish say about all this?" Dixie asked.

"I haven't told her."

"And just when did you decide you wanted to get back with Mary Sue?"

Barry shrugged. "It's been coming on for some time, but I guess I didn't really make up my mind until last night."

"Then maybe you're just emotionally overwrought. You need to think about it for a while, make sure that's really what you want to do. If you're sure you don't want to be with Trish anymore, move into an apartment. And help Mary Sue however you can. Be there for her while she goes through chemo again. But I'll tell you, Barry, you have your work cut out for you. You hurt her to the depths of her being. You killed her sparkle. You almost killed her. Mary Sue is the most loving, most forgiving person I have ever known, but I don't think she can ever forgive you, much less learn to love you again."

Dixie had to stop and blow her nose. Then she took a sip of the now tepid coffee and continued. "How can she trust you to love her, Barry? Mary Sue was always a pretty woman, but you left her for a goddess. You're a vain man, Barry. Are you sure you can really trade in your goddess for a breastless woman whose physical beauty is only a memory, no matter how beautiful her soul? Mary Sue's soul wasn't enough for you before. How can she ever believe that it would be now?"

Dixie took a deep breath. But still the words kept coming as she gave way to her anger. "Mary Sue is the dearest person I have ever known. She is good and kind to the core. You couldn't possibly have thought Trish was a finer person. You left Mary Sue for a trophy wife. You left her for a fucking trophy wife! Trouble is, Trish turned out to be as self-centered as you are. And that's just not working, is it? *Poor Barry.* No one makes him feel good about himself anymore. He looks in the mirror now and sees the selfish jerk that he really is. If I were Mary Sue, I'd tell you to go straight to hell. Or better yet, to go back home to the goddess."

Dixie rose and walked through the living room, toward the front door. For a minute, she was afraid Barry wasn't going to follow. But she heard him pushing back his chair. Heard his footsteps on the kitchen floor.

She opened the door, and he walked through. Neither of them offered a word of farewell.

Dixie went back inside and sank onto the staircase. She sprawled there, beating her forehead against a step. She didn't understand anything. Not anything at all. She wanted to scream obscenities to the heavens. Wasn't one bout with cancer enough? Was life just some sort of diabolical board game?

She tried to think of a reason to move as she watched dawn's first light began to seep through the windows and alter the room. As it always did. She felt suspended. Like a jellyfish in water. She might even have dozed for a while. She was still on the steps when Mary Sue arrived with bagels and lattes from Starbucks.

Dixie knew she wasn't a good enough actor to pretend she didn't already know about the lump in Mary Sue's breast and the appointment with the oncologist. And since there was only one person who could have told her these things, Dixie also had to explain that Barry had been here. Which meant she also had to explain what had precipitated his early morning visit. In the end, she found herself doing Barry's bidding, telling Mary Sue that the man who had hurt her more deeply than she had ever thought possible wanted her to take him back.

Chapter Twenty-three

$\mathcal{W}$hen $\mathcal{G}$retchen called, Dixie was putting the final touches on the last of a dozen centerpieces for a Junior League luncheon in the Marriott ballroom—rustic twig baskets filled with arrangements of sunflowers and yarrow with safari sunset for greenery. Normally she would have taken pleasure in the task, but today she was preoccupied. Her thoughts were with Mary Sue. A biopsy was scheduled in the morning.

"Hi, what's up?" Dixie asked, cradling the receiver between ear and shoulder, her voice a careful neutral, not knowing if Mary Sue had talked to Gretchen yet, if she knew about the lump in Mary Sue's breast.

"I need you to help me plan a small garden wedding for a week from Sunday," Gretchen said. Her voice sounded tentative, nervous.

"Oh? Whose garden?"

"Mine."

Dixie's mind raced. Oh, my God, was one of Gretchen's daughters pregnant and in need of a hurry-up wedding? "Who's getting married?" she asked.

"Me."

Dixie's mind took a minute to comprehend, to shift gears. *Gretchen was getting married?*

"You are kidding, aren't you?"

"No."

"Who's the bridegroom?"

"Remember last fall when I got my hopes up over a guy at the running club?"

"Yeah. He asked for your phone number, then went back to wherever it was he came from and never called."

"Well, he's back. This time for good—fully divorced and ready to start a new life in Garden Grove."

"But I saw you *yesterday,* Gretchen. Unless I was unconscious, I don't remember a word being said about plans to get married."

"He hadn't asked me yet."

Dixie put down her clippers and sat on a nearby stool. "Help me, Gretchen. I'm in shock. I need details."

"Well, I thought we'd use the arbor as a backdrop . . ."

"Stop it! You know what I mean. Who is this man?"

"His name is Yves Becker. Three weeks ago, he was watching for me when I drove up at the track. He hadn't called because he was trying to patch things up with his wife, but fortunately for me, that didn't work out."

"Why haven't you said something before now?"

"Pride, I guess. After Gus the Mustache Man, I wanted to be sure before I started talking about him again."

"What does Yves Becker do when he's not running?"

"He's a chef. He plans to open a French restaurant in Mission. His mother is French. He has all his grandmother's recipes."

Alarm bells went off in Dixie's head. *A drifter. No job.* She switched the receiver to the other ear. "How many times has he been married?" she asked.

"God, Dixie, I called you first because I knew you would be the toughest, but can't you at least be diplomatic?"

"How many times?" Dixie repeated.

Gretchen sighed. "He's been married twice. No children. His last wife has mental problems."

Dixie wanted to protest. To ask how she knew that Yves wasn't the one with mental problems. To say the fact that he was a runner didn't mean he was worthy. She was sure there were runners who were totally worthless, who abused their wives or were blatant womanizers.

Or Yves could be a fine human being, Dixie reminded herself. "Do you love him?" she asked, trying for a less challenging tone.

"My heart absolutely turned to mush when I saw him standing there by the gate. That night we went out to dinner in the city—at a fabulous place in the old train station. It was the first time I've dressed up in months. Of course, everything in my closet is dated. We're going shopping tomorrow for a dress for the wedding—Yves thinks I should wear blue. Something soft and flowing. Yves is nice-looking and under sixty. We had a moonlit dinner on his boat last night—he's been living there while he looks for a place to live. I've never had a man cook for me before and fuss over me. *Never.* It felt nice. He proposed. I accepted. We decided there was no point in waiting. He moved in this morning."

"Well, I disagree with you there. I think there's a lot of point in waiting—like getting to know each other."

"Look, Dixie, he can't be after my money since I have none. And he's six-foot-six. I feel positively petite next to him. He's going to fix up my house. He's already rearranged the kitchen."

"Did you want your kitchen rearranged?"

"What difference does it make?" Gretchen demanded. "The man's a chef and knows how kitchens should be arranged. How about saying something nice? How about being happy for me?"

"Are *you* happy?"

"All I want is to not be unhappy. I've been unhappy so long that I worry the condition is habit-forming."

"What do your girls say about this?"

"Robin said she'll love him if he's good to me and kill him if he's not. Debbie says she's withholding judgment. They're coming to the wedding."

"When do I get to meet him?"

"Tomorrow night. He's offered to cook dinner for my three best friends. Clay's invited, too, if he's up to it and Pamela wants him to come."

"Have you talked to Mary Sue?"

"Not yet. We're supposed to meet for lunch at the mall. I'm going to call Pamela as soon as we hang up. I hope she and Mary Sue show a little more enthusiasm than you have."

"I'm sorry, honey. But I worry about you. You need to move on, that's for sure, and I hope like hell that Yves Becker is the right catalyst. Tell me what you like best about him."

"He listens to me. I feel like I can tell him *anything* without him being judgmental."

Dixie drew in her breath. "You haven't told him about Walter, have you?"

"No, but I plan to. We agreed. There are to be no secrets."

"Gretchen, you listen to me. If you were the only one involved, divulging that particular secret would be your call. But you are not the only one involved. It's my secret, too. And Pamela's. It affects Mary Sue. *That* secret has to go with you to the grave."

Pamela was stunned by Gretchen's phone call. Of course, she would come to dinner tomorrow evening and be at the wedding a week from Sunday. Clay, too, if he was feeling well enough.

Then she had pumped Gretchen for details, learning all she could about the unemployed chef from St. Louis. He was born in Houston. Had been married twice before. Was an avid mystery reader, just like Gretchen.

"Have you checked up on him?" Pamela asked.

"What do you mean?"

"Like does he have any money or is he a freeloader?"

"*Pamela,* you are talking to a woman whose daughters are having to work their way through college. I was getting ready to sell my house because I can't afford to live here."

"Yes, a nice house in an upscale neighborhood. You might not have money in the bank, but you do own a major asset. I think you should call the restaurant in St. Louis where Yves says he worked and make sure he's telling the truth. If I were you, I'd want to talk to his ex-wives and find out their side of the story."

"First Dixie and now you. Why can't you just be happy for me?"

"If one of us were about to marry a man we'd just met, wouldn't you be advising caution?" Pamela asked.

"I don't know. Maybe. Or maybe I'd tell you 'nothing ventured, nothing gained.'"

"You haven't said anything to him about Walter Lampley, have you?"

"Jesus!" Gretchen yelped.

"You haven't, have you?" Pamela asked, genuinely concerned. Women did such stupid things when they fancied themselves in love. She herself had once cosigned a note for a man who was going to start a catering business and said he wanted to marry her. It took her years to pay off the debt. Even after she married Clay, she was still paying off that debt. It was one of the many secrets she had never shared with him and never intended to.

"No, I haven't told him about Walter," Gretchen said. "And you don't need to lecture me about the inviolate nature of shared secrets. Dixie has already taken care of that."

When she hung up, Pamela called a private investigator who worked for Clay's old law firm.

Then she started the dishwasher and walked down the hall to the study to tell Clay she was leaving.

She paused to survey the living room. Usually she couldn't resist plumping a cushion or adjusting a tablescape. Now, she just looked.

God, so much stuff. She thought of the hours she had spent accumulating all those paintings and objets d'art. All those throw pillows, some of which had cost as much as a work of art. And silk flowers. She had always hated anything artificial, yet she would let decorators talk her into using silk flower arrangements.

There was too much stuff, she realized. Too much furniture. Too many paintings. Too much opulence. The room looked like a display room at an upscale furniture store designed to entice wealthy women like her to buy, buy, buy.

Only weeks ago, she had been trying to convince Clay they needed to add a garden room onto the back of the house. Not that they needed a garden room; she had just needed another decorating project to fill her days.

Clay was still in his robe, working at his desk. He was still ashen but seemed to be getting stronger. Next week, he was going to start back to work a few hours each day.

"I'm leaving now," she told him.

"Where are you going?" Clay asked, looking at her over the top of his reading glasses.

Pamela sighed her exasperation. She had been telling him every day for the last week that today was the first day for her new job. "I am going to work," she said with a tilt of her chin. She had liked saying that. *Going to work.*

"You mean that museum thing?" he demanded, his voice gruff.

"Yes, *that museum thing.* I have five days of orientation, then I'll be working five hours a day, Tuesday through Friday."

"I told you I didn't want you to do that." His words were clipped. The displeased father speaking to an insubordinate child.

"And *I* told *you* I was starting today," Pamela said, amazed at her firmness. Normally when Clay used his stern voice, she backtracked. And now she got a rush from standing firm. Amazing.

"Who is going to fix my lunch?" he demanded.

"You're not helpless, Clay. There's sliced turkey for sandwiches or some of the lasagna left over from last night."

He took off his reading glasses and gave her the full force of his gaze. "Yes, *low-fat* lasagna that tastes like nothing. What if I decide to order a sausage pizza with extra cheese instead?"

Pamela held up her hands. "We've been through this already, Clay. If you want to eat hundreds of fat grams because you are mad at me, go right ahead. If you are *really* mad at me, you can even drink a couple of martinis and smoke a cigar after you finish the pizza. And not walk twenty minutes on the treadmill. But I won't be the one to have a second heart attack."

Clay scowled at her. Pamela squared her shoulders and met his gaze, waiting for his next challenge.

"We pay the yard man more than you'll be earning giving guided tours to schoolchildren," he said. "You have taken this so-called job to humiliate me."

Pamela felt a flush of anger but kept her voice calm. "Oh, come on, Clay, you sound like an old fogy. I have taken this very real job because I have a minor in art history, and I'm having an identity crisis."

"You're on thin ice, you know. I could throw you out on your ass."

"Not without a hell of a lot of litigation," she said, spitting out the words. "And if you succeeded, what then? Live here in this big house by yourself?"

"I could sell it and move to England to be near my daughters and grandchild. I could teach American jurisprudence at Oxford."

"Look, Clay, I'm not going to argue with you. For almost eighteen years, this marriage has been conducted according to your terms. Now, I need to establish some terms of my own. I was always willing to play by your rules because I enjoyed being your wife and enjoyed this wonderful house and our position in the community."

"So what has changed?"

"I grew up. Isn't that incredible? I will soon be forty-six years old and until just two weeks ago was still asking my husband if it was all right for me to go out with my friends. But I'm not blaming you, Clay. You are a creature of my own making. I let you rule the roost. I let you bar my brother from our home. I gave up my right to have children. I became the wife you wanted me to be. Then one day, there you were, telling me that I couldn't possibly understand how important becoming a grandfather was to you because I had never had children. And you didn't have a clue how insensitive that remark was. You never once asked me if I had any regrets about not having children, if I was still okay with that decision. You never once thanked me for making that sacrifice."

"I knew your behavior had to be some kind of menopausal thing," Clay said. "Maybe it's time you start taking hormones."

"Clay, don't make me sorry that I called nine-one-one."

His mouth hung open for several seconds before he managed to say, "God, Pamela, I don't even know you anymore."

"Then let's get acquainted," she said, sitting on a corner of the desk.

"Let's start over, Clay, and build a better marriage—one that will make us both happy."

She touched his shoulder, but he brushed her hand away. "If you want me to be happy, you'll forget about this stupid *job*."

"And if you want me to be happy, you'll be proud of me and wish me well."

"But I had a heart attack, and you're supposed to look after me," he said, trying to keep his voice stern, but tears of self-pity were welling in his eyes. "What happens if I pass out like before? I could just lie here and die."

Pamela hesitated, almost won over by the amazing sight of her husband's moist eyes. But the hesitation lasted for just a heartbeat or two. She had come too far. She could see landfall on the distant horizon. "I cannot be with you every minute. If you are truly afraid of passing out, you should arrange for a medical-alert device."

"Why do you all of a sudden hate me?"

"I don't hate you, but I have resented you for a long time. I resented you every time you made decisions that affected me without consulting me. You don't really want to live with a resentful woman, do you? With a woman who doesn't speak up because she's afraid not to? I still feel love for you, Clay, for the man you are sometimes and could be all the time. If you could just come down off your high horse, that love could grow."

She went to stand behind him, to lay her cheek against the top of his head, to stroke his shoulders and arms. "We're invited out tomorrow evening. Gretchen is getting married a week from Sunday, and her fiancé is cooking dinner tomorrow evening for her best friends. I plan to go, and I'd like for you to accompany me."

She could feel him gathering himself for a protest. She put a finger over his lips. "Don't, Clay," she said and repeated her words. "I plan to go, and I would like for you to come with me."

Chapter Twenty-four

*M*ary *Sue was late.* Gretchen was beginning to wonder if she was at the wrong end of the mall food court and decided to walk around and look for her. She was gathering up her purse and sacks when she saw Mary Sue standing at the top of the escalator, waving.

Gretchen watched her come down the escalator and weave her way through the tables. She felt almost angry that no one was taking notice of the small woman with big eyes and a lovely smile. Once heads would have turned.

Mary Sue was too thin. Her hair was not full and lustrous as it had been before. There was no bounce in her step. But the smile was still the same. Her big heart was still the same.

"What's going on?" Mary Sue asked as soon as she was seated. "You sounded like you were popping your buttons when you phoned. And you look absolutely radiant. Paul must have dropped dead or you won the lottery." Then she stopped and regarded Gretchen's face. "Or could it be that you're in love?"

"I'm getting married," Gretchen said shyly, and waited expectantly for the good wishes she trusted Mary Sue to provide.

"Oh, my God!" Mary Sue squealed. "Who is he? Do I know him? Is it Gus from the dating service? He turned out to be a nice man after all, didn't he?"

"No, it isn't Gus. He's the man I met last fall at my running club. Yves Becker. He's going to open a restaurant in Mission."

"I love him already," Mary Sue said, getting out of her chair to give Gretchen a hug. "I love him for making you look so happy."

Gretchen did feel happy, supremely so, just as she knew she would when she told Mary Sue. She knew that Mary Sue would not question her judgment, would not tell her she should wait. Mary Sue would celebrate with her. And Gretchen needed desperately to celebrate.

"I'm getting married a week from Sunday with my daughters and my best friends."

"A week from Sunday?"

"Yes. Is that a problem?" Gretchen asked. And then noticed the dark smudges under Mary Sue's eyes. And felt the skin on her face tightening, her flesh growing cold. "You said on the phone that you had something you needed to tell me, too."

"I'm scheduled for surgery a week from Friday," she explained. "Oh, God, Gretchen, I'm so sorry, but I won't be able to be at your wedding. I've got cancer in my other breast."

Gretchen had planned to rush home right after lunch to help Yves settled in. But she stayed on with Mary Sue in the bustling food court, neither one of them doing more than playing with her food. Mary Sue asked question after question—about how Yves proposed, what the girls thought about their mother getting married, what sort of restaurant he planned, whether Gretchen would be involved in the venture. She didn't want to talk much about the new cancer. The doctor said they would know more after a biopsy. She wasn't going to have a reconstruction. Maybe later. She didn't feel strong enough for that now. Not with another round of chemotherapy coming up. Dear God. *More chemo.* That was when she began to cry.

They walked then, slowly up and down the mall. The chemo would be stronger this time. This time, she would lose every hair on her body— even her eyelashes and eyebrows. But it was the lethargy she dreaded the most. Even more than the nausea and the constipation and all the other indignities.

"Do you believe there's a heaven?" Mary Sue asked abruptly.

"I'd like to think so," Gretchen said.

"I've never thought much about it before. I always figured my job was to live a good life whether there was a hereafter or not. Now, I'm finding it hard to face the prospect of nothingness. I'd like to think there would at least be a window so I could look back at my kids from time to time."

They talked on, about their changing image of God, about their children, their failed marriages. They talked about friendship and how much the four of them had all meant to each other. People would stare at the tall woman and the small one, walking arm in arm, pausing occasionally so one of them could blow her nose or wipe her eyes. They bought lattes at Starbucks and sat for a while by a fountain.

"I never thanked you for helping me after that football player . . ." Gretchen shrugged in lieu of finishing the sentence. "Calling you that night was automatic."

Mary Sue waved her hand. "You would have done the same for me. It still haunts you, doesn't it?"

"Sometimes. At least the motel isn't there anymore, and I don't have to drive by it every time I go to Lawrence. Mostly, though, I think about it less because what Paul did to me was worse. What that drunk ape did to me wasn't personal. I was just a convenient female stupid enough to get drunk with a man I didn't know. What Paul did to me was quite personal. He not only left me for another woman, he decided that he never loved me and had wasted twenty-two years of his life being married to me. If I had to pick which one of them should be drawn and quartered, it would be Paul."

"Do you love Yves as much as you loved Paul?" Mary Sue asked.

"No. I'm smitten. I want to be in love, but I'm not sure what love is anymore. I want this marriage to be a good thing for Yves and me, but I am not taking out my heart and giving it to him the way I did with Paul. I won't ever be able to trust a man like that again."

"Barry wants to come back home," Mary Sue said softly.

Gretchen could feel her mouth hanging open and had to consciously close it. Then she had to think of something to say. "He's leaving the tennis queen?"

"He already has. He's moved into a motel yesterday and wants to move back home. That's what he called it—'home.' He wants to be the one helping me after the surgery."

"Are you going to let him?"

"I think so. He brought dinner over last night. The kids were thrilled, with all of us sitting down together at the same table. When he left, I walked out to the car with him and let him put his arms around me. God, Gretchen, I can't tell you how wonderful that felt to have his arms around me again. I felt like I'd arrived home after crawling across a desert."

Mary Sue was sobbing now, her thin shoulders shaking. "I'd been so proud of myself at how strong I'd gotten and how well I was managing on my own. But this second cancer has taken the wind out of my sails. I'm not strong now, and when I'm afraid in the night, I want him to hold me."

Gretchen was stunned when she opened the front door of her house.

The living room had been completely rearranged.

And beyond the living room, the dining room table was now at an angle, with the china cabinet on a different wall. The pictures on the walls had even been moved. The rug from under the dining room table was now in the entry hall.

She heard Yves coming down the stairs. "What do you think?" he asked.

"I can't believe you did this without discussing it with me first."

"I wanted to surprise you. I'm working on the bedroom now." He took her hand and led her upstairs. "I didn't want our bedroom to be just the same as it was when you were married."

The bed was also at an angle. Which left a corner for a defined sitting area. It looked nice, she supposed, but it annoyed the hell out of her that he had just taken over like this.

"Look, the kitchen was one thing. And the garage really did need cleaning out. But you should have asked me before rearranging my furniture."

"Don't you like it?"

She wanted to tell him that it wasn't a question of liking or disliking, that it was her house and he had no right to take over like that.

But the words got caught in her throat.

She felt strange. Lightheaded. Her breathing was starting to come in gasps.

It was all too much. Mary Sue's cancer was back. And in eight days, she was supposed to marry a man she hardly knew. A man who had already moved his clothes into the empty closet where Paul's clothes had once hung. A man whose toothbrush and toiletries now occupied space in her bathroom. A man who wanted her to cut her hair and wear a darker shade of lipstick. A man who had cooked a huge breakfast for her this morning when she told him that she wanted only toast and juice. Maybe it wasn't such a good idea after all.

"Are you all right, darling?" Yves asked, looking intently at her face.

He had just a touch of an accent that cropped up from time to time and supposedly came from spending summers in France as a child, but now Gretchen wondered if it was an affectation.

He was a handsome man. Youthful. Superbly conditioned. A full head of graying hair. A good cook. But maybe his ex-wives had kicked him out because they couldn't stand him.

When he told her about the restaurant he wanted to start, she had imagined a joint endeavor. She would be the smiling hostess, greeting and seating the customers and supervising the wait staff. She envisioned a quaint place filled with antiques and candlelight. Now she wondered if she really wanted to spend every waking moment with this man. What if he expected her to mortgage her house to pay for the restaurant? She needed to ask him about that.

She also needed to explain to him that she didn't like the way he had commandeered her house, but when she opened her mouth to speak, no words came out. Just gasping.

Yves took her arm, led her to the bed that was now in a different place, directed her to sit down, and went racing out of the room. She kept opening and closing her mouth like a goldfish out of its bowl. She was frightened. *Very* frightened.

Yves was back at her side with a paper bag, which he placed over her mouth and nose. He told her in the most soothing, calming voice imaginable to breathe into it. *Slowly. Deeply. In and out. That's it. That's a good girl.*

She was having a panic attack, he explained. His first wife had panic attacks all the time.

When Gretchen's breathing was back to normal, he gently pushed her back onto the bed and began to rub her shoulders and arms. Then he rolled her onto her stomach and massaged her back.

Such strong, practiced hands. He really did give the most wonderful back rubs, a fact that had amazed Gretchen. Other women talked about back-rubbing husbands, but she couldn't remember Paul ever doing that. On their first date, even before they had made love, Yves had rubbed her back. And every night since.

Now he was rubbing away her panic attack and talking to her as one would talk to a hysterical child, telling her that everything was going to be just fine. She'd heard of panic attacks but had never had one—not even when Paul told her he was moving out, that he was leaving her for Mona, his big-busted, twenty-five-year-old secretary. She had screamed and thrown things, but she had not had a panic attack.

She needed to rest, Yves was telling her. She needed to calm down. She had just gotten too overwrought with all the wedding plans. She had been under such stress since her husband left her. She had borne so much pain. So much heartbreak. But he was here now. He would take care of things. He would look after her.

Finally, when Gretchen could feel herself beginning to drift off, she heard him unplug the phone and tiptoe out of the room.

She did allow herself a few minutes of dozing. Then she came awake with a start. And found herself thinking of her last visit to her lawyer's office. Joe Rollater had accused her of not allowing herself one iota of happiness, because if she did, it would be like saying it was all right that Paul divorced her. Was that what she was doing now—backing away from happiness so that she could go on blaming Paul for her unhappy life, so she could go on hating him? All Yves did was rearrange the furniture. Not a capital offense.

Hating Paul had become the center of her life force. It was what gave her strength. Her hate for him was stronger than her love for her daughters or anyone else. That was disturbing to her, but not something she could change.

Or could she?

She could never forgive Paul, but maybe she didn't have to keep on hating him. Maybe she could let the hate go.

Gretchen got out of the bed and went to the window. She wrapped her arms around herself and stared over the treetops, focusing on a distant bank of clouds. If she could let hate go, she would be free to put her daughters first. Free to find some inner peace after so much exhausting turbulence.

She had thought that finding another man was the only way to move on, the only way to get over Paul and deal with the hate that sometimes felt as though it were eating her alive.

Now she wasn't so sure. Maybe the only way to get over Paul was to stop investing so much emotion in hating him. All that hate didn't touch him, but it was destroying her.

Could she do that—let go of the hate?

She went to the dresser and stared at herself in the mirror. Then she went into the bathroom, scrubbed her face, and stared at herself again—at Gretchen, the woman who hated more deeply than she had ever loved.

Being romanced by Yves had given her such a high. Maybe a manic high. A man wanted to be with her. An attractive man. A man with whom she might even fall in love. The first time he had entered her, she felt whole, when so long she had felt empty. Her heart had sung, but her mind had been skeptical. She hadn't told her friends right away because she wanted to be sure, because Yves Becker seemed too good to be true.

Dixie and Pamela were right: She really didn't know the man at all. She should have checked up on him and had even entertained such a thought on her own. But then she pushed it aside. She might find out something that she didn't want to know.

However, whether Yves was as he presented himself wasn't the issue here. She didn't want to be married to a man who rearranged her furniture and commandeered her kitchen. She realized finally that she didn't want to be married to any man at all. Not now, at least. Maybe never.

Yves was in the kitchen chopping vegetables. Lots of vegetables. Making little mountains of chopped carrots, celery, onion, zucchini. "I just figured out that living alone is not the worst thing in the world," she told him. "I am going out into the backyard while you gather up your possessions and leave."

She carried her cellular phone with her, ready to call 911 in case Yves decided to kill her.

The pool and deck were immaculate. She couldn't find any weeds to pull. Yves had pulled them all. He had also pulled out all the marigolds, which had still looked perfectly fine to her but he said were past their prime.

She sat on the edge of the pool with her feet in the sparkling water. And took a deep breath. Breathing was wonderful. She'd never appreciated it quite so much before. She took deep breaths and felt the strength and health of her body.

She dialed Debbie and Robin's phone number in Lawrence. Debbie answered. Breathless. She just had gotten in from class.

"I thought I'd drive over later and bring dinner, if you girls are going to be there," Gretchen said.

"Just you, or you and . . ." She paused. "How do you say his name again?"

"'Eve.' Like Christmas Eve. He's gone." Gretchen studied the back of her house, the spacious yard, the pool. A smaller place would be a relief, she realized. Someplace she could take care of on her own.

"You're not going to get married?" Debbie asked.

"Nope. I asked him to leave. He's packing his things now."

"How come?"

"I started feeling . . ." Gretchen paused, searching for a word, "claustrophobic, I guess. Yeah, *claustrophobic*. Like I couldn't breathe. After years of thinking I would be less of a woman if I didn't have a man in the house, when Yves moved in, he just seemed to suck up all the air."

"Well, I'm glad you discovered this before you married him."

Gretchen gently splashed the water with her feet and admired the muscles in her calves. "Me, too, honey. Big time. So much so, I feel like celebrating. I finally found my way through the divorce maze and am standing at the other side. Poor old Yves was just the last wrong turn before the exit."

"You really think you're through divorcing?"

"Yeah, I do. I might succumb to momentary bouts of rage, but I need to wake up in the morning thinking about something other than how much I hate Paul Bonner."

After Debbie, she called her friends—Mary Sue first—to tell them there would be no wedding. The dinner was still on for tomorrow evening, but she would be doing the cooking.

The calling finished, Gretchen went to peek around the corner of the garage to see if Yves's Jeep was still there. It was.

She strolled about the backyard. She would definitely have to have the exterior of the house painted before she put it on the market, but at least the yard was shipshape.

She took another peek. The Jeep was still there.

Finally, Yves came to the patio door. "I'm leaving. Would you care to explain what the hell happened?"

"The timing was wrong," she said. "I'm sorry. Really sorry."

With the Jeep finally gone, she went back into her house. It took her hours to put the furniture back as it was before—even though it might have looked better the way he had it. While she worked, she planned a course of action.

Tomorrow, she would see what classes she needed to take to become certified as a physical education teacher. Maybe she could even coach track and field.

Maybe there would never be another man for her to truly love. She hoped there would be, but she could accept that there might not be. And it occurred to her that if she had to choose between having a man in her life and having grandchildren, she would take grandchildren.

❋   ❋   ❋

Pamela returned Mary Sue's call on the way home from the museum.

"How did it go today?" Mary Sue asked.

"I think art museums are sacred places," Pamela said. "I am going to be a high priestess of fine art. The guide job is just the beginning."

"Oh, I'm so glad," Mary Sue said so warmly that Pamela could almost feel her smile. "Hey, I need for you to call me back when you're not on the cellular phone. I don't want you to have a wreck."

"I'm only going ten miles an hour," Pamela said. "The traffic is backed up for miles."

"No, call me back."

Pamela exited from the highway and pulled into a grocery store parking lot. With Mary Sue back on the line, she said, "Talk to me. What's going on?"

"First of all, you need to call Gretchen. She's not getting married after all. I'm not sure why, but I think it's for the best. And the second thing is, I'm having surgery next Friday morning. I have cancer in the other breast."

Pamela didn't cry until she got home.

Clay had the table set and had a Schwan's casserole in the oven. He thought she was crying because she was touched by his thoughtfulness. He seemed almost angry when he realized it was about Mary Sue. But he turned off the oven and listened while she babbled on about unfairness and whether there was a god. Just when her own life was going so well, her dearest friend was facing another surgery, more chemotherapy.

"Do you really think your life is going well?" Clay asked hopefully.

Pamela took his hand and nodded. "Very well. But I need your help, Clay. I need this job. I need it very much. And I also need to be with Mary Sue every minute that I possibly can."

Clay stiffened. "So a friend with cancer is more important than a husband with coronary artery disease?" The look of displeasure on his face made him look almost menacing. As if he wanted to strike her.

"You're getting well, Clay. Josh said if you follow all the rules, you'll end up a healthier man than before. Of course, you never would have had the damned heart attack in the first place if you'd done the things he told you to do. He said that he'd warned you repeatedly about your cholesterol and blood pressure. And he said he had expressly told you not to take Viagra and to cut out the martinis and cigars. Mary Sue, who never broke any rules in her life, has an uphill fight ahead of her."

"You knew about the Viagra?" Clay said, his shoulders sagging.

"I figured it out. You must have ordered them online after Josh said he wouldn't give you a prescription until you got your blood pressure down. My God, Clay, did you think you were immortal? That you had special dispensation from the rules of healthy living because you are Clay Cartwright?"

"You knew?" he repeated.

"I never would have allowed you to take the stuff if I'd known about your blood pressure. Sex is nice, but it's not worth a heart attack. Now let's start working together instead of rowing in different directions. Maybe when you are healthy, you can use it again. Maybe not. But we can figure out something, Clay. I'd like a marriage based on honesty and respect instead of secrecy and intimidation. I should have stood up to you from the very beginning. We might have had a different marriage altogether if I'd dug in about having Danny at the wedding, but my mother kept warning me that you might be my last chance, and I was such a coward. I'm not a coward anymore. You can never bully me again. Never. If you do, I'll leave."

Pamela paused, giving him time to digest her flood of words. He looked so old, the poor darling, as if the starch had gone out of him. In spite of her bravado, she felt sorry for him.

"You have to get better before Janet has her baby," she said, "so that we can go to England."

"You'll go with me?"

"If you want me to."

He cleared his throat. "Maybe Danny would like to go."

She had frightened him, Pamela realized. Really frightened him. How incredible. How very incredible.

She took his face between her hands and kissed him. "A trip to Padre Island would be better for Danny, but thank you for the offer. I will remember it always."

She watched as he got the casserole out of the oven and served the plates, while he placed a platter of sliced tomatoes on the table. The balance of power had shifted in their marriage. She could feel it as surely as if the house had shifted on its foundation. He was more afraid of losing her and being alone than he was of losing control. Just as she had once given him power over her, he was now abdicating to her, which wasn't what she wanted at all.

At the end of the meal, they cleaned the kitchen together. A first in all their years of marriage. Pamela acted as though it was the most normal thing in the world for Judge Clay Cartwright to wipe the counters and carry out the trash. He needed for her to praise him, all but begging her for it, asking her if he needed to do anything else, if everything was okay. He even asked if she wanted him to go to the grocery tomorrow.

Was parity not possible in marriage? Pamela wanted their roles to be mutual, but she now wore an unwanted mantle of power.

Always before she had the option of leaving Clay and striking out on her own, but now she had no option. In spite of all her protestations to his physician and to Clay himself that she would not be his keeper, that was exactly what she was. And that meant she could never leave him, never abandon him to fend for himself. The power he had held over her had been an illusion of her own making. The power she now held over him was very real indeed, but it bound her to him more certainly than ever before.

Chapter Twenty-five

After Gretchen had put her house back into its pre-Yves state, she pondered briefly over the mountain of vegetables he had chopped, then assembled a chicken, vegetable, and rice creation that she divided into two dishes—one for tonight in Lawrence and one to feed her friends tomorrow evening. She also baked two no-fat pear cakes and packed grocery bags with staples to stock her daughters' cupboard.

With the exception of the concern she felt for Mary Sue, Gretchen enjoyed a feeling of almost euphoric well-being as she puttered about her kitchen, preparing for an evening with her daughters tonight and with her friends tomorrow night. She was healthy. She loved her daughters. She was blessed with good friends. She was unencumbered matrimonially, which she was beginning to realize could be a blessed state. And she was strong enough to have sent a man packing. She was the sole proprietor of her own space and her own life. She felt so positive that she dared feel hopeful for Mary Sue. Barry was by all accounts a savvy physician and well connected in the medical community and would take an active role in Mary Sue's treatment. Of course, he also was a self-centered piece of slime who deserved to be boiled in oil, but for now, Gretchen was glad he was back in Mary Sue's life. If he wanted to play the role of a repentant white knight, that was fine with her, if it helped Mary Sue. Trish the Tennis Queen, with all her buckets of money, must have really made life hell for him to come crawling back. Or maybe he had a latent streak of decency that had finally migrated to the surface.

She hadn't seen her daughters' apartment since the beginning of the summer session when the three of them had borrowed a truck and hauled two beds, two chests, and a table and two chairs. Robin and Debbie had painted the walls a pale green throughout and added several pieces of secondhand furniture. It still pained Gretchen that Debbie wouldn't be living in the sorority house this fall and Robin would not be going through rush. There were two cultures on the KU campus—the Greeks and the independents. The independents had to forge rudimentary social lives with other students who either disdained Greek life or couldn't afford that lifestyle, or both. Of course, Debbie was already a member of Chi Omega and even without living in the house could pay her dues and attend chapter meetings and social functions. But since her sister would not be joining the sorority, Debbie decided that the money would be better spent on rent and food.

Sitting at their wooden table, Gretchen told them about Mary Sue and was touched when both her daughters got tears in their eyes.

"Poor Michelle and Michael," Robin said. "They must be so frightened. And to think I'd actually felt jealous because Michelle's father is coughing up the money for her to go through rush and join a sorority."

Over dinner Gretchen learned that her older daughter had ended her relationship with the young man whose fraternity pin she had worn all last year. "Jay is a senior now and already interviewing with companies in Japan and Hong Kong," Debbie explained. "He wants to have a good corporate wife to take with him when he heads into the rising sun. I need to finish my degree and get started in a career before I give marriage a try."

"You could always finish school later," Gretchen pointed out, disappointment welling in her chest. Jay was brilliant, handsome, charming, confident, from a good family. He reminded her of Paul at that age. So why had she been so thrilled that he wanted to marry her daughter? A knee-jerk reaction, she supposed. Every mother wants her daughter to have a princess wedding with a princely groom and walk off into the sunset to happily-ever-after, when only a fool would give such an arrangement any more than two-to-one odds. And even if the marriage endured, it most likely would last because the daughter made all the same soul-eroding concessions to husband and marriage that the mother herself had made. Or sometimes it worked the other way around, Gretchen had to acknowledge. There were men who made concessions to domineering wives. She couldn't think of any, but she knew they were out there.

"I don't have a whole lot of faith in marriage," Debbie admitted, leaning toward the refrigerator, taking out another beer. Her tan had faded, but her hair was still a shade or two lighter from the summer sun. Gretchen thought she was beautiful, even though such a thought was probably a bit narcissistic since everyone said they looked so much alike. But Debbie's bone structure and features were finer. Gretchen was a racehorse; Debbie was a gazelle. "I want a degree and a career so that no matter what, I can take care of myself and not be left high and dry like my mother."

Robin was nodding, agreeing with her sister. She wore her lustrous dark hair longer now, so she could pull it back into a clip and not be bothered with it. The tousled look became her. She looked both sexy and vulnerable. With her dark hair and eyes, she was a lovely counterpart to her fair sister. Gretchen thought of them as her sun and moon. Her universe. "I hate to think you girls have a bad opinion of marriage because of what happened to me," she told them.

"To you, to your friends, to most women, it seems," Robin said. "A good number of all those ex-wives of doctors, dentists, and lawyers find themselves sans résumé and looking for jobs at forty or fifty."

"Yeah," Debbie added. "Most of the girls in the Chi Omega house still seem to think that finding Mr. Right is the key to a happy life, when at least half of them have stepfathers and stepmothers and step-grandparents up the kazoo. And the stepmothers are usually not much older than their stepdaughters. Like Mona. It's ridiculous for a woman to spend decades with a man, only to have him hide his assets and run off with his D-cup secretary."

"You ought to see those big tits of hers now," Robin said, her eyes full of mischief as she held her hands out in front of her, mimicking the state of

Mona's bust line. "And her belly looks like it would burst open if you touched it. She is so huge her belly button has turned inside out—you can see it pouching under her maternity clothes, which look like they were made by some tentmaker in Arabia. When she wears shorts, you can see the stretch marks on her thighs. I imagine her whole body is just one big stretch mark by now. She is completely miserable and making sure Daddy is, too. He has to help her out of chairs and wait on her hand and foot."

"They're going to induce her next Wednesday if she hasn't delivered by then," Debbie said.

"Did you know Grandma is coming to help out after the babies are born?" Robin asked her mother.

"I thought Darlene wasn't well," Gretchen said.

"She's not, but Daddy begged her to come for a couple of weeks—or months, or the rest of her life," Debbie said. "Mona's mom has moved to Hawaii with her new boyfriend and won't be coming back to serve on the feed-bathe-and-swaddle patrol. Daddy keeps telling Robin and me that he's counting on us to help out. He doesn't seem to comprehend that because the money we would have been using to attend college is now going into a college fund for his twin sons, we are working our way through and pretty much unavailable for childcare."

"Of course, we'll help out as much as we can," Robin added. "I can hardly wait to see the little guys. And Daddy's excited, too. He's already bought two sets of miniature golf clubs."

"And they bought a minivan to haul around the babies and all the paraphernalia," Debbie said. "He sold his beloved Thunderbird to make room for it in the garage. Mona said he all but wept when he watched some college kid drive off in his vintage T-Bird. I almost feel sorry for him."

Gretchen made no comment. Yes, Paul's life was insane right now. But he would have two precious babies for whom he would probably be a more attentive father than he had ever been for his daughters. That was the pattern. She found it amazing that Robin and Debbie weren't more resentful.

After Gretchen gathered up her things, she felt the need for a sentimental moment. She hugged her daughters and told them how proud she was of them, how much she loved them, how much she looked forward to helping out when they had babies someday. Even if she were off in Hawaii with a new boyfriend, she would come home for as long as they needed and wanted her.

"What if we decide to just get knocked up and forgo the husband part?" Debbie asked.

"Then I won't have to share my grandbabies with their paternal grandmother," Gretchen said, kissing them both goodbye.

"Tell Mary Sue we love her," Debbie said.

On the way back to Garden Grove, Gretchen sang along with Billy Joel and Rod Stewart. Her era. Her music. Paul used to have his own silly rendition of "Da Ya Think I'm Sexy?" She wondered if he had performed it for Mona, who probably didn't know Rod Stewart from Rod Serling. She wondered what Paul listened to in his new minivan—his music or Mona's? Fleetwood Mac or the Backstreet Boys? Debbie claimed Mona was a mental lightweight, but she had been smart enough to rein in money Paul should have given to his daughters and tuck it away for their sons.

Gretchen had such a low opinion of Paul and anyone male that she wondered how she would feel if she had a son. Dixie and Mary Sue adored their sons just as much as she herself adored her daughters. Someday she would probably have a grandson or two. How would she feel about them, knowing that someday they might very well hurt some woman the way Paul had hurt her?

Why did men allow themselves to fall out of love when so often a woman would hang on to love or the notion of love as long as she possibly could? Though she had willingly let go of the notion of loving Yves Becker. Gleefully let go. She was older now, of course. More cynical. But it had seemed like a question of survival. Was that how Paul felt about their marriage? That he had to get out of it if he were to survive?

When Gretchen unlocked her back door and entered her silent house, she felt far less euphoric than she had earlier in the day, after she had reclaimed her house from Yves. Yes, it was definitely time for her to move on. But would a different house seem any less lonely when she came home late at night?

This house was full of memories that once were fond but had become bittersweet or just plain bitter in the wake of children growing up and a husband leaving.

She had been standing here in this kitchen when Paul told her that he no longer loved her, but it was the bedroom where the demise of their marriage had first become apparent to Gretchen. She always had been too reserved in bed. She didn't know if this reserve was innate or the aftermath of twenty minutes in a motel room with Joe Markowski, but Paul used to tell her to loosen up. He complained that she never initiated sex. When he started becoming so distant, she tried. Once she had stepped into the shower with him, and he asked her what in the hell she thought she was doing. When she came to bed naked and brushed her bare breasts against his back, he rolled away from her.

Then there was the night he had proposed they have an open marriage. She could screw whomever she wanted, which meant he was free to do likewise. She had told him "no way." The only man she wanted to have sex with was her husband. She had cried and begged him to see a marriage counselor or minister or urologist or whoever it was that could help solve their problem. He had put on his clothes and left, muttering that the one thing he couldn't stand was a hysterical woman.

Of course, after she had reconstructed the chronology of his affair with Mona, she realized he had already been seeing her at the time he had presented his open-marriage proposal. She knew now that after Mona left her husband, Paul had rented a suite for her at a posh residential inn. One day Gretchen had arrived late for a luncheon at a tearoom next door and had to park in the inn's parking lot. That evening, Paul said he had been driving by and had seen her car there. He had demanded to know what she was doing there. Who was she seeing? Who was she fucking? Then he withdrew his suggestion of an open marriage. No way did he want *his* wife fucking another man.

"But you couldn't have seen my car from the street," Gretchen pointed out. "What were *you* doing in that parking lot?"

He had gotten very angry, telling her she didn't know what she was talking about. Then he had grabbed her and threw her on the bed. When he began ripping at her clothing, Gretchen froze. She was back in that Lawrence motel room with Joe Markowski pulling up her skirt, ripping off her panties. And she did something she hadn't been able to do that long-ago night. She screamed.

Almost instantly Robin and Debbie came running down the hall and burst into their parents' bedroom, Debbie carrying a baseball bat. Paul had told them their mother had been having a nightmare and, with his stunned daughters standing in the middle of the bedroom and his wife hysterical in the marital bed, had pulled on his trousers, grabbed his car keys, and left.

The girls had crawled into bed with her and offered what comfort they could. Gretchen got herself under control and told them everything would be all right. But she knew they didn't believe her.

When Paul came back the next afternoon to gather up his clothing, Gretchen begged him not to leave. She even told him he could have all the affairs he wanted if he would just stay married to her. When he told her she was pitiful, Gretchen ran at him and began pounding him with her fists, biting his shoulder.

To his credit, Paul had not hit her back. He simply backed out of the room, telling her she was not only pitiful, she was insane. He was able to walk out the door wearing a mantle of self-righteousness.

Ah, the ghostly memories this house held, Gretchen thought as she made her way up the stairs. She had lived some of the best and worst moments of her life here.

Gretchen supposed it wasn't so much a question of the memories moving with her when she sold the house as her dragging them along. They were a part of her. Still, it definitely was time for her and them to move on, leaving the house a blank slate for whomever came next.

Maybe she should get a scruffy little apartment in Lawrence, like her daughters. She could wait tables and earn a graduate degree in recreation sciences or whatever they called physical education these days. She could reinvent herself. She didn't want a husband, at least in the foreseeable future, but she wouldn't mind a middle-aged graduate student who was trying to reinvent himself and wanted to shack up every now and then.

But as appealing as that scenario was, Gretchen knew she didn't want to intrude on her daughters' independence by living in Lawrence. If she went back to college, she would enroll at the University of Missouri branch campus in Kansas City. She would be better off staying here in Garden Grove among the friends who had sustained her these many years. Especially Mary Sue. She couldn't leave Mary Sue now, no matter what.

Friday morning, in the hospital waiting room, Dixie had a feeling of déjà vu. Pamela and Gretchen were there. Michelle and Michael. Connie, Mary Sue's mother, had flown in from Florida. Once again the event that had brought them together was the surgical removal of Mary Sue's cancerous breast. The only difference was that Barry, wearing a physician's starched white coat, was sitting on a sofa between his children. Michelle clung to him. From time to time, Barry would drape an arm over Michael's shoulders, and Michael—with his bleached hair, earring, and left arm in a cast— would respond by leaning into his father's body.

Little conversation passed between Connie and her son-in-law. Or between Barry and his former wife's three best friends. Dixie hadn't the faintest idea what to say to him, and she was sure he felt the same about the three of them.

With no reconstruction being performed, the operation was over in less than an hour. When the surgeon came out, she addressed her remarks to Barry. Their conversation was conducted in medicalese until Connie stepped in and demanded the surgeon tell her how her daughter was doing.

Then there was the trek to her bedside in the recovery room. Mary Sue looked smaller and frailer than she had after the first surgery only ten months before. She opened her eyes. Smiled at them. With Barry standing on one side of the bed and the rest of them on the other, they stepped up in turn to kiss Mary Sue, and to offer words of love and hope. Then a nurse indicated their time was up, except for Barry in his white coat, who could stay.

"That's not fair," Gretchen grumbled as they headed for the coffee shop. "He acts like he's still her husband."

"I hear that Trish threw all his clothes out in the front yard and set fire to them," Pamela whispered, so that Michelle and Michael couldn't hear.

Dixie had to smile. Then she had to laugh out loud.

Chapter Twenty-six

Dixie had brought snacks and a video of a Julia Roberts movie. She, Pamela, and Gretchen were spending the evening with Mary Sue in her hospital room. The day after her surgery, Mary Sue was sitting up, going to the bathroom on her own. She planned to go home in the morning. With her out of the hospital, maybe Dixie wouldn't feel guilty about leaving on her trip.

Mary Sue's children and mother had come and gone earlier. She had sent Barry on his way. Now it was just the four old friends. The video went unwatched.

By her own admission, Mary Sue had not touched the bandages, had not even so much as glanced down at her chest when the nurse changed the dressing. She might consider a second reconstruction someday—if it looked as if she was going to live enough years to make it worthwhile.

Dixie winced when Mary Sue said that. So matter-of-factly she said it. The room went momentarily silent.

"Now I regret the first reconstruction," Mary Sue went on. "At least without it, the two sides would match. In the morning, when they let me take a shower, I'm going to look in the mirror. And I will weep." She paused a moment, having to compose herself at the thought of that first look. "Then I think I'll learn just not to look at it. At least it's not an arm or a leg. At least it's not something bad happening to one of my children. *This*, I can deal with," she said indicating the left side of her chest.

She paused again, reaching for a glass of water. Gretchen immediately jumped up and held the glass while Mary Sue sipped through a straw. Then she leaned back and continued her monologue. "When Barry asked if he could come back home, one of the many items I put on the table for discussion was my physical appearance. He's been married to a woman who could pose naked for *Playboy*. I've had both of my breasts removed and will once again be entering months of chemotherapy. I will become even thinner than I am now because most food will once again taste awful. I had just gotten back to the point where I could walk a mile and climb a flight of stairs without losing my breath. Soon I won't have any energy at all and will want to sleep all the time. If Barry and I walk into a restaurant together, people would think I'm his mother. I'm not sure I'm strong enough for that."

Pamela leaned forward and took Mary Sue's hand. "Don't let him bully you into letting him come back if it's not what you really want."

Pamela was actually wearing a pair of blue jeans. Of course, she still managed to look like a fashion plate, with the jeans accompanied by a pale yellow silk blouse, gold jewelry, fabulous belt, and Kenneth Cole crocodile slides, but none of them could remember the last time they had seen her in jeans. Not since she'd married Clay, certainly. She was a working girl now, she explained, and working girls wear jeans on Saturday.

Mary Sue had told her she looked peaceful. Which was true, Dixie decided. The tenseness was gone from Pamela's shoulders. Her hands were still. She didn't keep looking at her watch. She claimed that, in the wake of his heart attack, she and Clay had renegotiated the terms of their marriage.

Dixie found it incredible that Pamela, the classic kowtowing wife, was now telling Mary Sue not to let Barry "bully" her.

Mary Sue smiled and patted Pamela's hand. "I told Barry that I wasn't strong enough or big enough to forgive him and that a part of me would always mistrust him. But he holds the trump card. I *need* him. Having him back home would solve a number of problems. My mother has built a nice life for herself in Sarasota. And she now has a neurotic parrot that pulls out his feathers if she leaves him alone too long. She even has a gentleman friend who squires her around and has called her every day since she arrived here. I don't want her to feel like she has to stay with me indefinitely. I know you guys would take turns helping out, but I don't want to disrupt your lives indefinitely either. Dixie has the store to run, and she absolutely must spend August with Kirk in Italy. Pamela has her wonderful new job at the museum. And Gretchen needs to sell her house and either get a job or go back to college or both. Barry said he would sleep in the guestroom for now, and he plans to move in tomorrow unless I get some sort of legal restraining order. The kids both have begged me to let him come. Even Mom thinks I should give it a try, although she can hardly stand to be in the same room with him."

"But kids and your mom aside, distrust and past history aside, do you want him living in your house?" Gretchen asked. "When it came right down to it, I probably could have dated Yves indefinitely, but I realized I didn't want to live with him. Maybe I don't ever want to live with a man again."

"Your situation is different," Mary Sue said.

"Yeah, I hadn't been married to Yves before," Gretchen agreed. "Being married to him might have been better than my first marriage or it might have been worse, but I realized I no longer have the motivation or will to shape my life around a man's. Which is what I might have ended up doing—a thought that scares me half to death."

"No," Mary Sue said, shaking her head, "your situation is different because you don't have cancer. You are strong and can take care of yourself no matter what. Even though the oncologist tells me the biopsy showed this cancer to be a second primary and not metastasis, and theoretically, a second primary is no more ominous that the first, this tumor happened soon after chemo and in spite of tamoxifen. I don't know about lymph node involvement yet, but under the best circumstances, my health and even my survival are question marks. Barry is coming home to take care of me. I plan to focus on that and not the mistrust and pain. I need him to pay the bills, look after the house, and see that I don't starve. I won't even have to go downstairs on the days I don't feel like it. I won't have to feel guilty when the refrigerator needs cleaning, or when there are no clean towels. Barry's never taken care of stuff like that before, but with Michelle in Lawrence, he'll have to manage. And Michael will have to help. Whether he and Michael do the housework themselves or Barry hires it done, he will be responsible. And he will be the parent to tell Michael to do his homework. Maybe he can get Michael to stop skipping school and mouthing off every time he's asked to do something. I was tired before; now I'm going to be exhausted. And whether it's out of guilt or love or duty, Barry wants to take care of me. He says he wants us to remarry as soon as he's officially divorced from Trish, but I'm not even going to try to sort through that one. Not for a long time."

Mary Sue paused and nodded toward the water. Gretchen held the glass for her again, and Mary Sue took several long sips. Dixie used the pause to grab some tissue and discreetly wipe the tears from her eyes, and blow her nose.

Mary Sue held her hand out in a wordless request for tissue, and Dixie gave her a handful. They watched while she also wiped her eyes and blew her nose. "We went out to dinner night before last, and afterward we had sex at Barry's motel room," she said, her shoulders shaking with sobs. "And you know, he did a pretty damned good job making me feel like he really cared."

They all cried then. Dixie promised they would make life hell for Barry if he didn't do right by her. Then Mary Sue asked Pamela to tell the nurse she needed a shot for pain.

Once the shot had been given, Mary Sue said, "Give me a hug, Dixie, then go home and finish packing. I know you have an early flight in the morning. Someday I wish you would take your friends with you to Italy and show us why you and Kirk keep going back time and time again."

Dixie sat on the side of the bed and put her arms around Mary Sue. "I love you, honey. I always will. You are the dearest of us all."

Why she kept going back to Italy time and time again. Dixie thought about that as she walked through the parking garage. She had cringed a bit at the words. Best friends probably were not supposed to have secrets.

At first, Dixie had not told them about Johnny because they were all properly married. She alone had a failed marriage and worried that they thought the failure was through some fault of hers. Which would have been partly true. She had grown complacent.

She and Arnie enjoyed many of the same things—sports, politics, history, movies. They read many of the same books. They adored their son. They went to all Kirk's sporting events. They vacationed at places they thought Kirk should see—national parks, presidents' homes, Civil War battlefields. They planned for that someday trip to Europe—to Italy especially, with its art and beauty. They had sex two or three times a week.

Dixie thrived on routine. She wrote in the morning and ran errands, cooked, and cleaned in the afternoons. She played mahjong with lady friends every other Thursday afternoon and attended two monthly club meetings. She and Arnie had season tickets to the symphony, their favorite community theater, and the Bulls games. They called their parents every Sunday and went to Kansas often to see their folks and attend KU sporting events.

A good life. Dixie seldom dreamed of anything more. Of course, someday she might try to write something of substance—a biography probably, and to that end kept lists of possible subjects. But for the time being, she enjoyed the magazine pieces she wrote, enjoyed seeing her parenting and travel articles in print. Her small successes gave her a certain cachet among their friends, who had no idea how little she was paid for them. Being a published writer elevated her. She wasn't *just* a housewife.

Then everything changed. Arnie started coming home from work later and later, and when he arrived, he smelled of soap and aftershave, as though he had just stepped out of the shower, which she was quite certain was precisely what he had done.

She tortured herself tying to figure out who the woman was. And found herself imagining her husband having sex with almost every woman she knew that he knew. But she said nothing.

She knew from firsthand experience how an indiscretion could happen, which made her willing to wait until he got whoever it was out of his system and came home wiser and more committed than ever to their marriage.

When she had had an affair, she had barely known the man.

It had happened long ago. Arnie had refused to go to the annual KU alumni gathering in downtown Chicago. Dixie had a new outfit for the occasion and was hell-bent to go. That was about two years into the marriage—rocky times, with the first blush gone. Marriage did not automatically make anything happen. Neither of them was happier or more beautiful or richer for being married. Housework never stayed done. Arnie just wanted to sit in a chair in the evenings, clutching the channel changer. He never told her he loved her unless she said it first. When she suggested they join a coed softball team, he complained that she wanted them to be joined at the hip, that he still wanted to do things with the guys on weekends and putter around in the garage with the 1965 Morgan roadster he had bought for an outrageous price in spite of the fact that they were buried under credit card debt.

The alumni event was in the Hyatt Regency ballroom. The football coach was slated as the dinner speaker. The cheerleaders and a pep band entertained at the predinner reception. One of the people she recognized was a buddy of her brother's from the SAE house. Tom Henderson, his nametag said. He now worked for the KU Alumni Association. He flirted. She drank too much and flirted back. Just a little. Not blatantly. But she was, after all, furious with her husband for not coming and for having the gall to be angry with her because she had.

Tom Henderson told her his wife was a bitch and that he had a room upstairs. The whole episode had a surreal quality about it. She wasn't really getting in that elevator. She wasn't really kissing a man who wasn't her husband. Suddenly they were tugging at clothes, falling into bed. It was over almost before it began. For *that*, she had been an unfaithful wife?

Tom dressed and went back down to the party. Dixie had taken a shower and used lots of soap before putting on her clothes and heading straight for the parking garage.

As luck would have it, Arnie was feeling contrite about not going with her and had tidied up the house and put a bottle of wine on ice. Her faked orgasm had been the performance of a lifetime.

But that had been a one-time indiscretion. Whoever Arnie was fucking, he had been doing it for weeks. Maybe longer.

Every time he spoke to her, she cringed, thinking, *"Here it comes. He's going to tell me he's in love with someone else."* She lost weight and developed a headache that was with her every waking moment. She stopped going to mahjong and club meetings, not wanting to hear people ask if she was ill.

Arnie became impossible, criticizing everything she did and challenging every sentence that came out of her mouth, often in front of Kirk. He no longer liked her cooking, her hair, her driving, her jokes, her family. He brought up things from the past—the time she had been an hour late to pick him up at the airport, the time she had forgotten the name of his boss's wife. He found reasons to get mad at her and storm out the door.

Then suddenly Arnie was coming home on time and was less confrontational. They started having sex again. Dixie breathed a sigh of relief.

She began lightening her hair again and enrolled in a cooking class. When she told him he didn't have to go to her parents' golden anniversary celebration, he acted hurt. Of course he would go. He loved her parents. Later that year, Arnie surprised her with a second honeymoon trip to Buenos Aires. They even renewed their wedding vows.

She assumed they had weathered the worst thing that could happen in a marriage and survived. She fully expected to stay married to Arnie for the rest of her life. She *wanted* to stay married to him. Theirs was not the greatest love the world had ever known, but it was a comfortable, stable marriage that would endure. She felt smugly secure and even started thinking about where they would build their retirement home someday.

Then he started coming home late again. Almost every night. He didn't even try to make excuses. She waited until the next school holiday and sent Kirk to visit his grandparents in Garden Grove. When she got home from the airport, she called a locksmith and an attorney before going upstairs to pack Arnie's things. After the locksmith had changed the locks, she stacked the suitcases and boxes in the middle of Arnie's slot in the garage. On top of the stack she put an envelope with a brief note inside informing him about the locks and telling him her attorney's name and telephone number. Then she turned out all the lights and sat alone in her living room.

When the headlights lit up the front room, her heart began to pound so hard it was painful. She listened while the garage door went up, then heard the deafening silence that followed. She imagined him standing there, looking at what she had done, reaching for the envelope, opening it.

Finally there was movement. The sounds of him loading the car. The garage door going down. The car backing out of the driveway. The car lights once again filling the room.

Then she yelled and screamed and pulled at her hair. She ran through the empty house wailing like a banshee, crying out his name, cursing him, wanting him, wishing she could take this day back. Maybe tonight was the night he would have told her he was sorry.

He did say he was sorry. The apology came the next day in the form of a special delivery letter. He was sorry about the pain he had caused, but he had reached the point where he was just putting one foot in front of the other. He didn't think it was fair to her or Kirk to continue in a relationship that had grown stale and unfulfilling. He had fallen deeply in love with a wonderful woman. He and Cindy had tried to end the relationship several months ago but realized they could not live without each other. Cindy since had left her husband and was waiting for him to find the courage to leave Dixie. He was both sad and relieved that Dixie had taken the initiative. He ended the letter by wishing her well. His lawyer would contact her lawyer. He wanted to be fair, but he wasn't going to mortgage his future.

Even as she read Arnie's letter, she had felt a kernel of relief. At least it would be over.

As time passed, she felt not so much devastated as profoundly sad—for herself, for her son, and for Arnie. A new wife and a second marriage might cure his discontent for a time, but eventually that marriage, too, would become routine.

She had taken Kirk to Italy to show him there was life after divorce. Johnny had been completely unexpected. She was mistrustful of her attraction for the man. Either he was not as nice as he seemed or she was too vulnerable to know a worthy man from an unworthy one. Or both. Of course, Kirk was enchanted with him, but Kirk was just a kid.

She never could bring herself to admit to her three best friends that she indulged herself in a once-in-a-while affair with a married man, that she had become one of those loathsome "other women" and was no better than Cindy and Trish and Mona, even though she only borrowed Johnny from time to time and didn't want to steal him away from his shadowy wife two villages away, a woman whose name she did not know and did not want to know.

So she stored Johnny away in a secret compartment of her life known only to Kirk and guessed at by Mary Sue. Oddly the secret bound her more closely to her son, but she worried about the message she was sending him. She wanted him to believe in the sanctity of marriage. She wanted him to be a better person than his father or his mother.

But oh the glory of those trips to Italy! They sustained her as she watched the demise of Mary Sue's and Gretchen's marriages and watched Pamela trade her soul for a big house and jewels; as she dealt with flower brokers, credit card companies, and brides and their mothers; as she watched her father be happier with Myrtle than he had ever been with his wife. Johnny and Italy were about floating—not cut loose from the ties that bind, but out there on a very long tether.

Her friends had been wondering about her for years. And not just the trips. They couldn't understand why she wasn't out beating the bushes for a man and why she didn't loathe her ex. They speculated about her calmness when divorce had made Gretchen and Mary Sue hysterical and the prospect of divorce had filled Pamela's heart with dread.

Dixie knew she wasn't the only one with a secret. Something terrible had happened to Gretchen in college that only Mary Sue knew about. And the sudden return of Pamela's high school boyfriend to Garden Grove coincided suspiciously with her sudden emergence from under the wifely doormat she had created for herself. And there was the secret of Walter Lampley's death that they had kept from Mary Sue.

Best friends often shared their secrets, but not always.

Chapter Twenty-seven

They were sitting on the stone wall that surrounded the grounds of a small castle that rose above the tiny mountaintop hamlet of Verrucchio, with the coastal plain spreading out far below and blending into the distant haze that was the Adriatic Sea.

Did anyone ever become accustomed to all this beauty? Dixie wondered.

Much of Italy's panorama had been created by humankind, with all but the steepest hillsides and mountain slopes cultivated, with lines of stately cypress and majestic pine marching across the ridges of hills, around cemeteries, along roadways. The vineyards, orchards, and tilled fields; the picturesque villages and farms; the ancient hilltop churches and castles all seemed an integral part of the countryside, the entire tableau of a whole cloth, as though laid out in its entirety by some long-ago master designer so that in the centuries to follow it would inspire artists and other seekers of beauty.

Such vistas fed Dixie's soul and gave her a feeling of enormous peace. She sighed her contentment and patted Johnny's firm thigh——a thigh made muscular by a lifetime of physical labor. His hands and knees were callused, his fingernails stained. No one would ever mistake him for other than what he was——a man of the earth.

Kirk sat with them for a time, then grew restless and jumped down from the wall and went into the woods below. He called up to them that he'd meet then in the square in an hour for lunch. Dixie reluctantly looked at her watch so she would know when the allotted hour began.

When she arrived four weeks ago, she had programmed herself to enter as much as possible into a timeless world. She avoided clocks and calendars. She didn't count when church bells chimed the hour. She slept until she woke up, usually after Johnny was at work in the vineyard with Kirk. She and Johnny ate when they were hungry and went to bed when they wanted to make love. Usually she wasn't sure what day it was.

To give them privacy, Kirk had moved his things to the home of Johnny's cousin in the village, but he usually ate with them and accompanied them on excursions. Dixie was amazed, proud, and more than a bit jealous at how fluent in Italian her son was becoming. He apparently had an ear for languages and was young enough to make the most of it. She would try to follow his and Johnny's conversations for a time, but when the effort started giving her a headache, she would tune them out and enjoy watching the two of them as they discussed all manner of things—grape growing, politics, global warming, European history. And there was the continuing argument about which was the better game—soccer or American football. Eventually, though, she would call a halt and demand English only.

Almost daily she would open her Italian grammar and try to master the conjugation of yet another irregular verb. Conversationally, she seldom strayed from past, present, and future tenses and avoided the subjunctive altogether, even when she realized quite well that some other tense was called for in the sentence she was about to attempt. Kirk didn't worry much about grammar. He just absorbed. The language-learning synapses in his brain had not yet closed.

Kirk had changed. Not only was he tanner and more muscular, he looked older, more like a man than a boy, a realization that tugged at Dixie's heartstrings. When he spoke Italian, he adopted many of Johnny's expansive gestures. Like most Italians, Johnny talked as much with his hands and body as with his mouth. Kirk's lips even wrapped themselves around the words like Johnny's did. His eyebrows rose and his eyes widened with the inflection of certain words. Kirk's favorite expletive had become *Mio Dio,* which he said with a shrug, arms extended, palms up, eyes rolling heavenward. Johnny claimed that Kirk must have been Italian in a former life.

In the village, people smiled and called out to Kirk, making two syllables of his name. *Ciao, Kur-ka,* they would say, then ask him about the grapes and if his mother was having a good visit and whether he was coming back next summer. Dixie would enter into these conversations as best she could, with Kirk supplying words to help her along. Yes, she was enjoying her visit. Yes, Santo Stefano was *bella.* Yes, the weather was *bello.* Yes, Kirk spoke Italian *molto bene.* Such encounters made her feel awkward and limited, almost as though she were the child and Kirk the parent, and she was always relieved when they ended.

Of course, the fact that Johnny was married and everyone in the village knew it did not contribute to her comfort level. No one had ever indicated disapproval of the visiting American lady, but after all this time, she still felt as though she had a scarlet A on her chest. The word in Italian was almost the same: *Adultera.* An ugly word in any language.

They went to the village almost daily to make the round of shops—the butcher, baker, pasta maker, greengrocer, and a tiny *supermercato* for dairy products and staples. And most evenings they walked with Kirk to the *piazza,* where residents would congregate on a summer's evening to eat ice cream, watch the children play tag and ride the carousel, and keep an eye on their teenage daughters. As the evening wore on, the men would gravitate into one of the square's two bars, which were as much coffeehouses as places to consume alcoholic beverages. The men would watch sports on television and argue politics, leaving the supervision of the young to the women. Teenage boys and girls were allowed to pair off for strolls around the square but not to disappear from view. Kirk sometimes paired off but seldom with the same girl twice. Mostly he hung out with unattached boys, sailing a Frisbee back and forth or kicking a soccer ball up and down the empty streets.

Johnny insisted that in spite of supervision, the young people generally found ways to steal moments of privacy. And unlike in America, where boys were likely to have condoms in their billfolds and girls often took birth control pills, Italian youngsters were more likely to have unprotected sex.

According to Johnny, Italian girls often were pregnant—or *in stato interessante,* as it was so delicately put—when they got married. Because the young couple had no money, they usually lived with his or her parents. The young man found what work he could, usually for his father or father-in-law, and he and his wife both gave up any dreams they might have had for education, travel, or a career other than what the village had to offer.

She repeated all this to Kirk, who smiled and said Johnny had already given him his don't-get-a-girl-pregnant lecture, offering himself as an example of how a few moments of lust can lead to a lifetime of unhappiness. Kirk had given his mother a reassuring hug. "I'm not saying I'll never fall in love with an Italian girl, but right now I just want to go to college and enjoy being young and frivolous for at least four more years."

God, how lucky she was to have a son like Kirk, Dixie thought as she turned sideways on the stone wall, stretching her legs out in front of her, leaning her back against Johnny, lifting her face to the sun. He put his arm around her waist and buried a kiss in her hair. "It is good, no?" he asked.

"It is very good," she said.

Except that tomorrow *it* would end. In the morning, Johnny would put them on a plane, although a part of her—but only a part—wanted to stay forever. The rest of her was ready to go home to her friends and her store. And her father. Her dog. She might even be glad to see Myrtle.

And she could begin looking forward to the next trip. That was her pattern. But there was now a cloud on her Italian horizon.

Johnny's wife was not well.

Kirk said Johnny had left him in charge three days in July while he took her to a specialist in Bologna. And Johnny, too, had mentioned his wife's illness, saying that she was determined to see their daughter locked away in a convent before she died.

"And maybe that is the only place for her," Johnny said, "after her mother has taught her to be afraid of anything male, to be afraid of life."

"Does your wife have long to live?" Dixie asked, uncertain how she felt about this turn of events. After suffering mightily over her status as "the other woman," she had come to appreciate that there were advantages to the status quo. Because Johnny was married, she didn't have to struggle with the question of where their relationship was going. It wasn't *going* anywhere. It just *was*. And that, she had come to realize, was what made it last. Marriage was about day in and day out. She and Johnny were not suited for that. They were about once in a while.

The longer Dixie was unmarried, the more she wondered if she shouldn't just stay that way. Maybe in later life, she might form a geriatric relationship that was like a marriage, as her father had done with Myrtle to ward off the loneliness that seemed part of growing older.

But for now, her life was full. Of course, if there weren't a Johnny, she might feel different. Every time a man on her side of the ocean showed up on her radar screen, she asked herself if she were willing to give up her trips to Italy in order to enter into a relationship with him. And so far, the answer always had been no. After six years, however, she didn't bother much with radar. The blips were few and far between and probably not worth investigating anyway. She'd rather spend her time thinking about the next trip.

Dixie had come to depend on Johnny for the feeling of anticipation that he brought to her life. She had derived enormous, calming pleasure from the knowledge that something lovely was out there waiting for her. During odd moments, perhaps at work or driving down the highway, she would find herself thinking about that first glimpse of Johnny in the waiting crowd outside the airport customs hall and the joy of that first sweet embrace.

Johnny's wife made their relationship possible. If he were free, they would have to decide what happened next.

If he were free, his expectations surely would change.

How long did his wife have to live? Johnny had shrugged at her question. "The last doctor said she could live fifty years. The new doctor says she needs surgery in her neck where the blood cannot go, but she says no. She is weak and . . ."

He paused and, not knowing the word in English he wanted, mimicked fainting. "Faints," Dixie supplied.

"She is weak and faints sometimes," he continued, "and perhaps someday soon she will die. Perhaps not. She believes the Virgin is the boss of her
life and will decide the hour for her to die. Except she likes to go to the
doctor. For her, the doctors are very high, like the priests."

"So she is not actually dying?"

Again, he had shrugged, and mumbled harsh words in Italian Dixie did
not understand. The only time Johnny used that tone of voice was when he
was talking about his wife. The expression on his face would turn hard.
Dixie didn't like seeing the other side of him, didn't like knowing he was
capable of animosity. It made her think of Gretchen, whose lovely face
would be distorted with such hatred when she talked about Paul.

With her eyes closed and the solid presence of Johnny against her back,
Dixie listened to the lively voices of children heading home for lunch from
the nearby elementary school. She thought of Johnny's daughter, who had
never been allowed to go to school or to have friends, never had a chance
to live a normal life. In America, Johnny could probably have gone to court
and won custody of the girl. Dixie suspected that such a course of action
would be difficult in rural Italy and was probably not something that had
even occurred to him.

Poor Johnny. If ever a man should have raised children, it was he. In the
village, children would run up to him and hug him and dig in his pocket
for *caramella*. The little ones he would lift over his head. With the older children he would rough their hair and tease.

As though reading her thoughts, he put his mouth near her ear and said,
"Thank you for sharing Kirk with me. For three months I feel like a father
with a son. It is a good way to feel. And these weeks with you and your son,
I feel more happiness than in all my life."

"I feel happy but also sad because it has to end."

"When will you come again?" he asked, moving his hand so that his
thumb could rub against the underside of her breast.

"Soon, I hope. But I need to talk with you about something important,"
Dixie said, dangling her legs from the wall once again, her shoulder touching his. She selected her words carefully, using only ones she knew he

would understand. "You are still a young man, Johnny, not yet fifty years old. If your wife dies, you can marry again, have another child and have enough years to see this child grow up. Or you can marry a widow and help raise her child—or children. If you have the opportunity to marry again, Johnny, I think you should."

Johnny lifted her hand to his lips and kissed her palm. Then he turned it over and kissed the back. "And what about you and me?" he asked.

The breeze gently played with Dixie's hair. Cows were lowing on the hillside below them, a tractor mowing. The air smelled of newly cut hay and decaying leaves, of rosemary from the roadside hedges. It was a glorious day to be alive and to be sitting next to the man who had given her all this. If this were to be the last day she would ever spend with him, she would have no regrets. He had given her so much. So very much. She could never regret a moment of it.

"There is another side of this promise you want from me," he said. "It means you also would be free to marry another man. I think I like things just the way they are."

"Our relationship will end someday, you know. Old age or illness or death will end what we have."

He nodded and wrapped his arms around her. "Yes, all the things end. This happens if we think about it or do not think about it." He paused, a sly grin taking over his face. "Tell me, *mia cara,* you are happy to return to your Kansas?"

Dixie hesitated. She wanted to say that it was always good to go home, but she wasn't sure the word "home" for Johnny meant anything but *casa.* And it was more than her house that she would be glad to return to. She meant "home" in the way that Dorothy did when she told Toto, "There's no place like home." It meant her family and friends and homeland. It meant the place where she felt most herself.

As enamored as she was of Italy and the Italian man beside her, they did not and would never represent home to her. But rather than launch a discussion of semantics, she said simply, "I'll be glad to see my friends."

"Yes," he agreed. "You have called the sick friend many times."

Dixie nodded. "It did not feel right to be leaving right after Mary Sue had surgery and began cancer treatment again. I almost didn't come, but Mary Sue said she would feel terrible if I missed my trip because of her."

"And there are other reasons why you are glad to return to Kansas?"

"Well, sure. It's always good to return to my own house and get back to work at my store. I'll be happy to see my father—and even his lady friend. And there's an election coming up in Garden Grove—about a rule for new buildings in the center of town—that is very important to me. And when I'm gone, I always think of things I want to change. Now that Kirk is going to college, I think it's time for me move into the downstairs bedroom that was my parents'. It's time to stop being angry because my father no longer sleeps there. And I want to make part of my flower store into a place where people can come for coffee and conversation—like an Italian bar."

He nodded. "Now, you must ask me what I will do when you are gone."

"Okay, what will you do when I am gone?"

"First, I am less . . ." He reached in her purse for the dictionary and settled his reading glasses on his nose. Dixie waited until he came up with the word he was looking for. "I am less 'tidy' in my house. And when you are not here, I go every night to the bar to see my friends and to speak about the next important election in Santo Stefano and to argue why our soccer team is very bad. And in bed at night, I watch sport on television. And I count the days before we are together again."

Dixie started to giggle. Then to laugh. She laughed so hard Johnny grabbed her arm so she wouldn't fall off the wall. When she got herself under control, she asked, "Maybe a month is too long?"

"No, not too long, but long enough," he said, his eyes full of mirth.

And then Dixie said something unplanned. "Maybe it is time for you to come to Kansas," she said, then wished she hadn't. What if the fairy tale existed only here in this serene land?

Johnny tucked a finger under her chin and lifted her face to his. "Maybe someday," he said, and kissed her—a long and glorious kiss that promised one last night of lovemaking before they parted, before they once again went their separate ways.

Chapter Twenty-eight

S*o here she was again* with Mary Sue in the chemotherapy room, Dixie thought, when they were supposed to be done with chemo. It was the same but not the same. The feeling that came with being in this place was more ominous now, with Dixie less a believer in the chemical agents being dripped into Mary Sue's body. The chemical given first was bright red, like strawberry soda pop. The one being administered now was clear as water. In Dixie's mind, it was the obnoxious red one that nauseated Mary Sue and took away her energy and appetite.

With Mary Sue's veins in bad shape from the first round of chemotherapy, an indwelling port had been implanted near her left collarbone to receive the drip. She had begun this round of therapy with a thinner, frailer body. When Dixie returned from Italy, she was shocked at how much Mary Sue had changed. She was concentration-camp thin and almost completely bald. Her eyebrows were penciled on, and eyeliner helped fill in between her thinning eyelashes. With her newly evolved minimalist philosophy, Mary Sue had all but weaned herself from makeup and resented having to bother with it again. The good thing was, she quipped, she didn't have to shave her legs. Hairless and thin, she was still the same indomitable Mary Sue.

The elderly woman in the next recliner protested that Mary Sue was too young to be here at all, much less a second time in less than a year. Only old people like her should have cancer.

"Ah, but better me than some child," Mary Sue said.

They watched while the nurse removed the needle from the woman's arm and sent her on her way with a cheery "See you next time." The woman's husband took her arm, she kissed his cheek, and together they slowly shuffled their way to the door.

Mary Sue took a tiny sip of the apple juice Dixie had handed her, trying not to make a face.

"Would a Coke taste better?" Dixie asked.

"Actually, Sprite or 7-Up are about the only drinks that don't taste terrible. And my list of remotely tolerable foods has shrunk to mashed potatoes and once again my old friend canned chicken noodle soup."

After Dixie had handed her a cup of Sprite, Mary Sue smiled a bit too nicely. "Now tell me again, why is it we can't have my birthday party at the lake house?"

Dixie was saved from answering when Barry came strolling through the door wearing a crisp white jacket with his name stitched onto the pocket. *Barry Prescott, M.D.* He nodded in Dixie's direction, then knelt by Mary Sue's chair and kissed her, stroked her cheek, took her pulse. With his full head of thick hair and his smooth, tanned complexion, he looked obscenely healthy and handsome next to his former wife.

Dixie left them alone, crossing the room to the snack bar, where she poured herself a cup of coffee. While she was in Italy, Barry had taken Mary Sue to M. D. Anderson Cancer Center in Houston, and she had been put on an experimental protocol that allowed cancer patients to tolerate larger doses of chemo. She received the therapy here and was to return to Houston for periodic evaluation. Mary Sue said Barry was turning himself into an oncologist, spending hours searching medical sites on the Internet and calling physicians and researchers all over the world.

Barry was touchingly tender with her, Dixie had to admit. He was holding Mary Sue's hand, leaning forward with his face close to hers while he spoke—words of encouragement, most likely. Words of love. Plans for the future. Mary Sue said that he had cut back his hours at the hospital and completely taken over the household, which by her own admission was quite amazing. During the years of their marriage, he had taken care of the yard and seen to the cars, but she couldn't remember him ever going to the grocery for more than an emergency carton of milk or sixpack of beer. In her memory, he had never run the vacuum or mopped the kitchen floor. Now, he also kept track of her medication schedule and tried to anticipate her every need. Michelle came home from Lawrence on weekends to help, insisting she needed to do her part, and there would be plenty of time for parties and football games later, when her mother was well. Once again, Michelle and Michael were being nice to each other, with none of the jabs and taunts that had characterized their behavior toward each other since they were toddlers. It was as though they and their father were trying to heal their mother by being perfect in every way. The household had taken on a conventlike atmosphere, with all that goodness and everyone speaking in carefully modulated voices. "All that's missing is incense and chants," Mary Sue had pointed out.

Dixie had known Barry since junior high, known that he and Mary Sue would someday get married. Everyone thought they were made for each other. If the favorites elected by the senior class had included a "Best Couple," it would have been Barry and Mary Sue. Dixie could imagine the picture of them that would have appeared in the yearbook. It would have been taken on the front steps of the high school, with Mary Sue in her cheerleader's outfit perched on the railing and Barry in his letter jacket standing beside her, an arm around her shoulders. Two beautiful young people with smooth faces and healthy bodies, the promise of a rosy future enveloping them like an aura.

All through high school and college, Dixie had taken great pleasure in watching them together, is holding them up as her ideal. Someday she wanted to find someone she could love the way Mary Sue loved Barry, and who would love her in return the way Barry loved Mary Sue.

Dixie had wondered if Barry had been cheating on Mary Sue long before Trish came along. Ten years or so into his and Mary Sue's marriage, Dixie realized Barry had changed. There was something about him that hadn't been there before. Something predatory. Not that he ever hit on her personally, but conversations with him always seemed to lead to mention of sex and intimacy. He flirted relentlessly with waitresses and barmaids. More than once Dixie had seen him lean forward and say something intimate to an attractive woman at a social gathering. Dixie would glance at Mary Sue to see if she noticed. But Mary Sue still was wearing blinders when it came to Barry.

Once Dixie had even confronted Barry. She and Arnie always made the annual trek to Kansas to join her friends and their husbands for the Kansas–Kansas State football game. Even Clay joined them after he and Pamela had married. The game that year had been in Manhattan. At the pregame brunch in the student union, Barry had spent too much time talking to the voluptuous young wife of an assistant football coach. Later at the ballgame, with people cheering all around them, Dixie had put her lips close to Barry's ear and said, "If you hurt Mary Sue, I may have to kill you." She had actually said that. Of course, at least in part, it had been the Bloody Marys talking. What she should have said was that if he hurt Mary Sue, she would hate his guts forever and maybe even wish a truck would run him over. She wanted him to know that she knew he was either screwing around on Mary Sue or on the verge of screwing around on Mary Sue. She wanted him to have to look at himself through someone else's eyes. But probably he realized that she never would have voiced her suspicions to Mary Sue. None of them would. Mary Sue's friends tried to protect her to the end—even after Barry had begun his campaign to make Mary Sue fall out of love with him.

Comparing notes as they looked back, Dixie, Pamela, and Gretchen decided that Barry had been fooling around on Mary Sue for years before he left her for the ultimate trophy wife. Trish was the sort of woman who made heads turn—both male and female—when she walked into a room. She was the sort of woman who made every other woman in the room feel drab and ordinary and wish she could go home and change clothes and made her vow to lose ten pounds, lighten her hair, join a health club. Gretchen insisted that Trish was an alien. No real human being had skin that perfect. Trish had to have been manufactured in a factory on some distant planet.

Yet, now Barry had left flawless Trish. Filed for divorce even. Dixie felt mistrustful of his motivation. Had Trish been screwing around on him? If their marriage had been heaven on earth, she doubted that Barry would have come back no matter how remorseful he was about dumping Mary Sue.

Across the room, Mary Sue was smiling at something Barry had whispered in her ear. She lifted her face for a kiss before he left. Her eyes followed him out of the room. And the eyes of the two young nurses.

Carrying her coffee, Dixie went back to her place at Mary Sue's side. "Do you think you can ever love him again?" she asked.

"I never stopped loving the man he used to be, loving what we once had together. And I guess I need more than anything to believe in him now. I told him that if it took me getting cancer a second time to make us a family again, maybe it was worth it. He claims he'd already realized he'd made the worst mistake of his life even before the cancer came back, but he just hadn't had the courage to admit it before. But what it all boils down to is, if I am dying, we'll never know if he came back because he felt duty bound or because he really loves me. He will do a wonderful job of caring for me and making my last days as easy as possible. For me to live on would be the acid test. You saw how the nurses looked at him. He's a gorgeous man, still. Does he really want to live out his life with a woman who looks like the Bride of Frankenstein?"

"Oh, God, Mary Sue, don't talk like that!" Dixie said. "You are the same person you always were. You still have the same kind heart and beautiful smile. A little hair would help, and you need some meat on your bones. But those things will come."

Mary Sue leaned forward to offer Dixie a comforting pat. "Yes, they will," she said. "The hair I can't hurry, but I do wish I could eat more. Pamela made a pot of chicken noodle soup complete with homemade noodles, but it's too flavorful. The bland stuff out of cans goes down better. For my birthday, I guess you'll have to put a candle in a lump of mashed potatoes.

"And speaking of my birthday," she said pointedly, smoothing the throw that covered her legs, "I still don't understand why we can't have it at the lake like last year. This year I can't get soused because I won't be drinking anything but Sprite, but I like the idea of coming full circle. What an extraordinary year began that night! Just think about it. Pamela has regained control of her life. Gretchen has calmed down and even sold her house. Barry has come back home. Your business is doing well, as are our children, all of whom are now in college, except for Michael. And you have just come back tanned and tranquil from another of your mystery trips to Italy. Of course, I do have cancer once again and Walter Lampley is still among the missing, but thanks to Barry, I feel hopeful about the cancer, and whatever the verdict, I plan to live until I die. And do you realize that this fall is the fortieth anniversary of our friendship? So I do think a celebration is in order."

Mary Sue took another sip of Sprite, then put the can on the table beside her chair. "You know," she said, lowering her voice, "without a body or some other evidence that Walter is dead, his estate can't be settled for years. His children don't know what happened to their father and can't benefit from his estate. But, I guess we can't do anything about that, can we?" She shrugged and looked pensive for a second or two before adding, "Now tell me again, why we can't have my birthday at the lake house."

Cringing at Mary Sue's words, Dixie drained her cup and tossed it into the wastebasket. *Mary Sue doesn't know anything,* she reminded herself. Only three people knew what had happened to Walter Lampley, and they would never tell. They couldn't tell without creating havoc in their lives. "Like I told you, Daddy has been working for months getting the place ready to sell and is being real hard-nosed about letting anyone use it. Pamela and I think we should combine your birthday and a housewarming for Gretchen. Kirk is helping Robin and Debbie get her moved in this weekend."

"But I want one last slumber party out there for old time's sake." Mary Sue was using her firm voice, the voice she had once used to convey that she had decided they would play jump rope instead of kickball. She was, after all, through all the sweetness and demureness, the leader of the pack.

"I'll call your dad and talk to him about it," she said. "He won't say no to me. You know that he won't, so just belly up. That morning, I've got us all signed up for the Race for the Cure. Of course, Gretchen will be the only one actually racing. You and Pamela can do the two-K walk pushing me in a wheelchair. Then we can have lunch and head out to the lake."

"I think Gretchen would have her feelings hurt if we didn't come to her place," Dixie explained, all the while thinking that no way were they going back to the lake house. Just the thought of the four of them sitting on the screened-in porch staring out at the moonlit water—with three of them knowing the awful secret of what lay beneath the silvery surface—was too grim for words.

Mary Sue tilted her head to one side and gave Dixie an exasperated look, which she ignored and headed for the bathroom.

Mary Sue might not know anything specific about Walter's disappearance, Dixie thought as she locked the bathroom door behind her. What she did know was that they were keeping something from her.

Dixie stared at herself in the mirror and felt a pang of guilt. She looked pretty damned good, while Mary Sue looked haggard. Dixie couldn't begin to imagine what it would be like to be on the brink of one's forty-sixth birthday and facing cancer for a second time. Yet, she had never once heard Mary Sue whine, never once heard her say, "Why me?"

Michelle said that her mother, under the guise of housecleaning, had been having her sort through the contents of every drawer, every cupboard. And there was an envelope in her mother's jewelry box with the word "instructions" written on the front.

Dixie began to sob. Selfish sobs—not for Mary Sue but for herself. Growing old with her friends had seemed a given before. Now, the possibility that it was not to be was forcing itself upon her consciousness. Mary Sue was their center, and without her, the three remaining friends would drift apart.

Mary Sue was tidying up her life—just in case. And apparently the matter of Walter Lampley loomed large on her to-do list. She wanted the mystery of his disappearance cleared up for the sake of his children.

"Oh, God," Dixie groaned, putting a hand on each side of the sink to steady herself. How were they going to get through this?

When Dixie pulled up in front of Mary Sue's house, she was surprised to see Pamela and Gretchen's cars parked in the driveway.

"I asked them to drop by," Mary Sue explained. "Pamela was going to bring muffins and have the coffee ready."

They sat around the kitchen table making small talk, waiting for Mary Sue to explain the purpose of a called meeting.

Mary Sue didn't look surprised when the doorbell rang. Dixie stood, but Mary Sue told her to sit down. She would answer the door herself.

Shortly she returned to the kitchen. Behind her was Grace Corona, her red hair pulled back in a severe chignon.

Mary Sue didn't bother with an introduction. She cleared her throat. "I've asked Grace to drop by. She needs to tell you something."

Mary Sue sat on a barstool, allowing Grace to join Gretchen, Dixie, and Pamela at the kitchen table. That's why Mary Sue had put five coffee mugs on the table, Dixie realized as she poured Grace a cup of coffee. Her hand was shaking. Coffee sloshed onto the table.

Mary Sue wiped up the spill with a napkin, cleared her throat, nodded in the dentist's direction, indicating she was to begin. "Grace?"

Grace took a sip of coffee. Put the mug down. Sat up straighter. Sighed.

"I've known Walter Lampley since dental school," she began. "I had an affair with him back then and had gotten involved with him again in the months before his disappearance. I knew he was involved with someone else, but all we did was screw once in a while. I didn't love him. I didn't even like him very much, but I do like sex. My husband had surgery for prostate cancer and had been impotent for several years. You may find it hard to believe, but I loved my husband very much. Andy was the most decent, kindest man I have ever known. The night of Mary Sue's birthday party, he was in the hospital, scheduled to have a stent placed in a clogged coronary artery the next morning. After I left the hospital, I stopped by Walter's. He wasn't there, but I have a key. When I heard the garage door go up, I raced into the bathroom and pulled off my clothes, but when I opened the door, it wasn't Walter I surprised." Grace paused and took another sip of coffee before she continued.

"If there had only been one of you, I might have thought it was some other lady friend coming by for a late-night tryst, but a threesome wasn't Walter's style. When he turned up missing, I wondered if you two had something to do with his disappearance. I couldn't get involved, though, for Andy's sake. I think he realized I occasionally stepped out on him, but I didn't want him to have a face and a name. And I didn't want my affair with Walter to become public knowledge."

Grace looked away for a minute. Dixie could see the shine of tears in her eyes.

They waited.

Grace pushed her coffee cup aside and asked for a drink of water. They watched while she took several sips. She was a handsome woman. Great cheekbones and a real sense of style. Dixie couldn't imagine her being intimate with the likes of Walter any more than she could imagine Mary Sue with him. But then, she'd bedded a few losers herself.

Grace held on to the glass of water with both hands as she resumed her tale. "Walter had been missing about six months when I learned that his first wife was seriously ill. I've known Darlene since before she and Walter were married. She's kind of like Mary Sue—sweet and domestic. A really nice person. Her life revolved around Walter and their two children. He screwed her out of a realistic divorce settlement. She taught school until recently, but she needs a kidney transplant and is having a very difficult time financially. Her house is for sale. Her car is on its last legs."

Grace paused again, letting her words sink in. She looked at each of their faces in turn. "Darlene is the beneficiary of an insurance policy Walter took out as part of their divorce settlement, and whatever there is in Walter's estate will go to her and the kids. But the estate can't be settled because he isn't legally dead. If you ladies know any way to change that, I'd be willing to forget that I was in Walter's bedroom that night."

❋   ❋   ❋

On the way to the store, Dixie reached for her cell phone and dialed Kirk's number in Lawrence, where he had just completed his first week of classes. He wasn't in his dorm room, but the sound of his voice on the answering machine made her smile. *Better me than some child,* Mary Sue had said. Better any of them than one of their children.

Call her back, she told him. She'd like to drive over to Lawrence for dinner tomorrow evening if he was free. She loved him.

Telling him she loved him always seemed inadequate. She needed to invent some new word to express the range of feelings she had for her son. A word that included pride, respect, gratitude, and wonder.

Chapter Twenty-nine

Kirk came loping down the stairs of his dormitory and gave her a big hug. "I've decided to drop out of school and join the Hare Krishnas," he said.

"Great," Dixie said, linking arms with him as they walked out the door. "I've never seen you with a shaved head, but you do look wonderful in orange."

"An alternative plan would be for me to transfer to Kansas State second semester and major in agriculture."

"Are you serious? What about that MBA your father expects you to earn?"

Kirk made a face. "If last summer taught me anything, it's that I don't want to spend my life in an office."

Dixie handed him the car keys. "Take us someplace we can talk." In the car, she turned sideways to face him. *"Agriculture?"*

"I guess I got too much dirt under my fingernails in Italy. I find myself missing all that—being a part of the land, growing things. I'd like to own a vineyard someday and make wine. Of course, I'm just a kid and may change my mind, but right now that's what I'm thinking. Maybe Johnny could help out sometimes."

"My son, the winemaker," Dixie said, trying the idea on for size.

With her mind racing ahead, she tried to listen while he talked on. He probably would work in the California wine industry for a few years after he graduated. Or maybe in Italy. But someday, he'd like to have some land of his own; he liked the idea of raising kids in that environment. Probably he'd never be able to afford land in California, but vineyards were thriving in Texas, Arkansas, and Oklahoma. He was pretty sure the winters were too cold in Kansas, but he was going to check into it. Some North American grapes were pretty hardy.

"Of course, you have plenty of time to make up your mind, but it's an intriguing plan," she told him. "Your father won't like you going to Kansas State, but he'd get over it, I suppose. I'd hold off on telling him that you're planning to major in agriculture, though, until you feel surer of yourself. And maybe you should call it 'agribusiness.'"

The restaurant was a hole in the wall that Kirk assured her served great chicken-fried steak. He asked for a corner booth. The sound of pool balls and laughter came from the back room.

Dixie opened the menu with a pounding heart. At some point, she was going to have to tell him her reason for this visit. She tried to concentrate on the menu. She was too nervous for food, she realized as she took a sip of water.

She ordered a bowl of soup.

"What's on your mind?" Kirk asked when the waitress left.

Dixie looked around to make sure there were no listening ears. Then she took a deep breath. "What happened to the scuba equipment your dad bought you two or three summers back?"

"I loaned it to Michael Prescott. He wanted to try it out in his step-mother's oversize pool. I guess he still has it. Why do you ask?"

Dixie nodded. "Remember when Mary Sue's gentleman friend disappeared?" she began.

She started with the birthday party and her phone call to Walter. She told how he showed up barefoot and shirtless. She had gotten to the part about the video when the waitress brought the food. Kirk ate while she told him about the scuffle over the video.

He put down his fork. "I don't like where this is going," he said.

"Yeah. It's isn't good. Walter fell through the porch railing and hit his head on one of the rocks in your grandmother's rock garden. He broke his neck in the fall and died instantly, with scratches from Gretchen's fingernails on his arm and my teeth marks on his hand."

Kirk let out a soft whistle. "So where's his body?"

The waitress came to ask if there was something wrong with the food, and they waved her away.

When Dixie was finished with her tale, including the plight of Walter's ex-wife and children, and had explained her idea, she asked, "Do you think your mom and her friends are horribly wicked?"

Kirk stared down at his half-eaten food for a time, considering. Then he met her gaze.

"Stuff happens, Mom. Like when Dad left in a huff about something one morning, gunned the car down the driveway, and backed over the dog. Or the time a gang of us decided to put the principal's VW on the roof of the high school and Derrick Jacobson ended up having to have half of his foot amputated. You go back and relive stuff like that over and over again, thinking how you should have reacted and what you should have done, but all you can do is go forward."

"I'm sorry to get you involved."

"Hey, what are kids for?" he said, then added in a serious tone, "It's a good plan, Mom. I wouldn't get involved if it wasn't."

"I thought if it was you and your friends, it would seem innocent, not like if Gretchen and I suddenly discovered the body. You've been scuba diving out there before. We haven't."

"You're sure it's really down there? You guys weren't hallucinating the whole thing?"

"Actually, we went back later to see how deep the car was. Gretchen dove down there. She said it was about ten or twelve feet to the roof of the car. In murky water."

"Yeah, I remember. I was expecting beautiful underwater vistas, and I couldn't see much of anything."

Later, when she pulled up in front of the dorm, she took his face between her hands. "You are the greatest blessing of my life."

"Thanks. We do this mother and son thing pretty well."

The dog's name was Harry. Dixie thought about him on the drive home. A pound puppy that grew into an oversize, clumsy, lop-eared animal that dripped slobber wherever he went and became a beloved member of their little family. Arnie had been mad that morning because she had forgotten to pick up his blue suit at the cleaner's. He left without eating breakfast and to demonstrate his displeasure, backed down the driveway like a bat out of hell. She heard the screech of the brakes and went running out in her nightgown. Arnie was kneeling by poor Harry's crushed body.

Arnie's pain was real, and she comforted him as best she could, feeling more sad than angry. But Arnie never said he was sorry. All he said was if they got another dog, the animal would have to be kept penned up. She never chastised Arnie, never told him that he had to apologize to their son, that he must participate in the backyard funeral. She never held him accountable. But that was the story of her marriage. Its failure was just as much on her shoulders as Arnie's. Even if speaking up and announcing her own displeasure all those countless times when she had held her tongue had caused friction, even if in the end the marriage failed anyway, she would not still be wondering if it could have been saved had she been a different sort of wife.

At times she still sincerely missed Arnie and being part of a family with him. She did not regret the years they had together. But even now, after seven years as a divorced woman, she continued to have those epiphanic moments when she realized how truly satisfied she was with her life and would not have experienced a particular pleasure or joy if she were still married.

Maybe she was involved with a married man half a world away because it protected her from ever becoming a wife again.

Kirk brought his roommate and another buddy over for the weekend. Dixie fed them hamburgers before they headed for the Friday night football game between Garden Grove and De Soto. The boys were going to stay out at the lake house and get in a little water skiing tomorrow, maybe do a little scuba diving. Dixie had stocked the refrigerator at the lake house and made up the beds for them.

She was ill with apprehension. What kind of mother was she to involve her son in something like this?

But it had to be resolved. For almost a year, Walter's demise had been hanging over their heads. They were stupid to think Mary Sue wouldn't put two and two together. Stupid to think Grace Corona would fade into the sunset. Stupid not to have called the police in the first place. She should have marched to the phone that night and done just that. Except that doing so might have ended Pamela's marriage. And might have landed all of them in jail.

She was busy at the store Saturday morning, which was a blessing. Still, even though Kirk would call her on her cellular phone, she jumped every time the store phone rang, which was often. Miss McFadden asked if she was all right. Dixie blamed her jumpiness on too much coffee.

At two, after Dixie locked up, she checked her cellular phone for the umpteenth time, making sure it was on, making sure the charge was still strong, making sure she hadn't missed a call.

It was a bit cool today. Would the police be suspicious that boys were out scuba diving? Of course, they would be wearing wet suits.

She had asked Kirk if he felt like they were using his friends. He nodded, but insisted no harm would come of it.

"You don't think the experience will traumatize them? Or you?"

"Hey, we'll be telling and retelling the story fifty years from now—about the time we found the body in the lake."

Dixie hadn't told Gretchen and Pamela what she had planned. A year ago, they had talked her out of calling the police. This time it was she who asked them to wait, not to call the police yet, following Grace Corona's announcement a few nights earlier. This might not be the best way to handle it, but it was the only way she could come up with.

Of course, there was no question that something had to be done. Grace was right. Closure was needed. Mary Sue needed for Walter Lampley's disappearance to be resolved. And it was needed for his children's sake. Walter hadn't been much of a father or a husband in life, but in death he could help his children and their mother through a bad time.

Of course, there were no guarantees. Maybe Kirk and his friends wouldn't be able to find Walter's car. Maybe it had sunk completely into the mud and was lost for all time.

She stopped at a drugstore to buy medication for her nervous stomach.

Once home, she paced. The dog watched her with curious eyes as she circled the downstairs of the house over and over again, holding her cellular phone in her hand. Finally, to avoid eroding a hole her stomach, she fixed herself tea and toast and ate it standing up.

When the cellular phone rang, she yelped. Betty began barking.

Someone was with Kirk. His words were not just for her ears. "Mom, are you sitting down? Phil was diving about thirty feet out from the boat dock and found a submerged car. We've called the police. It's a Porsche. Wasn't that what that dentist was driving the night he disappeared?"

"I'm on my way."

She called Pamela and Gretchen from the car. And Mary Sue. She didn't tell them that she had asked Kirk to find the car, but if they asked, she would confess.

They didn't ask.

Pamela and Gretchen carried four lawn chairs down to the dock. The boys watched from the shore.

They watched throughout the afternoon as the tow truck and police department divers arrived. Dixie prepared sandwiches and coffee, which she carried down to the dock. Late afternoon, she brought a blanket from the house to put around Mary Sue's shoulders.

Sitting there, they told Mary Sue what happened that night. Everything. The video camera in Walter's bedroom. His behavior. His fall from the porch. His last ride into the lake.

Mary Sue listened quietly. When they finished, she said, "I latched on to Walter like a lifeline. And look at the result. He wasn't a worthy person, but he didn't deserve to die."

Of course, they assured her that what had happened was not her fault. It was no one's fault. It was just the way things turned out. Dixie used Kirk's line. *Stuff happens.*

At dusk, they held hands as they witnessed the ghostly sight of the car slowly emerging from the lake, as bright yellow as before. Dixie had thought it would be rusty and faded by now.

She held her breath while a plainclothes detective looked inside.

He walked toward them, his face grim. They stood.

"Which one of you was his girlfriend?" he asked. He was handsome. Thirtyish. Already on his way to portly.

Mary Sue stepped forward, clutching the blanket around her shoulders. "I'm Mary Sue Prescott."

The detective looked surprised, his expression saying that Mary Sue didn't look much like a girlfriend. He introduced himself as Detective Bill Sherman.

"Is Walter's body in the car?" Mary Sue asked.

"There are human remains in the car," the man allowed. "The coroner will make the identification." He paused, then asked Mary Sue, "And these other women? Who are they?"

Mary Sue introduced them, adding that the house belonged to Dixie's father.

"What was Lampley doing out here?"

Dixie took half a step forward. "We were having a birthday party for Mrs. Prescott. He was invited, but he never showed up."

"You never heard the car?" the detective asked. "It must have come over that hill at a pretty high rate of speed to end up where it did."

Dixie shook her head, feeling her pulse quicken at the shame of a lie.

"Had he been out here before?"

"No. I drew him a map and warned him about navigating the curving driveway in the dark. I'd asked him to come after dinner for birthday toasts. When he didn't show up, I called to remind him. He told me on the phone that he'd changed his mind. We opened the champagne without him and went to bed."

"So you never saw him at all?"

"It's all in the Shawnee police reports," Mary Sue interjected. "They investigated his disappearance."

He nodded. "Yeah, I talked to a female detective over there."

"When his body has been identified, will someone notify his ex-wives?" Mary Sue asked.

"Yes, ma'am. I'll see to it. There will be a coroner's hearing. I imagine you and Mrs. Woodward will have to testify."

They watched while he walked away. Then Mary Sue stumbled backward into her chair. "Poor Walter. I kept hoping it wouldn't turn out like this."

That night, the story made the 10:00 P.M. news. Scuba-diving college students came across a submerged car in a small private lake ten miles south of Garden Grove. A body in the car was thought to be that of Shawnee dentist Walter Lampley, who had been missing for almost a year.

The morning of Mary Sue's birthday dawned bright and clear. Gretchen picked them up in her vehicle, with a rented wheelchair for Mary Sue in the back.

It was a festive sight that greeted them at the fairgrounds, with balloons and Susan G. Komen Race-for-the-Cure banners everywhere, the high school pep band providing music, an aerobics group leading warm-up sessions, a health fair, and vendors selling all manner of refreshments, T-shirts, and running gear.

They were wearing their Race-for-the-Cure T-shirts with their official number pinned to the front. Mary Sue's T-shirt was pink and bore the words "I will survive" on the back. Her bald head was covered with a pink bandana.

Pink shirts were everywhere, each one worn by a breast cancer survivor. Dixie found their numbers sobering.

Gretchen, Pamela, and Dixie had pictures of Mary Sue pinned to the back of their T-shirts to show they were participating in her honor. Gretchen had taken the picture only last week, showing Mary Sue as she was now—thin but undaunted, giving the victory sign. Dixie placed a garland of daisies around Mary Sue's neck, and Pamela presented her with a vintage military medal she'd found in an antiques store. "You are our hero," Pamela said as she pinned the medal to Mary Sue's pink shirt.

And long may she survive, Dixie silently prayed as she joined in a tearful group hug. So many tears this past year, Dixie thought. So many poignant moments she had shared with these friends for a lifetime.

"I gotta go run now," Gretchen said. "I'm running for you, Mary Sue, and I'm going to try my damnedest to break twenty minutes."

Dixie, Pamela, and Mary Sue cheered from the grandstand as Gretchen and the five-K runners began their race. They were standing by the finish line jumping up and down when she crossed at 19:58, the second-place woman in her age group.

The three of them took turns pushing Mary Sue in the two-K walk, which went up Main Street, by the sports complex, and circled the high school. People along the side of the road waved. Some called out Mary Sue's name. Barry, Michael, and Michelle were in front of the high school with the video cam.

"Aren't they beautiful?" Mary Sue said as she threw kisses to her family. Then she got out of the wheelchair and pushed it past them, smiling and waving for the camera, turning her back to the camera and pointing to the brave words written on her back.

Dixie's heart ached with love for her.

Mary Sue walked the rest of the way, pushing the empty wheelchair. She looked better. Stronger. Barry said she was responding well to the treatments. She would be cured. He was sure of it.

As they reentered the fairground, she pulled off her bandana and began twirling it overhead and chanting the word "survive." Quickly the people lining the route took up her chant. *Survive. Survive. Survive.*

Dixie was overwhelmed with emotion as she called out the word. Tears streamed down her face as she and Gretchen and Pamela joined hands and lifted their voices to God or Whoever. *Please let Mary Sue survive.* And all those other women wearing pink T-shirts, all those women with friends and families who loved and needed them. *Let them all survive.*

When Mary Sue crossed the finish line, still pushing the wheelchair, her name was called out on the public address system: "Mary Sue Prescott, Survivor." Dixie tried to cheer, but the lump in her throat was too large.

After the awards ceremony, Gretchen placed her medal around Mary Sue's neck. "I'll hang it on my bedpost and touch it every morning for luck," Mary Sue promised.

With the festivities over, they drove once more out to the lake house. Pamela served chicken salad sandwiches and canned chicken noodle soup for lunch. After lunch, Mary Sue dozed on the sofa while they watched the first KU football game of the season. Nebraska won but the Jayhawks made them work for it. Dixie remembered other years when the four of them and their husbands would have been at the game together, with tailgate lunches before the game and hamburgers and beer afterward at a local tavern. Good years. Good times that should be remembered for what they were and not what came after.

Dixie had fretted about dinner. With Mary Sue's limited diet, it didn't seem right to prepare something special for the rest of them to eat. Mary Sue had anticipated her dilemma, however, and insisted she would be angry if they didn't have something good. Dixie dug in her seldom-used recipe box and prepared paella, complete with fresh mussels. She served Mary Sue a bowl of rice, its plainness softened with a parsley garnish. Pamela filled three wineglasses with a choice Chablis and one with Sprite. Gretchen had made the birthday cake—a practically fat-free angel food served with raspberries.

When it was time for toasts, they filled champagne flutes with Sprite and lifted their glasses to friendship, long might it endure. As part of their birthday toast, Dixie had planned to suggest that they celebrate Mary Sue's forty-seventh birthday in Santo Stefano, but that would require an explanation. And tonight belonged to Mary Sue. Maybe she'd tell them over breakfast. Maybe not.

After dinner, they walked down to the dock, with Dixie carrying the box containing Mary Sue's paraphernalia for the "ceremony." Walter's brother and ex-wives had decided against a funeral service, and his body had been cremated. Mary Sue, though, believed that everyone was entitled to a ceremony.

The box contained dozens of floating candles, which they lit and handed to Gretchen, who sprawled on her stomach to lower them into the water below. They stood side by side on the dock and watched the candles disperse across the glassy water. A magical sight.

"Rest in peace, Walter," Mary Sue said.

They parroted her words. The saddest thing was not that he was dead, Dixie thought, but that there was no one truly to mourn him.

Then Mary Sue began to strip. "Oh, honey, it's too chilly for that," Pamela said.

"Just for a minute or two, to commemorate having come full circle from last year to this," Mary Sue said. "It's been an incredible year, an incredible four decades of friendship, and I love you guys more than ever."

Wearing only her underpants, her scarred, bony, lopsided body looking honorable in the moonlight, the body of a warrior home from the wars, Mary Sue stood on her tiptoes and dove into the water with hardly a splash.

And there they were again, in the lake of their childhood, celebrating their friendship, celebrating life.

"Life is good," Mary Sue called out, her words echoing across the water, coming back to them again and again.

Printed in the United States
By Bookmasters